Michelle Douglas has been writing for Mills & Boon since 2007, and believes she has the best job in the world. She lives in a leafy suburb of Newcastle, on Australia's east coast, with her own romantic hero, a house full of dust and books and an eclectic collection of sixties and seventies vinyl. She loves to hear from readers and can be contacted via her website: www.michelle-douglas.com.

Stacy Connelly has dreamed of publishing books since she was a kid, writing stories about a girl and her horse. Eventually, boys made it onto the pages as she discovered a love of romance and the promise of happily-ever-after. When she is not lost in the land of make-believe, Stacy lives in Arizona with her three spoiled dogs.

She loves to hear from readers at stacyconnelly@cox.net or www.stacyconnelly.com.

Also by Michelle Douglas

Snowbound Surprise for the Billionaire
The Millionaire and the Maid
Reunited by a Baby Secret
A Deal to Mend Their Marriage
An Unlikely Bride for the Billionaire
The Spanish Tycoon's Takeover
Sarah and the Secret Sheikh

The Wild Ones miniseries
Her Irresistible Protector
The Rebel and the Heiress

Also by Stacy Connelly

His Secret Son
Romancing the Rancher
Small-Town Cinderella
Daddy Says, "I Do!"
Darcy and the Single Dad
Her Fill-In Fiancé
Temporary Boss...Forever Husband
The Wedding She Always Wanted
Once Upon a Wedding
All She Wants for Christmas

A BABY IN HIS IN-TRAY

MICHELLE DOUGLAS

THE BEST MAN TAKES A BRIDE

STACY CONNELLY

MILLS & BOON

First Published in Great Britain 2018
by Mills & Boon, an imprint of HarperCollinsPublishers,
1 London Bridge Street, London, SE1 9GF

ISBN: 978-0-263-26478-4

38-0318

MIX
Paper from responsible sources
FSC™ C007454

This book is produced from independently certified FSC™ paper to ensure responsible forest management.

For more information visit: www.harpercollins.co.uk/green

Printed and bound in Spain
by CPI, Barcelona

A BABY IN HIS IN-TRAY

MICHELLE DOUGLAS

For Beth,
whose quirky and offbeat sense of humour
always makes me laugh.

CHAPTER ONE

'WHAT I'M SAYING, Liz, is that someone has left a baby on your—*my*—' she amended, aware that Liz had already corrected her twice so far this phone call '—desk!'

'A baby?' Liz parroted for the third time, and Olivia Grace Gilmour closed her eyes and dragged in a breath—a long, deep, calming breath. In through her nose and out through her mouth. No matter how much she might want to, she couldn't take her twin to task for her incredulity. She could hardly believe it herself.

Except seeing was believing.

She peered once more into the baby carrier at the sleeping infant.

'Livvy, I…'

Liv waited but nothing else was forthcoming, and her heart rate kicked up another notch.

'Where's Judith?'

Judith was Liz's assistant. 'She called in sick.'

'Good.'

'Good?' She tried to keep the shrill note out of her voice. A partner in confusion and concern would be welcome at the moment. But Liz was right. It was just as well Judith wasn't here to witness her panic. Liv didn't want to give the game away. She swallowed and tried to modulate her voice. 'There was a letter addressed to your boss tucked into the side of the baby carrier.'

'*Your* boss,' Liz corrected. If a voice could sound green, hers sounded green.

'*My* boss,' Liv managed through gritted teeth.

Never had agreeing to stand in for her twin at her day

job seemed a crazier move than it did right at this very moment. But it was only for a week and Sebastian Tyrell—Liz's boss—was away. Not that he sallied forth all that often from his estate in Lincolnshire, from where he apparently oversaw operations. But with him being away it meant she shouldn't even need to speak to him on the phone. This week should've been non-eventful, mission possible, a walk in the park. Liz had promised her it'd be a piece of cake.

Except now there was a baby.

Somewhere in the back of her mind maniacal laughter sounded.

She stared into the carrier at the cherubically sleeping baby—the teensy-tiny baby. 'Heavens, Liz, it's little. She can't be more than four or five months old.'

'Oh, God.' If possible, Liz's voice turned greener. Liv grimaced. Her twin had never been good with babies. And now—

'Have you read the letter?'

Liv swung away from the baby, seized the letter and paced to the window overlooking a busy inner-London street, a sliver of the Thames in the distance, glinting silver in the afternoon light.

'Of course I've read the letter!' It was why she'd rung. It gave no clue whatsoever to the baby's identity. And she had no idea what to do. 'It says *"Sebastian"*—not *Dear*, not *Seb*, but *"Sebastian—I can't do this any more. It's not fair. You owe me. Do not let baby Jemima down!"*' She glared at the inoffensive-looking piece of paper. '*"Not"* is underlined three times. It ends in an exclamation mark.' She pulled in another long breath. 'It's not signed.'

'Not signed?' Liz's voice rose. 'Dear God, Livvy, I'm stuck in Turkey in the middle of a plane strike. It'll take me days to get home and—'

'Relax, Liz!' The words shot out of her with more confidence than she'd dreamed possible, but she recognised the panic in her twin's voice and needed to allay it. Liz was pregnant and she needed to stay calm. 'I'm not asking you to come home. You need to stick to your plan.'

What Liz didn't need was additional stress. Dear God, her sister had enough on her plate at the moment. Liv mentally kicked herself for troubling Liz with this except… except she'd panicked herself. 'Look, seriously, I can take care of everything at this end. I was just keeping you apprised of developments like I promised I would.' She dragged a hand back through her hair. 'And I thought you might have some idea where this baby had come from.'

'I haven't the foggiest. I can't think of a single baby he has in his life.'

'Well…obviously somewhere along the line he became a father.'

A strangled noise on the other end of the phone was Liz's only reply.

She swallowed. Did Liz's boss even know he had a child?

'Oh, what a mess! But Livvy, I can't shed any light on this at all. I wasn't joking when I said the most personal thing Mr Tyrell and I have ever shared was our mutual concern over an accountant I'd hired. I mean, I hardly ever see him, the only thing we ever discuss is work…and that as briefly as possible as a rule. He's not a chatty man.'

'Seriously? Nothing personal? Ever?' She still couldn't get her head around that.

Liz was silent for a moment. 'When I returned from my holiday he asked me if I had a nice time. I said yes. That was the extent of the discussion.'

The holiday where Liz had become pregnant to her hot mystery man?

'No passing comments about politics and the state of the

nation, or a book you've been reading, or a movie you've seen?' she persisted.

'*No!* We have a weekly phone call—the Tyrell Foundation is his baby and it's obviously close to his heart—but that's it. He's busy doing whatever it is lords running their estates are busy doing. It's the reason I was so convinced we could pull this switch off.'

They'd thought it so unlikely that Liv would even need to speak to him that they'd practically considered it a *fait accompli*. But now… She swallowed and nodded. She could do it. She could pull it off. After all, she'd had no trouble convincing Judith that she was Liz.

Still…deceiving the sixty-two-year-old Judith who did a solid job at maintaining the foundation's database but who was more interested in sneaking in a surreptitious game of Solitaire than gossiping with Liv was one thing. Deceiving a businessman in his prime was a different matter altogether.

'Livvy?'

'This new development might mean me and your Mr Tyrell have to come face to face.'

'Will you be OK with that?'

She could practically see the grimace on her twin's face. 'Yes.' She gave a silent scream and then stuck out her chin. 'But I'm not changing my hair.'

Finally Liz laughed. 'We already agreed I'd have to lop a few inches off mine before I came home. And in the unlikely event he even sees it, let alone mentions it, I'll tell him I've gone back to being blonde.'

For a moment she could almost picture her twin waving an unconcerned hand through the air, treating the issue of hair as a matter of little importance. Liv couldn't help smiling. She loved her hair. 'Right. We'll call that Plan A, then.'

'What are you going to do now, though? About the baby?'

She suspected what she should do was call the police, but…

'Please don't lose me my job, Livvy.'

But there was that—it was what she was here for. Everything else in Liz's life was up in the air and she was clinging to the security of her job like a lifeline. Liv couldn't jeopardise that.

And if Mr Tyrell did happen to be the father of this baby…well, it wouldn't be fair to call the authorities until after she'd spoken with him.

'I'm going to ring your—*my*—boss and ask *him* what *he* wants to do about the situation. I'll do my best to sound cool and efficient—' like her twin '—but if I sound a tiny bit flustered I think, given the circumstances, that'll be understandable.'

'Oh, Liv, are you sure you don't want me to come home? I can do my best to get back asap. Given this rotten plane strike, if Mr Tyrell is out of the country it could take him days to get home too. And in the meantime you could be literally left holding the baby on your own.'

'Which sounds like more fun than doing government grant acquittals. There's not been a peep from the little tyke. And before you ask—yes, she's breathing. I checked. Besides, I love babies—you know that. And thankfully they're not actually all that much trouble at this age.

'Except for the four-hourly feeds and the sleep deprivation.' Liv glanced down at the baby and grinned. 'Not much sleep deprivation happening here. Besides, Mr Tyrell is bound to know who Baby Jemima is and what I should do with her. We'll sort it out.'

'I'm so, *so* sorry, Liv. If I'd thought for a moment that anything like this would happen, I'd have never asked you to fill in for me.'

'I know. But don't fear—I'll muddle on through. You

just focus on sorting things out at your end. Don't worry about me, I'll be fine.'

Liv hung up from her twin and tucked her phone back into her handbag. She stared again at the sleeping baby and bit her lip. It *was* usual for babies to sleep a lot, right? She touched her fingers to the baby's forehead, but the baby didn't feel hot or feverish.

What on earth was the poor little mite going to think when she woke up and found her mother gone? 'Poor little chick.'

Right.

She planted herself in her office chair and pulled the phone towards her, punching in the contact number that Sebastian Tyrell had left…along with the instruction *Only to be used in the direst of emergencies.*

The phone rang three times before it was answered. 'Ms Gilmour.'

'Yes.'

'I trust this is an emergency?'

The cold, clipped tones told her it had better be or there'd be hell to pay. She took an immediate dislike to the man. 'Yes, I'm afraid it is.'

'My parents…?'

His tone didn't change and she disliked him even more. 'To the best of my knowledge they're in excellent health. This has nothing to do with your parents. It's to do with—'

Baby Jemima chose that moment to let loose with a loud wail.

Heavens! Who knew something so small could produce a sound so fierce? She stood up to peer into the carrier—still perched on her desk where it'd been left—but the sight of Liv seemed to startle the baby further. Baby Jemima's face turned red as she started crying in earnest.

Oh, heck!

Sebastian Tyrell's voice boomed down the line at her. 'Is there a baby in my office?'

Technically, it was her office.

Actually, it was Liz's office.

'Hey, there, little one, hush.' She ran her hand across the baby blanket—over the baby's tummy—in an effort to impart some comfort. 'Shh, it's OK.' She spied the dummy pinned to the blanket and popped it into the baby's mouth. Baby Jemima immediately stopped crying and sucked on it greedily. Oh! She must be hungry.

'What is a baby doing in my office?'

She hated that voice—the cutting ice of it. 'That, Se—sir…' She quickly caught herself. Liz had told her that first names weren't used in the office. *Ever.*

She closed her eyes and pulled in a breath. She had to keep her wits about her. Slip-ups were not allowed. She couldn't let Liz down. It was Sebastian Tyrell's reserve, his distance—both physical and emotional—that had made them believe they could pull this deception off. They could still pull it off. She and Liz were identical twins—at least on the outside. He'd never be able to tell them apart. She *could* do this.

'Continue, Ms Gilmour. Stopping partway through a sentence is not only unprofessional, but irritating.'

Her chin shot up and her nostrils flared. 'I was hoping you could shed light on this particular emergency, *sir*. You see, the baby *is* the emergency. It was left on my desk during my lunch hour…along with a letter for you.'

'What?'

She held the phone a little further away from her ear and refrained from pointing out that deafening one's office manager wasn't particularly professional either. Or that having her eardrums blasted was seriously irritating.

'You'll have to excuse me for having read your letter, but I deemed the situation warranted it.' She feared, though, that her tone told him she didn't give a flying fig what he thought about her having read his letter.

Air hissed down the line at her. 'Read it out loud.'

She did. Word for word. As few as they were.

Without being asked, she read the letter again, allowing him time to process it. She waited for him to respond. When he continued to remain silent she asked, 'What would you like me to do?'

'I'm thinking.'

She wanted to tell him to think faster. 'Do you know baby Jemima?'

'No.'

'Do you know who her mother might be?'

'Ms Gilmour, I'd appreciate it if you'd stop peppering me with questions.'

Jemima spat her pacifier out and set up a toothache-inducing wail. 'Mr Tyrell, there's a baby on my desk that is evidently hungry and probably in need of changing—a baby that has obviously been abandoned by its mother. You'll have to excuse my impatience, I'm afraid.' She pulled in a breath. 'If you don't know who this baby is or who she belongs to, then the sensible thing to do would be to contact the police and hand her over to Social Services.'

'No!'

She blinked. So…maybe he did have a clue?

'This child's mother obviously thinks there's some connection between us, between the baby and me.'

'Or someone could be trying to take advantage of your aristocratic heritage,' she felt honour-bound to point out. Sebastian was Lord Tyrell's only son. The Tyrell family had that enormous estate in Lincolnshire. Not to mention a London house and a holiday villa somewhere on the Riviera.

She rubbed Jemima's tummy again, and tried to entice

her to take her dummy—unsuccessfully. If anything the volume of her cries only increased.

'Going to the police has the potential to cause a scandal. The tabloids would have a field day.'

She rolled her eyes. What on earth was a scandal when a baby's welfare was at stake?

'And a scandal will affect the Tyrell Foundation. It's on a knife-edge already. I don't want to risk scaring away the benefactors I've been in negotiations with for the last few months. We've worked too hard for that.'

Sebastian's charity wasn't one of the glamorous ones featuring children or animals on their flyers. His charity assisted the recently unemployed in the over-fifties age bracket to find work.

From all that Liz had said, it was gruelling work too, and apparently Sebastian toiled like a Trojan. It wasn't something she'd have expected from an aristocrat's son.

We all have our peccadilloes, she reminded herself. She'd have never expected to be particularly fluent in office work, and yet here she was.

She tossed her head and gritted her teeth. She was glad she'd become skilled enough to help her sister out of a tight spot.

Baby Jemima's continual crying scratched through her brain, making her temples throb. 'Where on earth are you anyway?'

A heavy sigh came down the line. 'Australia.'

'Australia!' She said a rude word.

'Ms Gilmour, did you just swear?' There was no censure in his voice, just astonishment.

'I can't stand this crying another second. I need to change and feed the baby. I'll call you back.'

Without further ado, she hung up on him.

Don't lose me my job, Livvy.

She grimaced before pouncing on the bag the absent

mother had evidently packed for the baby. She'd searched it for clues earlier. It contained clothes, toys, nappies, formula and bottles, and, most importantly of all, a set of instructions. A quick glance at them told her that Jemima's next feed had been due fifteen minutes ago.

She crooned nonsense at the baby as she changed and then fed her. 'Don't you worry, little snuggly-wuggly Jemima. We'll have you fed and dry in no time. Would you like to hear a bit about me—my qualifications and what have you? Well, I'll have you know that I was *the* go-to babysitter when I was in high school. And believe me there were plenty of tots in Sevenoaks, Kent. And since then I've been made a godmother—twice! Once to baby Bobby and once to baby Matilda. So you see, I do have credentials. You're in safe hands.'

Jemima drank her bottle with an avid greed that made Liv laugh. 'You're simply lovely, little Jemima.'

The baby puked up on the sleeve of Liv's blouse when Liv burped her, and then promptly fell asleep again.

'Easy-peasy, nothing to it,' Liv murmured, gently placing her in the carrier again. 'If only I could curl up and go to sleep too. But no, not I. I now have to ring my sister's boss and apologise for hanging up on him. Grovel if I have to so he won't fire Liz. Wish me luck, little one.'

Without wasting any more time, she grabbed the phone and hit redial. It was picked up on the first ring. 'I'm sorry I hung up so abruptly, but I had to—'

'There's no need to apologise, Ms Gilmour. The noise was driving me to distraction as well and I'm not even in the same country, let alone the same room. It all sounds quiet now, though.'

'Baby Jemima has been changed and fed and, having thrown up on my blouse, is now blissfully asleep. All's well in Baby Land.'

'I'll replace your blouse.'

She blinked. 'That won't be necessary. It'll wash out.' She stared down at the sleeping baby and something inside her chest clenched. 'She really is the sweetest little thing. Would you like me to send you a photo?'

'Why?'

She shook herself. What was she thinking? Sebastian Tyrell didn't sound like the kind of man who oohed and aahed over cute baby pictures. 'Maybe…maybe she looks like her mother and that'll give you a clue to the baby's identity.'

'I…uh… OK.'

She was grasping at straws and they both knew it. Nevertheless she took a picture on her phone and sent it through to him.

A long silence ensued. 'Babies all look the same to me.'

She bit her lip. 'You don't have much experience with babies, do you?'

'No.'

She drummed her fingers against her desk. He'd ruled out the police, so… 'Do you want me to organise a nanny or some kind of babysitting service?'

'I may not know much about babies but I know business. Questions will be asked and the answers recorded. The baby's full details will need to be provided—a birth certificate may need to be produced.'

She doubted an actual birth certificate would be required, but she caught the gist of his concerns. They didn't know Jemima's full details. They barely knew any details at all! And if he was the baby's father…

Another long silence ensued—a silence that started to burn and chafe through her. 'Look, I don't know if you'll consider this any kind of solution, but Jemima can stay with me until you get back to London. How does that sound?'

'It sounds perfect.'

His relief was evident and it occurred to her now that those long silences of his had been strategic devices to lead her to the point of making this precise offer. She didn't know whether to be outraged or not.

'I understand this is a great imposition on you, Ms Gilmour, and you have my sincere gratitude.'

She chose not to be outraged.

'I also understand that you can't be expected to perform both nanny duties and office duties at the same time. Please organise a temp to take over in your absence. Judith performs her duties ably, but…' He trailed off. 'The woman you arranged to come in while you were on holiday was very good.'

'I'll check with the agency and see if she's available.' Playing nanny would be far more fun than playing office manager. And she couldn't help thinking that the further away from the office she was, the less the likelihood of her and Liz's deception being detected.

Win-win.

She glanced at the sleeping baby. Except what was baby Jemima winning? *Nothing.* She faced upheaval and an uncertain future. She bit back a sigh. Thankfully the baby was blissfully unaware of that fact.

'I hope your mother is all right,' she murmured.

'I beg your pardon?'

Oops! 'Oh… I was talking to the baby, but… Her mother must've felt in the direst of straits to leave her baby like this.'

And she'd left her baby in the care of Sebastian Tyrell. What did that show?

That she trusted him?

She swallowed. That he was the father?

'I'd prefer it, Ms Gilmour, if you refrained from enacting a Cheltenham tragedy.'

Her chin shot up. 'To be perfectly frank with you, *sir*,

I'm not sure it much matters what you'd prefer. I'd have preferred not to have come back from lunch to find an anonymous baby abandoned on my desk. There's not only a mystery to solve—' who was the child's mother '—but a couple of serious issues to be dealt with too. I can't help feeling time is of the essence.'

Don't lose me my job, Livvy.

She grimaced and waited for him to take her to task for her insolence. He didn't. Instead there was that darn silence again. She suddenly laughed. 'You don't feel that you can reprimand me at the moment because you're in my debt.'

'I have no wish to reprimand you. You're worried, understandably so, and I share your concerns. I will own, however, to a little…surprise over your fieriness.'

She winced. She needed to tread carefully—channel her more level-headed sibling. 'Babies bring it out in me,' she offered weakly.

'I see.'

'I should go and let you make your travel arrangements.' She blinked. 'I mean…you are planning to return immediately, aren't you?' She'd simply taken that for granted.

'Absolutely.'

'Or perhaps you'd like me to organise your travel arrangements?' She gave a silent scream. Were they part of her job description? She had no idea.

'The arrangements are already underway.'

The tap-tapping noises in the background suddenly made sense. She wondered how many devices he had open in front of him besides his phone—his tablet *and* laptop perhaps? Those strategic silences suddenly took on a different complexion.

A moment later she dismissed that thought. No, she'd bet her life on the fact that Sebastian Tyrell was a master of the strategic pause.

'I'll be back in London as soon as I can.'

'Travel safe, sir.'

'Wait!'

She wanted away from him—now! Though she couldn't explain why. 'Yes?'

'I'd like you and the baby to move into my house on Regent's Park.'

Not a chance! 'I'm sorry, Mr Tyrell, but I'm not comfortable with that. I'll go back to my—' she gulped back the word *sister's*, covered it with a cough '—flat. I know where everything is there.'

'I—'

'Please don't waste time arguing with me.'

'Very well.'

She winced at the tightness of his voice.

'You're going to incur expenses—the baby will need things. Please charge them to my personal account. I insist that I take care of all the expenses.'

'OK, will do.' She made a mental note to keep all receipts.

'I hope to see you very soon, Ms Gilmour.'

And then he was gone. Liv scowled at the receiver, miffed beyond measure that she hadn't had the chance to hang up first. She dropped the receiver back into its cradle. 'I can hardly wait.'

Liv sat bolt upright in bed and grabbed her phone before it could ring again. The clock by the bed read five forty-four a.m. *Please don't have woken the baby!* She held her breath but no answering wail met her expectant ears. *Thank you, God!*

'What?' she growled into the phone without the slightest bit of grace. It was too early and she was too tired.

'Ms Gilmour?'

Oh, God! 'Mr Tyrell?'

A sigh heaved down the phone. 'For the last five minutes I've been knocking on your door. I understand that it's early, but I'm starting to worry that I'm disturbing your neighbours.'

'Don't you dare wake the baby!' she whisper-hissed at him. 'Don't make another sound on threat of…of something dire!'

She leapt out of bed and shot to the front door of Liz's flat, reefing it open as quietly as she could. Her finger halted halfway to her lips when she took in the man that stood on the other side. Six feet two inches of solid-muscled man stood there, bristling with square-jawed arrogance and wide-legged impatience. Dark chestnut hair, lighter on the ends, stood up at odd angles as if he'd repeatedly run his hand through it. She had to fight the impulse to reach out and smooth it down.

She swallowed. Liz had never mentioned how handsome Sebastian Tyrell was. *Why not?* A pulse started up in her throat, making her breath choppy and uneven. Sebastian Tyrell wasn't merely handsome—the man was hot with a capital H!

'I know I look a mess,' he growled. 'But you could have the manners to pretend to not notice. I've come directly from the airport, and it's taken me more than fifty hours to get here, so what do you expect? And, I might add, you don't look much better.'

Dear God, she was standing in the open doorway in her pyjamas. They were perfectly respectable. They covered everything adequately. Some would argue *more than adequately*.

He continued to stare at her. 'What have you done to your hair?'

She tried to smooth it down. It probably looked like a rat's nest, though she knew that wasn't what he referred to. 'A…a change is as good as a holiday,' she mumbled.

He looked as if he were going to say something more,

but then blinked and shook himself. 'Are you going to let me in?'

'You *cannot* wake the baby.'

Sebastian took in the martial light in his office manager's eyes and raised both hands. 'Understood.'

He'd never seen Ms Gilmour so…undone, if that was the correct term. He could barely discern a trace of his cool, efficient office manager in the woman in front of him. Granted, he'd never knocked on her door at the crack of dawn and dragged her from her bed either.

And then there was her hair!

It took all his strength not to reach out and touch it, to track a strand's length to see if it contained some kind of magic.

He rolled his shoulders—jet lag.

To be fair, he'd never contemplated Ms Gilmour's life outside of the office before now either. To be brutally honest, he'd barely considered her at all beyond appreciating her myriad business skills and her efficiency…and feeling guilty about refusing her leave request a fortnight ago.

Damn it all to hell! She'd had no leave left. He'd needed her in the office overseeing things while he was overseas. He wasn't a tyrant, he was far from unreasonable, but he hadn't been able to shake off the memory of the desperation that had momentarily threaded through her voice. When the London office number had flashed up on his phone three days ago, he'd thought she'd rung to hand in her notice.

Had her hair been a response to her disappointment at having her leave declined?

He dragged both hands back through his hair. For heaven's sake, he'd not seen her in…what? Two months? She could've been wearing her hair like this the entire time.

He fought back a frown. He'd have sworn she wasn't

the kind of woman who'd ever dye her hair like that. Evidently he'd misjudged her.

But then he had form for misjudging women.

He glanced at her again.

And tried to ease the knots in his shoulders. Her hair looked great—*really* great. He hoped it'd given her some solace.

He dragged his gaze from her hair to her face. She was staring at his chest as if hypnotised. 'Ms Gilmour?'

She didn't move.

'Ms Gilmour,' he repeated, a little louder.

She gave a violent start before pressing her finger to her lips. 'Shh.'

She looked as jet-lagged as he felt. A frown built through him. 'How much sleep did you get last night?'

She held up two fingers.

He stiffened, but managed to keep his voice low. 'Two hours?' No wonder she looked so wrecked. For a crazy moment he had to fight an impulse to pull her into his arms and hug her, tell her to rest. He didn't, of course. It was a crazy notion. She'd probably slap him. And he'd deserve it. 'And the night before?'

Two fingers again.

He planted his hands on his hips. 'And the same the night before that?'

She nodded. 'Baby Jemima is a creature of the night. A demon. We—as in you and I—are not going to talk as we walk through the living room, because talking wakes her. We're not even going to look at her, because looking at her wakes her. You're going to follow me through to the kitchen and you're going to keep your eyes firmly forward the whole time. Got it?'

'Got it.'

Unfortunately eyes straight ahead meant his gaze was firmly fixed on her. Hips shouldn't move with such a provocative sway when encased in such ridiculously baggy garments. But apparently they could…and they did.

A pulse started up deep inside him and spread out until he throbbed with it. He wanted to dismiss it as jet lag, but he knew what it was—desire. And it had no place in his relationship with this woman. None whatsoever.

She gestured for him to take a seat at a small kitchen table, collapsing into the one opposite. 'I'm sorry,' she whispered, 'but I can't offer you coffee. The coffee machine is too loud. Apparently the kettle is too loud too, so I can't even offer you instant.'

He was dying for a coffee, aching for it. He now rued his decision to skip it at the airport to make his way here as quickly as he could instead. He wanted to sleep for a week, and yet he'd managed more sleep on the plane than she'd had in three days! 'I don't need coffee.'

'I do.' The words left her on a whimper. 'It's unfortunate on several counts. The primary one being that I don't function as a halfway decent person in the morning until after a shower and a mug of strong coffee.'

She dropped her head to her folded arms, every line of her etched in exhaustion. An answering exhaustion rose through him. He tried to smother a yawn. 'How much longer will the baby sleep for?'

She lifted her head to stare blearily at the clock on the wall. 'Probably another two hours…but it's one of those toss-a-coin things.'

Another yawn took him off guard. 'Maybe we should take advantage of that? Follow suit?'

She stared at him. 'Wow, you must be *really* tired.'

'Really tired,' he agreed. 'Spent.' But what he wanted was for her to jump back into bed and sleep until the lines around her eyes eased. 'Why don't you go back to bed and I'll stretch out on your sofa?'

'Reverse that and you have yourself a deal.' She shook

her head when he went to argue. 'This is a one-bedroom flat. I can't offer you a spare bed, and I don't want to think what Jemima's reaction will be if the first thing she sees when she opens her eyes is a strange man.'

Ah. Right.

He insisted she take her duvet. He stretched out on top of her covers. He only meant to lie there for a minute—just to help straighten out the kinks in his spine—before checking his emails. While he caught up on his emails he could try and think of a practicable way forward where Jemima was concerned.

What on earth was he going to do with her? He closed his eyes and Ms Gilmour's autumn-hued hair filled his mind. A glorious fall of hair shaded in horizontal bands from a deep, dark auburn through to gorgeous oranges and finally a pale blonde. Shaded dark to light, from root to tip.

Gorgeous.

CHAPTER TWO

SEBASTIAN WOKE TO the scent of coffee. His nose told him it was seriously good coffee too. He sat up gingerly, stretched… All the kinks were gone. His back didn't hurt, his shoulders didn't hurt, his head didn't hurt.

He couldn't remember the last time he'd woken up feeling so rested!

Obviously a nap was exactly what he'd needed. A couple of hours to—

His jaw dropped when he caught sight of the bedside clock. It was after one-thirty *in the afternoon*. He'd been asleep for over seven hours?

Dear God! What would Ms Gilmour think? He'd left her holding the baby…*again*!

He shot out of the bedroom and came to a halt. His office manager turned from pouring out two steaming mugs of coffee to send him a smile that momentarily dazzled him. She looked utterly together. She looked like his efficient office manager again. Except rather than a black pencil skirt and business jacket she wore jeans and a jumper, and that magical autumn hair. And the smile.

'Come and have a coffee.'

He forced himself forward. He was careful not to look into the living room as he went past, even though he was sure the 'don't look at the baby' embargo had been lifted.

Critical eyes roamed over his face and she gave a satisfied nod. 'You look much better.'

He collapsed into a seat and pulled a mug of coffee closer. 'So do you. You managed to get more sleep?'

'A blissful three hours.'

She poured milk into her coffee. Whenever he visited the London office she drank it black—like him. But… she preferred it with milk? She did know she was free to order milk in for her coffee, didn't she? Where the Tyrell Foundation was concerned he'd accept the charge of penny pinching, but he could stretch to milk for his office manager's coffee.

'You should've woken me.'

'Why?'

'Because we have things to sort out.'

'People make better decisions when they're well-rested.'

She looked so perky and chipper he felt at a distinct disadvantage. He leaned across the table towards her. 'The baby?' he whispered.

'Happily engrossed with her baby gym at the moment,' she answered at a normal tone and volume. 'She's an absolute angel during the day. It's only at night she turns into a demonic creature from the deep.'

How could she sound so cheerful? She'd been sleep-deprived for three whole nights. How could she look so… delectable?

'Drink your coffee, and then have a shower while I make us some lunch and—'

'I couldn't possibly impose on you more than I already have—'

'You can and you will. You can't just up and leave with the baby. Besides, Jemima is due for a feed soon and then she'll go down for a nap. There's really not much point in trying to do anything before then. There's a fresh towel for you in the bathroom.'

He supposed she had a point. And he was dying for a shower.

He collected a few things from his suitcase—left by the front door when he'd arrived earlier. On his way past he peeked at the baby. She lay on a quilted rug, batting at the soft toys suspended above her. Her head wobbled around to look at him, the tiny body went rigid and then she let forth with such a piercing wail he had to cover his ears.

Ms Gilmour came racing in from the kitchen. 'What did you do to her?'

'Nothing! I… I just looked at her.'

'And what were you told?'

'Don't look at the baby,' he mumbled, feeling all of two inches tall.

She leant down to sweep the baby up in her arms, cuddling the tiny body against her chest. Her jeans pulled tight around the soft swell of her backside and that damn pounding started up at the centre of him again, sending warm swirls of appreciation and need racing through his bloodstream.

He swallowed when she turned back around to face him.

'Did the big, bad man scare you, pretty girl? Did he sneak up on you and frighten you?'

He watched in amazement as baby Jemima snuggled into her rescuer, her crying ceasing as if a switch had been flicked. Ms Gilmour then blew a raspberry and the baby gave her a big smile and waved her arms about in evident delight.

'How…?' He stared at the baby and then his office manager. 'How did you do that? You took her from crying to laughing in seconds!'

She blew on her nails and polished them against her shoulder. 'Just call me Poppins, Mary Poppins.'

She said it in the same tones James Bond always used when introducing himself, *Bond, James Bond*, and he couldn't help but laugh.

She hitched the baby a little higher in her arms. 'Jemima, meet…' She frowned. 'What would you like her to call you?'

He had no idea. Did she have to call him anything? He

frowned. Hold on, she couldn't call him anything. She was too young and—

One look at his extraordinary office manager told him that wouldn't wash. 'What does she call you?'

'Auntie…uh… Liz.'

Her gaze slid away, and he understood why. He knew her Christian name was Eliza, but he didn't want to call her that. He wanted things to remain on as formal a footing as possible.

He let out a long, slow breath. 'Uncle Sebastian,' he clipped out.

'Right. Baby Jemima, meet Uncle Sebastian.'

She said his name impersonally and yet something inside of him stretched and unwound as she uttered it.

He did his best to ignore it.

'Well, say hello,' she ordered him. 'Talk to her.'

He shuffled a step closer.

'Don't frown or you'll make her cry again.'

He smoothed out his face and tried to find a smile. 'Hello, Jemima, it's nice to meet you.' He fell silent. The baby frowned at him. 'What do I say?'

'Say something nice. Tell her she's pretty. Tell her you've been on a big plane…recite a poem. It doesn't matter. She just needs to know you're friendly.'

A poem? He used to love poetry. Once upon a time. It felt like a hundred years ago now. He pulled in a deep lungful of air. '"The Assyrian came down like a wolf on—"'

'Good God, not Byron!'

Both woman and child swayed away from him.

'You'll scar her for life.'

Behind those honey-brown eyes he had a feeling she was laughing at him.

'Can't you think of something more…cheerful?'

Cheerful? Inspiration struck. *'The Jabberwocky!'*

He recited the entire poem and both woman and child stared at him as if mesmerised.

'Give her your finger.'

He did as bidden. Jemima stared at it for a moment or two, swaying in her protector's arms, before reaching out and clasping it in one tiny fist. Something inside of him felt as if it were falling.

She pulled it closer and then up towards her mouth, but he gently detached himself from her grip. 'You might want to wait until I've washed my hands first. You've no idea where these have been.'

Jemima stared at him and then gave a big toothless grin before letting forth with a sound partway between 'Gah!' and a gurgle.

He could feel his entire body straighten—his chin came up and his shoulders went back—and he couldn't help smiling back. 'She smiled at me. She…she smiled.'

He glanced at his office manager to find her staring at him as if she'd never seen him before. Something arced in the air between them, and colour flooded her cheeks. She shook herself and sent him a smile that didn't hide the consternation in her eyes. 'You've just been given the official seal of approval.' She laughed and suddenly seemed more natural again. 'Hold tight to the memory. You might just need it at two o'clock in the morning, and at three… and four.'

It hit him then that she'd been right. He couldn't just walk out of here with Jemima. He was going to need help.

Her help?

Something inside him chafed at the idea. He had a feeling it'd be best for him and Ms Gilmour to get back on a professional footing asap. He could hire someone else. He'd have to come up with a cover story for Jemima of course, but…

'Mr Tyrell?'

But first he had to stop staring at her! 'I'll, uh, just go have that shower.'

When he emerged from the shower, he found Jemima asleep and his hostess making sandwiches.

'Egg and lettuce,' she said, setting two in front of him.

They ate in silence. She kept glancing across at him and he knew he should initiate the conversation, but he didn't know where to start.

'Do you have any idea who her mother might be?' she finally asked.

'None whatsoever.'

She pulled in a breath. 'I know we're straying into dangerously personal territory, but...can you recall all of the women you've been...intimate with in the last twelve to fifteen months?'

He choked on his sandwich. 'I'm not Jemima's father!'

One eyebrow kinked upwards. 'How do you know that for sure?' Her lips twisted. 'Contraception isn't always a hundred per cent effective.'

He knew that, but... Something in her tone caught at him. He frowned. 'You sound as if you're speaking from experience.'

Her gaze dropped to her plate. 'Second-hand experience. A, um...girlfriend.'

'I'm *not* Jemima's father.'

She glanced back up at him. 'How can you be so certain?'

Because he'd not slept with anyone in two years! But he had no intention of confessing that to this woman. It made him sound priestly, saintly, celibate, and he was none of those things.

'Have you kept in contact with them all?'

He grabbed the branch she'd unknowingly handed him. 'Yes.'

She leant back and folded her arms, staring at him in outright disbelief. It rankled.

'I don't know what kind of man you think I am, Ms Gilmour, but there haven't been an endless parade of women in and out of my bed. I know *every* woman I've slept with in the past two years, and I've kept in contact with *all* of them. I can assure you that none of them have become pregnant—not with me and not with anyone else.'

She unfolded her arms, but he didn't know if she believed him or not. He didn't know why it should matter so much to him either way. She was his office manager, not his moral guardian.

'Jemima and I can get DNA tests done if it'll put your mind at rest,' he snapped out. 'A paternity test.'

Luscious lips—lips he'd never realised were luscious until this moment—pursed. 'Could you, though? You've not been made Jemima's legal guardian. You don't have the authority to give legal consent for such a test.'

He opened his mouth. He closed it again. She had a point.

'Which is why,' she continued, 'I'm not going to let you leave here with Jemima.'

He blinked. Had she just said…? 'I beg your pardon?'

'I'm not letting you take the baby.'

He stared at her. 'You can't stop me.'

Their gazes locked and clashed. 'Do you mean to take Jemima by force?'

His hands clenched to fists. Of course he wasn't going to take the baby by force! Was she threatening him with the police? He pulled in a measured breath. 'Jemima's mother entrusted her to my care,' he reminded her.

'You'll have to excuse me for not putting much faith in Jemima's mother's reasoning.' She'd leapt up and now proceeded to pace—back and forth in agitated circles. 'She left Jemima in my office during my lunch break. What if

I'd decided to take a half-day—to skive off because the boss was away?'

His head rocked back. 'You'd never do such a thing.'

'*I* know that and *you* know that, but she doesn't know me from Adam. So *she* couldn't know that.'

She had a point.

'She left the baby in your care but you were *out of the country.* What was she thinking? I mean, you *live* in Lincolnshire, not in London. Had she put any thought into this at all? Hadn't she done any research?'

He couldn't fault her reasoning.

She planted herself back in her chair. 'Look, this is all beside the point. I wish I wasn't involved. I don't want to be involved. But I am, and ethically and morally I can't just hand that baby over to you and walk away. Not when you aren't her father. Not when you know nothing about babies.'

He dragged both hands back through his hair. If their positions were reversed he knew he'd feel the same.

'Why do you want to take her anyway? Why do you feel so responsible for her?'

Finally they came to the crux of the matter. Exhaustion, disgust…and a still searing sense of betrayal momentarily overtook him. He dropped his head to his folded arms. Eventually he lifted it and met her gaze. 'I suspect Jemima and I are related.'

'Related?'

He forced himself to maintain eye contact. 'A niece perhaps.'

'But…you don't have any siblings.'

He had to swallow before he could speak. 'I have no siblings that I know about.'

'Ah.' She slumped back as if all the air had gone out of her.

'Or…' worse yet '…she could be my half-sister.'

'But—' she frowned and leaned towards him '—your father must be...'

'Sixty-eight—old enough to be her grandfather, yes.'

Liv ran a hand across her brow in an effort to shift the tightness that gripped it like a vice. The poor man looked exhausted. Not physically exhausted the way he had when she'd opened her door to him earlier, but deep-down-in-his-soul exhausted. 'I guess that explains the scandal you want to avoid.'

His head swung up to meet her gaze again. 'I've given up trying to quash scandal where my parents are concerned.'

Given how often they appeared in the pages of the tabloids, that was probably just as well. It might also explain why Sebastian wanted to present such a squeaky-clean image himself.

She wanted to see him smile again, the way he had when Jemima had smiled at him. It was probably crazy, but... 'I don't believe half of what the papers say. They inflate everything.'

His lips twisted—not into a smile. 'Where Hector and Marjorie Tyrell are concerned, you can believe pretty much everything that you read.'

She winced.

'My parents are selfish people, Ms Gilmour, and have been all their lives. Chasing their own pleasure is more important to them than anyone's welfare.'

Including their son's? A weight pressed down on her chest.

'I've no interest in protecting their reputations—they don't have reputations worth protecting. However, if Hector has taken advantage of some young woman and left her feeling *desperate*, then she does deserve protecting.

And until I can discover who she is, I mean to shield her from the spotlight.'

Liv lifted her chin. 'Good. Good for you!'

This time he did give a smile, though it was only a small one…and tinged with disillusion. 'In the meantime we—' he gestured first to her and then to himself '—have this problem to sort out.'

'No problem,' she assured him. 'You go off and find Jemima's mother. In the meantime Jemima can stay here with me. Ms Brady is doing a fine job holding the fort at the office. I've been checking in with her every afternoon.'

'No.'

No? What did he mean, no?

'Just as you're not comfortable letting me take the baby, I'm not comfortable leaving the baby with you.'

She couldn't prevent air from hissing out between her teeth. 'You didn't seem to mind her spending the last three nights with me when it suited you. From memory, I had your *undying gratitude*.'

'I believe that's a slight embellishment.' Just for a moment light danced in his eyes, making him look younger and less troubled. 'But you mistake me, Ms Gilmour.'

The formality of that *Ms Gilmour* was starting to chafe at her, but she didn't have an answer for it. She didn't want him calling her Liz or Eliza. Every time he did it'd bring home, all the more acutely, the deception she was playing on him. She was finding it hard enough to maintain the charade as it was, without an additional load of guilt every time he called her by her sister's name. At least she *was* Ms Gilmour.

It's a situation of your own making.

Yes, thank you—she knew that well enough. She pulled in a breath. She only had to survive for another few days. 'I mistake you?'

'I don't doubt your ability to look after Jemima, and I don't doubt your integrity.'

Darn it all! Why did he have to make her sound mean-spirited for doubting him? 'Then why aren't you comfortable continuing our arrangement?'

'Because you're getting no sleep. It's not fair to ask you to continue in this vein. You live in a one-bedroom flat. You haven't a spare room to put the baby in, let alone any additional help I might be able to provide for you.'

She wished she hadn't been so utterly shattered when she'd opened the door to him earlier. She'd sounded—and acted—like a mad woman. It was all she could do not to wince. She'd hoped he'd been too jet-lagged to remember, but…apparently not. The impression she'd made on him had evidently been indelible.

'I have a solution if you're willing to hear it.'

He had the most perfectly shaped mouth. She'd love to paint it and—

Stop it! She didn't want to think about painting or Sebastian Tyrell's mouth or anything. She didn't want to like him!

She rose and went to check on the baby. She returned to her seat only when she had her wayward thoughts back under lock and key. 'OK, hit me with it.'

He raised an eyebrow.

Oops, that was probably a bit informal for Liz. 'I mean, please outline your solution, Mr Tyrell. I'm all ears.'

He stared at her with pursed lips. 'I never imagined you'd be like this…outside of the office, I mean.'

His words had a texture and they brushed across her skin with a faint promise she didn't dare examine. It took all her strength to stop from chafing her arms. What did he mean? Like what? *Human?* She didn't ask. She didn't want to know. 'I wouldn't have expected you to think about what I was like outside of the office.'

He frowned and opened his mouth.

'Which is exactly as it should be,' she added.

He snapped his mouth shut, but his frown deepened. 'I want you to know that I'm more than happy for you to order in milk for your tea and coffee at the office.'

Oh! Liz took hers black! And he'd noticed that she'd added milk to hers earlier. *She was an idiot!* She tried to shrug. 'I chop and change all the time.' She shrugged again, overdoing it but unable to stop herself. 'Sometimes I prefer milk, sometimes I don't.'

His gaze narrowed in on her face. 'Well, on the weeks you do prefer milk you're to order it in. Are we clear on that?'

'Crystal,' she assured him.

Dear lord, that was sweet of him, and she felt an utter cow. She and Liz were the ones deceiving him. He had *nothing* to feel guilty about.

You're not doing it to hurt him. Besides, you're helping him.

She *was* helping him. And, given the events of the last few weeks, it was just as well that she was here rather than Liz. She was much better able to cope with a baby. Liz may, in fact, have gone to pieces. But that knowledge didn't make her feel any the less guilty.

'Well…ahem…tell me about this solution of yours.'

He set both hands on the table and leaned towards her. The scent of something rather lovely like spiced apples drifted across to her. 'We all leave together and go to my house on Regent's Park.'

Move in with him? Ooh, she really didn't want to do that. Instinct told her that the more distance she kept between herself and Sebastian the better.

'There's ample room in the house and you can still be Jemima's primary carer, but with the added benefit of having help near at hand.'

She bet he had an entire army of household staff. And a huge house. It was quite possible they'd hardly ever see each other.

'And…you'll do your best to find Jemima's mother?'

He nodded. 'That's the plan. I don't care what it takes, I *will* find her.'

Liv thought hard. She wasn't sure she could deal with too many more sleepless nights. If Jemima's mother had had to put up with that for months… With no help, no family… Liv repressed a shudder, understanding in a way she never had before how that kind of pressure could make a person snap.

But surely, after a little rest, Jemima's mother would come forward to claim her? And she'd find them quicker and easier if they were at Sebastian's house.

'If you think I'm being irresponsible in any way you can still carry out your original intent and go to the police.'

'Oh!' She shot to her feet. 'That wasn't a threat. It—'

'I know, and I understand. We have a duty to Jemima, a responsibility. You've been thrust into a role you didn't ask for, but you and the baby have bonded. And now you're understandably reluctant to abandon her to an uncertain fate. It's admirable.'

She paced back into the living room to stare down at the sleeping baby. She was an innocent in all of this. She knelt down beside her, brushed her fingers over a tiny hand.

The hand opened and gripped one of Liv's fingers convulsively before loosening again as she drifted back into a deep sleep. It was as if that little hand had squeezed Liv's heart. She'd known Jemima for all of three days, and yet she'd do anything now to protect her.

She rose and spun around to find Sebastian right behind her. She took an instinctive step backwards, the scent of cinnamon and something darker like aniseed wrapping about her. With a smothered oath he seized her shoulders before she could fall over the baby carrier.

'Careful.' He moved her three steps away from it.

'Sorry, I, um…didn't realise you were standing right there.' *So close!* 'You startled me.'

The warmth of his hands burned through the thin material of her jumper, sending a drugging surge of heat coursing through her blood. He stared down at her and his pupils dilated. This close to him she could see the lighter flecks—almost silver—in the grey of his eyes.

His hands dropped abruptly back to his sides and this time it was he who took a hasty step back. 'Sorry, I didn't mean to startle you.'

She swiped suddenly damp palms across the seat of her jeans. 'No problem,' she said, before gesturing that they should return to the kitchen.

She preceded him. When she turned back, she found him staring down at the baby with such gentleness her heart turned in her chest. He reached down to pull the cover up around the baby more fully. 'Don't you worry about a thing, little one. I'll find your mamma for you. I promise.'

'Yes,' she said before she even realised she was going to say anything.

He turned to stare at her, straightened. 'Yes?'

'To your solution. I think it's a good one. Just let me pack a bag.'

It took nearly half an hour in a black cab to drive from Liz's southside suburb to Sebastian's home—just off the outer circle of Regent's Park. The cab stopped in front of a neo-classical terrace—all white brick and imposing columns. 'You…you live here?' she breathed.

Sebastian didn't answer. He was already out of the cab, busy paying the driver and collecting up the various bags. She went to help him, but he shook his head. 'You just take care of Jemima.' He handed her a key and then hitched his head in the direction of the…*mansion*. 'Let yourself in.'

She stared at the black front door. Just…wow! Did he own the entire building or had it been converted into apartments? She glanced down at the key. She guessed there was only one way to find out.

She unlocked the door to find a large entrance hall complete with a fancy chandelier. A grand staircase curved gracefully to the upper floors. Reception rooms ranged off on either side. So…not a converted flat, then.

She moved the baby carrier to the other hand. 'Hello?'

'Who are you calling for?'

Sebastian came bustling in behind her. He set her bag, two of Jemima's bags and the portable cot that Jemima refused to sleep in down on the floor. His suitcase and several other bags still stood on the footpath.

'I… Your staff. I didn't want the appearance of a strange woman with a baby to make anyone nervous.'

'I don't have staff.'

He turned and headed back outside to collect the rest of their bags.

She could feel her eyes start from their sockets. What did he mean, he didn't have staff?

'Mrs Wilson comes in three days a week to clean,' he said, when he came back in. 'But I have no live-in staff.' He set the remaining bags down. 'I'm rarely in London.' He shrugged. 'It'd be indulgent, unnecessarily extravagant.'

And she was quickly coming to realise that he was neither of those things. Unfortunately that only made her like him all the more.

'You seem surprised.'

She moistened suddenly dry lips. 'So when you said I'd have help with the baby…?'

His face cleared. 'I meant me—that I'd help you. We can take it in shifts.'

A vision of spending the late hours of the night with him rose up through her mind with disconcerting clarity. Ooh, no…that couldn't happen and—

'That is OK, isn't it?'

But in the next instant she remembered the Jekyll and Hyde act Jemima pulled as soon as the sun went down and the image dissolved. There'd be no opportunity for any… funny business. Which was just as well, she told herself in her sternest voice.

'Ms Gilmour?'

She shook herself. 'Yes, of course that's OK. I just feel a bit of an idiot now for expecting staff.'

He hefted bags into his hands. 'My parents would tell you I'm the idiot.'

'They'd fill the place with an army of staff, I take it?'

'They would.'

She grabbed the nappy bag and followed him towards the staircase. 'You know what? I don't think I'd like your parents very much.'

'You'd be one of the few. They're widely considered… eccentric but charming'

She wrinkled her nose. 'Well, the likelihood of me meeting your parents, Seb—'

She froze at her slip.

He stilled.

Everything inside of her crunched up tight. 'Oh, God, I'm sorry. That was awfully unprofessional of me. Blame sleep deprivation. I promise it won't happen again, *Mr Tyrell*.'

He set his bags on the floor. He took the nappy bag and baby carrier from her and put both down—gently—as well. He turned her to face him, before planting his hands on his hips. Her mouth dried as she took in the long line of his legs—their latent power barely disguised by his business trousers—those lean hips tapering up to intriguingly broad shoulders.

'I think this is an issue we ought to clear up right now.'

CHAPTER THREE

'WE NEED TO sort this out,' Sebastian repeated.

'Sort what?' she squeaked.

She stared at him with wide eyes as if afraid he was going to give her a right royal rollicking. Damn it all to hell! What kind of grump was he to have her looking at him like that?

'I didn't say you were a grump!'

It was only then he realised he'd said the words out loud. 'You're staring at me as if you think I'm going to haul you across the coals.'

'Sorry, I—'

She broke off to press the heels of her hands to her eyes. He dragged a hand back through his hair and fought the urge to draw her into the circle of his arms and press her head to his shoulder where she could rest. She must be dead-on-her-feet tired. He'd got a good, solid seven hours' sleep, but not her. 'I'm *not* upset that you started to call me by my first name.'

She pulled her hands away, her eyes wary. 'You're not?'

'No.' He'd liked the sound of his name on her lips.

She pressed her hands tightly together in front of her and stared down at them. 'Nevertheless, I think it's important to maintain professional boundaries.'

His chest clenched tight. When had he become so self-absorbed? For the last two years he'd sought refuge in an impersonal distance in both his professional and personal life. He thought his coolness had created a corresponding coolness in all those around him, but it was obvious that, like him, Ms Gilmour sought detachment.

And he had no right to intrude further into her life than he already had, to ask anything more of her beyond the employer-employee relationship. Except…

Baby Jemima demanded more from both of them and it appeared they were both more than willing to unstintingly give the baby whatever she needed.

He just had to make sure that whatever price was paid, it wasn't too high for the woman standing in front of him.

'Several years ago I made the very grave mistake of mixing business with pleasure.' She stared at her hands as if they held the key to the universe. 'I don't mean to ever make that same mistake again.'

He pondered her words. From memory she was twenty-five. Several years ago she'd have been very young. She'd called it a *grave mistake*. His hands clenched into fists. Someone had taken advantage of her innocence and had hurt her badly. If he ever got hold of the man who'd done that he'd—

'Look, I'm not saying that's what I think is going to happen in our situation.'

She stared at his fists, her eyes going wide and worried. He unclenched his hands immediately. 'Of course not. I never thought for a moment that's what you were suggesting. I was just thinking of what I'd like to do to the man who hurt you.'

'Oh.'

She shot him a smile—so sweet and lovely, it melted through him like treacle melting into the honeycomb of a hot crumpet, softening all of the stony places inside of him.

It took all of his concentration to keep his breathing even. He had to be careful around this woman. Once you opened yourself up to a baby, other walls were in danger of coming down. He had to keep them standing firm—for all their sakes. He was better than his parents, and he had no intention of blurring the line between business and pleasure himself.

'I think we can both agree,' he started carefully, 'that this current *surprising* situation that we find ourselves in is not exactly a professional one.'

'No, not precisely professional,' she agreed.

Her eyes remained trained on him, waiting.

'But this,' he gestured to the baby, 'is only a temporary interruption from our usual professional routine. When we get Jemima's situation resolved things will go back to how they were.'

She pursed her lips and then pointed to herself. 'Ms Gilmour.' And then pointed to him. 'Mr Tyrell.'

'Exactly.'

'But in the meantime you're suggesting…?'

'That perhaps, while we're not in the office, we can unbend enough to call each other by our first names.'

Her nose wrinkled.

Someone had really done a number on her, hadn't they?

But as he continued to survey her, it occurred to him that it wasn't him she didn't trust, it was herself. Something primal tried to claw its way to the fore—something that wanted to force the issue, force her to see him as a man rather than her boss, force her to take a risk.

He stiffened and beat it back down. He and his office manager were *not* going to dance that particular dance, regardless of how attractive or surprisingly intriguing he found her.

He was not opening himself up to betrayal again. *Ever.*

He'd keep his focus professional and his libido under wraps. He'd learned an important lesson with Rhoda, and it was one he had no intention of ever forgetting. He fought a sudden exhaustion. He didn't have the heart—the energy—to venture down that path again. The part of him that had once welcomed the idea of love and family had been destroyed.

His office manager might be the complete opposite to Rhoda. But if she wasn't she'd be no good for him. If she were, he'd be no good for her. Either way someone would get hurt. He shook his head. *Not going to happen.*

Her need for distance and reserve should comfort him, but the thought of calling her Ms Gilmour in these circumstances rankled. 'You're not my office manager in this situation, you're…'

He watched the bob of her throat as she swallowed. 'I'm…?'

'Jemima's advocate, her friend…her Auntie Liz.'

She frowned and crossed her arms. 'You are *not* calling me Auntie Liz.'

She looked so suddenly schoolmarmish he had to choke back a laugh. 'How about I just call you Eliza?'

She huffed out a long breath, her lips pursed. She glanced away, finally giving a shrug before meeting his gaze once again, her expression strangely resigned. 'Fine. And I'll call you Seb.'

No one had ever shortened his name—not even at school. He liked it. At least…he liked it coming from her lips.

His collar tightened about his throat and he had to resist the urge to run his finger beneath it. He couldn't let this become too cosy. First names didn't mean they had to become too familiar with each other. It wouldn't do. He and Eliza were not going to cross any other boundaries.

She pointed a finger at him. 'But this is only temporary. When we're back in our respective offices we're reverting to Mr Tyrell and Ms Gilmour…and all of this will feel as if it happened to somebody else.'

'Absolutely.' This was only a momentary loosening of clearly defined roles that would be assumed again as soon as this adventure was over. But would it be as easy to slip back into their old roles of Ms Gilmour and Mr Tyrell—boss and secretary—as they hoped it would be?

He shoved his shoulders back. He had to make sure it was. End of story.

'You did this for three nights *on your own*?' Sebastian looked at his office manager with a new-found respect. Before tonight he hadn't known that a baby's crying could grind you down to your soul so quickly. He hadn't known that once it started it refused to release you.

He hadn't known it could be so *relentless*!

'Don't look at me as if I'm some kind of hero.' She didn't even look up from rocking the baby. 'It was a case of needs must and nothing more.'

From ten o'clock last night through to now—almost two-thirty in the morning—Jemima had slept in odd twenty- to thirty-minute increments, only to wake again screaming. It seemed he couldn't do any damn thing right, at least not according to Jemima. He'd bounced, dandled, crooned, rocked, played teddy bears and choo-choo trains. He'd changed her and tried giving her a bottle—none of it had worked. She'd continue to cry through all his efforts, making him feel like a low-down loser. The only thing that made her stop crying was being in her new acting nanny's arms.

'I can't believe you didn't give me a harder time when I rocked up on your doorstep yesterday.'

She turned that amber gaze on him and raised an eyebrow. 'I thought I did give you a hard time.'

That made him laugh. She was a rank amateur compared to his parents. Compared to Rhoda.

All mirth fled at that thought.

'I can't believe you didn't shove her at me and push us both out of the door.'

'Do you hear what the big, bad man is saying?' she crooned down at Jemima. He wondered where she found the energy for that smile. 'As if I'd do that.'

The baby stared up at her intently, working noisily on her dummy.

'You know, Seb, you ought to go to bed. There's no point in the both of us losing a good night's sleep.'

Not a chance. He wasn't leaving her to deal with this on her own *again*. Woman and child were ensconced on the sofa in the baby's room. He sat on the floor, resting back against it. He was hoping Eliza and the baby would drop off to sleep and then he'd watch over them—make sure the baby didn't roll off her lap or anything like that. At least then he'd feel as if he was pulling his weight.

He rubbed his nape. 'Do you think she's teething?'

'Babies don't usually start teething until they're six months. Her cheeks aren't pink and she's not rubbing at her mouth or pulling on her ears.'

'Then why…?' If he could find out what it was that was making Jemima cry, he'd set about fixing it. 'Should I call a doctor?'

She shook her head. 'I don't think it's anything physical—especially when she's so cheerful during the day. I mean, she's not hungry. Her nappy doesn't need changing. She doesn't have a temperature. And she stops crying whenever I pick her up.'

'So…comfort?'

She huffed out a long breath. 'Looks like it.'

'Then why won't she accept comfort from me?' It was unfair that Eliza had to bear the brunt of this.

'I suspect she will in a few days. Once she's more used to you. I suspect she's more familiar with women—or, at least, a woman—than men.'

He supposed that made sense.

Golden eyes met his. 'But I don't want to keep doing this. Sleepless nights are the pits.'

He couldn't blame her. But he wasn't sure how to help.

'I need a pram.'

He sat up a bit straighter. 'I told you to buy whatever you needed.' He winced at the glare she sent him. He probably deserved it. 'I'll organise one first thing in the morning.'

'Thank you.'

'You have a plan?'

She gave a hard nod. 'Jemima and I are going to spend a huge portion of tomorrow in the park…in the sunshine. I seem to recall that sunshine helps to regulate one's sleeping patterns.' Her brow crinkled again. 'Or is that an old wives' tale?'

For a moment she looked so disconsolate that all he wanted to do was buck up her spirits. 'It's not an old wives' tale. It's got something to do with melatonin.'

She stared at him as if he was speaking a foreign language.

'Daylight helps regulate one's body clock and melatonin is a hormone that makes us sleep well. They're related somehow. It has to do with our circadian rhythms.' He couldn't remember exactly how it all fitted together. 'I know because it's good for getting over jet lag too.' He made himself sound as confident and certain as he could—she looked in need of some certainty.

'Right. Good. It's spring. There's no better time for flooding this little body with as much natural daylight as I can than first thing in the morning. And I'm going to try and keep her awake as much as I reasonably can tomorrow—not let her sleep as much through the day as she has been.'

He lifted both hands and crossed his fingers.

'Which means she's going to be seriously grizzly come tomorrow evening.'

'I'll be here to help out.'

She shook her head. 'You need to focus on finding her mother. What's your plan?'

He shuffled upright a little more. 'I've thought about this from every angle.' He'd thought of little else…other than the dark circles under Eliza's eyes. 'I'm going to hire a private investigator. I know somebody discreet. He can start searching hospital records or the Department of Births, Deaths and Marriages for babies born in the last three to five months with the name Jemima.'

She raised an eyebrow. 'Do you know how many babies are born in the Greater London area alone in a single day?'

He had no idea but her expression told him it was a lot. 'I have to start somewhere. Do you have a better plan?'

She looked as if she might say something, but she re-adjusted the baby in her arms instead. 'No,' she sighed.

'And I need to make a phone call.' He didn't want to ring Rhoda, but he had to. He couldn't hide from that fact any longer.

He pulled the phone from his pocket, but before he could bring up his list of contacts a hand fell on his shoulder. 'You can't call anyone at this time of night!'

He stared at the clock before shaking his head, trying to clear the mist that had him in its grip. 'No. I can't. What on earth am I thinking?'

A giggle shot out of her. 'If sunlight is good for jet lag then you might want to make a point of getting a good dose of the stuff tomorrow too.'

And then they were suddenly both laughing—hearty, break-the-tension laughter. Jemima spat her dummy out and laughed too. A sense of wellbeing he had no right to feeling flooded every cell of his body, making him feel lighter and more buoyant.

When their laughter eased to hiccups he flicked a glance at the clock. 'It was about this time in Australia when you phoned to inform me of *the emergency*.' His lips twitched upwards, and a low laugh left him. 'The tone of your voice! I'll never forget it.'

'I was…nonplussed.'

'You were riled.'

'Panicked,' she countered. 'I mean, who just leaves a baby on a stranger's desk? I…' She shook her head and then bit a hangnail. 'My sister has just found out that she's pregnant, you see, so babies have been on my mind lately.'

He turned to face her more fully. 'You have a sister?'

Watch your mouth! She needed to guard her tongue during these cosy 'wee hours of the morning' sessions. 'Yes.' It was pointless saying otherwise now.

He surveyed her with those grey eyes.

Despite the intermittently screaming baby, the atmosphere was remarkably easy, almost relaxed.

She frowned. Was that a good thing?

'Is your sister happy about the baby?'

Liv's heart clenched. 'She's terrified.' She had no idea what Liz was going to do. But she sincerely hoped it wasn't something her sister would come to regret.

'Why?'

She stared down at the baby in her arms. 'It wasn't planned. She had a fling with a mystery man.' Which was so out of character for Liz it still made Liv's head spin. Not that she begrudged her sister a little fun, for letting her hair down for once and living a little. Liz deserved to be happy. Except an unplanned pregnancy was a big thing. Single motherhood was a big thing. It was inordinately difficult—emotionally and financially—for a woman to raise a child on her own. And she wasn't sure Liz had any intention of doing so. Which begged the question—what on earth *was* Liz going to do?

Her stomach churned every time she thought about it.

'A mystery man?'

She recalled the dreamy look on Liz's face when she'd described him and couldn't help but smile. 'A tall, dark and handsome stranger, apparently. Their eyes met across a crowded room. You know the drill.'

'How old is your sister?'

Liv stiffened at the implicit criticism. 'Old enough not to deserve the condemnation in your voice!' She glared at him. 'Why is it OK for men to have flings and not women? She's not in a relationship with anyone. She works hard and meets her daily responsibilities. She wasn't hurting anyone.'

He dragged a hand down his face. 'You're right. I'm sorry.'

He stared at the baby she held, the baby who, to all intents and purposes, *looked* asleep. Previous experience warned Liv, though, that if she tried to put Jemima into her cot she'd wake with a start and scream the place down.

He turned to face her fully, his eyes serious and his mouth grim. 'She has to tell the father she's pregnant.'

He was projecting. Because he'd want to know if he ever fathered a child. He'd want to be involved in his child's life.

How can you possibly know that?

Easy-peasy—look how seriously he was taking his responsibility towards Jemima and her unknown mother... when he wasn't even sure if there was a link between them yet.

'She has to tell him,' he repeated.

She glanced back at him. He really had a bee in his bonnet about it. 'She's going to...just as soon as she can track him down.'

He'd started to subside against the sofa, but now he stiffened with an oath. 'That's why you requested leave, isn't it? You wanted to help her? Why didn't you say?'

She swallowed, a weight pressing down on her shoulders. 'We don't talk about personal things in the office.'

'I… No.' His shoulders slumped. 'You must think me some kind of ogre. If you need to go and support your sister you have my blessing. Take all the time you need.'

A lump filled her throat. Why did he have to be so darn decent? She couldn't speak so she merely raised an eyebrow and glanced down at Jemima.

He lifted a stubborn chin. 'I'll cope.'

That made her smile. He probably would but… 'I love my sister to bits, Seb. She's not just my sister. She's my best friend too. I'd do anything for her—*anything*. But this is something she needs to do on her own.'

'If you're sure.'

She wasn't sure about anything.

A silence descended. They didn't speak, both evidently lost in their own thoughts. And then Jemima twitched and started to stir.

Liv stared.

Oh!

'Seb, are you still awake?'

'Yes.'

'Recite something—a poem, a prayer, a song. I don't care what. Nothing bombastic. Something gentle.'

Without hesitation he recited the words to an Elvis Presley song. As he did, she watched the baby carefully. The twitching stopped and Jemima seemed to settle…to fall back into a deeper sleep.

'I think talking soothes her…lulls her. I think it's silence that she doesn't like.'

He crouched in front of them and recited another song. When he finished he stared into her eyes, his own wide and excited. 'I believe you've cracked the puzzle.'

He was so close she could feel his heat, and her chest swelled at the admiration in his eyes. Then his gaze lowered to her lips and the grey in his eyes turned warm and smoky, the silver lights in them sparking and glittering.

An answering pulse kicked to life in her throat—an ache, an overarching thirst, stretching through her. She stared at the beckoning breadth of his shoulders, and her arms and legs went catch-me weak. Heat flooded her every cell.

His eyes darkened to a smoky storm, but one corner of his mouth kinked upwards—a ragged edge full of wolfish satisfaction. He recognised her hunger…he revelled in it. And she need only give him one sign and he'd be more than happy to assuage it.

She snaked her tongue out to moisten parched lips. It'd be so easy to run her hands across those shoulders, to learn their strength and latent power, to dig her fingers into the muscled flesh and pull him closer. Her breath hitched and her lips parted on an involuntary sigh.

Temptation coiled around her in ever smaller circles, shackling her to her body's demands. She wanted him to kiss her. She wanted it more than she could remember ever wanting anything.

Her heart pounded so hard she was amazed the vibrations didn't wake the baby.

The baby…

She blinked.

Liz…

Hell!

Reefing her gaze from his, she stared doggedly down at Jemima and started inanely reciting nursery rhymes. Her heart had led her astray once before. She wasn't giving it the chance to do so again.

Seb wasn't Brent, but he came from a different world to her, and it was just too…fraught.

Too foolish.

She'd lost too much last time.

Without another word, Sebastian rose and left the room.

She touched her lips to the baby's head, and tried to slow the pounding of her pulse. 'Oh, Jemima, there's a whole can of worms I need to keep a lid on here. I can't mess this up.' Messing up was not an option.

Liv woke to find sunlight flooding Jemima's room. She sat up and massaged the crick in her neck before pushing aside the blanket someone had placed over her. Sebastian?

She rolled her eyes. Obviously it was Sebastian. There wasn't anyone else here.

She rested back and pulled in a breath. It was so blissfully quiet.

She glanced at the clock and then did a double take. It was after nine o'clock!

She counted off on her fingers. That meant she'd had somewhere between five and six hours' sleep.

Thank you, God!

She was tempted to curl up and sleep for another two or three hours—she'd bet Sebastian wouldn't mind—but curiosity propelled her to her feet. Where were Seb and the baby? And how had he managed to keep Jemima quiet for so long?

She padded downstairs in her bare feet, and out to the kitchen with its attached conservatory. Seb was sitting at the table with Jemima on his lap and they were both eating…

Oh, God, eating! Was Jemima ready for solids yet?

She tried to ask the question, but as she rounded the table and caught sight of Seb properly, her throat closed over and nothing but a garbled sound emerged. Seb had changed out of his business trousers and button-down shirt and wore nothing but a pair of well-worn, low-slung jeans and a tight white T-shirt that outlined every lean, hard inch of him. The man was ripped and cut in ways she'd not imagined.

In ways she'd *tried* not to imagine.

And the reality made her mouth dry. She couldn't look away.

Jemima's squeal and her waving arms broke the spell.

Her evident excitement at seeing Liv filled her with warmth. She swooped in to give the baby a kiss, and then backed up again as the scent of hot, spicy man flooded her nostrils. She had the foresight to grab the jar of food Seb was feeding Jemima as she backpedalled, to read its label.

'Baby custard…for babies of three months,' he said, reaching over to take the jar back from her. 'She loves it.'

He fed Jemima a spoonful and she smacked her lips in evident enjoyment.

'You can't blame her. The stuff tastes great.' He popped a teaspoon of custard into his mouth, half closing his eyes in relish before dipping the spoon back into the custard and holding it out to her. 'You've got to try this stuff. It's out of this world.'

For a moment she was tempted, and then she frowned. Had she entered an alternative reality? Where had Liz's staid, remote boss gone? This scene—sexy man and cute baby, happy smiles and easy rapport…*ooh*, it was too attractive, too beguiling. She couldn't allow herself to get sucked into it.

Acid burned her stomach. Seb might not be twenty years older than her…as Brent had been, but he'd still be seven or eight years older. He was a man of the world, and there was little doubt he had far more experience than she.

And he was a lord to boot!

You know what happens when mere mortals fraternise with the gods.

Not that he was a god.

But she *was* a mere mortal. And she'd never fit into the life of someone like Sebastian Tyrell.

'No?' He held the spoon up a little higher, a teasing smile playing across those lips that had tempted her last night, and still tempted her today.

No! And she couldn't let him get sucked into this craziness either. He looked more than capable of looking after himself, but…

He was grateful to her. He trusted her. *And she was lying to him.*

'Ah.' His face cleared. 'Not human until after coffee and a shower. I remember. There's coffee in the pot on the hotplate over there.'

She drank her first cup black, and in silence, content to watch man and baby. They made a pretty contrast—the baby so small and fair and innocent, and the man so big and strong and—

Stop staring!

She drained the contents of her mug, set it on the table, and opened her mouth.

'Nope.' He pointed back the way she'd come. 'Go and take that shower. I'll put a fresh pot on to brew. It'll be ready by the time you're done, then you can drink another mug and then you'll be human.'

The kindness and warmth in his eyes made her chest burn. Without another word she turned and fled.

She stood under the stinging spray of the shower and recited over and over, *'Don't mess this up. Don't mess this up'* until her pulse returned to something approaching a normal rate.

She scrubbed herself dry with a soft, fluffy towel that caressed her skin rather than abraded it, all the while trying to ignore the sparks, the aches and yearnings that ebbed and flowed through her. Things between her and Sebastian Tyrell were becoming far too cosy far too quickly.

She wished they hadn't agreed to first names. She wished they'd maintained the formality of surnames—of Mr and Ms.

She finished dressing and then sat on the side of her bed, drawing in a deep breath. Bonding over the baby had evidently broken down barriers with an ease that wasn't the norm. Combine it with sleep deprivation…

She let the breath out slowly. But she was no longer sleep-deprived. They'd do their best to get Jemima sleeping through the night in four-hourly blocks, and she'd insist on them taking shifts—he could take the first half of the night and she'd take the second. Or vice versa.

No more cosy chats in the wee small hours. And no more sharing confidences. In fact, if she could get Jemima to sleep in four-hourly blocks, she wouldn't need Seb's help during the night at all.

She shot to her feet. It was time to badger him to start searching for Jemima's mother in earnest. That'd keep them out of each other's hair.

When she returned to the kitchen she found a steaming mug of coffee waiting for her, a small but sweet porcelain jug standing near by—probably a priceless heirloom—filled with milk. She carefully—*very carefully*—poured milk into her mug.

He smiled as if satisfied with something and eased back in his chair. She took a sip—such good coffee!—and he said, 'How do you feel?'

She wanted to laugh and say, *Human*, but a voice inside her intoned *Distance* in such stern tones she didn't. 'Thank you for letting me sleep.'

His eyes narrowed a fraction. 'You're welcome. You'd earned it.'

'How did you keep Jemima quiet?' She winced as a sudden thought hit her. 'Tell me I didn't sleep through the wailing and gnashing of teeth?'

He shook his head. 'Audio books did the trick. Both you and Jemima slept through E.M. Forster's *A Room With a View*.'

They had?

'Or, at least, a portion of it.'

He grinned. 'I'm saving the rest for tonight.'

It took all of her strength not to grin back.

'Though now we've a selection to choose from as I've bought a whole range of children's audio books. Mind you, I suspect it's the vocal rhythms rather than the content of what's being said that Jemima appreciates. I also bought a crate of baby custard, and the pram you requested.'

She glanced in the direction he pointed to find a gleaming pram standing there. How had she not noticed it earlier? It looked like the highest of high-end prams! 'How… how did you make that happen so quickly?'

'Online shopping. London. Express delivery.'

She'd bet that express delivery had cost him a pretty packet. 'Excellent. Thank you.'

His eyes narrowed a fraction more. 'You're welcome.'

'So that's Jemima and me taken care of for the day—sunshine in the park. What's your plan?'

'I thought I'd help you with the baby.'

Her heart clenched, but she hardened it. 'I don't need help with the baby.'

He stared at her, his mouth slightly open, and then he snapped it into a tight line and his face shuttered closed and she'd never felt like a bigger heel in her life.

She forced herself to go on. 'Have you hired your private investigator yet?'

His chin came up, all stone and disdain. 'I have.'

'And have you made your phone call?'

'Yes.'

She moistened suddenly dry lips. 'So…what did your father say?'

He frowned as if she'd lost him, the hauteur momentarily falling away. 'It wasn't my father that I rang.'

CHAPTER FOUR

NOT HIS FATHER? Then who—?

A woman?

None of your business.

She glanced at Jemima playing happily with her baby gym in the light-filled conservatory—and she offered up a silent prayer of thanks for all of that light—but… While it might not be her business, it was certainly Jemima's business. And as soon as she'd agreed to look after the baby, Jemima's business had become her business.

She glanced back at Seb, who surveyed her steadily, although no compelling smile now flickered in his eyes, no shared camaraderie softened the firm lines of his mouth.

She missed that. She wished she didn't, but she did.

She forced back an apology, and a teasing quip designed to open the way for their previous easiness again. It wouldn't do. She forced herself to concentrate on the conversation rather than her sense of loss.

He'd rung a woman? And yet she'd believed him when he'd sworn that none of his ex-girlfriends could be Jemima's mother. Maybe she shouldn't have, but she did. There was something innately honest about Seb. He was a man you could trust.

Unlike you.

She pushed the thought away. She might be lying to him, but she was also helping him. They mightn't precisely cancel each other out, but it had to help balance the scales a little bit.

She moistened her lips. 'Did your phone call give you any clues as to the identity of Jemima's parents?'

'No.'

She waited but he didn't expand further. Fine, she'd just have to come right out with it. 'Don't you think you need to speak to your father?'

One of his hands tightened to a fist. When he saw her staring at it, he opened it and started drumming his fingers against the table. 'My father can't be trusted.'

The glare he sent her should've charred her on the spot. *Whoa!* So this was the grumpy boss her sister had told her about. She lifted her chin and glared right back.

He slammed a finger to the table between them. 'What do you want from me?'

'I want you to find Jemima's parents!'

'No.' His glare intensified, his eyes narrowing on her face. 'You're angry with me and I want to know why.'

'You're talking rot.'

But her gaze slid away as she said it and something in his chest clenched up hard and tight.

'I'm not the least bit cross with you. But I do want this situation sorted.'

While he'd been looking forward to spending the day in the park with her and Jemima? He was a certifiable idiot!

He stilled, recalling the near panic that had flicked across her face when he'd told her he meant to spend the day helping her with the baby. He remembered that moment last night when they'd stared at each other with such naked hunger he'd almost combusted on the spot. A tiger had woken inside him and roared to full wakefulness. He'd been about to kiss her. And she'd wanted him to.

He'd been ready to take everything she offered him. He'd wanted her to offer *everything*. He'd been tempted to seduce her into mindless compliance so they could both lose themselves to the pleasure they could give each other, regardless of the consequences.

His lips twisted. Like father, like son.

He had to back away from that edge *fast*. He deliberately brought Rhoda's face to his mind.

'You're concerned about that moment last night when I nearly kissed you. It's playing on your mind.'

She opened her mouth as if to deny his words, but shut it again, her eyes clouded and troubled.

'It's been playing on mine too.' He leaned across the table towards her. 'You have my word that you've nothing to fear.' He kept his gaze, his attention, on her eyes. Not on her mouth, or the beguiling line of her throat, or that amazing hair. 'I promise that I will not try to kiss you or do anything else the least inappropriate.'

Her hands twisted together. 'It's just… You're still my boss.'

'And you don't want history repeating itself.' She'd trusted him enough to confide that, and her trust deserved a better repayment than him drooling all over her.

She drooled back.

That was beside the point!

'Seb, you're nothing like my previous…boss.'

That eased the burning in his soul a fraction.

'But I still don't want to have a workplace romance.'

'It's a recipe for disaster,' he agreed.

'Listen, we were both tired and it was the small hours of the night and—'

He gave a laugh, but it lacked mirth. 'That's nonsense and we both know it.'

Her eyes widened. Her throat bobbed as she swallowed.

'We can at least be honest with ourselves. I find you very desirable and I don't think the attraction is completely one-sided.'

'Oh!' She bit her lip and stared at him with deer-in-the-headlights eyes.

'But, being aware of it, we can take care to avoid fanning the flames…to tread with caution. Agreed?'

'Agreed.'

But her voice came out high and squeaky, and the need to kiss her roared through him. He gritted his teeth and clenched his hands…and waited for it to pass.

And kept right on waiting.

He unclenched his jaw a fraction. 'Yesterday you confided in me. Let me now make my position clear too. Like you, I've been burned by an…unhealthy relationship.'

Her throat tightened as she swallowed. 'Unhealthy?'

He had no intention of confiding the details of the betrayal he'd suffered at Rhoda's hands. He refused to relive the humiliation, the shame…the *degradation*. 'I won't bore you with the details. Suffice it to say that the aristocrat thing has a tendency to attract the worst kind of person. I have no desire to form any kind of lasting relationship. I have no desire to perpetuate the species or to keep my line running.'

Her throat bobbed once, twice…three times. 'Wow. Right. OK.'

'I choose my liaisons…carefully.'

She folded her arms, her eyes going hard. 'You prefer to fraternise with women of your own class.'

He opened his mouth to debunk her theory as snobbish rubbish, but closed it again. He thrust out his jaw. He didn't need to justify himself to her. Besides, if she thought that then maybe she'd feel safe. 'I refuse to risk my business relationships for the sake of scratching a temporary itch,' he said, deliberately crude. 'Sleeping with my secretaries would mean having to hire a new secretary every time the current one flounced off in a huff when she realised I meant it when I said I'd never marry.'

She blinked.

'Good help is harder to get than a good—'

'I get your point, Mr Tyrell! You don't need to explain it in any further detail.'

He tried not to wince at that *Mr Tyrell*. But the automatic way it came out of her mouth made him think that maybe, once this was all over, things would return to normal.

The thought should make him feel happier.

He lifted his chin. 'I just want us on the same page. I don't want you worried that I'll attempt to seduce you. You have my word that I won't.'

She laughed, but he didn't understand why. 'Don't worry, I believe you. And I appreciate your frankness, Seb.'

He had a feeling that she said his name to let him know she wasn't outraged at his revelation, that she didn't hold it against him. But he had to fight back a groan at the sound of it on her lips. The rightness of it.

'So I'm going to be equally frank.'

Dear God. How could this conversation get any franker?

'It still appears obvious to me that you need to speak to your father.'

Acid burned in his gut, tempering his lust.

'If he's the key to this mystery, as you suspect, then why are you delaying confronting him?'

The last of his desire dissolved. He shoved away from the table on the pretext of pouring himself more coffee. He held the coffee pot up towards her in a silent question, but she shook her head.

She continued to stare at him with relentless eyes. 'Well?'

He took a measured sip, leaning back against a kitchen bench as if the cares of the world weren't trying to pound him into the ground. 'I think it'll be best to wait and see what the private investigator turns up.'

'That could take days!'

'What is it you're really worried about?'

She shot to her feet, slamming her hands to her hips. 'What I want to know is why *you're* not more worried? In not reporting Jemima's situation, I suspect we're both skating on the wrong side of the law.'

It was unconscionable to have put her in this position.

'But apart from my fears about the legalities, there's a woman out there who obviously felt so far at the end of her tether she abandoned her baby to strangers. For Jemima's sake we need to find her and help her.'

'You're putting a singularly positive spin on it.' He shifted, trying to get comfortable against the bench. 'Jemima's mother could be a drug addict who'll contact us soon enough with menaces—demanding money.'

'If someone in your family is Jemima's father, her mother is entitled to financial aid in the shape of child support. Do you know how financially difficult it is for single mothers in this country? Do you know that across all developed countries in the world single mothers are among the poorest members of society?'

How did she know that? And then he recalled her sister's predicament. He suddenly saw how personal this situation must feel to her.

'And they can't win! If they have a full-time job they're bad mothers for not spending enough time with their child. But if they decide to be stay-at-home mums they're vilified for being welfare queens and a strain on society. Single fathers aren't viewed in the same way. They aren't subjected to the same prejudices. No!' She paced up and down, waving her hands in the air. 'They're patted on the back for going above and beyond. How can it be considered *above and beyond* when it's your own child? This world is set up to benefit and protect men, at the expense of women. It makes me so mad!'

Jemima gave a loud cry and Eliza immediately dropped

down on the quilted rug beside the baby, all smiles, making Jemima laugh with the aid of a teddy bear and a silly voice.

His gut clenched up tight. 'Is there anything I can do to help your sister?'

Her shoulders slumped. 'I'm not blaming you for society's ills, Seb. I'm not saying they're your fault or of your making.'

'I know that.' But it didn't change the fact that he benefited—unknowingly—from the way society was set up. 'But if there's anything I can do to help, then I want to.'

She glanced up at him and he couldn't read the expression in her eyes—it was a mixture of warmth, sadness, and feeling all at sea. 'You can't help my sister, but you can help the poor woman who left Jemima in your care.'

Her words sucker-punched him. He had to brace his hands on his knees for a moment to catch his breath. 'I haven't seen or spoken to my father in two years.'

Her mouth fell open. She snapped it shut. 'I'm sorry. I didn't know there was a rift.'

'You wouldn't.' He straightened. 'It's not a story that ever made the papers.'

She pursed her lips and then lifted the baby onto her lap. Woman and child stared at him and myriad emotions crowded his chest. He lifted his gaze to the ceiling and counted to ten before glancing back at her. 'What? Out with it.'

She grimaced. 'It's going to sound hard and—'

'I'm discovering, Eliza, that you have a propensity for uttering hard truths.'

'I don't mean to hurt your feelings.'

Those golden eyes were so wide and so worried he found himself biting back the beginnings of a smile. 'Understood and appreciated.'

She grimaced again. 'It's just that I don't believe your

pride should hold much weight in the face of Jemima's predicament.'

Ouch!

'Look at her, Seb.' She ran her hand over the crown of the baby's head as if he needed further convincing. 'She's so innocent…and so lovely. She deserves only good things, the best that life can offer.' She pulled in a breath. 'She deserves better than this.'

He wanted to point out that the baby currently had a roof over her head, food in her belly and two people at her beck and call, but it wasn't what she meant.

She was right. They needed to clear up this mystery and put things to rights as quickly as they could—for the baby's sake.

But…

'You don't seem to understand. Confronting my father will do no good.' Everything inside of him went cold. 'Hector is a liar and a cheat without an honest bone in his body. He won't tell me—or you—the truth. The sight of a baby won't move him. There are reasons we're estranged. Good reasons.' He and his father were done. For good.

She stared at him for a long moment, her eyes cloudy, and then rose with Jemima in her arms. 'Why don't we go for that walk?'

'I didn't think you wanted—'

'We're making a plan or, at least, trying to find a way forward. That's good…useful. We may as well make it in the sun in the pretty gardens.'

And just like that she made him feel less alone. It should've been impossible. And he probably shouldn't have revelled in the sensation, not even for a single second. But for a moment he simply couldn't help it.

Less than ten minutes later they were strolling in the park. It was a perfect spring day—warm with blues skies, the occasional ripple of white cloud drifting high above.

The gardens were bursting with colour and blooms. Tulips in myriad colours all vied to out-display each other. The scent of freshly mown grass and cherry blossom filled the air. Everything was warm, fragrant…idyllic.

Liv halted the pram to adjust the little sunhat Jemima wore and the hood of the pram to make sure the baby's face was properly shaded. 'I want her to get lots of light, but I don't want her to burn.' She straightened and glanced across at him. 'Is pushing a pram unmanly?'

'I have no idea.' And, frankly, he didn't care if it was. He took her place pushing the pram while she walked alongside staring at the cherry trees, the gardens…the squirrels. He sensed her mind racing, and he wondered how much of her surroundings she actually saw. He didn't interrupt her. He simply kept walking and waited.

'Seb?'

'Yes?'

She swung to face him. 'Look, I'm not going to ask why you haven't spoken to your father in so long.'

Ice tripped down his spine and a vice gripped his temples. Just as well, as he had no intention of enlightening her.

'But you obviously believe it's possible that he's either Jemima's father or grandfather.'

He stared straight ahead, but could feel the heat of her gaze. It seared his flesh. 'I don't believe for a single moment that my father will make any such admission.'

She didn't say anything and his flesh burned brighter and hotter.

'Eliza?'

'Yes?'

'Are you staring at me?'

He felt the release from her gaze as she swung forward again. He momentarily closed his eyes at the respite.

'You went all icy,' she murmured.

'Would you prefer I worked myself into a passion?'

She hesitated a beat too long. 'No!' The word emerged too breathy, too full of anticipation.

An anticipation that couldn't be explored. He ground his teeth together.

'There was an incident two and a half years ago.' He pulled in a breath, felt his nostrils flare as his stomach started to churn. He glanced at her. 'You understand this is just between you and me.'

She crossed her heart.

He turned his gaze back to the front. 'A young man came forward claiming Hector was his biological father. He was the son of one of our former housemaids.'

'And?'

'My parents threw him out of the house, with various insults and thinly veiled threats.'

Her breath hitched but he refused to turn and look at her again. 'And you?' she whispered.

'His story seemed…creditable. So I went after him.' His lips twisted. Oh, yes, it had been all too plausible. All his adult life Hector had used his charm and position to take whatever he wanted from whomever he wanted—including the sexual favours of his staff—before tossing them aside without thought or care. 'We had a DNA comparison done.'

'Oh! Did…did your parents know what you were doing?'

'Yes.' There'd been the most God-awful row. It was his first glimpse of Rhoda's true colours. He should've heeded them then.

'Well, good for you!'

From the corner of his eye he saw her plant her hands on her hips and give a decisive nod. She seemed to grow taller and for some reason it made him want to smile.

'So…the results? Was he your half-brother?'

'No.' Acid coated his tongue. 'More's the pity. I liked him.'

'Oh!' She stared up at him with throbbing eyes before reaching out and touching his arm, her fingers wrapping about his wrist, her eyes filling with warmth and sympathy.

The action slid in beneath his guard. And then the warmth of her hand registered and a pulse quickened through him, spreading heat and havoc.

He wanted to pull her to him. He wanted to shake her off.

He wanted to stop *feeling.*

'I'm sorry.'

They'd stopped and he forced his feet forward again. He told himself he was glad when her hand dropped away. 'My parents weren't. They were delighted at the outcome.' They'd crowed about their victory. 'But that was the moment I became aware that I could have several half-siblings I knew nothing about.'

'Did you ask them—your parents?'

Of course he'd asked them.

'Of course you asked them!' she said, echoing his unspoken words. 'But they refused to tell you anything—right?'

Exactly.

They both walked in silence for a while. 'I take it your mother wouldn't be of any help?'

'None whatsoever. She's as bad as Hector.'

'What about staff—do you have any allies there?'

He did. Brownie and George had been at Tyrell Hall his entire life. But they didn't believe in gossiping about their betters. If only he could make them see that they were worth ten Lord and Lady Tyrells.

'What about old records…diaries…photo albums?'

Would either of his parents have been foolish enough to keep records that might incriminate them, that would make them financially responsible for someone else?

He pursed his lips. It wasn't inconceivable. His father

in particular was reckless. It was a possibility. A remote one, but a possibility all the same.

'Seb?'

He shrugged. 'The odds are slim.'

'But better than what we have at the moment. Where would such things be kept? Here in London or at your Lincolnshire estate?'

'Lincolnshire.'

'Then…what are we waiting for?'

He halted halfway down the avenue of cherry trees. Here and there white blossom floated down through the air. Everything smelled fresh and sweet.

'You want to go to Lincolnshire?' He thought she'd been trying to get rid of him.

She huffed out a breath. '*Want* might be stretching the point a little. But I'm bullying you into finding Jemima's mother and it seems a little cold-hearted to send you off on your own.'

She wanted to give him moral support? For a moment he was speechless. He couldn't remember the last time anyone had tried to be so supportive of him.

Which was his own fault. He rarely gave anyone the chance. But…

'What?' She pushed her hair back from her face.

He started when he realised he'd been staring, forced his feet forward again. 'You haven't bullied me into anything. You simply pointed out—correctly—that I was dragging my feet. You've no need to feel guilty.'

She bit the side of her thumb and sent him a look that seemed far from reassured. 'Two heads are better than one; four hands are better than two. And I might be able to help in other ways too.'

It took a force of will, but he kept his gaze on the path ahead. The avenue of cherry trees with their spectacular blossom paled in comparison to the woman beside him. Every cell in his body strained towards her. 'Such as?'

'Babies catch at people's hearts. The sight of Jemima might make somebody talk or confide in us.'

'You're a romantic, you know that?'

'I am not!'

She looked personally affronted at the idea and it made him laugh. For the briefest moment it made him feel young.

'And...' She raised a reluctant shoulder. 'There are other less salubrious tactics we can resort to if needs be.'

'Such as?'

'Gossip.'

His stomach curdled.

'There are bound to be staff on the estate who've been there a long time...who might be able to provide us with a clue or two. Or neighbours or tradespeople.'

He stared down into the pram at the tiny baby. *How much am I going to be asked to sacrifice on your behalf, little one?*

'I see what you're driving at. You think that if you accompany me as Jemima's nanny it'll give you an inside track on any downstairs gossip.'

'It's a possibility, isn't it? It could at least be worth a try, don't you think?'

She didn't understand the ugliness she could uncover. Nausea made his stomach rebel and his head spin. He had to stop and brace his arms against the pram, concentrate on taking deep, cleansing breaths to keep it at bay.

A hand on his back sent warmth filtering into his veins, making the nausea recede. But replaced it with an ache that he dared not assuage.

'Seb, you're evidently not feeling well. Let's go back. You can lie down and—'

He captured her other hand in his and tugged her so close her perfume rose around him and he could see each individual eyelash—she smelled of gardenias and jam. 'Eliza, my parents have done some ugly things in their lifetimes. I've spent my adult life trying to make amends.'

The hand on his back moved to rest against his cheek. 'Oh, Seb, I'm so sorry. And here I am asking you to discover more potential awfulness.'

He needed some distance because he was in danger of breaking his promise and kissing her. He stepped back until her hand dropped away. 'If you come to Tyrell Hall with me I need to ask a favour of you.'

She stared at him wordlessly and then nodded. 'OK.'

'Whatever gossip you hear, whatever ugly things you learn, I need you to promise that you'll not go to the Press with the story.'

Her head rocked back. 'I'd never do such a thing! You have my word.'

Some of the tension drained from him. 'Thank you. You have to understand it's not my parents I want to protect, but the people they've hurt or taken advantage of.'

'I'll sign a waiver or contract or whatever to that effect. I've no desire to profit from this situation. I just want to see Jemima safe and settled, and—'

'I know. And I trust you.'

Shadowed eyes met his.

'Your word is good enough for me. I don't need you to sign anything.'

She glanced away. 'When do we leave for Lincolnshire?'

He wondered if she was already regretting her offer to accompany him. He turned the pram for home. 'How soon can you be ready?'

The closer they drew to Lincolnshire, the graver Seb became. The silence that had been mostly companionable—broken here and there with pockets of conversation—grew tight and tense.

Was he worried about what they might uncover once they started digging?

Of course he's worried!

Liv stared at the hands clenched about the steering wheel—those white knuckles—and wanted to fill the silence with chatter in an effort to distract him and ease his worries, if only temporarily.

But she didn't trust herself to chatter without giving Liz and herself away. For heaven's sake, she'd told him her sister was expecting a baby! What on earth would he think when in a week or so's time she—well, Liz, but he'd think it was her—told him she was pregnant too? Would he buy the coincidence?

She'd been meaning to keep a detailed journal outlining events as they happened and all of the things she and Seb talked about, but she'd yet to start it. Jemima had taken up all her time. Liz would need to know it all. Just thinking about the explanations, and accompanying justifications she'd feel compelled to add, left her feeling exhausted.

What on earth had she been thinking, offering to accompany *her sister's boss* to Lincolnshire? Why on earth hadn't she stopped to think for once? Being as far away from Seb as possible—and separate counties would've been perfect—would have made things so much simpler. Not to mention easier.

But the look on his face when he'd spoken about his parents… It had grabbed her heart and squeezed until she'd barely had breath left. He'd looked so *alone*.

She rubbed a hand across her chest. She was forcing him to delve into his parents' past—a course of action he had no appetite for—to poke a monster—maybe multiple monsters—that was probably better off left undisturbed. And she hated it! She hated being responsible for bringing that haunted, stony expression to his eyes.

Her phone buzzed as a text came through. *Liz!*

So sorry. I need a few more days. Please say you'll keep covering for me.

She texted back.

No prob. On way to Lincolnshire. Trying to track baby's mother.

What?

The word beamed out at her like an accusation.

How is your mission going?

She quickly sent the question to get her sister's mind off the predicament Liv had landed them in.

There was a long interval before her sister finally texted back.

I'll call you later.

Liv winced and shoved her phone back into her handbag, tried to slow the pounding of her heart. Was she making an utter hash of things here?

She bit her lip. How was Liz really doing? She'd said she needed a few more days? Did that mean she'd found her tall, dark mystery man? She wriggled, rubbing her shoulders against the plush leather of her seat. If she had…and they'd liked each other enough to spend five steamy days together…maybe—

'Is everything OK?'

She started when Seb spoke. 'Everything's fine,' she lied.

He sent her a brief, narrow-eyed glance. 'Regretting your offer to accompany me already?'

'No!' She shuffled upright. And then grimaced at the look he sent her—the man was too perceptive by half. 'A little,' she admitted. 'I don't have much experience with fraught family politics. My family is lovely.'

'You see a lot of them?'

'I do.'

The stark whiteness of his knuckles eased, so she continued. 'My parents live in Berkshire. They're both schoolteachers. Mum is Australian and they met when Dad was there on holiday.'

'She came back with him?'

That made her laugh. 'Absolutely not. She refused to relocate and upend her life on the basis of only two weeks' acquaintance. So he stayed and got a posting to a local high school there. When he'd proven his devotion, and she was sure of her feelings for him, they married before moving to England.'

'That's equal parts romantic and sensible.'

'They're devoted to each other…and to my sister and me.'

'Where does you sister live?'

'London…out towards Watford.'

'What does she do?'

The more relaxed his hands became on the steering wheel, the tighter the knot in her chest. 'She's an office temp.' It felt innately deceitful to speak of herself in the third person like this to him. *It* is *deceitful. You're going to hell.*

She bit back a sigh. She'd do anything for Liz, even this.

'She doesn't have a permanent position?'

'She doesn't want one. She likes the freedom temping gives her. And she says the money is good.' The truth was Liv didn't have the heart to settle for the monotony of a single day-in, day-out job.

'But there are no benefits in temping—no holiday leave or sick leave…maternity leave.'

'She, um…also designs jewellery.' Liv had needed a creative outlet when she'd dropped out of art school…after Brent. She loved working with silver and semi-precious stones, but it didn't come close to filling the gap left by painting and sketching.

'Is she any good?'

She shrugged. 'I've no idea.'

'Will it support her once the baby comes?'

'Seb, this is none of your business.'

He grimaced. 'Sorry. Focusing on your family is a more attractive proposition than focusing on mine.'

For him, maybe. Not for her.

He gestured at the windscreen. 'You'll get your first glimpse of Tyrell Hall when we top the rise up ahead.'

They'd left the motorway over twenty minute ago, and were now winding their way through low green hills on a single carriageway. Everything looked lush and gorgeous.

'To your left,' he said.

She looked and her jaw dropped. 'Oh, my God! It's massive, huge…enormous. It looks like something straight out of an Austen novel! And I've loved Austen since…*forever*!'

CHAPTER FIVE

TYRELL HALL SAT amid rolling green fields. A large number of outbuildings trailed out to its right, but it was the hall itself that held Liv's gaze...and her awe. In gorgeous grey stone, Tyrell Hall preened with an unselfconscious acknowledgement of its own grace and grandeur. For the briefest of moments her fingers ached for her sketchpad and charcoals.

But while the hall was more than aware of its charm, the grey stone and elegant lines were both weathered and warm rather than cold and uninviting. It stood three storeys high with two wings branching out either side, creating a U-shape that formed a large central courtyard. A fountain with frolicking Greek-style nymphs held pride of place in the centre. White-gravelled, rose-lined paths radiated out from it in eight different directions.

Just...wow!

She pointed to the main building. 'How old?'

Seb stared at it with shadows in his eyes and she realised that, rather than a beautiful historic building, he saw ghosts. Unhappy ghosts. She bit her lip. Evidently, growing up here hadn't been a happy adventure.

Not the house's fault. But still...

'It dates from the sixteenth century.'

'It's really beautiful.'

He blinked as if coming back to the present. 'You think so?'

'Absolutely!' She wanted to remove those shadows. 'Seb, regardless of anything else, empirically your house is amazing—graceful, elegant, not to mention historical… and just plain gorgeous!'

He stared at her with such evident disbelief she had to reach behind to scratch an itch between her shoulder blades. 'At least that's what my artist's eye tells me.'

'You have an artist's eye?'

'I do. A very good one.' Even if her fingers didn't want to work any more. 'Still, I understand that a house may be one thing, while its inhabitants are the polar opposite.'

He stared back at the house. 'It *is* considered rather fine in most circles,' he murmured as if only just remembering that fact. 'I…it's been a while since I looked at it properly. Sorry.'

He sent her a half-apologetic smile that twisted her heart.

'I'm afraid one takes it all for granted after a while.'

She didn't believe he took any of this for granted—not for a moment.

A sudden, rather awful thought struck her. She swallowed as they pushed out of the car. 'Seb?'

'Mmm?'

'Your parents don't still live here, do they?'

He physically recoiled from her. 'No!'

'Sorry.' She tried to swallow her wince. 'The house is so big I thought that maybe they lived in one wing and you lived in another and never the twain shall meet.'

He shook his head, those shadows alive and dangerous. 'No. This all belongs to me now.'

She didn't ask him how. It was none of her business. But he really needed to start making some happy memories here to shake away those ghosts from his past.

'Hector and Marjorie live in Monte Carlo.'

'Good.'

He raised an eyebrow. 'Good?'

She lifted the baby carrier out. 'It means I won't have

to run into them, which therefore means I won't have to give them a piece of my mind.'

He laughed. It wasn't a deep belly laugh, more a quiet chuckle, but Liv counted it as a win.

Twelve wide stone steps led up to a grand portico. A portly middle-aged woman dressed in black stood waiting with an ominously straight back at the double-door entrance.

'Brownie!'

'Master Sebastian.'

Seb's grin of greeting, and the other woman's smile, the way they embraced, dispelled Liv's trepidation.

'Brownie, I'd like you to meet my office manager-cum-nanny, Eliza Gilmour.' He turned towards Liv and his lips twitched. 'Also known as Mary Poppins.'

Oh, those lips could do seriously dangerous things to a woman's blood pressure.

Brownie pressed her lips together in evident disapproval, though her eyes seemed to smile in spite of her. 'I'm Mrs Brown.'

Liv found herself smiling too. She gestured to the baby. 'And this is Jemima, who is currently blissfully asleep.'

Brownie glanced at the baby and then at Seb with a question in her eyes.

Seb shrugged and glanced back at Liv. 'Brownie—Mrs Brown—has been the housekeeper here at Tyrell Hall for as long as I can remember. She made sure I was fed and clothed, and let me know when I stepped out of line.'

She saw it all in an instant. Mrs Brown had been Seb's surrogate family. She'd done what she could to prevent a small boy from feeling too lonely in this enormous house. She'd been someone the younger Seb could turn to for comfort and a measure of security.

'I'm *really* pleased to meet you, Mrs Brown.'

Liv meant every word and the sharp look the housekeeper sent her told Liv she knew it too. She didn't know if that was a good thing or not. But one thing was clear—if she didn't stop revealing her personal feelings so unreservedly, she'd be making things a lot harder for Liz when she returned.

'Excuse me, Ms Gilmour, but I've never been one for taking nonsense. Master Sebastian, will you kindly tell me what you're doing with a baby?'

'It's a long story...and we're weary travellers in much need of sustenance.'

She chuckled. 'Come on in with you both. George!'

A man appeared and he and Seb shook hands, big smiles lighting their faces.

'Tush, enough of that! George, bring in the bags and garage the car.' As George left, she turned back to them. 'If you'd like to rest yourselves in the green sitting room, I'll—'

'Not a chance, Brownie. We're coming into the kitchen with you.'

Liv followed Seb and Mrs Brown out towards the back of the house and learned that George was Mrs Brown's husband—and, yes, his lumbago was doing just fine thank you very much, especially now he'd started seeing a new man in the village for some fancy kind of newfangled massage therapy—and that, between the two of them, they kept the place running.

Liv stopped dead when they came to the doorway of the kitchen. Something inside her chest expanded. The room was generously proportioned with an old-fashioned cast-iron cooker set into one wall alongside a more up-to-date oven. The stone-flagged floors might've been cold if not for a large blue and white rug that looked completely at home beneath an enormous wooden table, which had pride of place in the centre of the room.

She started when she realised the conversation had

stopped and both her employer and the housekeeper were staring at her.

'Is everything all right, Ms Gilmour?'

'Everything is perfect.' She stepped into the room and gestured around. 'I think I've just fallen in love.'

'Aye.' Mrs Brown's eyes lit with warmth. 'It's the nicest kitchen I've ever worked in.'

'It the only kitchen you've ever worked in,' was Seb's wry reply.

It was nice seeing him in these surroundings, seeing him so at home with himself and the people here. Everyone deserved a place where they could feel at home.

She set the baby down, recalling the shadows in his eyes when they'd first arrived. At least they hadn't reappeared here in the kitchen. She glanced around again and it occurred to her that this might be the only room in the entire house where he did feel so unabashedly at home.

The thought burned through her, making her hands clench. She flexed her fingers. He worked from here, which meant he had to have an office somewhere near by. He'd have made that his own too. There had to be at least two rooms in this sprawling mansion he felt at home in, right?

Mrs Brown planted two steaming mugs on the table along with a plate of still-warm date scones. She pointed at Seb, and then the coffee and scones, and then a chair. 'Now you can start filling me in on this long story of yours.'

With a twist of his lips, Seb motioned Liv to a chair before taking the one next to her. She drank coffee and ate a scone as he told the housekeeper all about the events of the past few days.

'Well, now, this is a pickle and there's no denying it.'

'Any thoughts?'

Seb reached for a scone, his hands steady, but Liv sensed the tension in him.

Mrs Brown shook her head, glancing at him and then

at the still sleeping Jemima. 'I can't abide gossip or telling tales outside of school.'

'Oh, but this isn't like that!' Liv couldn't hold the words back. 'This is… I mean, there's some poor girl out there who—'

Jemima wriggled, gave a loud yawn and then her eyes popped open. A smile wreathed her face when she saw Liv.

Liv's heart expanded to the size of a beach ball. 'Hello, lovely, snuggly-wuggly Jemima. Come and meet Mrs Brown…and Mr Brown,' she added when George came through the back door.

Under the influence of the baby, Mrs Brown's show of stiffness melted. 'Oh, look at you, you wee poppet.'

She was rewarded with a big smile and much waving of arms.

Liv slid a glance at Seb, to find him staring at the baby. His face had softened, making him look younger and less buttoned-up. Her insides turned to mush. She swallowed and glanced back at Mrs Brown, who was playing peekaboo with a delighted Jemima. 'Mrs Brown, would you mind holding Jemima for me while I warm up a bottle? She's due for a feed soon.'

She watched the other woman wrestle with duty and desire—in other words, what she saw as her duty, which was to heat the bottle herself, and her desire, which was to hold Jemima. Liv held her breath.

Holding the baby won out.

Liv heated the bottle.

Seb filled George in on the tale of Jemima.

When Liv returned to the table, Mrs Brown motioned her back to her chair. 'You finish your coffee, lass. I can feed the little one.'

Liv watched and waited. She helped herself to another scone. Eventually Mrs Brown lifted her head to meet Seb's gaze. 'Over the years two women that I know about have come here to the house claiming that Lord Tyrell fathered their children.'

Seb stiffened. 'Do you remember their names?'

The older woman sighed. 'I have them written down. It might take me some time to search them out. I should have them for you in the morning.'

'Thank you, Brownie.'

'You have to understand that those accounts could be false, so don't go getting your hopes up. They were never taken any further. You don't need me telling you the sort of tricks a certain kind of woman can play when she has a mind to.'

A look passed between Seb and his housekeeper that made Liv's heart thump. She guessed it had something to do with that *unhealthy* relationship he'd mentioned.

She recalled the stone-cold angles of his face when he'd spoken of it and had to repress a shudder. He'd warned her off—it'd been under the guise of sharing a confidence, but she had every intention of heeding that warning. There was no way she was falling for someone so…frozen, someone who'd simply replace her when she flounced off *in a huff*. She didn't know how men could be so cold-blooded when it came to sex, but it appeared they were. One day she'd fall in love again *with a nice man*. Sebastian Tyrell *wasn't* that man.

And yet the shadows in his eyes continued to plague her. She shook her head. She should be concentrating all her efforts on Jemima. Not Seb. Seb could look after himself.

'We need to find her mother.' All eyes turned to her. 'It's the only decent thing to do.'

'Aye.' Mrs Brown nodded. 'Unfortunately, Ms Gilmour, not all mothers are created equal.'

Was she talking about Seb's mother? Liv swallowed, not daring to look at him—even as the memory of haunted eyes taunted her. 'I know, but…' She tilted her chin. 'I'm going to keep an open mind about Jemima's mother until we know the facts.'

'Aye.'

She couldn't stand it any longer. She turned to Seb. 'Are you OK?'

His head went back and his nostrils flared. 'Of course I am. Why wouldn't I be?'

Oh, Seb. 'Because you just found out that you have two potential siblings.'

'Half-siblings,' he corrected.

Did he really think that made any difference?

She turned back to Mrs Brown absurdly close to tears. She needed to keep busy and she suspected Seb did too. 'We were wondering if there might be old letters, diaries… photo albums that we could scour for possible clues. I know it's a long shot,' she added when Mrs Brown opened her mouth, 'but we need to start somewhere.'

Mrs Brown glanced at Seb, and Liv had a feeling she'd come to the same conclusion—give Seb an occupation. She handed Jemima back to Liv. 'If you'd like to follow me…'

They walked through an array of rooms—rooms that probably had names like the Morning Room, the Green Sitting Room, and the Breakfast Room—and up the sweeping grand staircase into a room that led directly off the landing. It was large and preposterously ornate, and she had to bite back a gasp of awe. Its perfect dimensions, high ceilings and the row of tall windows marching down the length of the room and reflecting the view outside made her ache to set up with paints and easel. The furniture, though… ugh! She managed not to scowl at it—just. They were all delicate pieces of white and gold nonsense that looked as if they'd break upon contact. There was only one substantial piece of furniture in the room, and that was a leather armchair that sat by the fireplace. Seb's chair, she'd bet.

Mrs Brown went to a long cabinet and pulled forth

a wooden box, several folders and four large photo albums. She set them on one of the larger tables. Liv held her breath, but the table bore their weight without crumpling. 'That's probably as good a place to start as any,' the housekeeper said before bustling over to start a fire.

It wasn't really cold enough to warrant a fire, but Liv, for one, welcomed its cheer.

She set Jemima's carrier down on an oriental rug—Jemima was busy munching on a teething ring—and seized the box to shove it into Seb's hands. 'Why don't you start with that?'

She didn't want to read personal letters addressed to his family. She collected up the photo albums, glanced around, and then sat cross-legged on the floor beside Jemima.

Seb halted half in his chair. 'You don't have to sit on the floor.'

'I like the floor.' She pointed at the furniture. 'Besides, none of that looks like it's actually made for sitting in. And I don't want to break it.'

He followed the direction of her hand and his nose wrinkled. 'It won't break, but, I agree, it looks far from comfortable.'

It was his house…his furniture. If he didn't like it, why didn't he change it?

He stood. 'You can have my chair.'

'No, no, I'm fine on the floor, I promise. I like it. I can stretch out as I like. Besides, the rug is thick and soft. It's all good.'

He stared at her for a long moment. She resisted the impulse to check her face. 'What?'

'You like to…stretch out?'

Oops. 'I don't *stretch out* in the office, if that's what you're worried about. When I'm at the office I'm all buttoned-up and professional with not a hair out of place.' She stuck out her chin and tried not to glare at him. 'But, as you've no doubt noticed, we're not currently in the office.'

'No.' He subsided back into his chair.

She seized the top album and opened it, effectively bringing their conversation to an end. She didn't want him looking out for her comfort, she didn't want him looking at her, and she didn't want to keep remembering the shadows in his eyes!

She worked her way through the first album. She frowned. Her heart started to thump. She worked her way through the second, the third…and finally the fourth. She closed it with a snap and her hands clenched up so tight her arms started to shake.

'Eliza?'

She leapt up and raced over to one of the windows, dragging big breaths into her lungs. Those albums!

'What's wrong?' He raced across to her. 'What have you found?'

She swung around and the concern on his face pierced her to her marrow. She pointed a shaking finger at the offending albums. 'Where are you?'

Her own family's albums were so different. *So different!*

He blinked. 'What do you mean?'

'Where are you in those photographs?' It was all she could do not to stamp her feet. 'There are pictures of parties and holidays and concerts and yachts and all sorts of amazing things, but you're not in a single one of them!' Because he hadn't been there. Because his own parents had excluded him.

He stilled and then pressed the fingers of one hand to his forehead and rubbed, as if trying to shift a headache. The anger that had whirled through her like a dervish settled into a low burn in her belly. She had to fight the desire to fling her arms about him and hold him tight, to tell him he'd deserved more—so much more.

'There are official photos of my birth, christening… things like that.'

'They're not the pictures I'm interested in.'

He nodded and met her gaze. 'My parents didn't want children.'

That was evident! 'Then why…?'

'It was the one dutiful thing they did do—produce an heir to carry on the family name.'

'Oh, well, let's just pin a medal on them, shall we?'

Her throat thickened. Funny, wasn't it? Here he was, so responsible and conscientious…and yet, producing an heir was the one duty he wasn't interested in fulfilling. She swallowed, hating the reasons that must've led him to that decision. 'So they had you and…what, just abandoned you?' They'd abandoned him as effectively as poor Jemima had been abandoned.

His lips twisted and he shook his head. 'Abandoned me to an army of household staff and a life of privilege. It's not exactly a hard-luck story.' He sent her a small smile. 'And despite everything, I am rather glad to be alive.'

Was he? Then why wasn't he living life…*more*?

She shook that thought off. How could his parents have done it? How could they have treated him so…? A hundred words rallied for selection, but one stood out above the others: coldly. How could they have had so little regard for his feelings? What dreadful people they must be.

He'd deserved so much more than what they'd given him. She wished there were some way it could all be made up to him, but she knew there wasn't. And that seemed like such a tragedy.

Sebastian wasn't quite sure what to make of the expression in her eyes. 'Don't take it so much to heart, Eliza. I don't.' Not any more.

'I'm sorry.' She shook herself and gave a funny little hiccup. 'You deserve so much better than that.'

'Hey…' He bent down until he was on eye level with her. 'Are you crying?' She averted her gaze, but he swept a thumb gently beneath one of her eyes and it came away wet. 'Hey, don't cry. It's OK.'

'No.' She shook her head. 'It really isn't.'

That was when he finally interpreted the expression in her eyes—heartbreak. Heartbreak *for him*! A lump lodged in his throat. He gathered her in and held her close until her head rested against his shoulder and the scent of gardenias and jam rose up all around him. Her free arm slid about his waist and she hugged him back.

Holding her like this felt right in a way that nothing else ever had. He dropped his cheek to her hair and just breathed her in. He wasn't sure for how long they stood like that…or how long they'd have continued—he'd have been content to stay there the rest of the afternoon—but Jemima gave a loud squawk, demanding attention, and, reluctantly, at least on his part, they eased away.

'I'm sorry,' she murmured, moving across to pick up the baby and cuddle her.

'No need to apologise.' She'd cried for him? He couldn't quite believe it. It touched him deep in some centre he'd never known he had. It made his heart beat more firmly. It sent the blood rushing through his veins with renewed vigour. And it made his skin hyper-sensitive.

Desire?

Yes.

And no.

He had a feeling that where this woman was concerned desire would always figure in the equation. But this was something apart from that…something…

Unsettling. But was it good or bad?

His fingers flexed. *It could be dangerous.*

The thought whispered through him. Gooseflesh lifted all of the fine hairs on his arms.

'I was expecting a certain…decorum in the photos, with your family being nobility and whatnot, but I wasn't expecting you to be invisible. I was expecting something…'

'Something?'

'Something *more*. Some show of affection or regard for you. Something of worth!'

Jemima's face crumpled at her nanny's outraged tone and Eliza did her best to hush and comfort her.

Sebastian's stomach churned. 'I can see why you'd be disappointed.'

'Disappointed?'

Air whistled out from between her teeth, telling him she considered that the understatement of the century.

'Better words would be appalled…horrified. I—' She broke off to stalk back to the baby carrier. She rummaged among the blankets and emerged with a disposable nappy. 'Your…your parents should be—' she waved the nappy in the air, evidently searching for a suitable fate '—put in the stocks!'

It was fascinating to see her so riled. Energy crackled from her like static electricity. He glanced at her autumn hair, and then at the way her legs barely seemed to contain her outrage—moving back and forth, feet tapping. He swallowed and a pulse kicked to life at the base of his throat. An answering pulse started low in his groin. He shifted, biting back a groan.

'I wish I could take you home to my parents. They'd make a proper fuss of you like you deserve.'

Warmth flooded through him. Who knew that beneath all that efficiency his PA had such a kind heart?

She stilled. 'I mean… I didn't mean that as…'

He took pity on her. 'I know.'

She glanced around the room. 'I think I hate this house.'

And then she spread out one of Jemima's blankets on the Persian rug and placed the baby on top, changing her nappy with a deftness that made him blink. He stared at those hands, imagined them on his body…

He wrenched his mind back to find her dropping the wet nappy in a plastic bag she'd pulled from her pocket. She rose easily, as if dealing with babies and their paraphernalia were the easiest thing in the world. As if it were second nature to her.

He took the baby blanket and plastic bag from her.

'Eliza.' He reached out and pressed a finger to her lips. Their softness, the caress of her breath against his skin… the way those lips parted the slightest fraction at the pressure of his touch had him clenching up tight.

With a gasp she took a hasty step back, and his hand dropped to his side. 'Yes?'

Her voice came out too breathy and too fast. It was all he could do not to reach for her. He clenched his hands to fists and ordered himself to re-establish normality between them quick smart. 'I…'

He cleared his throat and tried again. 'Don't let my peculiar upbringing poison any of the beauty you find here. Seeing Tyrell Hall through your eyes when we first arrived—through your highly honed artist's eyes,' he teased, his stomach unclenching a fraction when she smiled back. 'It made me see that's what I've been doing. This house is a masterpiece…set in magnificent surroundings. Just because a couple of reprehensible people happened to live here for a while shouldn't blind anyone to the beauty the estate has to offer.'

She stared at him and then gave a nod, her chin coming up. 'You're right.'

She went to say something else but Brownie bustled into the room. 'Ms Gilmour, I thought you might like to see your room…freshen up and take care of the little one.'

'That'd be lovely.'

Not ready to be left alone with his thoughts, Sebastian seized the baby carrier and trailed after them. He smiled when they stopped at the door of the Rose Bedroom. It was the loveliest of the guest bedrooms.

'Oh!'

Eliza's eyes went wide when they entered. Very carefully she set the baby on the bed to turn on the spot and take in her room. 'I'm going to feel like royalty sleeping in here.'

The room had a four-poster bed with a smoky-pink silken canopy, the hangings embroidered with blue, white and yellow roses. The same accents were picked up in the curtains at the two windows. The walls were painted the palest of pinks and a rug of pink and white made a warm contrast to the dark floorboards. Her windows looked north over fields to woodland.

'It's absolutely and utterly divine! But—' She swung around. 'Mrs Brown, I'm just the nanny. Surely I—'

'Nonsense! This room rarely gets used. It'll be nice to have someone in here enjoying it for a few days.'

That was when Sebastian spotted the cot in the corner. He pointed to it. 'There's been a mistake. The cot needs to go into the room next door. I'm sharing night-time baby duties with Ms Gilmour.' He glanced at Eliza. 'My bedroom is two doors down, which will work out perfectly.'

Eliza planted her hands on her hips, unintentionally directing his attention to how those hips flared gently in the soft woollen trousers she wore. The collar about his throat tightened. His hands itched to trace her outline from neck to waist…and further. His fingers craved to sink into the softness of the flesh of her backside and to—'

'No!'

His attention snapped back. The colour high on her

cheeks betrayed her awareness of his scrutiny. He swallowed. 'I beg your pardon?'

'I said *no*.'

She was saying no to…?

'You're paying me to be Jemima's nanny, and that's exactly what I mean to be.'

The thread that held him tight released him when he realised she was referring to her role as nanny. He pulled in a breath and tried not to look too relieved.

'It was an altogether different thing when I was thrust into the role with no warning and then had three sleepless nights. But I'm better rested now.'

But not fully rested.

She lifted Jemima back into her arms. 'I've kept this little monkey awake for a greater part of the morning. And I mean to do the same for the rest of the afternoon.'

He shuffled his feet. 'But—'

'And now we have those talking books I expect things will start to fall into place.'

He tried to think of an argument to convince her to let him help.

'You'll have oodles of time to play with her tomorrow.' She shot Brownie a grin. 'This little miss has him wrapped firmly around her little finger.'

'Well, she's such a sweet thing.' Brownie cast an undeniably hopeful glance at Eliza. 'If you need any assistance at all, Ms Gilmour, I'd only be too happy to help out.'

'Oh, that's kind of you.'

'I took the liberty of unpacking the baby bag and I've made up a couple of fresh bottles. So if you'd like me to take her back down to the kitchen…'

He saw the exact moment Liv registered Brownie's yearning to fuss over the baby—if only for half an hour. She glanced at her watch. 'Are you sure you wouldn't mind? I'd kill for a shower.'

Brownie promptly took Jemima from her arms. 'It's no problem whatsoever. Why don't you have a nice long soak in the tub instead? Me and the little one here will have a fine old time getting to know one another.'

'A bath? Ooh, you're an angel, Mrs Brown.'

'You take your time, Ms Gilmour. Master Sebastian, show Ms Gilmour where to find the bathroom and then come down to the kitchen so I can tell you about all the local happenings.'

'I've been away less than a fortnight; I—' He broke off with a nod and a half-grin at the glare she sent him. 'Yes, ma'am.'

'I'm timing you,' she shot at him as she stalked from the room.

'That was a nice thing to do,' he said once Brownie was out of earshot.

'It was nice of her to offer. Besides, she's lovely.'

'Still, you could've kept Jemima all to yourself and nobody would've blamed you. It's kind of you to share.'

She frowned. 'Seb?'

'What?' He had to resist the urge to move closer to her. Moving closer wouldn't be wise.

Her frown deepened, countered by the worry in her eyes. 'I know we both feel a great deal of responsibility towards Jemima, but you can't forget that she doesn't belong to us.'

A scowl built through him. He rolled his shoulder. 'I know that.'

'Do you?' Her eyes refused to release his. 'If we do this right we'll reunite Jemima with her mother. After that it's possible we'll never see her again.'

An unexpected pain slipped in between his ribs.

She tapped a fist against her mouth. 'I… I just want you to be prepared.'

Never see that little baby again? Never know if she was

safe and happy? Everything inside of him rebelled at the thought. 'How is it possible to prepare for that?' It took all his strength not to shout the words.

She sucked her bottom lip into her mouth and he sensed the same turmoil roiling through her. 'By believing it's what's best for Jemima.'

He pulled in a breath and nodded, tried to regulate his breathing. 'Yes.'

But what if Jemima's mother was like his own?

She moved towards the door, but paused beside him. She touched his shoulder. 'It's just… I'd hate to see you get hurt.'

The warmth of her hand did strange things to his insides. She pulled her fingers back as if suddenly burned and sent him an over-bright smile. 'Now, show me where the bathroom is. A long, hot soak is exactly what the doctor ordered.'

He led the way and refused to fantasise for a single moment on what her naked body would look like sliding into a tub of steaming water.

CHAPTER SIX

LIV DIDN'T SEE Seb at breakfast the next morning. Last night they'd sat up going through the documents Mrs Brown had dug out, but they were left none the wiser. The documents and letters hadn't divulged any deep and dark secrets. She glanced across the rim of her coffee mug. Had the housekeeper provided Seb with those names this morning? Was he holed up somewhere brooding…and haunted?

She set her mug down. He might simply want some solitude from his too-bossy, too-chatty office manager. The thought made her wince.

When Mrs Brown didn't give her any message from him, she refused to ask his whereabouts. It wasn't as if she didn't have plenty to do looking after Jemima. And she really ought to get started on that detailed outline on events for Liz.

She didn't need to send it yet. Liz didn't need the worry. But her sister would need to know more than just the basics before she returned.

Liz hadn't phoned last night as she'd promised either. Liv didn't know whether to be relieved or worried. She'd sent Liz an email asking her how things were going…and when she thought she'd be coming home.

She was still waiting for a reply.

'What are your plans for the day, Ms Gilmour?'

Liv snapped herself back into the present. 'I'm going to take this little one,' she jigged Jemima who was currently ensconced on her knee, 'out in her pram for her daily dose of sunshine.' She took a big sip of coffee. The sooner she was out in the day the better. She felt in serious need of sunshine herself.

'You should stroll up to the artists' co-operative.'

Her ears pricked up. 'Artists' co-op?'

'Aye. Master Sebastian had the barn and a few of the other outbuildings converted into studios with spaces for local artists to sell their wares. He wanted to showcase local talent.'

She stared at Mrs Brown, her mug halted halfway to her mouth. 'Really?'

The housekeeper chuckled. 'You look surprised.'

'I...' She blinked and lowered her mug. 'I had no idea he was interested in art.'

'Ah, well, he's not. Not personally. But a large portion of the estate had to be sold off to cover the debts that had accrued.'

Debts incurred by his profligate parents, no doubt.

'A great chunk of farming land had to go—land leased to local farmers.' The older woman shook her head. 'It was a terrible business. A lot of good folk lost their livelihoods.'

Because of the selfishness of two negligent, unprincipled snobs? Her hands clenched and she had to concentrate on not jiggling Jemima right off her knee.

'So Master Sebastian, in an effort to help reinvigorate the local community, had the outbuildings converted and offered the spaces to local artists and craftspeople.'

He was trying to make amends for his parents' lavish spending. He was trying to make a difference. A good difference. He was a good man.

'Aye, that he is.'

She blinked and realised she'd said the words out loud.

'The public are invited to drop in during business hours to see the artists at work and to buy what they've made. You won't be disturbing anyone if you go up there. They're a lovely bunch, always up for a natter.'

It was obvious that Mrs Brown was proud of the initiative and Liv didn't need any further convincing. She drained her mug and stood. 'It sounds perfect.'

Ten minutes later Liv was pushing Jemima's pram along the neat gravel path that led towards the artists' co-op. The collection of buildings was located to the north-east of the hall, and as she drew closer she saw that the complex had its own separate entrance from the road and its own small car park, which was already a third full.

She glanced down at Jemima, busily chewing on her teddy bear. 'This could be fun, Jemmy Jemima Jo-Jo.'

Jemima gurgled her delight and appreciation at Liv's sing-song silliness.

She'd not had a good dose of arts and crafts in an age. She might not paint herself any more, but it didn't stop her from admiring the work of others. She regularly frequented the galleries and exhibitions of London to get her fill, by proxy, of creativity, artistic endeavour and beauty. It replenished her in a way that nothing else could.

And as always happened, the closer she drew to the gallery—or in this instance, the artists' co-op—the lighter she became, as if just being near art freed something inside of her. All her worries temporarily lifted from her shoulders. She glanced up at the sky and smiled. It was almost impossible to cling to her anxiety in the face of such beautiful weather in a rural idyll like this, especially with the promise of such a treat in front of her.

The proverbial cherry on the cake, though, was that she'd been seen coming from 'the Big House'. Once it was established that she and Jemima were friends of Mr Sebastian's, they were welcomed with unstinting warmth that spoke volumes of the high regard Seb was held in by the members of the community here.

The blacksmith and his apprentice snaffled her first

to tour their forge in a separate building set slightly apart from the others. They showed her the beautiful cast-iron candlesticks and bookends they made and had proven such a hit with the general public. 'We're starting to take orders via our website,' they told her proudly.

She could've stayed there for hours except that the potters bore her off to the main barn building. There she marvelled at decorative glazed tiles and plates, and drooled over the jugs, vases and beer steins. 'We have a kiln and pottery wheels in a part of the old coach house. It's ideal.' She promised to come back if she had time later in the week and try her hand on the pottery wheel.

Between them, the weavers and leather workers explained how they paid a nominal rent for their spaces, but that the money wasn't ploughed back into the estate. Instead it was used to maintain the complex and make any improvements that the members voted on—like the café that was currently under discussion. Liv asked them to put away a woollen shawl and one of the leather-tooled journal covers for her and she'd come back tomorrow with the money. She added a tie-dyed silk scarf in the most amazing colours to her growing list of purchases. 'It'll match your hair,' the dyer laughed.

She moved along to the next studio—a jewellery maker. One glimpse at the wares and Liv came to the crushing conclusion that her own attempts were embarrassingly amateur.

Oh, well. She only did it for fun.

Finally—with the leather worker's assistance with the pram—she ascended to the mezzanine level to view the paintings and sketches that the three local artists were working on, and the finished artworks they had for sale. Her chest burned when she glanced at an easel complete with a readied canvas just waiting for an artist to start work. But she had no time to brood as Naomi, Helen and Dirk—the artists—introduced themselves.

They fell into an immediate and rapt conversation. She quizzed Naomi on her use of light and shade, fascinated with the effects she'd created among sun-dappled leaves and mist-shrouded tree trunks in her woodland collection of paintings. She and Dirk then became engrossed in a discussion about structure and perspective. With Helen it was modernism and her bold choice of colours that they analysed. It left her feeling alternatively breathless and invigorated. She hadn't felt this alive in...*years*!

'C'mon, then.' Helen held out a sketchpad with a grin.

Liv crashed back to reality. 'I...' She swallowed. 'What do you mean?'

'Don't give us that,' Dirk chided. 'It's obvious you're an artist too. You've an artist's eye, not to mention an artist's vocabulary.'

'I... I just love art.' At their raised eyebrows, she gave up. 'I don't paint any more.' Her heart thumped with bruising power as she said the words.

The three artists exchanged glances. Helen swung back. 'You don't have to paint.' And then she frogmarched Liv to a stool and set the sketchpad on an easel in front of her.

'Oh, but—'

'Sketch,' she ordered her.

She swallowed. 'I don't do that any more either.'

'Artist's block,' Naomi diagnosed. And at her words all three of them sprang into action. Naomi flipped the sketchpad open, while Helen selected a pencil and pushed it into Liv's hand, neither woman giving her the chance to dither over the choice.

Dirk wheeled the baby closer. 'Sketch the baby,' he instructed. 'She's asleep, so it'll be a doddle.'

She glared at him. 'A doddle? Babies aren't a doddle, they're—'

'Don't think, draw,' he ordered.

With a sigh, she gave in and started a sketch. As soon as they saw her pitiable efforts they'd retreat and leave her in peace. She started but soon made a mistake. Naomi turned the page of the sketchpad, not giving her any time to dwell on her mistake. 'Start again.'

It happened twice more—stupid mistakes that in her heyday she'd have never made—but Naomi refused to allow her to dwell on the errors, just kept urging her forward.

The feel of the pencil in her hand was as familiar as the rise and fall of her own breath. And as she stared down at Jemima, remembering her in all her moods, the pencil started to fly across the page. She sketched and she shaded and then she turned the page, seized a stick of charcoal and did it all again in a bolder style.

And then she stopped to survey her handiwork. She stared at it and her throat closed over. She couldn't have uttered a word if her life depended on it.

This sketch…it was a halfway decent effort. Better than anything she'd attempted in the last four years.

Her heart starting to beat hard. Actually, it was better than all right. It was…*good.*

She gripped her hands together so hard they started to ache. She was too afraid to hope, too afraid to let the wild exhilaration spinning through her free. But… Had her gift come back?

How?

Was it even possible?

Her mind spun.

The three other artists passed the pad from one to the other silently. 'This isn't just good,' Helen finally said, her voice full of awe. 'This… You have an amazing talent.'

She stared at them, lifted her hands and let them drop, absurdly close to tears. 'I thought I'd lost it.'

'You don't just *lose* a gift like this,' Dirk told her.

When had it come back? How? 'If you three hadn't bullied me I might've gone the rest of my life not realising I could still do this.' And the thought now seemed too awful to consider.

'That wouldn't have happened. You'd have picked up a pencil again. You'd have not been able to help yourself. How long since…?'

'Four years.'

The three artists stared at her in varying shades of shock and horror. 'Four years,' Dirk finally said. 'Where were your artist friends? Why weren't they pushing and nagging you?'

'I…' She'd pushed them all away, cut herself off from them, too ashamed to face them.

'Never mind that now,' Naomi said with a smile. 'What's your preferred medium—oils or watercolours?'

'Oils,' she whispered.

Naomi nodded at the sketchpad. 'Would you like to give that a whirl on canvas?'

A smile rose through her. 'Yes, please.'

Sebastian came to a halt, his foot resting on the last riser up to the mezzanine level in the refurbished barn. Brownie had sent him across to the co-op in search of Eliza…and it seemed his search had come to an end.

She stood in front of a canvas *painting*, and his heart started to thump. She somehow managed to look completely alien and totally familiar, both at the same time. Yet…he'd never seen her like this before—totally immersed in the project in front of her, her brow crinkled with a kind of intense concentration that was interspersed with bursts of fiery movement.

What on earth had happened to his sensible office manager? How could he have got this woman so wrong? For a moment he couldn't move. All he could do was stare.

She looked… Powerful.

Energy coursed through her—setting her lips with purpose, curling her fingers about the brush and rag she held as if they were part of her. Energy crackled all around her, as if she had her own electrical force field.

A beat started up at the centre of him—a pulse that had the same intensity, the same sense of purpose. He didn't know what it meant or what it signified. He only knew that for long, deep moments he couldn't move, couldn't look away, couldn't even breathe, as he felt the world shifting and himself falling through space…all while his feet remained planted firmly on the floor.

A glance about the room told him he wasn't the only one mesmerised. A crowd stood around in an expectant hush—the three artists and several potential customers. The only one not the least concerned was Jemima, who nestled in Dirk's arms—he had three little ones at home—intently sucking on her bottle.

Naomi glanced across at him. Putting a finger to her lips, she beckoned him over. As a child he'd learned to walk silently to avoid his parents' notice. He brought those skills into play now as he moved to Naomi's side several feet behind the absorbed artist at work, where he'd get a partial view of the painting in progress.

What he saw made the pulse in his throat pound while his lips parted to drag in more air. He didn't need to be fluent in art appreciation to realise that what he saw on that canvas wasn't just good—it was amazing. He raised an eyebrow at Naomi, who shook her head and shrugged.

Eliza had all but completed a painting of a sleeping Jemima, but the bold strokes and the texture of the paint didn't just capture the innocence and peace of the sleeping baby—it also captured Jemima's mischievousness, her laughter…but something darker was hinted at too in the colours bleeding out at the edges of the canvas. Those colours suggested turmoil…mourned a paradise lost. He couldn't capture or explain all of the emotions that flashed back and forth through him—he only knew that Eliza's painting seized him in a fast grip and then shook him like a rag doll.

Jemima finished her bottle and Sebastian gave up silent thanks that Eliza refused to sally forth without a ready-made bottle to spare…just in case. Dirk lifted the baby to his shoulder to burp her, but Jemima saw Sebastian and gave a squeal of delight, making everyone jump.

Eliza didn't jump, but it did pull her from whatever world she'd inhabited. She turned slowly as if emerging from a dream. Those golden eyes rested on him for a moment before surveying the rest of the room. She had a smudge of pink and white paint on her cheek, and her right hand was covered in the stuff. He watched as astonishment and then consternation passed across her face, before she swung back to her painting and stilled.

All of them held their breath as she surveyed her artwork.

She set the brush and rag down to a nearby workbench and folded her arms. She unfolded them a moment later to plant her hands on her hips. She moved from one side of the painting to the other—bent at the waist to examine a detail here and there, moved back to study it from a distance. Eventually she turned to face the small crowd behind her and lifted her hands before letting them drop back to her sides. 'It's good.'

'Good?' Naomi sprang forward. 'It's amazing!'

And then Sebastian found himself holding the baby while the other two artists rushed to join Naomi, the four artists hugging each other and talking at once, and all Sebastian could do was watch and wish he could be a part of it.

Which was crazy. He shifted and jiggled Jemima.

'I want to buy it!' One of the customers leapt forward, pulling his wallet from his back pocket. 'How much?'

Every muscle he possessed stiffened. 'It's not for sale!'

The customer bristled. 'I offered first and I'm not going to let you undercut me. Let the woman speak for herself. Who do you think you are anyway?'

Helen pointed back the way Sebastian had come. 'He's Lord Tyrell's son…he owns this place.'

'Oh.' Crestfallen, the customer shoved his wallet back into his pocket.

Eliza met Sebastian's eyes. 'It *isn't* for sale.' And he realised that she was talking to him, telling him he couldn't have it either.

He opened his mouth to protest. He wanted that painting with every fibre of his being. But the customer—who evidently wanted it as much as Sebastian…and, who knew, maybe they had identical expressions on their faces?—leapt forward with a second wind. 'I'll pay good money.' And then he named a sum that made Sebastian's eyes water.

Eliza shook her head. 'I'm sorry this particular painting isn't for sale. But if you come back next week, who knows what you might find?' she said with a smile to soften her refusal.

Dimly he was aware of her making arrangements for the painting with the other artists and then she was at his side, taking Jemima from his arms and settling her back in her pram.

'I'm starving! It must be time for lunch.'

He kicked himself out of his stupor. 'Brownie sent me to find you. She said you'd been gone for hours.'

She flicked a glance at her watch and her eyes widened. 'She's right. Heavens! Come on.'

He helped her manoeuvre the pram back to the ground floor, noted the friendly waves she exchanged with everyone, before turning in the direction of the hall. They were halfway along the gravel path and his pulse still hadn't returned to its right rhythm, the ground beneath his feet still hadn't stopped shifting. 'Are you going to explain that?' he finally burst out.

She halted to stare up at him. It was only then that he realised her appearance of calm was a sham. Behind the gold of her eyes everything raced and boiled.

'I mean I thought you were a super-cool and efficient PA.'

The gold in her eyes dimmed a fraction.

'But then you transformed into… Mother Earth.'

'Oh, that's hardly an apt description.'

'And now…now you're *an artist*?'

Those eyes were abruptly removed from his. 'Not…not an artist, but… I used to like to paint. A lot.'

'Of course you're an artist. I just witnessed it with my own eyes!'

Her shoulders inched up towards her ears. 'Well, as I said, I used to like to paint, but… I stopped for a while and…and I thought… I thought I'd lost it.'

How could you lose…*that*?

'But it appears I haven't.'

In an instant her shoulders unhitched and it was as if she couldn't keep her smile in for another moment, it blazed out full of life and hope, and Sebastian found his heart beating hard and fast. For the briefest of moments she tossed her head back to beam at the sky and as he stared at the long, lean line of her throat something pierced into him, making him hungry for…for something that was more than sex. Something he couldn't name.

'Thank you for bringing me here, Seb.' She reached forward to seize his hand. 'You've no idea what it means to me.'

'I'll accept the painting as payment.' He had no idea he'd meant to say that until the words shot out of his mouth, but that painting had reached out and grabbed him by the heart, much as Jemima had.

She dropped his hand and he immediately wished the words unsaid. Her hair fanned out about her face as she shook her head. 'I'm sorry, but that painting is mine. You've no idea how hard-won it was.' Clouds chased themselves across her face. 'That painting will make sure I *never* forget.'

She smiled so suddenly it momentarily blinded him and he wondered if his heart would ever return to normal again.

'But I'm awfully chuffed you like it so much. I'll paint you something else,' she promised.

An ache started up deep down inside him. 'You say you thought you'd lost it?'

She nodded and started pushing the pram again.

'What did you mean? Will you explain it to me?'

She bit her lip. 'Oh, I'm not sure there's much to explain. I…'

He didn't buy that for a single moment. 'Over lunch.'

Brownie seated them out in the courtyard in the sun and served them steaming bowls of vegetable and barley soup, crusty bread and a jug of beer before whisking Jemima back into the kitchen with her.

Liv grinned at the food. 'This doesn't exactly look like lord-of-the-manor fare.'

'Brownie knows what I like.' He poured her a glass of beer, and then paused. 'If you'd prefer something else—'

'No, no!' She sampled the soup and closed her eyes in appreciation. 'This is perfect.'

He didn't want to waste time on preliminaries. 'So… what did you mean earlier?'

She didn't pretend to misunderstand him but nor did she allay his curiosity. 'You first.'

She had to be joking! Seeing her paint had shifted something inside of him, changed him in a fundamental way he didn't want to examine too closely. And it had changed her too. He sensed it. And yet she wanted to talk about—

'Did you get those names from Mrs Brown?'

And just like that the world slammed back into place—the way it had been before he'd seen her paint. She was right. They were here to find Jemima's mother. Anything else was of little importance, and yet he continued to let himself get distracted.

He let *her* distract him.

His heart pounded with a sick realisation. He'd been wrong about Eliza Gilmour. She wasn't some cool and efficient, buttoned-up office manager, no matter how much she might assume that façade at work. It didn't mean she couldn't be trusted, but it reminded him of all the ways he'd misjudged Rhoda, of how he'd let his desire for family and belonging blind him.

He wasn't making that same mistake again.

He had to be careful. Lust and desire were evolving into a dangerous fascination he couldn't afford to entertain. He had to resist it. He set his spine. He *would* resist it. For God's sake, Eliza was an employee. He *did not* take advantage of his staff. He *was not* his father.

'Seb?'

He pulled in a breath. 'Soup good?'

'Delicious.'

They sipped their soup, eyeing each other over their bowls with watchful caution. He reached for the bread, cutting off a wedge and slathering it in butter. 'Brownie provided me with the promised names first thing this morning. An internet search hasn't kicked up any additional clues so I've given the names to Jack, my PI.'

She stared at him but he had no idea what was going on behind the golden amber of her eyes. He recalled the way she'd cried the previous afternoon and had to swallow.

'So…you might have two siblings.'

His mouth dried. 'It appears a possibility.'

'Do you, um…want to know them?'

Once he'd ached for family, but now… 'I don't know.'

'It must be a lot to take in.'

He didn't want to talk about it. 'I just want to find Jemima's mother. That's all I'm prepared to focus on at the moment. We now have two potential candidates, which means we're closer to the truth than we were yesterday.'

She abandoned her spoon to slump in her seat. 'These are only the women Mrs Brown knows about, the ones who've come forward. There could be others.'

Countless others.

She grimaced. 'Another thought occurred to me while I was up at the co-op.'

She picked up her spoon again, ran it back and forth through her soup, not meeting his eye. He set his bread down. 'What is it?'

She pulled in a breath. 'Mrs Brown explained to me earlier that to save the estate you had to sell off a large portion of land.'

He promptly lost his appetite. 'I sold hundreds of acres of farmland. To a conglomerate.' He'd needed to find a large sum fast.

'I understand that created hardship for…for some of the farmers who'd been leasing the land from you.'

'Yes.' The single word coated his tongue in bitterness.

'Oh, Seb, it's not your fault.' She reached across the table towards him, but stopped short of touching him. 'You saved what you could.'

It wasn't how it felt. He should've found a way to curtail his father's spending years ago.

'Is it possible that Jemima could belong to one of them?'

He stared at her. The thought had never occurred to him. Had he made some young mother homeless? He shot to his feet and made for the house.

'Where are you going?' she called after him.

'To ring Jack.'

CHAPTER SEVEN

LIV WAITED, BUT SEB didn't come back to finish his barely touched lunch. Famished, she ate her soup and a good portion of the bread. Losing herself to a painting always made her hungry. She contemplated the events of the morning, trying to make sense of them, swinging between euphoria one moment and fear the next.

What if it was a one-off and the next time she picked up a paintbrush she froze again?

What if it wasn't and what if she didn't?

Had her gift been there all this time, hiding from her, just waiting for her to put in the effort to unearth it?

Why hadn't she kept trying? Why hadn't she proven herself to her muse sooner?

She swallowed. Why had she let shame and guilt conquer her so completely?

"'The bad stuff is easier to believe,'" she murmured, quoting a line from one of her favourite movies. It was easier to believe the worst of oneself rather than the best.

And still Seb didn't come back.

She glanced around the walled garden—the kitchen garden rather than the more formal gardens on the other side of the warm grey stone. The staked tomatoes and runner beans provided a flourishing backdrop for feathery carrot plants and other vegetables she couldn't identify. Heads of lettuce gleamed in the sun and lemon balm and thyme scented the air from nearby pots. Everything looked lush and vigorous. *She* felt lush and vigorous. She felt full rather than empty.

She glanced over her shoulder. Why hadn't Seb come back?

She frowned, going over their lunchtime conversation—what little there'd been of it. Something had changed in him and it took a while for her to pinpoint the exact moment it had happened. It wasn't when she'd started quizzing him about selling the farmland as she'd first thought. It was when she'd told him he had to go first—to bring her up to date on Jemima's situation.

'Oh!' She stiffened. Had he thought she'd been unwilling to confide in him?

It wasn't that at all! But she'd needed to remind herself what they were doing here, what their priority was—Jemima. She'd been playing for time. She'd love to confide in him, but… How on earth could she and Liz maintain their charade if she did?

But she hadn't meant him to feel excluded, or think she thought him an unworthy confidant.

The bad stuff is easier to believe.

She glanced up at the house. He'd grown up with those vile parents who must've made him feel excluded and unwanted every single day of his childhood. He'd been honestly interested in what had happened to her this morning. Mystified too, and curious, but interested in a way a friend would be interested—perhaps even a little invested as this was his home and he'd been the one to bring her here. He'd sensed it was a big thing, a turning point, a personal miracle. And so much else here at Tyrell Hall obviously had hateful associations. Rather than sharing her good fortune with him, her excitement and gratitude, she'd dragged him back to ugly realities.

'Oh!' She shot to her feet. She hadn't meant to be mean-spirited! No wonder he hadn't come back.

She raced their two bowls back into the kitchen.

'Don't you wake her,' Mrs Brown ordered when she peered into the pram. 'She's only just gone off.'

Liv picked up the empty tray sitting on the table. 'You

have yourself a deal as long as you let me clear away the rest of the lunch things.' When she returned with a laden tray, she said, 'Do you know where Seb went?'

Mrs Brown pointed upstairs. 'I think you'll find him in the drawing room.'

With a swift smile she headed upstairs.

Seb stood by one of the tall windows, staring out at the park, his tall frame silhouetted in all its lean, hard glory. A pulse in her throat kicked to life. She had to swallow before she could speak. 'Seb?'

He swung around. 'Yes?'

The word was clipped out, all the lines about his mouth tight and firm and yet that couldn't hide the natural sensuality of those lips. Not completely.

She moistened her lips and stared at that mouth. She couldn't help wondering—fantasising—how would it feel on hers? How—?

She dragged her gaze back to the fire, her heart pounding. The fire was totally unnecessary in this weather, but she had to admit that it was pleasant. It was the fire flaring to powerful life inside her that was both unnecessary and unpleasant.

No, not unpleasant so much as inconvenient.

'You didn't come back to finish your lunch.'

He waved a hand towards his laptop, open on a nearby coffee table—one of those ridiculous pieces of frivolous nonsense. 'There were several very unhappy people when I sold off that farming land. I kept a record.' His face didn't change by the movement of a single muscle and yet she could sense the tension coiling through him. 'Unfortunately, when you're in a position like mine, you do receive the occasionally threatening and, or, unpleasant letter or email.'

She could imagine. And delving into these particular ones had forced the lid on unpleasant memories.

'I've sent the information to Jack, but...' He shook his head, a frown burrowing into his brow. 'I know it's a legitimate lead, but I can't help feeling we'll have no joy from that area.'

Good. She glanced down at her hands then back up at him. 'Remember my plan to gossip with the estate workers and anyone else I thought might be of use?'

His head swung up. 'Yes.'

'I hadn't been up at the co-op for two minutes before I realised how totally fruitless that would be. You're held in the very highest of regard there.'

He waved that off as if it was of no concern. 'It doesn't change the fact that selling off the farmland left people unemployed. I should've found a different way to deal with it! It's my fault those—'

'Rubbish! You're not the spendthrift here. Whose debts were they? Your parents'? If anyone's to blame, they are. Holding yourself responsible is crazy, Seb. I imagine you were lucky to save what you did.'

But she could tell her words barely touched him. She moved across and shook his arm. 'You've nothing to beat yourself up for. What you've done with the co-op is amazing. Why can't you focus on that?'

He raised a mocking eyebrow, detaching himself from her grip. 'If you tell me I take my responsibilities too seriously, I'll tell you that you sound like my father.'

She took a step back from him.

'And if you claim I take my sense of duty too far, I'll tell you that you sound like my mother.'

She took another step back and nodded, swallowed back the lump that wanted to lodge in her throat. 'Right. Well. I know you must be busy so...'

She turned to leave.

'No! *Stop!* I'm sorry.'

She turned back to find him dragging a hand down his

face. He looked so momentarily haggard that her heart went out to him.

'That wasn't fair of me. I…' He lifted a sheaf of paper he'd dropped to the window seat and rustled it in her direction, his lips twisting. 'I've just been rereading the last correspondence between my father and myself. I thought there might be some clue in it that I'd missed.'

She took in the expression on his face, the shadows in his eyes, and in that moment she hated his parents.

'Being confronted with one's shortcomings is far from edifying. Let's see…' He glanced down at the page. 'Now, it's after the piece about the Cresley-Throckmortons being *"frightful prigs"*. Ah, yes, here we go. Apparently I'm a *"dreadfully dull dog who wouldn't know how to have fun if it jumped up and bit me on the nose..."* I have *"a lamentable lack of charm..."* and I'm apparently *"the death of any party"*—which, they believe, is the worst insult that could be levelled at anyone.' He glanced back down at the letter and shrugged. 'I could *"cast a pall over Christmas and they're so very pleased never to have to clap eyes on me again."*' He folded the letter and pushed it back into its envelope. 'It's put me out of…temper.'

She stared at him in growing horror. 'But that's…it's nothing but mean-spirited spite! Because you bailed them from financial ruin and then refused to continue financing their high living.'

'It is indeed.'

But it seemed their attitude still had the power to hurt him.

'And it's no excuse for my shortness to you just now. You didn't deserve it. I apologise.'

'Apology accepted.' She moistened suddenly dry lips. After three beats she said, 'They're wrong, you know.'

Both of his eyebrows shot up towards his hairline. 'But, my dear, the Cresley-Throckmortons *are* frightful prigs.'

She choked back a sudden and entirely inappropriate laugh. 'You know what I mean.'

He sobered, with a shrug. 'It's also true I don't like parties.' He strode across to the fireplace. 'I've no talent for them. They bore me silly.'

She rolled her eyes. 'That just means you haven't been to the right kind of party.'

He stirred the fire with the poker and sparks shot up the chimney.

She stared at him. She planted her hands on her hips. 'It's possible to be honourable, responsible *and* fun, you know? And you are.' Or, at least, she was pretty certain he could be.

'Thank you for the vote of confidence.' His lips lifted but his smile held no real warmth and she could see that he didn't believe her.

Damn and blast and damn!

He glanced up, paralysing her to the spot with those piercing grey eyes. 'Was there something you wanted to talk to me about? Is that why you came looking for me?'

Her first instinct was to deny it, to give him some space, but the words took too long in coming.

He straightened. 'There was.'

'It's nothing that can't keep.'

'And yet there's no time like the present.'

Being the sole focus of those intense grey eyes did seriously unsettling things to her insides. She swallowed and tried to appear unaffected. 'It's just that we didn't finish our lunchtime conversation and I didn't want you thinking I was trying to put you off or deflecting you from asking about what happened this morning at the co-op…with the painting and stuff,' she added in a rush.

He seemed to wrestle with himself for a moment and suddenly she felt like a prize idiot. It could be that he hadn't pursued the topic because he simply wasn't all that interested, and now here she was making a big thing about it and—

'I didn't want to pry into out-of-bounds territory.'

Her heart started to thump. It should be out of bounds.

'But I'd love to know what happened this morning. It seemed…momentous.'

Oh, but he has such awful parents.

She swallowed and then lifted her chin. 'It was. It's hard to describe.'

She couldn't just keep standing here when he stared at her like that—with such intensity. It was too… She just couldn't do it! 'Does Tyrell Hall have one of those wonderfully long galleries lined with portraits of ancestors that one sees in period films?'

'Follow me.'

He took her to a wing at the other end of the house. They passed dim rooms where dustcovers enveloped the furniture. They went up a flight of stairs and she sensed that she stood at one end of a long space, but it wasn't until Seb went along and opened the shutters at the multitude of tall windows that the gallery's glory came to life.

'Oh, my,' she murmured as she moved further into the gallery and glanced up at the first couple of portraits. 'This is splendid.' She pointed along the wall. 'I recognise some of these painters.'

'Would you like a potted history of the Tyrell family?'

She smiled. 'I would, but not today.' She didn't need him to treat her like a child and create an atmosphere where she'd feel comfortable confiding in him. He looked after enough people. He didn't need to look after her too.

She needed to be careful. She needed to keep these details as general as possible. Nothing she told him could conflict with Liz's CV. She pulled in a breath and pointed at the painting above them. 'I can't remember a time when I haven't loved to paint and draw.'

The truth was she'd attended a prestigious art college in London. Big things had been expected of her. Dropping out in her second year hadn't been one of them. Her parents had paid a great deal of money to make sure she'd had a chance to follow her dream. Money they could've spent on Liz's education. Money they could've spent on themselves!

They moved along to the next portrait. She stared at the painting, not at him. 'After I finished secondary school I took some art classes…night classes.' That wasn't a complete lie. Some of her classes had been scheduled in the evening.

'You have an exceptional talent. You should've gone to art school.'

She tried not to wince. 'I wanted job security. And being an artist is not a proper job.' *Liar.*

'So, you took some art classes…?'

She moistened her lips. Now came the difficult part.

'What happened?'

'I loved them.'

'But?' he prompted when she faltered.

She'd wanted to confide in him because she wanted him to know that she saw him as someone worth confiding in, that she valued him, because she wanted him to feel good about himself. Oh, but her confession was so shameful!

He was no longer pretending to gaze at the portraits. He was staring at her, and she could no longer ignore his silent demand that she meet his gaze. The very air about her seemed to throb. 'But I had a torrid affair with my teacher.'

He stilled. 'How old were you?'

She swallowed. 'Nineteen.'

His nostrils flared and his eyes grew hard and flinty. 'How old was this teacher?'

She nodded. 'He was more than twice my age, but very good-looking and suave.' She pulled in a breath and sent him an apologetic smile. 'He seemed so…sophisticated. I can see now how he took advantage of my relative inexperience, but at the time I was smitten.'

He reached out and seized her shoulders. 'You've nothing to feel guilty about. Do you understand me? There are men out there that prey on young women and—'

He released her to pace to the window. He stalked back, his hands clenched. 'What was his name? He should be exposed...punished...horsewhipped.'

At that moment he looked more than capable of doing exactly that. The momentary heat from his hands continued to burn through her, and the thought of him exacting revenge on her behalf had her tingling all over. She moistened her lips, suddenly thirsty for a taste him.

She had to stop thinking of him like this!

As if aware of the direction of her wayward thoughts, he stilled and then his gaze lowered to her lips. They darkened with a barely disguised hunger, and wind roared in her ears. She had to fight the urge to run her tongue over her lips again, to taunt him into action. At the last moment she wrenched herself away and moved to stare unseeingly out of the window.

It was a moment before he spoke again. 'Do you still care for him?'

She swung around at that. 'No!'

'But he hurt you.'

She couldn't deny it. She tried to control the pounding of her heart, tried to keep the conversation on track. 'At the time I was convinced he'd broken my heart and that I'd never recover.' She twisted her hands together, fighting the shame that wanted to devour her. 'But he did something far worse than break off our affair. He poked fun at my paintings, undermined my confidence, told me I'd never amount to...to anything.' And she'd been stupid enough to believe him. 'Why would he do that?' She still didn't understand it.

She watched in fascination as his hands clenched into fists. 'He sounds as small-minded and contemptible as my parents. I suspect he was jealous of your work, probably felt like a failure when he compared it to yours.'

'Oh, surely not! He was successful and I… I was a nobody.'

She suddenly wanted to smash something. 'I should've kicked up the biggest fuss! But at the time I felt too ashamed and…and I just fled with my tail between my legs.'

'Have you not picked up a paintbrush in all of this time?'

'Of course I have! I've tried many, many times, but my efforts were appalling—so clumsy and awkward…that…' That she'd lost heart.

'His words were still in your head.'

They'd been all she could hear.

Until today.

'And that's why you thought you'd lost your talent.'

'Until today,' she whispered.

'And now you're going to follow your passion and continue painting?'

Yes! Except she couldn't forget that at this moment she was supposed to be Liz, not Liv. 'I mean to take great pleasure in a much-loved hobby again.'

He started to laugh. 'Hobby, huh? I have a feeling that in the not too distant future I'll be losing the services of my favourite office manager.'

She froze. *Dear God!* 'No!' *When had the conversation taken such a drastic turn? Where had she gone so wrong?* She had to make things right again.

Swallowing, she pursed her lips and channelled Liz at her primmest. 'Office work suits me just fine, thank you very much.'

Seb just laughed again. 'You heard what that man was prepared to pay for your painting this morning. All it's going to take is one good exhibition and your name will be made.'

Everything inside her crunched up tight. 'Nonsense. Painting is a hobby, nothing more.'

His eyes never wavered from hers. 'I saw you paint, Eliza. We both know that's a lie.' He moved to stand in front of her, those compelling eyes piercing the depths of hers, and her heart seemed to stop…to hang between beats. 'You've been denying your talent for what…four years?' He cupped her face in his hands. 'Don't you think it's time to follow your dreams?'

His words, his touch, unbalanced her, robbing her of breath. Her hands shot out to grip the sides of his waist, to stop herself from falling into him. The life she'd thought closed to her—the one she'd thought she'd ruined—had magically opened up again at her feet and anything, *everything*, seemed possible.

Heat burned her palms through the thin material of his shirt. Her pulse thrashed and fluttered. It was all she could do not to press closer to that warmth and the intriguing lean firmness of him. She'd bet she'd fit inside the circle of his arms as if she'd been made for them—as if he'd been made for her.

He stared down at her for a long moment. His eyes darkened, but very gently he released her and stepped back. She swallowed and told herself that she was glad.

His phone rang, and he excused himself to answer it. She watched him as he strode away from her down the length of the gallery, phone pressed to his ear. When he disappeared from view she closed her eyes and tried to douse the crazy burning in her blood. He might be the most tempting man she'd met in a long, long time, but she was lying to him. To kiss him would be unforgivable.

It was all she could do not to grab a fistful of hair in both hands and give a silent scream. Dear God, what was

Liz going to say? She was making a hash of everything! How on earth was she going to fix this?

Liv retraced her steps to the drawing room and her gaze rested briefly on that awful letter from Seb's father. Damn those parents of his! Seb was honourable. Thank God he was honourable or heaven only knew where they'd be right at this very moment!

She squashed the images that rose in her mind.

The thing was, they had him convinced he couldn't be fun or amusing or…or even interesting. Her mind raced as she made her way back down to the kitchen. 'Mrs Brown, do you know when Seb's birthday is?'

The other woman cocked her head to one side. 'It's in five weeks' time.'

Hmm…that was too far away. She fell into a chair at the table.

Mrs Brown glanced at her. 'Is everything OK, lass?'

She wrinkled her nose. 'Seb has this ridiculous notion in his head that he's not fun-loving.'

The housekeeper raised an enquiring eyebrow.

Her shoulders slumped. 'Look, I know he's not some latent party animal, but…there's more to life than duty and responsibility.' Having a bit of fun wouldn't turn him into his parents.

'That's very true.'

She drummed her fingers against the weathered wood of the table. 'It's his parents' fault. They have him convinced he's dull and boring.'

Shrewd eyes met hers across the table. 'And you think they're wrong.'

'I *know* they're wrong. And he's just got it all mixed up in his head—responsibility and fun are *not* mutually exclusive.'

In bringing her to Tyrell Hall he'd inadvertently changed her life. For the better. He hadn't set out to, of course, but all the same he was sincerely happy for her. Surely she could return the favour? In a tiny way.

She lifted her chin. He had a poetic soul. And in her experience poetic souls loved a good party. 'Which is why I have a favour to ask.'

Sebastian stomped up to his bedroom. *Dress for dinner?* He scowled. What bee did Brownie have in her bonnet now? Eliza was on his staff, not someone for whom he dressed for dinner. Even if kissing her was becoming harder to resist.

The thought didn't improve his temper.

And none of it changed the fact that *dressing for dinner* was utter nonsense.

He resisted slamming his door—just. He kicked off his shoes and prepared to throw himself down on his bed when he saw the zippered suit bag laid across it with a crisp white envelope resting on top. What on earth…?

He flicked his thumb beneath the envelope's flap and pulled out a one-sided card.

The Honourable Eliza 'Poppins' Gilmour
requests the pleasure of
Mr Seb 'Elvis' Tyrell's company
this evening from eight o'clock.
For celebration, revelry and shenanigans
to commemorate the return of long-held dreams.
Theme: fancy dress.
Gifts: optional.

He found himself shaking his head…a slow grin spreading across his face. For a moment he let himself remember the way she'd beamed up at the sky—the momentary joy that had radiated from her. He recalled her heated denials of the accusations his parents had levelled at him. And then the expression on her face when she'd confided her ill-judged love affair with her teacher.

No wonder she was one thing in the office and another out of it. She was living a lie. But it wasn't the same kind of lie that Rhoda practised.

Today had been an extraordinary day for her and she deserved the chance to celebrate. With something akin to dread, he unzipped the garment bag and pulled forth a signature Elvis outfit. He shook his head. She'd remembered the song he'd recited to try to hush Jemima. So…would she dress as Mary Poppins? The thought made him smile.

It might be crazy. It might even be a little dangerous, but she deserved to celebrate and he had no intention of raining on her parade.

He glanced at the card again. It'd been decorated with pictures of balloons and a disco ball—in colour pencils rather than paint, but it still captured her signature style. It'd probably be worth thousands in a few years. Not that he'd ever sell it.

Gifts: optional.

He tapped the card against his hand, thinking hard. In the next moment his brow cleared and he gave a laugh. Perfect.

Half an hour later, Sebastian stood outside the party room—dubbed so by his parents, not Eliza. It ran the length of the entire ground floor of the western wing. He pulled in a deep breath.

You're the only one who can celebrate with her. Don't let her down.

He raised his hand and knocked.

The door was flung open almost immediately and the

moment he clapped eyes on her, his jaw dropped. She twirled on the spot. 'What do you think?'

'I...' He could barely form a coherent sentence. 'I thought you'd dress up as Mary Poppins.'

She tossed her hair—well, not her hair so much as the blonde wig that she wore. 'I always had a sneaking suspicion that under Mary Poppins' strait-laced exterior lurked the heart of a vamp.'

'A...' He swallowed again. 'A Marilyn Monroe vamp?'

'But of course, darling,' she said in a breathy Marilyn Monroe whisper that curled around him, making his pulse race and firing an ache of need to life deep inside. 'Is there any other kind?'

Grabbing his arm, she hauled him inside and promptly handed him a glass of champagne. She touched her glass to his. 'Bottoms up, darling.'

She wore a replica of that infamous white halter-neck dress—the one in the photograph where Marilyn stood above the grate—and it outlined her shape to... His mouth dried. It outlined it to utter perfection. He'd never known that beneath her severe suits she had such delectable curves, such generous...

He started when she poked him in the shoulder. 'My dear Elvis, it's far too early to start ogling the hostess. That's reserved for much later in the evening, surely?'

Dear God! 'I'm sorry! I—'

'Relax, Seb.' Her eyes danced. 'We look extraordinary, and probably faintly ridiculous.'

She didn't look ridiculous.

She shrugged. 'It's hard not to stare.'

And then she eased back and did exactly that. Everything inside him went hot and tight as her eyes darkened in appreciation and her lips parted on a sigh. 'Oh, you make a mighty fine King of Rock 'n' Roll.' She grinned and fanned her face. 'Whoa!'

And just like that she removed the last trace of self-consciousness that he felt.

She leaned forward to nudge the bottom of his glass. 'Drink up.'

Colour tinged her cheekbones pink and her eyes sparkled, but whether with delight or from champagne he couldn't tell.

'Come on over and take a seat at the bar.'

He followed her and that was when it hit him—she had the sound of a party coming through the speaker system. He swallowed a grin and pointed. 'You wanted to set the right tone?'

'Oh, the things you find on the internet! Listen to this…'

She was streaming the sound from her tablet and she leaned forward to click a button. The next moment whale song filled the air. She grinned at him and clapped her hands. 'Now we're partying with whales and dolphins. Groovy, huh? Check it out.'

She pushed the tablet towards him before setting out bowls of crisps and nuts. He pushed the item labelled 'Trappist Monks' and the sound of chanting filled the air. They stared at one another before bursting into laughter. 'We'll save that one for the speeches. It has a suitably solemn tone.'

He reached for a crisp. Would there be speeches?

'This one's fun.'

She pointed and he clicked. The sound of fireworks exploding sounded through the room. 'Very…' He searched for a suitable word.

'Loud?' she offered.

'Invigorating,' he said. 'Perhaps we'll save that one for the close of the evening's proceedings.'

'Wise,' she agreed.

They kept playing with the multitude of soundtracks while nibbling on the snacks and sipping at their champagne until he realised with a start that somehow between them they'd finished the bottle.

'I bought you a gift.'

'Oh!' She eased back to stare at him. 'That wasn't necessary. It was just me being silly.'

He pulled the gift from his pocket and handed it to her.

She took it, and then her face turned reverent. '*Pride and Prejudice.* Oh, but Seb, this looks like a very old edition.' She gulped, her eyes going wide. 'Please tell me this isn't a first edition.'

'Not a first. A fifth edition from 1902 with illustrations by H M Brock.'

'Who has signed it!' Her fingers moved over the inside cover. 'I'm sure I shouldn't accept this.'

'I'm sure you should. I can't imagine anyone who would treasure this more. You love Jane Austen *and* as an artist you'll appreciate the illustrations.'

'I…' She swallowed and her eyes shimmered. 'I can't believe you remembered that.'

He remembered everything about her. *Dangerous.* He shook the thought away. 'Perhaps it'll remind you of the adventure you once had in an Austen-eque house.'

She stared up at him. 'It's beautiful. It's the best present I've ever received.'

They stared at each other for a long moment, and something arced between them. They swayed towards each other…

But then a knock sounded on the door and both of them jumped back. Eliza pointed to the tablet. 'Choose us some good party music.' And then she went to answer the door.

Recalling the decoration on his invitation, he chose a disco playlist. Disco was silly, fun…not romantic. He gritted his teeth. It set the perfect tone.

'Excellent!'

She sent him a grin over her shoulder as she sashayed

to the door and it threatened to undo him completely. He ached to sweep her up in his arms and kiss her, to pull that ludicrous wig from her head and thrust his hands into the softness of her hair and—

'Help yourself to another drink.'

He crashed back to earth to find she'd wheeled in a trolley laden with party food.

'And eat up. Mrs Brown has made enough to feed an army!'

She had champagne, beer and soft drinks on ice. He chose a beer. He ate party pies and sausage rolls, mini spring rolls and meatballs, pigs in blankets and tiny pizzas until he thought he'd burst, while Eliza regaled him with stories of the infamous parties she'd attended at college. There'd been an unofficial school motto—*Work hard; play hard.* And she and her peers had apparently taken a great deal of pride in living up to it.

They played pool on the billiards table—his grandfather would be turning in his grave. She made him dance the twist, and he taught her the jitterbug.

She'd unearthed the karaoke machine and gave an eye-watering rendition of an eighties power ballad. She might be able to paint, but she couldn't sing to save her life. He sang an Elvis medley and she clutched her heart and pretended to swoon.

She dragged him back to the bar. 'You have to make me a cocktail.'

'What would you like?' He'd make her anything she wanted.

'No, no, it doesn't work like that. It has to be a surprise.' She frowned. 'Except, no tequila.'

Right.

'And I'm going to make one for you. We're making original concoctions, you see. And we have to give them appropriate names.'

Uh-huh. He glanced at her from the corner of his eye as she gathered ingredients. Neither of them was drunk, but they were both pretty merry. 'Can I request no cream?'

She beamed at him. 'Of course you can.'

A few minutes later he presented her with, 'A Magnificent Marilyn.' It was a combination of white rum and cranberry juice.

She clapped her hands together. 'It's pink!' She took a careful sip. 'And delicious. Here's yours. It's called, um… Graceland.'

He sampled it. Brandy, a hint of orange liqueur and dry ginger ale. 'Superb.'

She flopped down on the sofa, putting her bare feet up on the coffee table—she'd kicked off her shoes on the dance floor. He eased down beside her and followed suit. 'What happened at your old parties at this point in proceedings?'

Her cocktail floated through the air as she gave an elegant wave of her hand. 'Oh, we'd play ridiculously serious music and lie around being all mellow and artistic and insufferably pretentious.' With mischief alive in her face, she leaned forward to grab her remote. The sound of Trappist-monk chanting filled the room.

He rested his head against the soft cushioned back of the sofa and grinned. 'I thought you were saving that for the speeches.'

'Oh!'

The sofa cushions beside him dipped as she struggled to her feet, and she rested a hand against his thigh for a moment to gain her balance before clambering in her stockinged feet onto the coffee table. She tapped the remote against her glass as if to gain the room's attention.

'Everybody, everybody…if we could have a little hush.'

She'd put the crowd noise back on, but turned it off

again now and he couldn't help grinning—her sense of fun was contagious.

'I only want to say a few words. I won't keep you long from your revels. First of all I'd like to thank the wonderful staff here at Tyrell Hall for pulling this event together so seamlessly at such short notice. But most of all I want to thank all of you for coming here tonight to celebrate with me. You have no idea how much it means to me.'

Something in his chest clenched. The smile faded from his face.

'But even more than that I want to thank Seb here for…'

His heart surged against his ribcage. His feet hit the floor as he shuffled into a sitting position. *For...?*

'For bringing me to Tyrell Hall, because if he hadn't I might've spent the rest of my life not truly living.'

He hadn't done anything!

'And I want to thank him for being so kind and encouraging…and for being the best party companion anyone could ever have.'

His spine straightened when he finally saw what she'd done.

She met his gaze. 'Your parents are wrong, Seb.' A smile trembled on her lips, vulnerability flashing through her eyes. 'You're quite perfect just as you are.'

His heart gave another giant kick. He rose and set her drink to the table beside his before taking her hand and helping her back down to the floor.

And then he folded her in his arms and kissed her.

CHAPTER EIGHT

THE SURE PRESSURE of Seb's lips on Liv's, the way his fingers cradled her head as if she were made of something fine and precious, completely undid her, crumbling any resistance she might've put up.

Resistance? There was no thought of resistance. Kissing Seb was the most exciting, wonderful thing she'd ever done! She flung her arms around his neck and kissed him back with everything she had.

For a moment he seemed to bend under the onslaught of her wholehearted enthusiasm, like a tree in the wind, but he came back with a force that had the potential to fell them both.

'Seb.' His name whispered from her lips. She couldn't help it. She wanted to say his name over and over. She wanted to whisper it to the stars.

Warm lips pressed kisses to her throat, teeth scraping gently across the delicate skin there. Her knees trembled, her legs threatening to buckle beneath her, but his arm slid about her waist to hold her upright…and so very close. She pressed herself even closer. Under her hands, his shoulders flexed—broad and strong. She traced her hands up the strong column of his neck, the stubble on his cheek scraping her palms as she urged his mouth back to hers.

He kissed her so thoroughly, so completely and shockingly explicitly that a fire burst into flaming life and engulfed them both, and all she could do was hold on and try to keep up with him.

Kissing him was like being on a roller coaster. And yet it was like being wrapped in a warm blanket too. It was like flying, but it felt like the most natural thing in the world. Exotic and forbidden scents should be swirling all around them…as well as the scent of baking bread and sunshine-scented soap. She expected to hear fireworks exploding…alongside birdsong. Kissing Seb was all things exciting…and all things warm and welcoming.

It made no sense, and it made all sense.

She fitted into his arms perfectly, as she'd known she would. And she knew that if they were naked they'd fit even more perfectly. And she wanted that. She craved it with every atom, sinew and fibre. Ecstasy sparked to life wherever he touched…and aches and burnings and yearnings. She pressed herself against him to try and assuage the need engulfing her.

'God, Eliza.'

It wasn't his ragged breathing or the hoarseness of his voice that made her freeze. *Eliza.* She wasn't Eliza. She wasn't who he thought she was.

She pushed away from him with all her strength. 'No!'

The single word rang around the room, dispelling her ludicrous notion of fireworks and birdsong. He released her immediately. 'Eliza…?'

She'd let him kiss her when he thought she was someone else. She'd kissed him back. What kind of person did that make her?

She pressed her hands to her cheeks, trying to get her racing pulse back under control. She met those dark, fathomless eyes, her heart pounding so hard it felt bruised. 'This can't happen,' she choked out.

Those smoky eyes narrowed. 'Nothing need happen that you don't want.'

She knew that. Her hands clenched into fists. He'd never force himself on her.

He adjusted his stance. 'Look, Eliza, if you're worried

that I've had too much to drink, I can assure you I'm not drunk.'

She wished he'd stop calling her that!

What would you have him call you instead?

She swallowed. 'Neither one of us is rolling drunk. But we've both had more than is wise, and alcohol definitely clouds one's judgement.'

He raised a contentious eyebrow. 'I wanted to kiss you before I had a drink. I've wanted to kiss you for days… And I think you've wanted to kiss me.'

'That doesn't make it right,' she hissed at him, trying to ignore the way her stomach curled in delicious spirals at his words.

'What's wrong with two consenting adults…?' He broke off to drag a hand down his face.

She edged towards the door before she did something foolhardy and threw all caution to the wind. If she did that…it'd be unforgivable. 'Can…can we talk about this in the morning?'

Hooded eyes gave nothing away. He said nothing, just gave a nod.

She turned and fled. She needed to email Liz. She needed to bring an end to this charade as soon as possible. They had to tell Seb the truth.

There was no reply from Liz the next morning.

Liv bit her lip and then seized her phone from the bedside table and dialled her sister's number.

It rang. *Finally!*

And was answered.

'Livvy, I was just going to call you, but…'

Liv dispensed with pleasantries. 'Are you OK?'

'No.'

The tears in her sister's voice—Liz hardly ever cried—

squeezed her heart. She leapt up and started to pace. 'Are you safe? Do you need me to call the police?'

'No, no—it's nothing like that. It's just…things are more complicated than I imagined.'

'How?'

'Dear God, Liv, he's an emir!'

She plonked back down to the bed. 'You mean, like an…um, desert king or something?'

'I mean *exactly* like that.'

She couldn't think of a single word to say.

'So you can imagine what a scandal me being pregnant could cause him.'

She frowned. 'You've seen him and spoken to him, haven't you? He's treating you well?'

'He treats me like a princess—nothing is too much trouble. I can't believe how kind he's being. I'm getting the very best of everything—accommodation, food, medical care.'

Her chin shot up. 'Why medical care?' She couldn't keep the sharpness from her voice. 'Lizzy?'

'I've had a little bleeding. It's nothing to be alarmed about but, well, Tariq insists on taking every precaution.'

As he should!

'How are things there with you and Mr Tyrell?'

She gulped. 'Oh, they're fine.' What else could she say?

'Have you found the baby's mother yet?'

'No, but we've a couple of good leads, so we're hoping to solve the mystery soon. Jemima is such a lovely little thing.'

Liz remained silent.

Liv bit back a sigh. 'Lizzy, you're kind and generous and clever and all good things. You *will* make a wonderful mother. I know you don't believe it, but it's true. You just need to have faith in yourself. And if you can't do that then have faith in me and all of the people who care about you and know you.'

'I have to go, Livvy. I can't thank you enough for what you're doing for me.'

Liz disconnected and Liv stared at the phone before falling backwards on the bed to glare up at the canopy. Right, so… Evidently she'd have to keep up the charade for a little longer. At least until she could be assured that Liz's health wouldn't suffer from the shock of finding out how badly Liv had messed up here.

She huffed out a breath and forced herself upright. First things first. She had to get downstairs and relieve Mrs Brown of babysitting duties. If Jemima had had an unsettled night…

She needn't have worried. She found Mrs Brown ensconced in a comfortable chair by the combustion stove, feeding Jemima. Both of them seemed inordinately pleased with each other.

'She was an angel,' Mrs Brown said. 'A delight. We had a lovely time.'

Liv noted the way the older woman smiled at the baby and something in her stomach clenched. As casually as she could, she helped herself to coffee and took a seat at the table. She moistened suddenly dry lips. 'Mrs Brown, I don't suppose you have any…suspicions of where Jemima came from, do you?'

Shrewd eyes glanced up. 'You're thinking that because I'm fussing around the little one like this that I might be her grandma?'

'Oh, no! I—'

'God didn't see fit to give George and I children. It's a shame as we'd have dearly loved a couple of kiddies, but…'

'I'm sorry, I didn't mean to imply anything.'

'It's OK, lass. I'm enjoying playing grandma by proxy.

You want to find Jemima's mum and that's understandable and a good thing to be doing.'

What a strange world they lived in. Women became pregnant every day—some of them unexpectedly, like Liz, and some of them with dire results, like Jemima's mother—while other women yearned for the opportunity. It didn't seem fair.

'So if you need to focus on finding the girl who left this baby in Master Sebastian's office, then you need have no fear of leaving the baby with me. I'm more than happy to help.'

Liv bit back a smile. Mrs Brown would evidently be content for Liv to leave Jemima with her all of her waking hours.

'Morning, Master Sebastian.'

She froze. *Look normal. Act normal.* Impossible when her heart was trying to beat a path out of her chest. With a jerky movement she lifted her mug to stiff lips and managed to drink, though she didn't taste a drop.

'You're both up early this morning. But if you give me a tick I'll get your breakfast and—'

'No rush,' Seb assured her. 'I thought I'd take a walk before breakfast. Care to join me, Eliza?'

The sooner they got this over with the better. 'Sounds lovely.' She drained her coffee and rose to her feet.

They walked across the fields in the opposite direction from the co-op towards a copse. They walked in silence and she simply let the peace of the early morning seep into her.

She sensed the moment he turned his head.

'I have a secret,' she blurted out.

As if by prior agreement, they both came to a halt.

'I'm sorry.' She pushed her hair off her face. 'I meant to start this conversation more elegantly, but—'

'I don't care about elegance. I'd prefer honesty.'

She huffed out a laugh. 'And I can't even give you that.'

'You have a secret…?' he prompted.

'Yes…and until you know what it is then nothing can happen between us. Nothing more,' she amended. 'Not that you want a relationship, I know that, but… I mean fling-wise, kissing-wise…nothing can happen.'

Was she really considering having a fling with this man, if they ever sorted this muddle out? She clenched and unclenched her hands. His kisses might be scorching hot, but his heart was on ice. She'd sworn to never get involved with a man like that again.

His hands went to his hips and he stared at a spot in the distance. 'I take it you're not prepared to tell me what this secret is.'

A light breeze lifted a lock of his hair from his forehead. An ache started up at the centre of her. She swallowed and shook her head. 'Not yet.'

His gaze speared back to hers, and there was a fierceness in it that made her mouth dry and prevented her from moving a muscle. 'And this is a secret you believe will matter to me?'

She gave a laugh that held no mirth whatsoever. 'Oh, yes, it's going to matter to you.' She swallowed again. 'I'm sorry, I should never have let you kiss me.'

He swore and swung away, took a few angry strides up the hill before coming back again. 'I promised not to kiss you. I promised to keep things businesslike between us. If I choose to act like my father, then I deserve the consequences!'

'You're nothing like your father!' She tried to temper her voice. 'Besides, things sometimes just happen.'

He glared at her. 'Like your speech last night! It was so damn adorable.'

Oh!

'It's no excuse, I know that, but… Nobody has ever put themselves to so much trouble for me before.'

Double oh!

She couldn't speak. He traced a finger down her cheek. 'You really can't trust me with your secret, Eliza?'

'I…' She gulped. 'The thing is, Seb, it's not really my secret to tell.'

She went to move away, unable to think when he touched her like that, but his fingers suddenly seized her chin in a relentless grip, forcing her eyes to his. 'Do you know who Jemima's mother is?'

'No!' She stared at him, horrified. 'My secret has nothing at all to do with Jemima. I swear it.'

He nodded and released her, evidently satisfied.

She rubbed her chin, feeling as if he'd branded her. 'The secret was never designed to hurt you. You weren't even supposed to know about it, but…'

'But?'

'But you got to know me. And I got to know you.'

He muttered an imprecation under his breath. 'I swore never to get involved with another unsuitable woman.'

'I'm… I'm unsuitable?' Her voice wobbled.

He glared at her. 'You have a secret.'

He was right. She nodded and moistened her lips.

He stared up at the sky for a moment. 'Are you married?' He didn't look at her when he asked it.

Her throat closed over. 'No,' she managed to choke out. 'Please don't question me further. I'm not going to say any more.'

'You think I'm going to let this rest?'

His every line was etched in anger and frustration. He seemed to boil with it. It made her tremble—not with fear but excitement.

Still, she couldn't afford to have him digging into her—or Liz's—background. 'Haven't you ever had a big secret,

Seb? One that didn't seem so bad at first, but then seemed to grow? A secret you couldn't escape from?'

He dragged a hand down his face. When he pulled it away again he looked haggard. 'I made the mistake of thinking that you and I had become friends. Evidently I was wrong.'

No, he wasn't!

'I think the less time we spend in each other's company, Ms Gilmour, the better.'

With that he turned and strode back towards the hall.

With stinging eyes, Liv set her face in the opposite direction and continued tramping up the hill. What an absolutely rotten time to discover she'd fallen in love with him.

Sebastian knew the very moment Eliza appeared in the doorway of the drawing room. He knew it with a throbbing awareness that travelled up his arms to burn in his chest.

Yesterday she'd done as he'd bid. He hadn't clapped eyes on her for the rest of the day. It seemed he wasn't going to be quite so lucky today. Still, he refused to look up from his laptop. He pretended to be unaware of her presence.

Not that it helped slow the thumping of his heart. He counted the beats that pounded through him while she stood there hesitating on the threshold. He held his breath and waited for her to turn and leave.

The fact she wouldn't trust him with her secret rankled. It made him want to hurl his laptop into the fireplace with all his might.

The night of her party—that ridiculous party—she'd made him feel like someone who mattered.

Yesterday she'd shattered that illusion.

Today…

He ignored the cramping in his chest and continued blindly scrolling through the document open on his computer screen.

Eventually, when he thought he would finally have to turn and stare at her—order her from his sight—she cleared her throat. 'Seb?'

She still said his name as if—

He cut the thought off. 'What?' he barked, glancing up, his blood leaping at the sight of her.

But she wasn't looking at him. She was staring about the room with wide eyes. 'Wow! This looks great!'

Yesterday he and George had moved all the fussy furniture that his parents had favoured out of this room and had replaced it with pieces that had lain dormant and abandoned in far-flung corners of the hall—pieces he remembered from his childhood when he'd taken refuge in rooms far away from his parents. It'd taken them most of the day, but he'd welcomed the distraction.

He glanced around. The room now felt like his. He didn't know why he hadn't done it the moment his parents had vacated the place.

But he didn't need his office manager's approval or the warmth it sent scuttling through him. 'I'm glad you like it,' he drawled in a tone deliberately meant to imply the opposite. 'What do you want?'

'Oh, yes. Sorry.' She swallowed and he couldn't help but watch the line of her throat as it bobbed. 'The thing is, it's occurred to me that…'

Her golden eyes skittered from his to stare at the rug at her feet, leaving him nothing to read except the pallor of her face. His heart clenched at the sight of it. He wanted to tell himself that it served her right. Instead he found himself battling the urge to fold her in his arms and tell her everything was OK.

It wasn't OK.

She had a secret and he was sick to death of secrets, sick to the stomach with the impact they'd had on his life.

'What has occurred to you?' He didn't bark the words, but his voice came out grim and remote. He couldn't help it.

She folded her hands at her waist and stared at his knees. 'It's occurred to me that I'm surplus to requirements here.'

What?

She moved further into the room, her hands clenched tight. 'Mrs Brown is more than capable of looking after Jemima. You and your private investigator are doing all you can to find Jemima's mother.' She lifted her chin and finally met his gaze. 'You don't actually need me here at all.'

He shook his head in automatic denial. 'No.'

'But… I'd be more use to you at the office.'

'No.'

'Why not?'

He widened his stance. 'Have you heard the saying: Keep your friends close and your enemies closer?'

Her eyes flashed sudden fire. 'Am I supposed to be the enemy in this scenario?'

He gave an eloquent shrug. 'Time will tell…once I discover the truth about you.'

Her chest lifted on a sudden intake of breath. 'So all the ways I've helped you and all the things I've done mean nothing?'

They'd meant too much! That was the problem. He needed to find a way to pull back.

She hitched her chin higher. 'You can't keep me here against my will.'

'I've no intention of doing any such thing!' he bellowed.

She took a step back and he tried to moderate his voice. 'Running away, Eliza?'

She sucked her bottom lip into her mouth and stared at him. 'More a strategic retreat,' she finally said.

'I want you to remain here.'

Something flared in her eyes—hope?

'It'll be best for Jemima. I don't want her unsettled any further than she has been already.'

She snapped away from him, strode across to one of the tall windows, but not before he'd seen the light in her eyes disappear. Maybe it'd been cruel of him, but he needed to shore up his defences around her. He needed to keep his wits sharp and honed. Not dulled with desire.

'Will you stay?'

She didn't speak for a long moment. 'For the time being.' She didn't turn around and before he could extract more from her, she gestured outside. 'It appears you have company.'

Footsteps sounded on the stairs and Brownie appeared in the doorway, Jack at her heels. She puffed herself up. 'This...*gentleman* refused to give his name, Master Sebastian, but he insisted on seeing you.'

'Thank you, Mrs Brown, it's OK.' He moved forward, hand outstretched. 'Jack, you have news for me?'

Brownie harrumphed and stomped back down the stairs. From the corner of his eye he saw Eliza stiffen in recognition of the name, and then sit unobtrusively in the window seat...as if she thought he might forget that she was there. As if that were even possible!

'I do have news and I thought you'd want to hear it as soon as possible.'

He motioned the private investigator to one of the sofas. 'You didn't need to deliver it in person.'

'Sometimes it's best. In the interests of privacy.' Jack glanced around at Eliza and then at Sebastian again, raising an eyebrow.

'Jack, this is Ms Gilmour, my office manager. She's been helping me with this...situation.'

'I didn't ring or send an email,' Jack said carefully, 'because there are times when a client might prefer for there to be no record of certain...discussions.'

His heart started to thump. Jack had found out the truth. And it was ugly. He wanted Sebastian to be sure of any potential witnesses to this conversation before they continued.

A part of him was tempted to send Eliza away—as a punishment for her reticence. But he recognised the impulse for what it was—petty and unfair. Her secret, whatever it was, gave her no joy. He was sure of that.

And if he sent her from the room she'd go and pack her things and leave.

He wasn't ready for that. Not yet.

Not ever?

He pushed the thought away.

'Eliza can stay. She can be trusted.'

Her head shot up, but he refused to meet her gaze.

He motioned again to a sofa, taking a seat on the one opposite. 'What do you have for me?'

Jack set his briefcase on the coffee table, snapped it open and withdrew several documents. 'I followed up on the leads you gave me but they didn't prove fruitful. The woman you were concerned about—Rhoda Scott—she's not borne a child in the last six months. And if she had it certainly couldn't be your father's as he's now infertile. He caught a bad case of something nasty five years ago. He's been infertile ever since.'

Sebastian blinked. 'I see.'

'Naturally I continued to follow other lines of enquiry.'

Acid burned the back of his throat. How many other women had emerged from the shadows claiming that Lord Tyrell had fathered their children? Why hadn't they persisted—forced the point with paternity tests and lawsuits? They deserved support—financial *and* emotional support. 'You've discovered that I have…siblings?'

'Your parents have paid two women significant sums to…'

'Keep quiet?'

'Legal contracts were signed. In return for the money the women had to agree to never divulge the name of their child's biological father. Both women had daughters.'

He pushed a folder across to Sebastian. Seb didn't ask him how he'd acquired the information.

'All of the details are there.'

So if he wanted to follow up, make contact with these two half-sisters, then he could.

But would they want to know him?

'Unfortunately, neither woman has a child of Jemima's age.'

So he'd gained two half-sisters in the space of three minutes, but was no closer to discovering the identity of Jemima's mother. He dragged a hand down his face. When he pulled it free he found Jack staring at him, holding out a large A4 envelope.

'I also found this.'

For the life of him, he couldn't reach out and take it. 'What is it?' he croaked.

'A birth certificate.'

His heart leapt. 'Jemima's?'

'Not Jemima's.'

Jack continued to hold it out to him. Swallowing, he took it. His hands were surprisingly steady as he pulled the single sheet of paper from its envelope.

He stared at it. It took him a moment to make sense of the print on the page. His head snapped up. 'You're sure?'

'Yes.'

He slumped back, the air leaving his body in a rush.

'It's all detailed in my report.' Jack set a large packet on the table. Glancing at Sebastian again, he pursed his lips. 'You had no idea?'

He shook his head.

Liv moved across to the sofa, the warmth of her hand

on his arm, pulled him back, her golden eyes full of concern. 'Can I get you anything? I know it's early, but maybe a brandy or…?'

He shook his head and wordlessly handed her the birth certificate. She read it and her brow knitted. 'This doesn't make sense. It—'

She broke off, her eyes widening. 'Marjorie Heathcote? Marjorie is your mother's name.'

'Heathcote was her maiden name. She's used her maiden name on that documentation, even though she was married at the time.'

She stared at Sebastian and then at Jack. 'Lady Tyrell gave birth to a daughter just over seventeen years ago? How…how old would she have been?'

'Forty-two,' Jack answered.

She turned back to Seb. 'How old were you?'

'Eighteen.' He'd already calculated it. 'In my last year of boarding school before starting university. I didn't come up to Tyrell Hall at all that year. I spent the summer with a school friend and his family on their estate in Cornwall. My parents spent the summer in Switzerland. I spent Christmas in London.' On his own.

She pointed at another name on the certificate. 'And the father…this Graham Carter?'

'A tennis coach,' Jack said. 'At the time Lady Tyrell became pregnant he was working at the local tennis club.'

'Wow.' She slumped back against the sofa as if all the air had been punched out of her. 'Seb, your parents are seriously messed up.'

She could say that again.

She straightened and glanced at Jack. 'Have you met them?'

He gave an emphatic shake of his head. 'And I don't see that there'll be any necessity for that either.'

'Amen,' she muttered.

For some reason that almost made him smile.

'Lady Tyrell had her daughter adopted?'

He wanted to hug her for asking all the questions he seemed currently incapable of forming.

'She did.'

'Right.' She let out a long breath and glanced back at the birth certificate. 'So this Catherine Elinor Heathcote is Jemima's mother?'

'It appears so. She gave birth to a little girl five months ago in St George's Hospital, and called her Annabelle Jemima Gordon. Gordon is the name of her adoptive parents. It appears they've become estranged. I've been able to trace Catherine to a squat in London. She's living rough.'

'Sad,' Eliza murmured.

They all remained silent for several long moments.

'A sister,' Eliza finally said. She sent Sebastian a sudden smile. 'You have a sister called Catherine and a little niece called Annabelle Jemima. I know it's a shock, but… sisters are great.'

He had a sister... In fact, he had three.

'Well, come on, then.' She dusted off her hands. 'We have a rescue mission to perform.'

CHAPTER NINE

HE STARED INTO her eyes and Liv found it suddenly difficult to breathe. He was staring at *her* again, rather than through her or beyond her, and she wanted him to keep looking at her like that for the rest of her life.

But then the light in his eyes snapped off and he looked away, and a hard stone settled in her stomach.

'You'll stay here and take care of Jemima.' He rose. 'Jack and I will go to the squat and bring Catherine back.'

She folded her arms. 'You do realise you'll scare her half out of her wits? She'll probably bolt. What will you do then? Chase her…kidnap her?'

He swung back with a frown.

She stood then too and did her best to glare down her nose at him, even though he was half a head taller. 'She's a young girl living by her wits—so desperate she left her baby with total strangers. How do you think she's going to react when confronted by two intimidatingly large men storming into her squat, one of whom is insufferably bossy?'

Seb muttered a curse under his breath.

'Even if you manage to prevent her from bolting, you're going to terrify her. And I can assure you that's not the ideal way to build a sibling relationship.'

He glared at her. 'And you think you can help?'

She lifted her chin. 'Of course I can.'

Liv stared at the Fulham address scrawled on the piece of paper in her hand and then at the house in front of them. 'This is it.'

Air whistled out from between Seb's teeth. 'It doesn't look too bad…for a squat.' He switched the engine off and turned to her. 'What's the plan?'

'We go in there and we talk to her. We're non-confrontational. I expect she'll recognise you, but I think you should let me do most of the talking.'

'But—'

'This is an emotional situation for you, Seb, and I understand you want to pick her up and take her away from here as soon as humanly possible.' His eyes darkened at her words. 'But we're not going to railroad her. She needs to feel she has some autonomy…some agency.'

His face twisted and his hands clenched into fists. 'She needs to be away from here and with her daughter!'

'We're not going to bully her. Instinct tells me she's been bullied enough. Do you really want to align yourself in her mind with all the other people she's had to fight against? Do you want her to see you as another enemy?'

'Of course not! I…'

He dragged his hand down his face and her heart went out to him. 'Let's give the softly-softly approach a try first, all right?'

'But if that doesn't work…?'

'Have some faith,' she chided. 'Stop playing the worst-case scenario game.' She studied the photo Jack had provided of a slim girl with dark hair—she looked so young! 'Ready?'

They pushed out of the car, Seb seizing a torch. They were still enjoying bright spring weather and it was only mid-afternoon, but the windows of the house were boarded up and no doubt the electricity had been cut off.

'Have you been in a squat before?' she asked as they picked their way to the front door.

'No.'

'I have.' She didn't knock on the door, but pushed

straight in to reveal a cluttered corridor with rooms off either side. A young man—skinny with greasy blond hair that hung past his shoulders—materialised. Liv refused to appear intimidated, even if she had started shaking inside. 'We're looking for Cathy,' she said without preamble.

'Don't know no Cathy.'

She shrugged. 'Katie, then.'

Something flickered in his eyes and she thrust the photo under his nose. 'Small, dark hair…blue eyes.'

He glanced at Seb and back at Liv. He eased back a step as if getting ready to run. 'Who're you? I don't want no trouble.'

'Neither do we. I'm Katie's cousin and he's,' she gestured back behind her, 'my boyfriend.' She held up a twenty-pound note. 'I have a message for her.'

He stared at the money and licked his lips. She couldn't help wondering when he'd last eaten.

'She's out the back.' And then he snatched the money and hustled out the front door. Seb went to grab him, but she shook her head and he let him pass.

'Was that wise?'

'No idea.'

She headed straight for the back of the house. The kitchen was empty but coughing sounded from a room leading off it. Liv followed the sound to a small figure wrapped in a blanket, lying on a dirty mattress on the floor. Seb sent the light from the torch about the room and swore softly.

Liv knelt beside the figure, touched a shoulder through the filthy blanket. 'Katie?'

Eyes sprang open immediately. She stared at Liv and shot upright. 'Is Jemima OK? I left her with you. I saw you go back to the office. I saw you leave with her. You're supposed to be looking after her!'

A fit of coughing overtook her. When it was over Liv

said, 'Jemima is in the best of health. She's a lovely little girl but she misses you.'

The young girl saw Seb and shrank back. 'How did you find me? That woman gave me her word. She said you wouldn't find me here.'

Seb shook his head. 'What woman?'

'She said her name was Rhoda.'

There was that name—Rhoda—again. Liv watched Seb swallow, watched him fight the protective impulse to pick Katie up and take her away from here…watched him fight with some other internal demon.

Eventually he just shook his head. 'We had to find you for Jemima's sake, Katie.'

Katie's face crumpled. 'I can't look after her. I lost my job and…and my adoptive parents wanted me to have her adopted and wouldn't speak to me when I refused, so… Jemima deserves better! I wanted her to be with…family.'

Liv sat back on her heels. 'You deserve better too, Katie. And I think with a little bit of help from your brother, you and Jemima are going to be just fine.'

Katie stared at Seb. Her hands tightened about the blanket. 'You know the truth, then?'

'I only just found out. I had no idea. I wish I'd known sooner.'

Liv heard the suppressed emotion in his voice and wondered if Katie could hear it too.

He knelt down beside Liv and held out his hand. 'I'm Sebastian and I'm very pleased to meet you.'

She hesitated before putting her hand in his. 'I'm… Katie.'

'Look, Katie, I want to take you away from here right now and—'

Liv placed a hand on his thigh. He'd gone into full fix-it alpha mode and Katie's eyes had widened in alarm. 'Seb, it's about what Katie wants rather than what you want.'

'But…'

She watched him struggle with her words, but he finally gave a nod.

'This is what we were thinking, Katie. We thought you might like to come back with us to Seb's London house—it's where we're staying tonight. You can have a bath and we can all eat a nice hot meal…and it might be an idea to have a doctor round to give you a quick once-over, as I don't like the sound of that cough. And then, tomorrow, if you want, we can travel up to Lincolnshire to see Jemima.'

'But…'

'If you want to come back here tomorrow, you can. We'll bring you back any time. It's entirely up to you.'

Beside her, Seb made a strangled noise in the back of his throat. She patted his knee to keep him quiet. They couldn't force the girl against her will. No matter how much they might want to. If they did that, the minute their backs were turned she'd bolt again. They needed to make her feel safe, and confident that she had some measure of control.

'Katie, this isn't about charity. It's about family.' She leaned in closer. 'And he might not like me saying this, but your brother needs family every bit as much as you and Jemima do.'

Something in Katie's eyes shifted and stilled. 'You have a family?' she whispered to Liv.

Liv nodded. 'I wish everyone could have a family half as wonderful. My sister is my best friend.' She smiled at Katie before hitching her head at Seb. 'I think you'd make him a fine best friend.'

The younger girl's eyes filled. 'Why are you being so nice to me?'

Her throat thickened. 'We all need a hand sometimes. I had one earlier in the week that changed my life. Also, I adore Jemima and I want what's best for her—having her mother there is what'll be best.'

'You think so?'

'I know so. And…'

'And?' she whispered.

'And I care about Seb. I know how much he wants to build a relationship with you and Jemima. It's…it's what friends do—they help each other. So what do you think of our plan, Katie? Would you like to come with us?'

'Yes, please.'

It was the cue Seb had been waiting for. 'I don't mean to frighten you, Katie, but I want to get you out of here and safe and warm as soon as I can.' With that he lifted her straight into his arms.

'Do you want to take anything with you?' Liv said before he could stride with her from the room. If Katie had managed to hold on to any of her belongings it was because they meant something to her. And Liv didn't want to have to come back here ever again.

'My bag!' She pointed to the bag she'd been sleeping with on the mattress. 'And…and would it be OK to leave the torch for the others? It gets so dark in here at night.'

Seb shifted so that Liv could take the torch from his hand. She set it on the kitchen table on their way out. When they reached the car she dug into his jeans pocket for the car keys, trying not to focus on the strength of his thighs beneath her fingers. 'Why don't you sit in the back with Katie? I'll drive.'

'I need to thank you.'

Liv glanced up from what had become her favourite chair in the drawing room—close to the fire, opposite Seb's. It was a wingchair, plush and welcoming, and it fitted her perfectly. She loved what Seb had done with this room, but the peace she'd been seeking was shattered by his presence. His very life force seemed to pulse around her, a blanketing energy that engulfed her whenever he was near.

She unfolded her feet from beneath her and clutched a cushion to her stomach. Her posture probably looked ridiculously defensive, but it meant that her hands were accounted for—busy with other things, like picking at a loose thread. It stopped them from doing something stupid and betraying her. 'You've already thanked me.'

They'd brought Katie to Tyrell Hall two days ago. Jemima had been beside herself with excitement, while Mrs Brown had taken Katie firmly under her wing. And then Katie had told them her story. Mrs Brown had cluck-clucked. Seb had grown grim. And Liv had refused to ask questions. *None of her business.*

According to Katie, a woman once closely associated with the Tyrell family—a woman named Rhoda—had approached her two months previously. She'd handed her a photocopy of a birth certificate—Katie's birth certificate, which had revealed the names of Katie's biological parents. Rhoda had urged her to make the story public and demand financial compensation. She'd told her the family had treated her shabbily and that Katie deserved better. 'She had my birth certificate and my adoption papers. She even had my biological father's death certificate. She seemed to know all about me.'

At the time, Katie had been living in a rented flat with two other girls, but when the flat had been sold they'd been given two weeks' notice to vacate the premises. It appeared nobody wanted to share a house with a baby, and she hadn't been able to find a bedsit she could afford.

Her adoptive parents had given her an ultimatum when she'd become pregnant—give the child up or they'd disown her. They'd had plans for her to follow in their own academically successful footsteps. Rather than a daughter, they'd wanted a carbon copy of themselves. Unable to turn to them for support, on impulse Katie had rung Marjorie.

'Dumbest thing I ever did,' she'd confided. 'She was horrible. She said Rhoda had stolen her private and personal documents and that if I tried to profit from them I'd find myself in serious trouble with the law…and so would Rhoda. I didn't want to profit. I just… I just wanted a family to give Jemima. But she didn't ask me how I was…she didn't want to know me.'

At this point in the story, Katie had buried her face in her hands. A few moments later she'd lifted her head and continued. 'Something about Rhoda frightened me. I knew she was trying to make trouble, but after talking to Marjorie I didn't really blame her. I figured Marjorie had done something awful to her too. Rhoda kept saying they needed to learn a lesson, and that they shouldn't be allowed to treat people so badly. She told me about you, Sebastian. She told me that I deserved to have a portion of what you had.'

She'd bitten back a sob then. 'I didn't believe that. I didn't want your money.'

But it had led her to research the family, and the more she'd read about Sebastian, the more she'd liked him. She'd watched him from afar the last time he'd been in London—just before he'd gone overseas.

'I wanted to approach you, but after speaking with Marjorie I was too afraid to,' she'd confided. 'I was on welfare benefits. I hadn't been able to find a flat. If I'd had a job and proper place to stay, and was doing OK with money and things…well, that would've been all right. But I had nothing and I thought… I thought you'd despise me like Marjorie did.'

Seb had paled at those words. 'I'd have helped you.'

She'd nodded, tears in her eyes. 'I know that now.'

She'd blown her nose and continued. 'Rhoda kept telling me to confront you and demand what was my due, but I couldn't see that you owed me anything. But then Social Services wanted me to come in for an interview and my welfare payments were stopped until I did…and I knew that if they found out I was living rough they'd take Jemima away from me. Rhoda told me that's exactly what they'd do. But she swore if I left Jemima with you, you'd look after her…that you wouldn't go to the authorities because you'd do anything to avoid a scandal.'

At that point Seb had cursed, making them all jump. 'Sorry,' he'd muttered. 'What happened then?'

'She said once I'd done that, she'd help me get back on my feet—find a flat and a job. That it'd be so much easier without Jemima in tow. I didn't want to leave Jemima—I hated leaving her like that—but I was afraid if I didn't do something drastic she'd be taken into foster care and… I couldn't bear it!'

Seb, Liv and Mrs Brown had all assured Liz that they understood, and that they didn't blame her for anything.

Katie had stared up at Seb with those big blue eyes of hers. 'I knew you'd take good care of her. And your secretary had such a kind face. I'd watched her for three days in a row. She bought sandwiches for the homeless family in the park every single day. I knew I could trust her.'

That had made Liv's throat thicken. Seb had turned to her, but she hadn't been able to meet his eyes. 'It was nothing,' she'd mumbled. 'Tell us what you were doing at that squat. Wasn't this Rhoda supposed to be helping you find a flat?'

'I never saw her again after I left Jemima in your office. Not once.'

Seb had nodded, as if far from surprised. 'Rhoda is a malicious piece of work. She wanted nothing more than to cause trouble. She's as bad as Marjorie and Hector. She took advantage of you, Katie, and I'm sorry, but I'm glad it led you to me.'

'I was going to get back on my feet—get a job and find a place to stay—and then I was going to come and see you. But you found me first.'

'I'm glad I did. And now everything is going to be just fine, you'll see.'

Katie was still a little shy around Seb, but it was evident that she had a bad case of hero-worship…and he was slowly but surely winning her trust. He was all she could talk about when she, Jemima and Liv had their daily ramble up to the co-op.

Liv was fiercely glad that Seb finally had a family who looked up to him, who appreciated him the way he deserved to be appreciated, who were going to love him the way he deserved to be loved.

He folded his frame into the chair opposite. 'I haven't thanked you properly.'

She frowned. What did he mean by that?

'When you told me you had a secret that you couldn't share, I acted like a two-year-old and went into a ridiculous sulk.'

Her fingers worried harder at that loose thread. 'It wasn't ridiculous. You were hurt. I totally understood it because we're more—'

She broke off and dug her fingers deep into the plushness of the cushion.

His eyes darkened and he nodded, his eyes never leaving hers. 'Exactly. We're more than just colleagues.'

'Yes,' she whispered.

'But we can't move forward until you deal with this *thing* that you can't tell me about yet.'

She couldn't speak. She could only nod. Though she didn't really know what he meant by moving forward.

He'd made it clear that a romantic relationship didn't figure in his future.

Unless he'd changed his mind?

Fat chance! He's talking about sex. Just sex.

She bit her lip, heat flicking through her. But…sex was nice. There was nothing wrong with sex.

But would it be enough?

'It's something you believe can be dealt with, yes?'

'God, yes!' *And soon!* Liz's situation seemed to have reached a more even footing, her health stable. She and Liz had to tell him the truth. Between them all they'd sort the situation out. Beneath the shelter of the cushion, she crossed her fingers.

He stretched out his legs, but she had a feeling his assumed nonchalance was just a front. 'From the very beginning of this strange adventure, you've acted with nothing but integrity, kindness and generosity. Why should I doubt your word now? You tell me you can deal with this unknown *thing* and I'm choosing to believe you. I've no reason not to trust you.'

'Oh!' Her fingers dug so hard into the cushion she was afraid she'd poke holes into it. In the next moment she shot to her feet and flung the cushion back to the chair. 'I… I need to go and make a phone call *right now* and—'

'It can wait.' He motioned for her to sit. 'There's something I want to tell you.'

She sat. She had a feeling she'd do anything he asked of her at the moment.

'You asked me if I'd ever been under the shadow of a secret.'

Her mouth dried. 'Is this about the unsuitable woman you mentioned?'

'Yes.' His lips cracked open the merest fraction to utter that word and Liv's stomach performed a sickening somersault. 'I suspect you've worked it out by now. Her name was Rhoda.'

Her heart stuttered in her chest. 'The same Rhoda Katie spoke of?'

'One and the same. I met her just over three years ago at a business function in London. At the time I didn't question what she was doing there. I know now that she was there to meet well-heeled men.'

Her stomach clenched. 'You started dating?'

'Yes.' The lines bracketing his mouth momentarily deepened. 'She was beautiful, fun…and she played me to perfection.'

Liv's mouth dried. She had no idea what that last bit meant, but it sounded cold-blooded…clinical…awful.

His mouth twisted as if he'd read the confusion in her eyes. 'She discovered my weaknesses and she played on them. I imagine it didn't take her too long to work out what I really wanted, which was a family and a quiet life. So… she turned herself, outwardly, into my ideal woman. And I fell for the charade completely.'

A lump lodged in her throat. He'd fallen in love with her. And then she'd broken his heart and left him completely disillusioned. Even more disillusioned than Brent had left her. At least she hadn't given up on love altogether. She'd always expected to fall in love again one day.

'What I didn't see at the time was that all she wanted was my money and my title.'

She swallowed the lump. It lodged in her stomach, heavy and indigestible. 'How…?' She swallowed again. 'How did you find her out?'

His face had gone grey and he now pressed fingers to his eyes, as if to push back a headache. 'I tried to keep her and my parents separate for as long as I could. I didn't want them tainting the one bright spot in my life.' He gave a harsh laugh, his hand clenching. 'They're snobs, they're unkind, and… I didn't want them to hurt her.'

Her stomach churned. He'd wanted to protect her and she'd obviously thrown it back in his face. Her chin shot up. 'It sounds like they'd have been kindred spirits, bosom buddies!'

His lips lifted into a mockery of a smile. 'Funny you should say that.'

She went cold all over at the expression in his eyes. 'What do you mean?' she whispered.

Sebastian stared at the woman opposite. She was nothing like Rhoda. She'd never set out to seduce a man with one eye always on the main prize. In fact, she'd been doing her level best to do the exact opposite and resist the attraction flaring between them. She'd never use a man the way Rhoda had.

'Seb?'

He opened his mouth and forced the words out. 'Rhoda and my parents hit it off splendidly. So splendidly in fact that I found her in bed with my father.'

He tried to toss the words off lightly, as if none of it mattered any more, but the expression of horror that spread across Eliza's face brought his overwhelming sense of betrayal, and all of the ensuing pain that had ripped through him, to full-bodied life. Rhoda, the woman he'd loved, the woman he'd planned to marry, had betrayed him. *With his father!* A part of him still couldn't believe it.

Eliza stared at him, her face losing all its colour. And then she shot across the small space, dropping on her knees in front of his chair. 'Oh, Seb! I'm so sorry…so very, *very* sorry.'

'She was appalled that I'd found them out.' The sight of their limbs entangled—it was an image he'd never erase from his mind. 'All of her hard work undone in a matter of moments.'

'I can't even...' Eliza trailed off with a shake of her head.

'She begged me to overlook it...she begged for forgiveness...she swore it would never happen again.'

'But you couldn't overlook it,' Eliza said quietly.

'No. I didn't want the kind of *sophisticated* marriage my parents had, but it was clear that's exactly the kind of marriage Rhoda had in mind. And in that moment it was as if the scales had been lifted from my eyes.'

Eliza surveyed him, her face pale, though her eyes were steady. 'Is it too much to hope that she went quietly?'

'It is. She hurled every insult at me she could lay her tongue to. At least she now no longer had to marry the most boring man in England; my father was ten times more fun, et cetera.' If not edifying, it had certainly proved enlightening. 'So she embraced the role of Hector's mistress instead, hoping no doubt to gain some financial benefit from that arrangement...and perhaps some leverage to use against any of us at a later date.'

'Like the documentation she showed to Katie.'

'Exactly.'

His chest clenched and his stomach churned. The episode had left him reeling. It'd left him feeling lonelier than he'd ever felt in his whole damn life.

Eliza's face turned fierce. She gripped his knees. 'She was a liar and a cheat and good riddance to her!'

But then she pulled in a breath and blinked hard—blinking back tears for him, he suspected. 'But I know it wouldn't have felt like that at the time.' She gulped back something that sounded suspiciously like a sob. 'At the time it would've felt as if everything you'd held dear had been ripped away.' She shook her head, her brow creasing. 'How could she have done that to you? How could *he*? That's not an ordinary betrayal it's…so *callous*.'

He'd always known his parents were ruthless and inconsiderate, he'd known he didn't count for much in their emotional landscape, but he'd have never thought his father could break faith with him so completely. It had staggered him. It still did.

The pressure of her hands on his knees pulled him back from the edge of the black pit that opened before him. 'Seb, this is a reflection on them and their warped morals, their…their twisted depravity, not you. You know that, right?'

How could her faith and the vision she had of him temper his pain? He'd never thought he'd be free of it, but something in her face pushed it back and kept it at bay. He didn't understand it. He didn't know whether to be grateful or whether he ought to flee.

She stared back at him as if he were the centre of the universe, and it was all he could do not to take her face in his hands and kiss her until neither one of them could think straight.

He couldn't do that until she told him her secret.

'Do you wish you'd never found out? Do you wish you'd married her?'

He shook his head. 'I'm glad she's out of my life. I'm glad I found out what she was before I made a bigger mistake and married her.' Once they'd married, Rhoda would've worked on getting pregnant as soon as she could. And she'd have wielded that child like a weapon. It made him sick to his stomach thinking about it.

Eliza let out a slow breath. 'What happened afterwards?'

'My parents were living here. *On my charity*. So I threw them out.' He shrugged, fighting an inappropriate grin—

not because of the momentary satisfaction it'd given him, but because he knew Eliza would appreciate the gesture.

She stared at him and then her lips lifted in an answering grin. 'Good for you!'

'Part of the settlement—when I extracted my father from his financial straits—was that he and my mother could keep the apartment in Monte Carlo, but everything else had to be signed over to me. They all packed their things and flew there that very day.'

'What?' She frowned. 'Even Rhoda?'

'Even Rhoda.'

'Didn't your mother mind?'

He shrugged. 'She always turned a blind eye to my father's affairs.'

She opened her mouth…and closed it again.

He sympathised. There really were no words to do the situation justice.

'I understand the arrangement between Rhoda and my father lasted for several months before my father tossed her over without a penny. I suspect she'd been trying to get pregnant.'

'Oh, my God! You thought Jemima might be…?'

'That was the phone call I made. I asked her if she'd had a child…that I would make her an allowance if she had. Her reply was a very bitter *no.* She ordered me instead to make recompense for all the anguish she'd suffered at my family's hands. I told her to take a hike and then I had Jack double-check all the facts where she and my parents were concerned. But as my father is now infertile her plan would never have worked.'

'But if it had…' She pulled in a breath. 'She'd have taken your father for all the money she could?'

'Yes.'

'I'd have had no sympathy for him if that had happened, but…'

'But?'

'She'd have had you where she wanted you too, wouldn't she? You'd have done anything to protect that child.'

Exactly. But thank God it hadn't come to that.

'Instead she tried to cause mischief for you through Katie.'

'If she has any inkling how that's ended, she'll be gnashing her teeth.' And it served her right.

Eliza reached up and touched his face. 'And now you need never bother with her again,' she whispered. 'Instead you've gained a sister and a niece who adore you, and who'll look after you.'

He couldn't help it then; he hauled her onto his lap and buried his face in her hair. Her arms went about him and she held him tight. He had no idea how long they remained like that. He only knew that it helped, that it pushed away the darkness that had raged inside him for the last two years.

He eased back to glance into her eyes, and then at her lips—full and plump. They parted a fraction and her breath hitched as if she suddenly couldn't get enough air into her lungs. Adrenaline surged into every muscle, priming him for action.

One of his arms was about her waist, but with his other hand he traced the length of her leg from knee to hip. She shivered and shifted. 'Seb.'

Her voice held a warning note that he ignored as he trailed his hand from hip to shoulder, his hand brushing the side of her breast. She trembled and half smothered an exclamation. Her nipples beaded and peaked through the thin material of her blouse and hunger roared in his ears.

'I told you my nasty little story because you deserved to know it all after everything you've done for Jemima and Katie…and me. Not telling you became too hard.' His voice rasped from him, low and husky…and full of desire.

Her eyes darkened in answer and he felt her press her thighs tight together to counter the same desire he knew coursed through her too.

How had he lived without this for so long—the feel of a warm woman in his arms, a woman he liked and respected… and desired?

'As soon as you sort out this issue of yours, I'm taking you to my bed where—'

Her hand pressed against his lips, silencing him. 'You don't want to make any decisions about me yet,' she whispered.

He trailed his fingers along her collarbone and the delicate skin of her throat, back and forth until her eyes grew dark and slumberous. 'What do you think you're doing?' she finally rasped out.

'One kiss.' He cupped her jaw, lifting her face to meet his. 'One kiss can't hurt.'

Hunger flared in her eyes. 'Seb, I—'

He swallowed her words, his lips closing over hers with a fiercer hunger than he meant them to. She wanted to resist him. He could feel it in the way she tried to hold herself stiff and still. Her hand went to his chest as if to push him away.

He cupped her face in both his hands, his lips moving over hers gently, reverently. He wanted to tell her in a language that needed no words how beautiful he thought her.

A shudder racked her entire frame and rather than push him away, her hand tangled in his shirt to pull him closer as she kissed him back with a vigour that made the blood stampede in his veins.

He lost himself to the sensation and freedom of kissing her. There were no games or hidden agendas—just pure mutual desire and respect, and he revelled in it.

The sound of someone clearing their throat in the doorway had them crashing back to earth.

He dragged his lips from Eliza's, stared into her stunned eyes, before glancing around to find Katie grinning at him from the doorway. 'Sorry, I didn't mean to interrupt anything.'

'You're not interrupting!'

But Eliza's voice came out on a squeak. She tried to scramble off his lap, but he held her fast, refusing to relinquish her. 'I'm just trying to convince Eliza here that she should date me.'

Katie laughed. 'From where I'm standing, she's looking pretty convinced.'

'Oh, the two of you!' Eliza stopped struggling, and wrestled to hide a smile instead. 'I was taken off guard. You can both just stop it.'

That only made Katie laugh again. The sound gladdened his heart. He had a sister, and a niece…and very soon he meant to have Eliza.

'I just popped my head in to say goodnight.'

'Goodnight, Katie.'

'Sleep well,' Eliza called after her.

She turned her gaze back to Seb. He wanted to kiss her again, but he didn't trust that he'd be able to stop. He reached up to wind a lock of her hair about his finger. 'I do want to date you, Eliza. I hope you'll agree.'

She swallowed.

'We'll take it slowly.' He wanted to get it right this time.

She folded her arms and lifted her chin. 'Whenever a man says he *wants to take it slowly* that just means he wants to take the emotional commitment slowly. He still usually wants to jump into bed as soon as possible.'

He stared at her, fighting a scowl. *What on earth...?*

She sent him a smile that held a world of hurt…and he hated that he might have somehow put it there. 'Guilty as charged, huh?'

He thrust out his jaw. 'I want you physically. I have no

desire to deny it. As for the rest…' He lifted a shoulder and let it fall. 'It's too soon to know.'

She nodded, but whether in agreement or not he couldn't be sure. Why did women always want assurances and promises? He could give her neither.

This time when she scrambled off his lap, he didn't try to stop her.

Soon, he told himself. Soon.

With a growl of frustration, Liv threw her phone to her bed. Why did Liz have her phone turned off *still*?

Seizing her laptop, she checked her emails. There was nothing from Liz. Pulling in a deep breath, she started typing.

Dear Liz,
I've fallen in love with your boss.
I'm sorry, I didn't mean to.
I need to tell him the truth.
Please get in touch with me asap.

She signed off and waited.

And waited.

She didn't fall asleep until the wee small hours.

She woke in the morning to her ringing phone. She glanced at the screen—*Liz*! She pressed it to her ear. 'Where have you been? I've been trying to contact you for days! I—'

'Oh, Livvy, I'm so sorry! Have you seen today's newspapers?'

'No, why…? I've only just woken up. Hold on…' She grabbed her laptop, turned it on and then scanned the newspaper headlines, her heart dropping like a stone to her stomach. 'Oh, God.'

Had Seb seen these yet?

She shook herself. 'Is it true?'

'Um…yes.'

'You're engaged?'

'Look, it's complicated. I'll explain later, but first you need to get to Sebastian and tell him the truth before he sees these headlines.'

Dear God, Liz was right!

'Good luck, Livvy.'

She had a feeling she was going to need it. 'I'll ring you later.'

CHAPTER TEN

LIV THREW ON the nearest clothes to hand. She tried Seb's room first, but received no answer to her knock. The room was empty. She started for the kitchen but redirected to the drawing room first.

He glanced up the moment she entered. She saw the newspaper open in front of him—with the news of Liz's engagement to King Tariq splashed all across it.

She covered her face. Why hadn't she followed her instincts and told him the truth last night?

She pulled her hands away. 'I was hoping I'd get a chance to explain before you saw that.'

'You can explain this?'

The coldness in his voice made her recoil. 'Yes,' she replied, but her voice barely emerged above a whisper.

'If this—' he lifted an edge of the newspaper '—is Eliza Anne Gilmour, former office manager of the esteemed Tyrell Foundation,' he quoted, 'then who are you?'

She wanted to go and sit beside him, but his coldness forbade it. She twisted her hands together. 'I'm Olivia Grace Gilmour, born twenty-two minutes after Eliza Anne. Liz is my sister...my twin sister.'

He stared at the paper rather than at her—as if the sight of her disgusted him.

She swallowed. It wasn't disgust. It'd be too easy for her to hide behind that, to get all uppity and defensive and use it as an excuse to fight against his reaction. It wasn't disgust that he was experiencing, but betrayal and pain. This lie had hurt him. As she'd known it would.

Oh, she hadn't known that at the beginning, of course.

But she *had* known it since they'd had such fun together at their private party…*since that kiss.*

And yet you still didn't tell him the truth.

Which made her a fool!

He still refused to look at her and panic clawed at her belly. She pressed her hands to her stomach and tried to keep it at bay. With him refusing to look at her, she wasn't sure what to say next…or what to do.

'I'm sorry.' She couldn't keep the emotion from her voice. She didn't even try to.

She hesitated and then perched on the sofa opposite, her knees shaking. She gestured at the newspaper. 'Eliza—Liz—met King Tariq on her holiday to Greece. She didn't know who he was—he was travelling incognito—but they had a holiday romance. It wasn't until Liz was back home in London that she found she was pregnant.'

His head lifted, but not an ounce of warmth filtered across his face. 'That's why she asked for more leave—to find him and tell him that they were expecting a child?'

'Yes.'

His hands clenched and his eyes blazed in his face. 'Why didn't she tell me the truth?'

She tried not to flinch at the accusation ripping through his words. 'Because the two of you are as reticent as each other.'

He shot to his feet. 'So this is my fault?'

'Of course not!' She shot upright too. 'But, just for a moment, look at it from her point of view. She was scared witless at finding herself unexpectedly pregnant. And she was frightened of losing her job.'

'I would never—'

'And she wasn't thinking as clearly and logically as she'd have normally done.'

He gave a harsh laugh. 'So she called on you for help.'

She couldn't stand it any longer. She raced around the

coffee table to stand in front of him, so close waves of heat beat at her. She ached to touch him, but she didn't dare. 'The switch wasn't even supposed to have an impact on you.'

His jaw dropped. 'Not have an impact…?' And then he ground his teeth together so hard she winced.

'You were overseas…and Liz was only supposed to be away for a few days. My role was to simply keep the office running smoothly until she came back—something I am actually qualified to do, by the way. We had no intention of defrauding you. And Liz had every intention of being back before you returned.'

'But your nasty little scheme didn't go to plan.'

She swung away, strode to the window. 'There was nothing nasty about it. We weren't trying to steal from you or rob you. Your office was being taken care of…and you were never supposed to know—what you don't know isn't supposed to hurt you, right?' *Wrong.* 'It wasn't supposed to hurt anyone!'

She turned back. How naïve that all seemed now. 'But Tariq's being a king complicated everything. Then there were plane strikes…and an anonymous baby was left on your desk.'

He strode across to her, his eyes flashing silver fire. 'The scheme turned nasty the moment I kissed you and you still didn't tell me the truth.'

She swallowed and nodded. 'Yes.' She hated being so far in the wrong, but she hated the fact that she'd hurt him more. 'It was wrong of me…really wrong.'

'I understand your wanting to help your sister. I can even understand your agreeing to stand in for her at the office, but the rest of it…' He shook his head.

He stared at her as if he didn't know her, and that stung. 'The only thing I lied about was my name,' she whispered. 'Everything else was the truth.'

He gave a laugh so devoid of mirth that nausea burned

the back of her throat. 'You expect me to believe that?' And then his eyes went horrifyingly blank. 'You're just as bad as my parents. You're just as bad as Rhoda.'

'That is not true!' Fear and anger swirled through her, making the edges of her vision darken.

'I want you to pack your bags and go back to London. I never want to see you or your sister again.'

No! She pulled in a breath. 'I know you feel betrayed and hurt, Seb, and I don't blame you. I know you're angry at the moment, and rightly so. I know what I did was wrong—big-time wrong. But are you really going to throw away what we could have because you refuse to give me another chance? I swear I'll make this up to you. I swear I'll never let you down like this again.'

She held her breath. He'd made her no promises last night. That had been painfully clear. But he had at least been willing to explore the potential for something more.

'What we could have?' He raised a mocking eyebrow. 'My dear Ms Gilmour, a few pleasant kisses does not a relationship make.'

The words were designed to draw blood…and they did. But she lifted her chin. 'It was more than that and you know it.' Her hands clenched. 'If all we'd shared was nothing more than *a few pleasant kisses*, you wouldn't be feeling this cut up now.'

His nostrils flared. 'I do not envisage a future with a woman who has lied to me about her very identity.'

Which is why he was trying to cast her in the same mould as Rhoda and his parents. Well, she wouldn't let him! She reached out and placed her hand over his heart. He stiffened, but he didn't move away. 'I know you in here, Sebastian Tyrell. I know the real you.' He paled at her words. 'And you know me in exactly the same way, regardless of whether you call me Eliza or Olivia.'

His eyes, dark and hard, bored into hers. 'It's not what

it feels like. It feels like I don't know you at all. It feels like I never did.'

The words emerged from white lips and she reefed her hand back, her heart pounding, hope lying in tatters at her feet. 'I love you.' She hadn't meant to say the words out loud, but now that she had she didn't try to retract them.

'I'm sorry, but I'm going to go with my gut instinct on this one.'

Her words hadn't penetrated even a millimetre beneath the armour he'd wrapped securely about him.

'I'm afraid my idea of love is different from yours. As soon as you have your bags packed George will take you to the station.'

She swung away to stare blindly out of the window. She'd wrecked everything.

She listened to him walk away, but he paused in the doorway. 'How could you be persuaded to do something so deceitful?'

She swung around, her fists clenching. 'You were too!' If he wanted to see the world in such black and white terms she'd give him a dose of his own medicine. 'You kept Jemima's plight from the authorities.'

'That's nowhere near as bad as you lying about your identity!'

'You can only say that because you weren't caught!'

They met in the middle of the room like combatants, both of them throwing any veneer of civility out of the window.

She thrust her chin out. 'Why is what I did worse than what you did?'

'Because I had Jemima's best interests at heart,' he bellowed. '*You* didn't have *my* best interests at heart.'

'Oh, and what do you think a judge would make of that defence—*I had the baby's best interests at heart, Your Honour*—if Katie had panicked and reported that you'd kidnapped her baby…or if she'd never been found and the authorities discovered you were harbouring an unknown child? Huh? *Huh?*'

She stood on tiptoe as she *huh*-ed him, straining to meet him eye to eye. No doubt later she'd die a thousand deaths at her childishness, but for the moment she'd lost all semblance of control.

He opened his mouth, but it took several moments before words emerged. 'That didn't happen! You're creating hypothetical scenarios based solely on their dramatic impact—'

'The police, a judge, all of those people wouldn't consider it any defence at all. As for hypothetical situations, well here's another one for you. What if I'd told you the truth last night?' As she'd been so tempted to do. 'Would you be feeling like this now?'

His eyes narrowed. 'But you didn't tell me last night and—'

'You got lucky! I didn't!'

She shouted the words. She shouted them more loudly than she'd ever shouted anything.

They stared at each other, both breathing heavily.

'You got lucky with Katie, but I didn't get lucky with you.'

He didn't say anything, not that she expected him to see their situations as in any way similar. The shouting felt good. Although she knew it was only a temporary panacea. Still, it was better than dissolving in a flood of tears at his feet.

'And I'll tell you something else—' she jutted her chin aggressively again and hoped it hid the way her bottom lip wobbled '—I've helped you a whole lot more than I've harmed you.'

His face set in mutiny but she refused to give him a chance to speak. 'Liz wouldn't have been able to cope with an abandoned baby. You're lucky you got me instead.'

'What the hell—?'

'Yes, lucky! Liz would've called the authorities like any sane person would've done…except I was *persuaded* to do otherwise.'

He blinked.

'And I expect a defence of "I did it because my boss asked me to" wouldn't hold much water with the authorities either. Were you thinking of *my* best interests in that situation?'

The tightening of his mouth told her that arrow had found its mark.

'And I stopped you from making a hash of things with Katie and scaring her out of her wits, which now means you're getting the chance to form a decent relationship with her.'

He stared at her, his eyes throbbing, but he remained tight-lipped and all the fight left her. Still, she refused to let her chin drop. 'I was trying to help my sister—a sister I love. Why on earth do you think you deserve my loyalty over her? I've known her all my life and I've known you for all of five seconds.' She folded her arms. 'You can remain as cold and distant and unbending as you want, but I know the truth.'

'And what truth is that?'

'That I *have* helped you, Seb.' She moistened her lips. 'And that I am deserving of your forgiveness.'

He didn't say a word and her last hope died. She'd been so sure that he'd *liked* her—that their souls had understood each other on a primal level—and that what they'd shared had been more than a physical attraction. But maybe that had been a chimera, wishful thinking on her part, because if he had truly *liked* her, then surely she should be able to reach him.

She pressed a hand to her brow. 'Is there anything else you want to say, other than goodbye?'

His lips cracked open briefly. 'No.'

The room blurred. 'Right, I'll go and pack my bags then.'

She turned and left. She pulled in a breath. She would not cry. She pulled in another breath. She would not cry. She pushed all the pain to the periphery of her being. She'd try and find a way to deal with it when she got home.

Her phone rang. On automatic pilot she pressed it against her ear. 'Hello?'

'Livvy, how are you? How did things go with Sebastian?'

Don't laugh. She had a feeling that laughing would open floodgates she'd not be able to close again in a hurry. 'Oh, about as well as either one of us expected. I'm sorry, Liz, but you've been fired. I can't talk now. I'll call you tonight.'

She rang off, found her suitcase and started throwing her things into it.

'As soon as Ms Gilmour is ready I want you to drive her to the station.'

The four occupants of the kitchen—Brownie, George, Katie and Jemima—all snapped to attention at his sergeant-major tone. Newspapers littered the kitchen table and he wanted to collect each of them up and shove them into the wood-burning stove.

Except that'd reveal the extent of the storm raging through him, its ferocity.

He wanted to open his mouth as wide as he could and yell with all his might. But what good would that do? It'd only frighten everyone.

'Very good, Master Sebastian.'

His back teeth ground together. For God's sake, why couldn't they just call him Seb the way Eliza did?

Her name isn't Eliza!

The formality isn't their fault.

Don't take this out on them!

He shot one last blistering glare at the newspapers and then made for the door. 'I'm going for a walk!'

He left before anyone could say anything. Questions would be asked and explanations would need to be given, but he didn't have the heart for it at the moment. Maybe after lunch…or tomorrow…next week.

To hell with it. Maybe he'd shut the topic down—declare a ban and order a blanket of silence on it.

It's not curiosity. They care.

The voice that echoed through him sounded suspiciously like Eliza's. He stopped and braced his hands on his knees, drew in several deep breaths.

I've helped you more than harmed you.

He shot upright and surged forward again, his legs eating up the distance between the house and co-op buildings. He veered to his left and vaulted the fence, making for a copse at the top of the hill. He didn't want to see anyone. He didn't want to speak to anyone.

She'd lied to him and the size of the lie made his chest constrict until he could barely breathe—as if a giant hand had reached out and wrapped about his middle and was trying to break him. He couldn't ignore the pain. He just did his best to breathe through it.

When he reached the top of the hill, he was breathing hard and cramping all over. He threw himself down onto a fallen log and rested his head in his hands.

I love you.

His head jerked up, pain knifing behind his eyes. What kind of love lied so…completely? He'd started to believe…

He was a fool!

When he'd found Rhoda with his father, it'd horrified him. But Eliza's duplicity devastated him to a whole new level that he didn't understand. She hadn't just lied about what she'd done. She'd lied about who she was.

And yet, even now, he wanted to believe in her. What kind of fool did that make him?

'What the hell?' He shot to his feet only to see Naomi—one of the co-op's artists—marching up the hill towards him.

She stopped about twenty feet away when she realised he'd seen her. Keen eyes scanned his face and then she moved the last few paces towards him. 'I saw you trekking up here and I came after you.'

'Why?' He didn't mean to sound unfriendly, but he couldn't help it. Did everyone at the co-op know he'd been played for a fool too? Had they all read the newspapers this morning, seen that his former PA was now engaged to King Tariq? Had they joined the dots of a complicated deception, just as he had?

'There's something I think you should see.'

He set off back down the hill. 'I'm not in the mood.'

'I wouldn't have troubled you if I didn't think it was important.'

He halted and glared at her.

She didn't betray by one flicker of an eyelash what she was thinking. 'I wouldn't have troubled you if I didn't think you might…regret not seeing this.'

He huffed back a growl of pure frustration. 'Fine!'

Without another word, Naomi led him down the hill and into the main co-op building…up the stairs to the mezzanine level. She didn't try to engage him in conversation, evidently sensing his current aversion for idle chitchat. Not that it'd take a rocket scientist to work that one out.

She led him out to the artist's workspace and gestured to a painting awaiting framing. There was no denying the identity of the artist.

Eliza.

His hands clenched. *Olivia Grace Gilmour.*

The picture was of the hall's kitchen garden. It was bright, vibrant and pulsing with energy.

'She's donated this to the co-op. She's requested that

the proceeds be split between the co-op and the Tyrell Foundation charity.'

He turned to stare at her. 'When did she organise that?'

'Earlier in the week.' She glanced back at the painting. 'It's a handsome gift.'

His mind whirled.

'She's promised us a new painting every year for the next five years. It'll put this place on the map.'

Why? Why would she do such a thing?

Balm to a guilty conscience?

But… That didn't ring true. She hadn't known earlier in the week that this situation would explode in her face.

He recalled her jubilation—her elation—at painting again. He closed his eyes. Gratitude—she wanted to thank them…wanted to share that jubilation and joy with them.

It was part of who she was.

He rolled his shoulders. As well as being a liar.

His heart started to thump against the walls of his chest. How different would he be feeling today if she *had* told him the truth last night?

But she hadn't…

'The painting I really wanted to show you is over here.' Naomi halted in front of a large easel covered in a dust cloth. She hesitated. 'I hope I'm doing the right thing…'

And then she pulled the cover free. Everything inside of him froze.

It was a picture of him.

Olivia had painted him.

And the impact of the image had him rocking back on his heels. In the painting he held Jemima against his chest, but the baby had turned to stare up at him—wonder alive in her eyes. While he… He gulped. In that painting he looked alive and animated and full of plans for the future.

And yet the picture was deceptive, its mood shifting and changing as he moved in front of it. At certain angles the lines of his shoulders reflected a restless energy rather than relaxation. The lines of his mouth that appeared at first glance soft took on an edge that looked almost… carnal. He ran a hand across his chest to try to ease the tightness there.

In the painting he wore one of his white business shirts, and it should look starched and professional. Instead it hugged the outline of every muscle he possessed and a fleeting impression of intense sexuality sizzled across his eyes…gone again in a flash…and then there again.

She'd made him look raw and vital and beautiful. And complicated, protective and desirable. All at the same time. He sure as hell didn't look boring.

His heart beat hard. He was missing something. The painting was trying to tell him something. But what? He moved a few paces to his right and then his left. He moved in closer and then eased back out, never once taking his eyes from it.

'She's left instructions for this to be delivered to you on your birthday next month.'

She'd promised him a painting.

And she'd kept her word.

And that was when he saw it. From a certain angle Jemima's eyes looked like Eliza's eyes—*Olivia's* eyes.

Blood drummed in his ears. Was that baby Jemima at all…or a child she'd imagined having with him?

Did Olivia look at him—view him—with the same sense of wonder that the baby did?

The only thing I lied about was my name.

The truth of those words felt like a physical lessening of all the tension inside him—a letting go of anger and pain and the bitterness of disappointed hopes.

What right did he have to judge her so harshly, to be so fiercely angry with her, when he hadn't made her a single promise? He hadn't given her any assurances. He hadn't hinted at how much she'd started to mean to him. Why not? Because he'd hidden the truth from himself. He hadn't been honest with her, so how could he blame her for keeping her sister's secret? He'd given her no incentive to do otherwise!

He turned and left the studio at a run, clattering down the stairs and heading for the hall. Had George already left with her? He crossed his fingers and hoped his interfering sister and bossy housekeeper had insisted she needed to eat first, had delayed her with surreptitious questions. He put his head down and ran faster.

He was breathing hard when he approached the back door. Relief, when her voice drifted outside to him, made him sag while he tried to catch his breath.

'Look, none of this is Seb's fault, and you aren't to give him a hard time about it.'

She was defending him? He shook his head.

'He's an idiot if he lets you go.'

That was Katie and he could picture the outrage on her face.

'You've helped me and Jemima *so* much.'

'And so has he. Please, Katie, he's not to blame for this. It's my fault. I lied to him, and hurt him.'

'Ah, but lass, you didn't mean to.'

'It doesn't change the fact that I did, though. I don't blame him for not forgiving me. I don't think I'll be able to forgive myself.'

OK, enough. He refused to let her suffer a moment longer. She *had* helped him—more than he'd ever had the right to expect. She'd given him everything that she had to offer and he had no intention of throwing it back in her face.

'You will come to the party, won't you?'

He faltered, one step from the door. What party?

'I mean, you're the one who's organised it. And he won't still be angry with you by then. He'll have got over it.'

'Oh, Katie, it's really not the kind of surprise I was aiming for when I suggested we throw him a surprise party.'

She was giving him a party?

He surged into the kitchen. They all turned to look at him, but he only had eyes for Eliza.

Her mouth dropped open. She snapped it shut and then chafed her arms. 'I'm sorry, I meant to be gone before you got back.'

She wasn't going anywhere, but he didn't want an audience for all the things he wanted to say to her. Reaching forward, he seized her hand and pulled her out of the door and all the way into the walled kitchen garden.

He could identify each and every plant she'd painted.

'Seb, what do you think you're doing? I think we've yelled at each other enough and—'

He spun her around, seized her face in his hands and kissed her. He wanted to be gentle, but he felt too much like the picture she'd painted of him—restless, primal and filled with need.

Her lips yielded beneath his, a moan dragging from her throat, her hands clutching fistfuls of his shirt to keep her upright.

He lifted his head to stare down into her dazed eyes. She unclenched her hands from his shirt, smoothed out the material and ran her tongue over her swollen bottom lip. 'I…' Her throat bobbed as she swallowed. 'I couldn't read that kiss at all.'

Because she was afraid. Just as he'd been too afraid to see the truth earlier.

Liv stared up at Seb and her heart pounded so loudly that for a moment she couldn't hear anything else. A wild hope tried to spring free, but she roped it back down. He might not be as furious with her as he had been an hour ago, but it didn't mean…well, it didn't mean he ever wanted to see her again after today.

She shook her head. 'You don't like me any more. You hate me.'

'I don't hate you.' He stared down at her with those grey eyes that seemed to pulse with an inner light. 'I just saw the painting you've donated to the co-op.'

'Ah.' She clasped her hands together and tried to ignore the burning in her chest. That'd explain why his anger had abated. It explained why he didn't want to part from her on such unpleasant terms. 'It was the least I could do. Naomi, Dirk and Helen have helped me so much. It's just a small thank-you.'

The light in his gaze smouldered and sparked, and she tried not to read too much into it. Her paintings had often filled viewers with an enthusiasm that searched for immediate release. That was all this was now. Plus, Seb was the kind of man who always took the time to thank others, to let them know when a gesture was appreciated.

Beneath all of that he'd still be wrestling with his anger. Not that she blamed him.

'I also saw the picture you painted for my birthday.'

'Oh!' Wow. OK. She took a step back and lifted her chin. She didn't ask him if he liked it. 'Did you see anything in that painting?'

His eyes darkened. 'I saw the truth.'

'What truth?' She wanted her voice to come out strong and unflinching, but it didn't. It came out the exact opposite. She wanted to turn and run away, but his eyes held her captive.

'I saw that you loved me.'

A lump lodged in her throat. 'I've already told you that.'

'I was humbled when I finally let myself see how you saw me.'

Very slowly, she nodded. 'Good.' It was better than nothing, and probably more than she deserved.

'I realised, despite all of the other confusions going on, you never hid your real self from me.'

Everything inside her stilled. She felt as if the smallest breeze might knock her over. She couldn't speak. She couldn't do anything except stare at him.

'I realised it didn't matter if your name was Eliza or Olivia or Rumpelstiltskin.'

That was the moment when she finally started to hope… and when she recognised at least a part of what emotion lay in those smoky eyes of his. She took a step towards him. 'You…you *don't* hate me.'

A smile hooked up one side of the mouth that had become so dear to her. 'I've already told you that.'

Her pulse kicked up a notch as she continued to read his eyes. 'You *like* me.'

'Olivia Grace Gilmour.' He took her face in his hands and his touch was like water to a thirsty plant. 'I love you.'

He loved her?

He loved her!

She pulled his mouth down to hers and kissed him with everything she had—with every crazy emotion roiling through her body.

When he lifted his head, long minutes later, his eyes were dark and ravenous. He traced a finger down the vee of her shirt, sparking a path of fire that arrowed to her centre. 'I hope you don't have plans for the rest of the day.'

'Oh, I have plans all right.' She tossed her head. 'But they all include you.'

For a moment she thought he was going to sweep her up in his arms then and there and stride up to his room. She burned at the thought.

Instead he towed her across to a garden bench and

pulled her down onto his lap. 'I want to apologise for my anger earlier.'

She smoothed her hand down his cheek, relishing the scrape of his stubble against her palm. 'You were entitled to your anger, Seb. I don't blame you for it.'

'I refused to listen to reason, I refused to trust you and—'

'Oh, but—'

He pressed his fingers to her lips. 'Let me finish.'

She pressed a kiss to his fingers before nodding. His eyes darkened, but he didn't kiss her. She understood why. He wanted to explain and she needed to hear what he had to say, to understand. Before their relationship moved to the next level, they had to make sure that there were no more barriers or misunderstandings—that the air was clear and the path at their feet unobstructed.

'You've heard the stories about my parents. You know what Rhoda did.'

Her heart ached for him. She'd give him so much love it'd make up for the pain of his past.

'So you'll understand what I mean when I tell you that my default position whenever receiving unpleasant news is set to disaster mode.'

She thought about that. It made sense. 'You immediately leap to the worst-case scenario?'

His lips twisted. 'Where my parents are concerned that attitude usually saves time, heartache and money. With them I've learned not to expect or hope for any extenuating circumstances.'

How old was he when he'd learned that lesson—twelve? Ten? Even younger? She pressed a hand to his cheek. 'I'm sorry.'

He covered her hand with his own. 'It's not your fault, sweetheart.'

Her toes curled at the endearment. He was a wonderful man with a huge heart. He only deserved the best life had to offer. 'So this morning when you saw the newspaper headlines you immediately leapt to the conclusion that...' Her heart squeezed tight. 'That I'd taken you for a ride, taken complete advantage of you, and that I'd lied about everything.' She pulled in a breath. 'You must've thought I didn't have an honest bone in my body.'

'I couldn't think straight.' His eyes throbbed with remembered pain and confusion, and she wished she could wipe it away. 'I lashed out at you, too afraid to believe anything you said.'

'I'm sorry,' she whispered.

He lifted his head. 'And then I saw the picture you'd painted of me and I realised you'd never meant to hurt me.'

He traced a finger across her cheek making her blood leap. 'In that moment I understood that your sister had put you in an untenable position.'

'She didn't mean to.'

'And that I'd put you in an untenable position too. Not informing the authorities of Jemima's situation could've backfired badly...and yet you chose to trust me and to help me—to help Jemima—because that's the kind of person you are. You have a heart of gold, Olivia Grace Gilmour, and I love you.'

Her chest filled until she thought it would burst.

'If I'd told you that sooner, you'd have told me the truth.'

She dragged in a breath and blinked hard. 'I love you, Seb. But I do understand if you want to take things slow.'

He shook his head. 'I don't want slow. I just want you.'

She had to pinch herself.

He grinned down at her and she had a feeling he felt as light and free as she did.

A smile burst to life inside her. And then she pulled his head down for a kiss that sealed every silent promise their hearts had just made to each other.

EPILOGUE

One year and five weeks later...

A FAMILIAR HEAT radiated through Sebastian when Olivia came up behind him and slid her arms about his waist, resting her chin on his shoulder. For a moment they both silently watched the revels taking place in front of them.

'Surely *this* is your favourite party?' she said, pressing a kiss to his cheek. 'Though…it has to be said…we did have a rather fine party for our wedding.'

They'd married five months ago. 'We did,' he agreed. 'And this too is a very fine party.'

She frowned up at him. 'But?'

His smile grew. 'But nothing will ever top our Marilyn and Elvis party.'

She tossed her glorious autumn-toned hair. 'I mean to make it my life's work to eventually throw you a party that bests it, you know?'

Impossible. That was the night of their first kiss. The night he'd fallen in love with her. Nothing could ever beat that. 'I look forward to it,' he said instead. It might not be possible to beat it, but he meant to enjoy the ride.

He still couldn't believe he'd come to love parties so much, but he'd discovered a party with Olivia by his side was a thing to be cherished. He half turned so he could slide an arm about her shoulders and draw her closer to his side. 'And I promise you that I'm loving my birthday party tonight.'

She smiled and pointed. 'You're not the only one. Philippa is having a grand old time.'

At thirty, Philippa was the oldest of his half-sisters and a mischievous extrovert, not to mention an outrageous flirt and confirmed bachelorette. The two of them were complete opposites and yet they'd hit it off splendidly. Currently she was holding court in a circle of half a dozen of the most eligible bachelors in England. He couldn't suppress a grin. 'No surprises there.' He searched the room. 'What about Laurie? Please tell me she's not hiding in some dark corner.'

'Of course not. She's in earnest conversation with a group in the room next door. They're playing cards but it's just a pretext to discuss politics.'

Laurie was his middle sister, much quieter than Philippa and shyer than Katie. They were getting to know each other—slowly. More slowly than he'd like, perhaps, but he was grateful to have her in his life and he suspected she felt the same.

He sent up a silent prayer for the information Jack had been able to unearth. And another for the fact that his sisters had agreed to meet him, and had agreed to become a part of his life.

His youngest sister's laughter reached him from the nearby billiards table. As there were eight of them playing they'd obviously made up a new set of rules for the game. 'It's been great having Katie and Jemima down for the weekend. I've missed them.'

Olivia pressed closer to his side. 'Me too, but she's so happy.'

Two months ago Katie had taken up an administration position at the Tyrell Foundation when Judith retired. She had plans to take over the running of the office in the next few years. She worked so hard he had no doubt she would too.

He glanced at the couples swaying on the dance floor. 'I've enjoyed having Eliza and Tariq to stay too. Your sister seems very happy.'

Olivia followed his gaze and her smile softened as she

watched Eliza and Tariq swaying in each other's arms. 'I miss her terribly now that she's living so far away. But she *is* happy and I'm so pleased for her. She, Tariq and little Ahmed make the perfect family for each other. I just knew she'd be a wonderful mother. And Ahmed is such a delicious baby!'

That made him grin. 'Brownie is in her element tonight looking after not just one, but two babies.'

He harboured no grudge for the deception the sisters had played on him. He'd forgiven Eliza the moment he'd held her tiny baby and she'd pronounced him Uncle Seb. 'We'll return the visit in a couple of months,' he promised.

He turned Olivia to face him more fully, both arms circling her waist. 'You haven't given me my birthday present yet.' She'd been working on it for weeks. 'Is it finished?'

A smile he couldn't read touched her lips. 'Oh, it's finished, but I thought you might prefer a private viewing rather than a public one.'

'Why?'

She took his hand and he followed silently as she led him through the house and up the stairs to their bedroom. A picture covered with a cloth hung on the wall opposite their four-poster bed.

He swallowed.

'Ready?'

He nodded.

The cloth fell away and he couldn't suppress a quick intake of breath. She'd painted him. Again. Nude.

He stared at it and his spine grew straighter, his shoulders broadened and his chin came up. 'You've made me look… You've made me look like the king of all I survey.'

She didn't say anything—just watched him as he continued to stare at the portrait.

It wasn't just that he looked supremely satisfied with his kingdom… 'You've made me look noble.'

'You are noble.'

While she'd painted him in a pose reminiscent of some mythical Greek god, the man in the portrait was unmistakably human—virile and alive. He looked like a king. He looked noble. And yet he pulsed with unmistakable sexual desire.

That same desire flooded every inch of Sebastian's being now—raw and scorching. He loved all the ways she saw him—all the ways she forced him to see himself. Not one of them was boring. She made him feel powerful and loved, and he wanted to give her everything.

He swung to her. A smile spread across her lips at whatever she saw in his eyes. 'You like it, then.'

'I love it,' he growled, advancing on her until she was backed up against one of the bedposts. He trailed lazy fingers down the deep neckline of her dress. The pulse in her throat fluttered to pounding life, and a primal triumph flooded him. 'I want to ravage you.'

She lifted her chin and her eyes glittered with desire. 'That's fortunate, because I'm in the mood to be ravaged.'

He claimed her lips and the passion between them flared to instant life—its intensity still had the potential to take him off guard.

When he lifted his head, long moments later, her eyes were as dark and needy as his must be.

She swallowed. 'I've been thinking…'

'I don't want you thinking,' he rasped. 'I want you mindless with sensation and pleasure.'

She huffed out a laugh, but her pupils dilated. 'You're a wicked man.'

He bit back a grin. 'Yes, but I'm your king.'

She tilted her chin. 'And I'm your queen.'

That was true. 'And what is it that my queen desires?' He pressed in closer, leaving her in no doubt what he desired.

He revelled in her quick intake of breath. His hands

travelled the length of her back, his fingers digging into her hips to draw her closer. 'I just thought,' she panted, 'that it could be time to start adding to our family...to try for a baby.'

He stilled. He found it suddenly difficult to breathe. He craved a child with every atom he had, but... 'I don't want to rush you.'

She kinked an eyebrow. 'Maybe I want to rush you.'

No rushing necessary. Not on his part. He was almost too afraid to hope—he had so much already and... 'Are you sure?'

'I'm very sure.' She pulled his head down to hers, a smile in her eyes. 'Happy birthday, Seb.'

He kissed her with everything he had. He held her the way he meant to hold her for the rest of their lives. He loved her with a fire that would never go out.

'Are you sure,' she murmured against his mouth, 'that this isn't the best party you've ever had?'

Sebastian found himself laughing. 'What if I tell you it's one I'll never forget?'

Her eyes danced. 'That'll do, for now.' And then she pulled him down on the bed with her and it was a long time before either of them spoke again.

* * * * *

I

THE BEST MAN TAKES A BRIDE

STACY CONNELLY

To all my fellow romance readers out there
and the ongoing search for happily-ever-after…
in (and out) of the pages of a romance novel!

Chapter One

This was going to be a disaster.

Jamison Porter eyed the dress shop with a sense of dread. Early-morning sunshine warmed the back of his neck and glinted off the gilded lettering on the plate glass window. Frilly dresses decorated with layer after layer of lace and ribbons and bows draped the mannequins on display, a small sample of the froth and satin inside. All of it girlie, delicate and scary as hell.

The forecast promised a high in the low seventies, but Jamison could already feel himself breaking into a sweat.

He swallowed hard against the sense of impending doom and fought the urge to jump in his SUV and floor it back to San Francisco. Back to his office and his black walnut barricade of a desk, matching bookshelves lined with heavy law books, and rich leather chairs. All of it masculine, substantial—the one place where Jamison never questioned his decisions, never doubted his every move—

He felt a tug at his hand and looked down at his four-year-old daughter's upturned face. Big brown eyes stared back at him. "I wanna go home now."

Never felt so useless as he did when he was with Hannah.

His daughter's barely brushed blond curls tilted to one side in a crooked ponytail. Her mismatched green T-shirt and pink shorts, both nearing a size too small, were testimony to the crying fit that ended their last attempt at clothes shopping. Jamison at least took some small comfort that Hannah had been the one to leave the store in tears, and not him. Because there were times…

Like now, when he didn't even know which home Hannah was referring to. Back to Hillcrest House, the hotel where they'd be staying for the next couple of weeks? Back to his town house in San Francisco? To her grandparents' place? To the house where she'd been living with her mother…

"I know, Hannah Banana," he said, fighting another shaft of disappointment when the once-loved nickname failed to bring a smile to her face. "But we can't go home yet," he added as he set aside the question of where his daughter called home for another time. "We're here to meet Lindsay, remember? She's the lady who's getting married to my friend Ryder, and she wants you to be her flower girl."

Hannah scraped the toe of a glittery tennis shoe along a crack in the sidewalk. "I don't want to."

Her lack of interest in playing a role in Lindsay Brookes's wedding to Ryder Kincaid didn't bother Jamison as much as her patented response did. Not because of all the things Hannah didn't want, but because of the one thing she did.

The bell above the shop's frosted-glass door rang as the

bride stepped outside. Dressed in gray slacks and a sleeveless peach top with her dark blond hair caught back in a loose bun, a smile lit Lindsay's pretty face. "Hey, you made it! Not that I thought you wouldn't." She waved a hand, the solitaire in her engagement ring flashing in the sunlight. "I mean, it isn't like any place around here is hard to find!"

Ryder had told Jamison his hometown near the Northern California coastline was small, and he hadn't exaggerated. Victorian buildings lined either side of Main Street and made up the heart of downtown. Green-and-white awnings snapped in the late-summer breeze, adding to the welcome of nodding yellow snapdragons, purple pansies and white petunias in the brick planters outside the shops. Couples strolled arm in arm, their laughing kids racing ahead to dart into the diner down the street or into the sweet-smelling café across the way.

It was all quaint and old-fashioned, postcard perfect and roughly that same size. Jamison figured it had taken less than five minutes to see all Clearville had to offer even while obeying the slower-than-slow posted speed limit. "No trouble. Didn't even need to use the GPS."

Finding the shop had been easy. Making himself step one foot inside, that was a different story.

"Good thing," Lindsay said with a laugh, "since cell coverage can be pretty spotty around here."

Jamison fought back a groan. In a true effort to focus on Hannah and leave work behind, he hadn't brought along his laptop. But he'd been counting on being able to use his phone to read emails and download any documents too urgent to wait for his return. "How does anyone get things done around here?" he grumbled under his breath.

She lifted a narrow shoulder in a shrug. "Disconnecting is tough at first, but before long, you find you don't miss it at all."

"Can't say I plan to be in town long enough to get used to anything," he replied as the driver of an SUV crawling down Main Street called out to Lindsay and the two women exchanged a quick wave.

And despite his own words, Jamison couldn't help thinking that, back in San Francisco, had a driver shouted and stuck an arm out the window, the gesture wouldn't have been so friendly.

"That's too bad. Clearville's a great town. A wonderful place to raise a family," she added with a warm glance at Hannah, who dropped her gaze and retreated even farther behind his back.

So different from the adventurous toddler he remembered…

He sucked in a deep breath as he tried to focus on whatever Lindsay was saying.

"But why don't we get started? I'm here for my final fitting, and I've picked out some of the cutest flower girl dresses. Our colors are burgundy and gold, but I think that would be too strong a palette for Hannah since she's so fair. Instead I've been leaning toward a cream taffeta with a sash at the waist—"

Catching herself, Lindsay offered a sheepish smile. "Sorry, Ryder's already warned me I tend to go into wedding overload on even the most unsuspecting victim. The other day, I talked a poor waitress's ear off and all she asked was if I wanted dessert. If there's something else you need to do, you don't have to stay—"

"No! Daddy, don't go!" Hannah's hands tightened in a death grip around his as she pressed closer to his side.

Lindsay's expression morphed into one of sympathy that Jamison had seen too many times and had grown to despise over the past two months.

But not as much as he hated the tears in his daughter's

eyes. "I'm not going anywhere," he vowed, disappointed but not surprised when his promise didn't erase the worry wrinkling her pale eyebrows.

"Pinkie promise?" she finally asked, holding out the tiny, delicate digit.

Jamison didn't hesitate as Hannah wrapped him around her finger. Love welled up inside him along with the painful awareness of how many times he'd let her down in her short life. His voice was gruff as he replied, "Pinkie promise."

"Your daddy can stay with you the whole time," Lindsay reassured Hannah gently. "I bet he can't wait to see you try on some pretty dresses."

Jamison had thought Hannah might enjoy being a flower girl, but the truth was, he didn't have a clue what would make his little girl happy anymore. Sweat started to gather at his temples along with the pressure of an oncoming headache. "Look, Lindsay, I appreciate you thinking of Hannah and wanting her to be part of the ceremony, but I don't—"

"Sorry I'm late!" The cheery voice interrupted Jamison's escape, and every muscle in his body tensed. That need to run raced through him once more, but his feet felt frozen in place. Still, he couldn't help turning to glance over his shoulder, bracing himself for the woman he could feel drawing closer.

The wedding coordinator.

Ryder and Lindsay had introduced them not long after he'd checked into the sprawling Victorian hotel. He'd been exhausted from fourteen-hour workdays, worn out from the long drive from San Francisco and far more overwhelmed by the idea of taking care of Hannah on his own than he dared admit even to himself.

That was the only logical explanation he'd been able

to come up with for why that first meeting with Rory McClaren had sent a lightning bolt straight through his chest. Her smile had stopped him dead in his tracks and her touch—nothing more than a simple handshake—had shot a rush of adrenaline through his system, jump-starting his heartbeat and sending it racing for the first time in… ever, it seemed.

But logical explanations failed him now. One look at Rory, and Jamison was blown away all over again.

Big blue eyes sparkled in a heart-shaped face framed by dark, shoulder-length hair. A fringe of bangs, thick lashes and arched eyebrows drew him even deeper into that gaze. A sprinkling of freckles across her nose kept her fair skin from being too perfect, and cherry-red lipstick highlighted a bright smile and a sexy mouth Jamison had no business thinking about again and again.

A white sundress stitched with red roses revealed more freckles scattered like gold dust across her delicate collarbones. The fitted bodice hugged the curves of her breasts and small waist before flaring to swish around her slender legs as she walked.

She looked as fresh and sunny as a summer's day, and Jamison almost had to squint when he looked at her, like he needed sunglasses to shield him from her stunning beauty.

He sure as hell needed some form of protection, some barrier to establish a safe distance from this woman and the unexpected, unwanted way she made him feel. If his disastrous marriage had taught him one lesson, it was that he far preferred being numb.

"Mr. Porter, nice to see you again."

Her smile was genuine, but Jamison couldn't imagine her words were true. He'd been abrupt the day before, unnerved by his reaction and bordering on rude. "Ms. McClaren. I didn't know you'd be joining us this morning."

"All part of Hillcrest House's service as an all-inclusive wedding venue," she said with a smile to Lindsay before turning that full wattage on Jamison. "But we are a hotel first and foremost, so I hope you enjoyed your first night under our roof."

He'd heard his share of come-ons in his lifetime. There was nothing the least bit seductive in her smile or her voice. But his imagination, as suddenly uncontrollable as his hormones, had him picturing an intimacy beyond sleeping under her roof and instead sleeping in her bed…

Jamison didn't know if his thoughts were written on his face, but whatever Rory saw had enough color blooming in her cheeks to rival the roses on her dress. Her lips parted on an inhaled breath, and Jamison felt drawn closer, captured by the moment as the awareness stretched between them until she dropped her gaze.

"And Hannah!"

That quickly, the enticing image was banished, but not the pained embarrassment lingering in its wake. He wasn't some gawky teenager lusting after the high school cheerleader. He was a grown man, a father…a father with a daughter he was terrified of failing—just like he had her mother.

"How are you this morning?" Undeterred by the lack of response, Rory's lyrical voice rose and fell, and Jamison didn't want to think about the slight tremor under the words. Didn't want to think she might be as affected as he was by the chemistry between them. "Do you like your room at the hotel? You know, the Bluebell has always been my favorite."

The Bluebell...

What kind of hotel designated their rooms by a type of flower?

"It's all part of Hillcrest's romantic charm," Rory had explained.

He had no need for romance or charm or bright-eyed brunettes. He wanted logic, order. He wanted the normalcy of sequential room numbers, for God's sake!

But the Bluebell was one of the hotel's few two-room suites and, while small, it offered a living space and tiny kitchenette. The comfortable room was subtly decorated in shades of blue and white.

If only it wasn't for the name…and the reminder of flowers that had him thinking far too often of Rory's dark-lashed, vibrant blue eyes.

"I like purple," Hannah answered, surprising him too much with her willingness to talk to a virtual stranger for him to point out bluebell wasn't a color.

"Me, too," Rory agreed as she caught on to his daughter's twist in the topic.

Hannah's forehead wrinkled. "You said you like blue."

"Actually, Hannah, rainbow is my favorite color…" The wedding coordinator bent at the waist so she and Hannah were almost eye to eye as she shared that piece of nonsense with the little girl. "That way I never have to pick just one."

A lock of her hair slid forward like a silken ribbon and curved around her breast. The dark strands were a stark contrast against the white fabric, but it was the similarities that had Jamison sucking in a deep breath. Soft cotton, soft hair, soft skin…

Realizing he was staring, he jerked his gaze away. Falling back on good manners now that good sense seemed to have deserted him, he ground out, "Hannah, you remember Ms. McClaren?"

His daughter nodded, her eyes too serious for her still-baby face as she peered up at the wedding coordinator. She wrapped her index finger in the hem of her shirt, holding on the same way she had to the pink-and-white blanket Jamison remembered her carrying with her everywhere when she was a toddler. “She’s Miss Lindsay’s fairy godmother.”

Jamison blinked at Hannah’s unexpected announcement. “She’s… Oh, right.” That was how Lindsay had introduced the woman. The bride had sung Rory McClaren’s praises, complimenting her on finding the perfect music, the perfect flowers, the perfect menu—as if any of that attention to detail would lead to the perfect marriage.

Jamison knew better. He was cynical enough to wonder if Rory knew the same, but not cynical enough to believe it. Everything about her was too genuine, too hopeful for him to convince himself it was all for show. But even if the wedding coordinator believed what she was selling, that didn’t mean Jamison was buying.

“She’s not really a fairy godmother,” he told his daughter firmly.

“Of course not,” the dark-haired pixie said with a conspiring wink at the little girl, who gazed back with shy curiosity. “And you can call me Rory.”

Jamison’s jaw tightened. No doubt Rory thought the shared moment with Hannah was harmless, but the last thing he needed was for his daughter to put faith in fairy tales. Especially when the one thing Hannah wanted was the one thing no one—not even a fairy godmother, if such a thing existed—could give her.

Rory’s smile faltered when she glanced up into his face. Straightening, she rallied by getting down to business and glancing between Lindsay and Hannah. “So, are we ready to start trying on some gorgeous dresses?”

“I can’t wait!” Lindsay announced, clapping her hands in front of her as if trying to hold on to her excitement.

"I've picked out some of the cutest dresses, and you have got to help me decide which one to choose."

"That is what I'm here for. Anything you need, all you have to do is ask!"

And with statements like that, Jamison thought, was it any wonder Hannah thought the woman was some kind of fairy godmother? Even he half expected a magic wand to appear in the delicate hand she waved through the air.

Better to leave now before he—before *Hannah*—could get sucked any further into a belief in fairy tales and happily-ever-afters.

"About that. I think Hannah might be a little too young for all of this."

Lindsay sank back onto her heels, her earlier excitement leaking out of her. He wasn't a man to go back on his word, but he never should have agreed to have Hannah in the wedding in the first place. With his in-laws pointing out the need for a female influence in Hannah's life, he'd thought—hell, Jamison didn't know what he'd thought. But the whole idea was a mistake. "Trying on clothes isn't her idea of fun."

This time, though, the wedding coordinator's smile didn't dim in the least. If anything, an added spark came to her eyes. "The shopping gene hasn't kicked in yet?"

"I'm hoping it skips a generation."

Rory laughed as though he'd been joking, brightening her expression even more, like a spotlight showcasing a work of art. "You and all fathers everywhere."

It was a small thing—Rory categorizing him as a typical dad—but some of the pressure eased in his chest. Maybe it wasn't so obvious from the outside that he was at such a loss when it came to his own daughter. Best to quit while he was, if not ahead, then at least breaking even.

But before he could once again make his excuses, Rory

turned to Hannah. “Well, maybe Miss Lindsay can go first. What do you think, Hannah? Are you ready to help?”

“Ms. McClaren—”

“Why does she need help?” It was Hannah who interrupted this time, coming out from behind him far enough to look from Rory to Lindsay. “She’s a grown-up, and big girls should be old enough to get dressed by themselves.”

Jamison closed his eyes and wished for a sinkhole to open up in the sidewalk and swallow him whole at his words coming out of Hannah’s mouth. *Crap.* Was that really how he sounded? So…condescending and demeaning?

“Hannah…” He’d only pulled out the big-girl card because Hannah was so filled with ideas of what she would do when she was older. Or at least she had been.

But if Rory was ready to take that “typical dad” title away from him and flag him with “worst father ever,” she didn’t let it show as she knelt down in front of his little girl. Close enough this time that he could have stroked her hair, as dark as Hannah’s was light, and he shoved his free hand into his pocket before insanity had him reaching out…

“You know, Hannah,” Rory was saying, her voice filled with that same touch of sharing a secret she’d conveyed earlier with that wink, “funny thing about being a big girl…sometimes we still need help.”

As she spoke, she reached up and slipped the bright pink band from Hannah’s hair. With a few quick swipes of her hands and without a comb or brush in sight, she had the little girl’s curls contained in a smooth, well-centered ponytail. “Not a lot of help. Just a little, just enough to make things right.”

To make things right… Jamison didn’t have a clue how to go about making things right in his daughter’s world. Especially not when he saw the open longing and amazement in Hannah's face as she reached up to touch her now-perfect ponytail.

"So what do you think?" Rory asked as she straightened, her full skirt swirling around her legs. The roses on her dress might have been embroidered, but somehow Jamison still caught a sweet, fresh scent, as if she'd risen from a bed of wildflowers. "Do you want to help Lindsay with her dress for the wedding?"

Hannah hesitated, and Jamison braced himself for the "I don't want to" response. Instead, she surprised him, nodding once and sliding a little farther out from behind him.

"And maybe, after Lindsay's done, we could find a dress for you. Just to try on—you know, like playing dress-up. And then you can put your everyday clothes back on, because who wants to wear dresses all the time?"

Hannah reached out and brushed her tiny hand over Rory's skirt. "You do."

Rory tilted her head to the side as she laughed. "You caught me. I do like wearing dresses. But not *all* the time."

Jamison might have only met the woman, but he already sensed how Rory's clothes—elegant and old-fashioned—suited her. He had a hard time picturing her in anything else.

Now, if he could only stop himself from picturing her wearing nothing at all…

Chapter Two

When Rory McClaren was five years old, she went through a princess phase. Her cousin Evie would likely say she never fully recovered from her belief in true love and happy endings and fascination with gorgeous ball gowns. Or the hidden longing to wear a tiara. On a Tuesday. Just for fun.

And while Rory had denied those longings throughout her adult life, her new position as wedding coordinator for Hillcrest House brought out every once-upon-a-time memory. She might have laughed it off when Lindsay Brookes had introduced her as a fairy godmother, but it was secretly how she viewed her job.

Of course, Rory also knew what Evie would say about that.

Coordinating weddings is a serious business, not a game of pretend. And Hillcrest House isn't a fairy-tale castle, no matter what you thought as a kid.

Neither she nor Evie had planned on this recent stay in Clearville, but the two of them were in this together—doing all they could to keep Hillcrest House running while their aunt was going through cancer treatments. Evie, a CPA, was handling the books and the staff while Rory was taking on a guest relations role as well as event planning for the venue.

So far, Lindsay Brookes had been a dream to work with, but her wedding to Ryder Kincaid came with some extra pressure. Not only did Rory consider Lindsay a friend, the pretty businesswoman also worked for Clearville's chamber of commerce. She was constantly promoting the small Northern California town and its businesses.

Rory wanted to prove all the brochures and promotions touting Hillcrest House as *the* all-inclusive wedding destination were as good as gold. The weight of responsibility pressed hard on her shoulders, but she was determined not to crumble.

She could certainly withstand a reticent best man and his shy flower girl daughter. Despite Jamison's claims that she didn't enjoy shopping, Hannah was gazing at the elegantly posed mannequins and racks of lacy dresses lining the walls of the small shop while her sharp-eyed father watched from close by.

With her tiny hands clasped behind her back, the little girl was clearly familiar with the phrase *look but don't touch.* Under her breath, she named off the color of each dress she came across in a singsong voice, and Rory didn't think it would take much to rid Hannah of her uncertainty in her role as a flower girl.

Her smile faded, though, when she caught sight of the storm clouds gathering in Jamison's eyes. Something told her erasing *his* concerns wouldn't be so easy.

Rory had hoped her initial impression of Ryder Kincaid's best friend had been a rush to judgment. She'd told herself that with a good night's sleep and a chance to relax and unwind, Jamison Porter would be a different man. A man she could handle with professional competence as she guided him through the duties of the best man from suggestions for a fun yet tasteful bachelor party to tips on a heartfelt toast.

But Jamison Porter was still every bit as intense and edgy as he had been the day before—and not a man easily handled.

It wasn't the first time Rory had been to this shop with a reluctant man in tow. Not every couple held to the superstition that the groom shouldn't see the bride in her gown. But none of the men had seemed so out of place as Jamison did. At over six feet, with rich chestnut hair and cool gray eyes, all rugged angles and sharp planes, he wore the tall, dark and handsome label to perfection. The airy dresses around him seemed as insubstantial in comparison as dandelion fluff, ready to disintegrate with a single puff of breath from his lips.

Not that Jamison Porter's lips were anything Rory should be thinking about…

"So, you're the best man," she said, cringing at the exuberant sound of her own voice.

"That's what Ryder tells me."

The hint of self-deprecating humor loosened a strand in the single father's too tightly laced personality. One that made him even more attractive than his classically handsome good looks.

But that was the last thing Rory needed. Their first meeting, as abrupt and tension filled as those moments had been, had sparked an awareness that had her thinking of the handsome single father far too often.

And just now while standing outside the bridal shop,

when she asked what she'd thought to be an innocent question about his first night at Hillcrest…

The intensity in his expression served notice there was nothing innocent about Jamison Porter. Everything about the man had Rory on high alert, raw nerve endings leaving her jumpy and out of sorts. Off her game at a time when she needed to be at her best.

Evie had taken a leave of absence from her job at the accounting firm to help out their aunt, confident they would hold her position for her, and had sublet her fabulous condo in Portland.

Whereas Rory—

Rory had nothing left. She couldn't afford *not* to come to Clearville. Back in LA, she had no boyfriend, no apartment, no job and a reputation left in tatters all thanks to her professional—and personal—failure.

Pushing thoughts of her short-lived interior design career aside, she focused on the most important aspects of the wedding.

"Ryder and Lindsay make such a wonderful couple. It's amazing the way they've reunited after so many years, and seeing them together… Well, they're crazy about each other."

Jamison gave a sound that wasn't quite a laugh. "*Crazy* is one word for it."

"And what word would you use?"

He paused for a moment, and Rory had a feeling he was searching for the least offensive description. *"Sudden,"* he said finally. "They just got engaged."

"True, but they've known each other since high school." Lindsay had filled Rory in on the couple's history, how she had been a shy bookworm with a huge crush on the popular quarterback. "They went their separate ways after graduation, but from what Lindsay says, she never stopped loving Ryder."

And while Ryder had gone on to marry another woman, Rory had no doubt he was in love with his future bride.

"She's a wonderful person. A great mother..."

The dark clouds in Jamison's eyes started flashing lightning and Rory's voice trailed away as she realized that was one box she shouldn't have opened. Unable to leave well enough alone, she couldn't help asking, "Have you met Robbie?"

He gave a quick nod. "I have."

"He's a great kid."

"One Ryder didn't even know about until a few months ago."

Rory sucked in a startled breath. Okay, so Jamison was breaking out the big guns to take on the elephant in the room. Fortunately, the curtain to the dressing room opened and Lindsay stepped out before he had time to reload.

Hannah's breathless voice broke the silence that followed. "You look beautiful."

This was the first time Rory had seen Lindsay in her wedding dress, and she couldn't hold back a whisper of her own. "Oh, Lindsay. Hannah is right. That dress is perfect."

Having worked on the flowers, the music and the table settings for the reception, Rory knew Lindsay had an elegant, timeless vision for the wedding, so it was no surprise her dress reflected that same taste.

The sheath-style gown was gorgeous in its simplicity; lace sleeves capped a straight column of white satin, and a hint of beadwork decorated the bodice and the lace insert that veed out into a modest train.

Lindsay gave a self-conscious laugh as she glanced at the silent member of the group. "It's not bad luck for the best man to see the bride in her gown, is it?"

To his credit, Jamison tipped his head at Lindsay. "You make a beautiful bride."

Lindsay blushed at the compliment, but while the words were right, Rory knew in her heart Jamison thought Ryder and Lindsay getting married was wrong.

A gentle tug on her skirt distracted Rory from the troubling thought. "Miss Rory, is it my turn to dress like a princess?"

She smiled down at Hannah. She was an adorable little girl with a riot of blond curls, big brown eyes and a shyness that tugged at Rory's heart.

But it was the expression on Jamison's face that had grabbed hold and wouldn't let go. A mix of love and uncertainty that held him frozen in place, as if he, too, were bound by the *look, don't touch* mantra.

"It sure is, sweetie," Rory said, injecting a positive note into her voice though she didn't know which of the Porters needed her encouragement more. "Miss Lindsay has a whole bunch of dresses for you to try on." Tilting her head in the direction of the changing room, Rory asked Jamison, "Do you want..."

Looking torn between Daddy duty and a man's typical reaction of running as far as he could from anything girlie, he said, "I, um, think I'll wait out here."

"What do you think, Hannah?" Rory asked when the little girl hesitated. "See, your daddy wants the princess dresses to be a surprise, so he'll wait in that chair over there."

Like father, like daughter. Hannah looked indecisively from her father to the curtained dressing room and back again. Finally her blond head bounced in a nod. "You wait there, Daddy, and no peeking."

Rory wouldn't have thought Jamison Porter could look any more uncomfortable than he had two seconds ago, but his daughter's instructions for him not to go peeking into the women's dressing room had a slight flush darkening his cheeks.

Rory fought to hide a smile, but judging by the narrowing of Jamison's eyes, she didn't succeed.

Biting the inside of her lip, she shot a stern look in his direction. "You heard the girl, Mr. Porter. No peeking."

For a split second, their eyes met, and Rory's smile faded as something electric and powerful passed between them. Heat flared in Jamison's eyes, a warning beacon, and she swallowed hard. He might not have looked behind the curtain, but when it came to her attraction to him, Rory feared he saw way too much.

The jingle of metal rings cut through Jamison's relentless pacing, and he glanced over in time to see Rory slip through the curtain.

The one his little girl had warned him not to peek behind. His faced started to heat again at the thought. Not because his own kid made him out to sound like some kind of Peeping Tom—she was only four, after all. But because of the moment that had followed.

The moment when Rory had echoed his daughter's words and his gaze had locked on hers and there'd been nothing—nothing—in his power that could keep him from mentally pulling back that curtain and picturing Rory McClaren wearing something far less than the old-fashioned dresses she favored.

Judging by the way her eyes had widened, she'd known it.

Clearing his throat, he asked, "Is Hannah—"

"She's fine. The seamstress is taking some measurements, and Hannah wanted me to make sure you're still waiting for her. She was a little nervous at first, but I think she's getting into the spirit of things. So, please…" She nodded her head at the waiting chair. "Sit down and relax."

He all but glared at the floral-print cushions that might as well have been covered with sharp thorns. Without some outlet for his excess energy, he'd likely explode. "Relaxing doesn't come easy to me."

"Really?" Rory drawled.

"That obvious, is it?" He supposed he shouldn't have been surprised. Maintaining a single-minded focus and blocking out the world around him had been a reflex since he was a kid.

His parents' divorce—hell, their entire marriage—had been a battlefield, his childhood collateral damage. The fights, the cold silences, the endless digs when the other wasn't around—Jamison had hated it all.

That volatile home life had made Jamison even more determined to keep the peace in his own marriage. He'd worked hard to give Monica everything she could need, everything she could want, everything she'd asked for and more.

And none of it had been enough to make her—or their marriage—happy.

Monica had always complained about the long hours he put in. Of course, Monica had complained about so many things that work became even more of a refuge.

A sweet giggle came from behind the curtain, and Rory murmured, "She's a beautiful little girl."

The innocent comment slammed through him. He needed to spend this time away from work with his daughter. He needed to find a way to reconnect, but he was at a loss to know how. And it galled him, he had to admit, how easily, how naturally Rory related to Hannah when for him it was all such a struggle.

"Thank you," he said stiffly, wishing he could take more

credit for the amazing little person Hannah was. But she even looked like Monica, a tiny carbon copy of his blond-haired, doe-eyed wife.

"She'll make an adorable flower girl," Rory said.

"I'm sure she will," Jamison said. "I'm just not sure about this whole wedding thing."

Rory cocked a questioning eyebrow. "The *whole* wedding?" she asked.

"Hannah's role in it," he amended, knowing he'd already said too much.

"I can see how she'd be nervous, walking down the aisle in front of all those people. But you'll be standing at Ryder's side, so all she has to do is keep her eyes on you, knowing you'll be watching her the whole way, and she'll do fine."

"You make it sound so easy."

"I have faith," she said lightly.

Of course she did. The Hillcrest wedding coordinator had faith, hope and light shining out of her. "Still, it's a lot of pressure to put on a little kid."

"Oh, I wasn't talking about Hannah. My faith is in you."

"In me?" Jamison echoed. "Why would you—" why would *anyone* "—put your faith in me?"

"Because I see the trust Hannah has in you. All you have to do is show her you'll be there for her, and she'll find the courage and confidence to move forward all on her own."

All you have to do is be there for her. Little did Rory know how seldom he'd been there for Hannah during her short life. First because of how hard he'd been working, and then because of Monica... But now he, as Hannah's only parent, was responsible for her health and happiness.

The weight of that responsibility pressed on Jamison's chest until he struggled to breathe. And he couldn't help wondering if his in-laws were right and if they weren't so much better equipped to raise Hannah…

"Ever think maybe you put too much faith in people?" he asked Rory, his voice rougher than necessary and so out of place in this shop filled with feminine softness.

"Sometimes," she admitted, surprising him with the candid answer. "And sometimes they let me down."

"Rory—" A hint of sadness clouded her beautiful features. And that restless energy inside him changed into an urge to close the distance between them, to pull her into his arms and wipe the lingering shadows from her blue eyes…

"Daddy, look!" His daughter's excited voice broke the moment, saving him from making a huge mistake, as she popped out from the dressing room. "It's a real princess dress! Just for me."

She giggled as she spun in a circle, the cream-colored lacy skirt flaring out around her tiny legs and glittery sneakers. The happy sound only magnified the ache, the guilt, pressing down on his chest. When was the last time he'd heard Hannah laugh?

"Just for you, Hannah," he vowed.

From now on, everything was just for his daughter.

Because if there was one thing he'd already done far too many times, it was let the females in his life down.

So despite the attraction, despite the knowing, tender look in the wedding coordinator's gaze, Jamison was going to keep his distance.

Chapter Three

"Oh, my gosh! Didn't Hannah look so cute?"

Seated at a wrought iron bistro table outside the café, Rory smiled as she listened to Lindsay describe every detail on the flower girl's dress. Not that she minded. The time with the sweet little girl was still playing through Rory's thoughts, as well.

Which was much better than thinking of the girl's not-so-sweet but undeniably hot father…

The bride-to-be's recitation stopped on a sigh as she paused to take a bite of a double-chocolate muffin. "Why did you bring me here?" she demanded. "That was supposed to be my final fitting, and after eating this dessert, I'm going to need to go back and have the seams let out at least two inches."

Eyeing Lindsay's slender frame, Rory laughed. "I think you're safe, and besides, we're splitting, remember?" she asked before breaking off a piece of the moist top rising above the sparkling pink wrapper. She gave a sigh of her own as rich chocolate melted in her mouth.

"Perfect, so the seams will only need to be let out one inch." Despite the complaint, Lindsay went in for another bite.

"You have nothing to worry about. Ryder is going to take one look at you walking down the aisle and be blown away."

The other woman smiled, but as she wiped her fingers on a napkin, Rory could see her heart wasn't in it. "Hey, everything okay? I know how busy you've been between the wedding and the benefit next week."

As part of her job promoting Clearville and its businesses, Lindsay was helping Jarrett Deeks with a rodeo at the local fairgrounds. The benefit was aimed at raising funds and awareness for the former rodeo star's horse rescue.

"Everything's on track. Jarrett lined up enough cowboys to compete, and local vendors have been amazing about donating their time and part of the proceeds from their booths." Despite the positive words, worry knit her dark blond brows, and she crumpled the napkin in her fist.

"So then what's wrong…and what can I do to help?" Lindsay was a Hillcrest bride, but she was also a friend. "Whatever you need, I'm here for you."

"You might wish you hadn't made that promise."

"I never make promises I don't keep," Rory vowed, her thoughts drifting back to her ex, Peter, and his many, many broken promises, but she shoved the memories away.

"Okay then," Lindsay exhaled a deep breath. "Here goes… It's Jamison. He and Ryder have known each other for years, and I can tell by how Ryder talks how close they are. He's already told me there's nothing he wouldn't do for Jamison, and I'm sure Jamison feels the same."

The last part was said with enough worry for unease to worm its way into Rory's stomach. "And what do you think Jamison's going to do?"

"I'm probably being paranoid. But my relationship with Ryder... Well, let's just say we didn't get off to the best start." The bride gave a shaky laugh at the understatement behind those words.

Rory might have moved to Clearville recently, but her frequent visits as a teenager had given her a taste of small-town life. Everyone knew everyone's business. Which was why it was still something of a shock among the local gossips that Lindsay Brookes had managed to keep her son's—Ryder's son's—paternity a secret for so long.

"But the two of you are together now," Rory reassured her friend, "and that's all that matters."

She might not know the whole story of how Lindsay and Ryder had worked out a decade of differences, but she'd seen for herself how in love the couple was. The way Ryder looked at Lindsay—

Rory pushed aside the pinpricks of envy jabbing at her heart to embrace the positive. If Ryder and Lindsay could overcome such odds and find their way back to each other, then surely there was hope for her. True love was out there somewhere, but right now her focus was Hillcrest House and helping her aunt. Her own happily-ever-after would wait.

"I know. Things are going so well, but I can't shake this feeling that something's going to go wrong. Like I'm waiting for the other shoe to drop."

"And you think that shoe's a size-eleven Italian loafer?"

Lindsay laughed. "You noticed that, huh?"

"I think it's safe to say Jamison's strung a bit tight for a guy who's supposed to be on vacation."

And was it any wonder she was determined to ignore

the instant, unwanted attraction? If Rory had a type, she certainly didn't want it to be Jamison Porter. He was a corporate attorney, for heaven's sake! A shark in a suit when she was looking for more of a—a puppy.

Someone sweet, lovable…loyal. Someone willing to defend her and stay by her side.

"From what I've heard from Ryder, Jamison doesn't do vacations. Ryder really had to push him to take this time off. I guess Jamison has some big deal in the works, but I think if he would take a day or two to relax, it might give him a different perspective on the whole wedding and, well, on me."

"Lindsay, Ryder loves you. And as for Jamison, I think he and Ryder need to go out for a couple of beers and a game of pool over at the Clearville Bar and Grille. They can do the whole high-fiving, name-calling, competitive guy thing, and all will be well."

Even as she said the words, Rory had a hard time picturing Jamison Porter at the local sports bar. He seemed like her ex, Peter, who was more interested in being seen by the right people in the right places. But then again, so much about Peter had all been for show…

"And Ryder's asked, but Jamison won't go. He doesn't want to leave Hannah."

And *that* did not sound like Peter at all. Maybe Rory had been too quick in making her comparisons.

"She's had a hard time since the accident."

"Accident?"

Lindsay nodded, sympathy softening her pretty features. "A car accident a few months ago. Hannah sustained a mild concussion and a broken arm, but she was the lucky one. Her mother was killed instantly."

"Oh, no." That lost look she'd picked up on in Hannah… and in Jamison. Rory had assumed it was nothing more than a single dad on his own with his daughter, far away from the comforts of home. She should have realized it was something deeper… "Poor Hannah. And Jamison, to lose his wife."

"They were separated, and from what Ryder's said, things hadn't been right between them for a long time. But still…"

"I guess you can't blame him if he has his doubts about love and marriage."

"That's what Ryder keeps telling me. Not everything going on in the world revolves around our wedding."

"You're the bride, Lindsay. Everything *does* revolve around the wedding."

Lindsay dropped what was left of the mangled napkin on the table and leaned forward with a relieved smile. "I knew you'd understand, Rory! You're the best wedding coordinator ever, and I knew I could count on you to help."

Rory's eyes narrowed. "What exactly am I helping with?"

"Well, with Jamison, of course. I thought if you could show him around town, spend some time with him—"

"Wait! What?" she asked in alarm. "Why me?"

"You have such a way with people. Of keeping calm and helping them relax. Not to mention how taken Hannah is with you. You saw that, and I know Jamison did, too."

Yes, Rory had noticed Hannah's shy fascination. Knowing the little girl had lost her mother added a sense of heartbreak to the tiny fingers that had wrapped around her hand. But it wasn't enough to erase the memory of the dark, disapproving clouds brewing in Jamison's gray gaze.

She'd dealt with enough parental disapproval in her relationship with Peter to last a lifetime.

"I don't think that's such a good idea, Lindsay. With everything Hannah and Jamison must be going through—"

"That's why this is so perfect!" her friend insisted. "Back home they're surrounded by memories, but Clearville—and you—are a clean slate. I know this isn't some miracle fix for what they've lost. No one expects that. All I'm asking is for you to show them around town. Give them a tour of Hillcrest House. You're always saying how magical the place is."

"So no miracles required, just performing a little magic," Rory said wryly as she sank back in her chair. But she was already caving despite Jamison's disapproval, despite her own reluctance to spend time with a man who made her heart skip a beat even when he was frowning at her.

Because once upon a time, Rory had found magic at Hillcrest House, and while her belief might have wavered a time or two over the years, it had never left her.

And when she thought about Hannah and the seriousness in her big brown eyes, Rory couldn't help thinking that belief in happily-ever-after was what the little girl needed.

As for Jamison… Well, there was some magic Rory wasn't sure even a fairy godmother could perform.

As a corporate lawyer at Spears, Moreland and Howe, one of the most prestigious firms in San Francisco, Jamison Porter was at the top of his game. He was vying for a promotion that would make him the youngest junior partner in the firm's history. He had a track record of success and negotiated million-dollar deals for breakfast.

So why was it he couldn't win an argument with his daughter when it came to *eating* breakfast?

"I want pancakes."

Still in her ladybug pajamas, her hair a tangled mess of curls—proof of another battle he'd already lost this morning—Hannah slouched in the dining room chair in a classic pout.

"Hannah…"

The key to winning any negotiation was coming to the table from a place of power, and in this, Jamison had none. Zip. Zilch. Nada. Not after he'd given in to her request for pancakes the day before.

But how was he supposed to say strong when his daughter's willful tantrum broke down and she'd whispered, "Mommy let me have pancakes," with tears filling her eyes?

And so he'd given in and learned the hard way a sugar rush was not a myth. Hyped up on the sweet stuff, Hannah had talked almost nonstop after leaving the bridal shop—mostly about the very woman Jamison was trying so hard not to think about.

"Rory says I can wear ribbons in my hair.

"Rory says I'll get to carry a basket filled with roses and can throw them like it's raining flowers.

"Rory says…"

But no matter how much his daughter talked, it was Rory's voice Jamison heard. Her smile that flashed through his mind time and again. Her challenge to him to reassure Hannah that everything would be okay and her misplaced confidence that he would succeed.

His daughter didn't need him to encourage her to walk down the aisle and be the best flower girl she could be. Rory had done all that on her own. Jamison doubted there was much the woman couldn't talk a person into if she tried.

Sometimes people let me down.

Whoever the man was—and Jamison would bet the partnership up for grabs that it was a man—he had to be the biggest kind of fool to put that shadow of disappointment in Rory's eyes.

And Jamison was no fool. He learned from his mistakes and the biggest one he'd made was in believing he could make a woman happy. So he'd be smart and keep his distance from the pretty wedding coordinator before she could learn the hard way he could only be another man who would let her down.

Jamison scraped a hand over his face, feeling the stubble he had yet to shave away. He'd grabbed a quick shower that morning, but Hannah had been up by the time he'd gotten dressed. He had hoped she might sleep in, but she awoke first thing…looking as bright eyed and well rested as if she hadn't taken ten years off his life when she woke up screaming in the middle of the night.

His mother-in-law, Louisa, had warned him about deviating from Hannah's schedule. *She's been through so much. She takes comfort in a stable routine.*

In that, they were alike, but lately he'd noticed his daughter's routine—or more specifically, Louisa's routine for his daughter—left very little time for him to spend with Hannah.

After the accident, he'd welcomed his mother-in-law's help. Though not life threatening, Hannah's injuries had left her bruised and broken, and Jamison had almost been afraid to touch her. Louisa, a former nurse, had the knowledge and experience Jamison lacked. But now that Hannah had healed, it was time for Louisa to take a step back—whether she wanted to or not.

Which was one of the reasons he'd insisted on this extended trip with Hannah. He'd thought his mother-in-law had exaggerated the problems he might cause, but now he had to wonder.

The first night at the hotel, bedtime had been accompanied by multiple requests for night-night stories, drinks of water and trips to the bathroom. Had those delay tactics been something more than a child's typical resistance to bedtime in a strange location? Were the nightmares that haunted Hannah enough to make her afraid to close her eyes?

Jamison hated the helplessness that gripped him and how the sound of her cries took him back to that horrible day.

On the phone fighting with Monica, Hannah crying in the background…his wife's shrill scream, the sickening crash of metal and after that…nothing. Just a dead phone clutched in his hand.

Eventually Hannah had drifted off to sleep, her breathing still shaky from lingering tears. But Jamison hadn't slept a wink. Blinking through blurry eyes, he figured he looked every bit as rough as that sleepless night had felt.

He was relieved Hannah didn't seem to be suffering any ill effects, but the sense of anxiety that had kept his eyes wide-open still lingered. The monster under the bed ready to jump out at any minute, even during the day with the sun shining.

"I've already ordered breakfast," he reminded her now as he sank into a chair and was met with her pouty face.

Stick with the routine, he reminded himself.

When he first read through Louisa's list of approved foods, dominated by fruits and vegetables, he'd wondered if his mother-in-law wasn't setting him up for a fall. Really, what kid wanted oatmeal for breakfast? But the pancake incident and last night's nightmare made him realize he didn't need to blame Louisa for his failures.

He could fail spectacularly all on his own.

"But I want—"

A quick knock on the door interrupted the brewing

tantrum, and Jamison wasn't sure when he'd felt more relieved. "See, there's room service now with breakfast."

"Pancakes!" Hannah finished in a voice loud enough to have him cringing as he opened the door. And then cringing again at who was on the other side.

"Morning!" Looking bright, chipper and far too tempting for so early in the morning, Rory McClaren met his frown with a beaming smile.

Her dark hair was pulled back in a high ponytail that made her look even younger than he guessed she was and brought to mind old sitcoms set back in the '60s. So did the halter-style dress with its soft floral print and full skirt. His mind still foggy from a sleepless night and too many hours spent thinking of her, Jamison could only stare.

After Hannah's nightmare, Rory looked like something out of a dream. As the rich, strong scent of caffeine hit him, he belatedly noticed the silver serving cart in front of her.

"What are you doing here?" Still on some kind of sleep-deprived delay, the question didn't form until Rory had already wheeled the cart between the floral-print couch and coffee table in the living area and into the dining room.

She shot a questioning glance over her bare shoulder. "You did order room service, didn't you?"

Her blue gaze was filled with wide-eyed innocence, but Jamison wasn't buying it. Realizing he was still holding the door open, he let go and followed her inside. "Yes, but I didn't expect the wedding coordinator to deliver it."

She waved a dismissive hand. "Small hotel. Everyone pitches in." Smiling at his daughter, she asked, "Are you ready for breakfast this morning, Miss Hannah?"

Despite her earlier fascination with the woman, Hannah retreated back into shyness. She drew her bare feet up onto the seat and wrapped her arms around her ladybug-covered legs, looking impossibly tiny in the adult-size chair. “I want pancakes,” she repeated, her voice more of a whisper this time.

Instead of a wave of embarrassment crashing over him, Jamison couldn’t help feeling a little smug as Rory’s cheery expression faltered a bit.

“Um—” she glanced at the ticket tucked beneath one of the covered trays “—it looks like the chef made you oatmeal this morning.” She lifted her gaze to Jamison for confirmation.

He nodded. “Oatmeal’s good for you. Healthy.”

At least that was what his in-laws thought. It wasn’t something his mother would have fixed when he was a kid. Not that his mother fixed much of anything in the way of meals—breakfast or otherwise. Jamison had mostly been on his own and, in all honesty, more than content with sugary cereal eaten straight from the box, parked in front of morning cartoons.

“Good for you. Right…” Rory drew out the word as she pulled the cover off the bowl of plain, beige cereal. No fun shapes, bright colors or magically delicious marshmallows there. “What do you say we make this oatmeal even yummier, Hannah?”

Somehow, Jamison should have known a bowl of mush wouldn’t be enough to throw her off her game.

“How?” A wealth of doubt filled that one word, and just like that Jamison’s amusement vanished.

Yesterday, Hannah had been ready to believe Rory was a fairy godmother who walked on flower petals. And okay, so he didn’t buy into Rory McClaren’s brand of happily-ever-after, but his daughter was still a little girl. Did he want her doubting something as simple as breakfast couldn’t somehow get better?

“I’m guessing Rory has an idea about that,” he murmured.

He caught her look of surprise before pleasure brought a pink glow to her cheeks. "That's right. Thanks to your daddy, who also ordered some fruit, we are going to turn this into happy oatmeal."

"Happy?"

"Yep. This oatmeal's a little sad and plain right now," she said as reached for the platter of fruit beautifully arranged in the middle of the tray. "But with a little bit of color…" Her hands, as delicate and graceful as the rest of her, sliced up the fruit as she spoke. A moment later, she'd outlined a blueberry smiley face in the bowl of oatmeal, complete with banana-slice eyes, a strawberry nose and an orange-wedge smile.

Scrambling up onto her knees, Hannah peered into the bowl Rory set in front of her and let out a soft giggle. "Look, Daddy, the oatmeal's smiling at me."

And his daughter was smiling at him. Jamison would have liked the credit, but Rory McClaren had the magic touch. A woman who thought rainbow was a color and turned plain beige oatmeal into a bright, happy-faced breakfast.

"I like smiley-face yummy oatmeal." Grabbing the spoon, Hannah leaned over the bowl, ready to dig in, her blond hair falling into her face.

"Oops, hold on a second, Hannah."

Skirting around the whitewashed oak table, Rory reached up and pulled the peach-colored band from her ponytail. Jamison's mouth went dry as she gave her head a quick shake and sent her dark hair tumbling over her bare shoulders.

His tongue practically stuck to the roof of his mouth; he fought to swallow, assailed by the image of that silken hair spread out against a pillow or tumbling over *his* shoulders as Rory leaned down to kiss him…

"Thank you, Miss Rory." Her riot of curls contained, Hannah beamed up at the beautiful brunette.

Cupping her chin in one hand, Rory bent down until they were eye to eye. "You are welcome, Miss Hannah."

Hannah giggled at the formality before digging into her breakfast. She bounced up and down in the chair in time with chowing down on a bite of banana, drawing an indulgent smile from Rory.

"And what about you, Mr. Porter?" she asked as she walked back over to the serving tray and waved a hand. "I don't see another bowl of oatmeal for you."

"Coffee," he said abruptly, still trying to get the erotic images out of his mind.

Mistaking the reason for his short response, her earnest gaze met his. "I'm sorry if I overstepped with the ponytail. My only excuse is to say it's an occupational hazard."

"So, wedding coordinator, room service attendant and hairstylist?"

"Oh, I'm not a professional stylist by any means. But in my short time as wedding coordinator, I've learned to be a jack-of-all-trades when it comes to last-minute emergencies. Whether it's figuring out how to turn three bridesmaids' bouquets into four because the bride made up with her best friend at the last second or pulling out a hot-glue gun for a quick repair to a torn hemline, I feel like I've already been there, done that. And now it's like I can't help fixing things… Not that Hannah's broken or you need help and—I have got to learn to keep my mouth shut and my hands to myself!"

Rory wasn't the only one with that second problem, but it wasn't his daughter's hair Jamison longed to get his hands on. "It's all right," he said gruffly, even though it wasn't. Her actions were innocent. His intentions…not so much. "About the ponytail thing, I mean. Anyone can see I can't get it right. And I do mean anyone, since even Hannah tells me her hair looks funny when I'm done with it."

"I'm sure you're doing fine."

"Are you?" The sympathy in her eyes told him he and Hannah had been a topic of conversation once they left the bridal shop. "Because I'm not sure of a damn thing."

He half expected some meaningless platitude, but instead she reached for the carafe on the serving tray and poured a cup of steaming coffee. "Rough night?" she asked as she handed him the mug.

His fingers overlapped hers, the warmth seeping through coming more from her soft skin than from the hard ceramic. For a brief second, they both froze, connected by the fragrant cup of coffee. And he found himself desperate for someone to confide in.

"Nightmare," he admitted as Rory released the mug and took a quick step back. She set about tidying the serving tray, her lashes lowered as she avoided his gaze.

"You or Hannah?"

Jamison gave a quick laugh. "Hannah," he said as if he hadn't had more than his share of bad dreams over the past months. Not about Monica, like the dreams that had Hannah crying out for a mother who would never again kiss away her tears, but ones about the accident.

He'd seen pictures of what remained of the run-down sedan Monica had been driving—a mangled wreck of metal Hannah had somehow survived. As if those images weren't bad enough, his subconscious tormented him even further. In his nightmares, the car burst into flames, plunged into a river or fell from a cliff while he could do nothing but watch.

In reality, Jamison hadn't seen the accident, but he'd heard it.

Worse, he'd caused it.

Chapter Four

"Oh, Ms. McClaren, I have to tell you we just got back from the wedding-cake tasting, and every one of them was to die for. I think all those tiny little bites added up to an entire cake by the time we made up our minds."

Rory smiled as the beaming, sugar-filled bride-to-be rushed to her side in the middle of Hillcrest House's elegant, dark-walnut-paneled lobby. She had offered to take Jamison and Hannah on a tour of the grounds, but so far they hadn't made it out of the hotel. She'd been stopped a handful of times either by guests or employees with questions about upcoming events.

Susannah Erickson was the latest interruption. "I'm glad you enjoyed the tasting. I learned within my first few days here not to accompany brides to the bakery. Too much temptation."

And why, oh, why did she have to say *temptation*? Just speaking the word out loud had her thinking about that morning, and not about food. The image of Jamison opening the door, dressed but fresh from the shower, was seared in Rory's mind. The scent of soap and shampoo had clung to his skin, and his damp hair had been rumpled from a quick toweling. Add to that the dark stubble he'd yet to shave away, and all she'd been able to think about was the seductive rasp of that rough skin against her own…

Almost against her will, Rory sought Jamison out. He stood off to the right with Hannah at his side, but Rory had already known that. She'd felt hyperaware of his proximity since he'd opened the door. Telling herself in the intimate setting of the Bluebell suite, of course she would notice the overwhelming presence of a masculine, six-foot-something man.

But even now, surrounded by guests and employees in the spacious lobby, she was still conscious of him. Of the way his gray gaze focused on her. Of the way the air crackled with electricity when their eyes met. Of the restless energy that seemed to pulse inside every inch of his broad-shouldered frame.

As Rory spoke with the bride-to-be about menu options and table settings, her words trembled and tripped on her tongue as though she were the one experiencing a high-octane sugar rush. Fortunately, her client didn't seem to pick up on her nerves and promised to call back and book Hillcrest for her wedding as soon as she had a chance to talk with her fiancé.

After saying her farewells to Susannah, Rory braced herself to face Jamison again. He had taken the opportunity to shave and comb his hair during the time it took for her to return the breakfast dishes and serving cart to the kitchen. Too bad she didn't find that strong, smooth jawline and the hint of an expensive, spicy aftershave any less attractive.

But the clean-cut version was a good reminder of who the man was. In the suite this morning, he'd been a harried father who'd needed her. A man dealing with the heartache of raising a child on his own. A man her heart urged her to help…

This, though, was Jamison Porter, Esquire. A businessman in control of himself and immune to his surroundings as his thumbs flew over his phone. Including, she feared, the daughter twisting restlessly at his side.

Rory knew what it was like to be pushed aside, forgotten, ignored…

She'd been a few years older than Hannah when tragedy struck her family. As an adult, she understood that her parents loved her every bit as much as they loved her brother, Chance, but in the weeks following his accident she'd felt like a ghost wandering the hospital halls—unseen, unheard.

Shaking off the memories, she scolded herself for projecting her own past onto the father and daughter in front of her. *Focus, Rory. Jamison Porter is part of a wedding party and dealing with him part of* your *job.*

Pasting a professional smile onto her face, she apologized as she joined them. "Sorry about all the interruptions."

"If there's one thing I understand, it's work." He thrust the phone into the pocket of his slacks, but Rory couldn't tell if he was reluctant or relieved to break the connection. "I'm good at what I do."

Rory frowned. The words didn't sound like bragging as much as they sounded like…an apology? She wasn't sure she had that right until his gaze dropped to the top of his daughter's head and his throat worked in a rough swallow.

Suddenly the puzzle pieces fell into place. Successful businessman, not-so-successful family man. His fingers tapped on the outside of his muscular thigh, and Rory could sense his need to reach for his phone again—tangible proof of the predictable, logical world he'd left behind.

"Jamison—"

"I want cake for breakfast," Hannah cut in, her tone grumpy enough for Rory to know the little girl hadn't totally gotten over having to eat oatmeal that morning.

"Only brides get cake for breakfast," her father answered quickly.

"I wanna be a bride."

His daughter's comeback was even faster than his and left Jamison groaning in response. Rory couldn't help but laugh. "Relax, Dad, that's one worry you can put off for a few years." Gazing down at Hannah, she asked, "Do you want to go see where Miss Lindsay is going to get married? You can practice being her flower girl."

Hannah was quiet for a second before her eyes lit up. "Do flower girls get cake?"

"They do—but not for breakfast."

After heaving a sigh at the unfairness of that, Hannah nodded. "Okay."

"All right then. Let's go!"

"Wait, Miss Rory," the girl demanded. "You hafta hold my hand."

Hannah held out her left hand, her right already wrapped around her father's. Rory hesitated even though she knew she was being ridiculous. In her short time at Hillcrest, she'd held more than her share of little and big girls' hands leading up to a wedding. This was nothing different. But with Jamison on the other side, his daughter joining the two of them together, Rory felt a connection that went far beyond a professional capacity.

Something about the corporate lawyer, something in the shadows lingering in his silver eyes, grabbed hold of her. She'd been telling the truth when she said she'd become a jack-of-all-trades with a quick fix for prewedding emergencies. But she had to be careful. She'd be foolish to think she could step in and fix Jamison and his adorable daughter. Foolish to invest too much of herself when their time in Clearville was temporary. Foolish to think he'd want her to.

Though Rory didn't want to be so in tune with the man just a child's length away, she sensed the deep breath he exhaled as they stepped out into the cool morning air. Hannah bounced between them down the wraparound porch's front steps, but it was Jamison who seemed to have released a negative energy bottled up far too long.

As they walked down the gravel path leading from the house, Rory couldn't help glancing back over her shoulder. Even though she'd been back for almost three months, the sight of the Victorian mansion never failed to steal her breath.

She loved the history and old-fashioned elegance of the place. The way it brought to mind a simpler time. With its high peaks, glorious turrets and carved columns and balustrades, an air of romance surrounded the house and property.

Not that romance was anything Rory should be thinking of—at least not as her gaze met Jamison's.

"Um, did you know Hillcrest House was built in the late 1800s? The original owner made his fortune decades earlier down in San Francisco during the gold rush. Not that he ever found gold, but he was one of the enterprising men who figured out the more practical side of gold fever. The thousands of men dreaming of striking it rich were going to need tools and equipment, and he was one of the first on the scene to set up shop."

"Let me guess...at ridiculously inflated rates?" Jamison

asked, the corner of his mouth lifted in a cynical smile that still managed to trip up Rory's heartbeat.

"Oh, but he wasn't just selling metal pans and shovels and pails… He was selling the miners the tools they needed to follow their dreams." Catching the look of utter disbelief on Jamison's face, Rory let out the laughter she'd been holding back. "Yeah, okay, even I can't pull that one off. He robbed the poor suckers blind, selling on credit and then cashing in on their claims when they couldn't pay him back."

"So much for the romance of a time gone by."

Rory started, feeling as if Jamison had read her thoughts moments earlier. "Well, uh, if it's any consolation, karma did bite back, and he ended up losing his fortune—and Hillcrest House—when the stock market crashed."

"Hmm, sounds like cosmic justice but, again, not very romantic."

"Ah, but that's when the house's luck changed. After it stood empty for years, a wealthy industrialist from back east came to California and fell in love with a young woman. He bought Hillcrest as a wedding present for his bride. The story goes that their plan was to have a dozen or so kids—"

"A dozen?"

"At least," Rory emphasized, smiling at the overwhelmed expression on his face as he glanced down at his lone child. "Sadly, they were unable to have children, but as time went on and more and more people were traveling to California and taking vacations along the coast, they decided to turn Hillcrest into a hotel so its rooms could still be filled with families and children and laughter—even if those families only stayed for a short time."

The reminder was one Rory needed to focus on. Jamison and Hannah were only staying for a few weeks.

She couldn't allow herself to be drawn in on a personal level, to let herself start to care too much, too quickly. But with the little girl's hand tucked so trustingly in hers as she sang under her breath, Rory couldn't help wondering if it was already too late.

Hannah's shy sweetness reminded Rory of a kitten she'd once rescued. The frightened Siamese had been all eyes in a skinny body covered with matted fur. It had taken time to build up enough trust for the kitten to allow her to pet it and even more time for the tiny bundle of fur to completely come out of its shell. To learn to run and play and chase. But Rory hadn't given up, because even at the beginning, underneath all the wariness, she had sensed the playful kitten longing to come out.

And as much as the kitten had needed to be rescued, Rory had needed something to save. She couldn't compare her experience as a child to what Hannah was facing in losing her mother so young, but Rory understood a little of what the girl was going through.

That beneath the sadness and loss, a silly, playful girl was struggling to break free.

"And what's your family's connection to the hotel?"

The summer breeze blew a lock of chestnut hair across Jamison's forehead and let loose a flurry of butterflies in her stomach. He was so good-looking, she forgot the question, forgot everything as she met his gaze over his daughter's head.

"Rory."

Heat flooded her cheeks as she tore her attention from the heat shimmering between them and back on what should have been her focus all along. "Right…my family's connection to the hotel. Um, the couple owned the hotel for decades, but with no children to leave it to, they put it up for sale. My grandparents met at Hillcrest—"

"Another romantic story?"

"Exactly," she answered, pleased with his guess despite the cynical tone of the question. "My grandmother was working the front desk and my grandfather was a guest here. Years later, when they heard the hotel was available, they bought it as an investment. They visited all the time but never lived here.

"My father and my uncle both worked here when they were younger, but the hotel and the hospitality industry were never their calling. Not like it was for my aunt Evelyn. Everyone knew she would run Hillcrest one day. She's smart and strong and independent."

Rory's worry over her aunt's health stung her eyes, but she blinked, banishing the tears before they could form. Her aunt wouldn't appreciate Rory getting teary in front of a guest. Not even if that guest was ridiculously handsome with the kind of broad shoulders and strong arms where a woman would be tempted to find comfort.

"And you and your cousin are here helping out?"

That was the explanation she and Evie had been giving people. Their aunt kept a strict line drawn between her personal and professional life, and she didn't want anyone outside of family to know of her health problems.

"Hillcrest House has always been a popular location for weddings with the locals in Clearville and Redfield," Rory said, naming another nearby town, "but last year my aunt decided to expand Hillcrest as a wedding destination. The couples now have the choice of an all-inclusive ceremony, with the hotel handling everything from the cake to the music to the photographer."

"And that's where you come in."

"I work with the couple to get a feel of the type of wedding they're looking for and design all the elements to match that theme."

Jamison shook his head at the notion of a wedding theme, which had Rory wondering what his wedding to Hannah's mother had been like. Not that she was about to ask.

"You're good at this."

Feeling her cheeks heat at the surprising compliment, Rory shook her head. "I've had Hillcrest House facts drilled into my head since I was a little girl. I could recite this information in my sleep. A couple of times, in the midst of wedding madness, I think maybe I have!"

"Not just the tour. I mean the way you dealt with the guests and the staff earlier. You're friendly and encouraging but firm enough to get your point across."

"I—thank you," Rory said, far more pleased by the compliment than she should have been. She didn't like thinking of herself as hungry for approval, but after her failure at the interior design firm in LA, finding success—especially at Hillcrest House—was so important to her. "I didn't expect..."

"Expect what?"

She gave a small laugh. "You and my cousin Evie have quite a bit in common when it comes to the whole wedding thing."

Jamison and her by-the-book cousin likely had more in common than their negative views on weddings and marriage. A CPA, Evie was smart, well educated, as razor sharp as the blunt cut of her dark, chin-length hair. She was practical, pragmatic and more than a little cynical—the kind of woman Rory figured would impress a successful businessman like Jamison.

Ignoring the stab of jealousy at the thought of Jamison and her cousin forming their own mutual-admiration society, Rory said, "Evie's a genius when it comes to handling the books and the last person to believe in fairy tales, but sometimes she acts like I pull off these weddings with nothing more than a wave of a magic wand. She doesn't seem to notice the hard work that goes into them."

"Look, Daddy!" Hannah's impatient tug on their hands brought the conversation to a halt as they reached a curve in the pathway. An intricate lattice-arched entry led to the rose garden—a favorite spot for many brides and grooms to say their vows. Pink, red and white blooms unfurled amid the dark green bushes and the thick, rich lawn.

Turning to Rory, Hannah asked, "Is that where you grow the flowers for the flower girls?"

Not about to ruin the moment for the child, especially when she saw some of that curiosity shining through in her big brown eyes, Rory said, "It sure is. Why don't you go look for the perfect flower? But don't touch, okay? Some of the roses have sharp thorns."

Hannah's pale brows furrowed as she glanced between the rose garden and back again. "Will you stay right here, Daddy?"

"I'm not going anywhere, Hannah Banana."

A small smile tugged at the little girl's lips, and Rory swore the sweet expression was somehow tied to the strings around her heart. She couldn't help smiling as Hannah tucked her hands behind her back before racing—somewhat awkwardly—over to the garden.

But it was Jamison and the unabashed tenderness in his eyes as he gazed at his daughter that had Rory's emotions all tangled up in knots.

He was a guest. And like any other guest who passed through Hillcrest House, Rory would quickly forget all about him. She'd forget all about this day, about walking with Jamison and Hannah beneath a cloudless sky. About the warmth of his skin as his arm brushed against hers. About the rich, masculine scent that tempted her to move closer and breathe deeper. About the longing to reach out and take his hand, knowing how something as simple as entwining her fingers with his would form a bond she would feel right down to her bones…

Yes, indeed, she would forget all about that. Might just spend the rest of her life forgetting all about that.

The strict talking-to had Rory straightening her shoulders and adopting a polite smile, neither of which were any protection against the power behind Jamison's gaze.

"I'll say it again, Rory. You're good at what you do," he repeated, the intensity behind his words preempting any denial she might have made. "Anyone who doesn't appreciate you is a fool."

"Like this, Miss Rory?" Hannah asked over her shoulder as she placed a single rose petal on the verdant green grass.

"Just like that!"

Jamison shook his head at the beautiful brunette's unrelenting encouragement. "You do realize, at that rate, it'll take her an hour and a half to walk down the aisle?"

"She is the flower girl, and they are her flowers. She has every reason to enjoy her moment."

How was it that Rory McClaren seemed to enjoy every moment? A hint of pink touched her cheeks, and he couldn't help wondering if it was from the midmorning sun—or in response to the words he shouldn't have spoken.

Mouth shut and hands to yourself, Porter, he repeated, glad he'd at least stuck to the second part of the mantra despite the serious temptation she posed at every turn. His finger itched to discover the softness of the dark hair that trailed down her back, to trace the splash of freckles across the elegant line of her collarbones, to strip away the strap of her dress marring the perfection of her shoulder…

He hadn't touched, but he couldn't seem to stop himself from speaking. He'd seen the self-consciousness she tried to hide as she talked about her aunt and cousin—smart, successful women—as if she were something less. And everything in him had rebelled at hearing it.

Yes, Rory was beautiful, but desire was something he could control. Listening to her put herself down, even if the words had been unspoken, that was something he couldn't let go. Not after all she'd done for Hannah in as little as two days.

And yeah, it scared the hell out of him, when at times his daughter still felt like a stranger to him. When he felt at such a loss for what to do or what to say. When he felt himself start to shut down like he had when he was a kid and his parents' fighting was enough to send him underneath the covers—or sometimes even underneath the bed—where he'd cover his ears and close his eyes and wish himself away.

But right now, in this moment with Hannah jumping from one spot to the next, playing some kind of flower-petal hopscotch, he wouldn't have wished himself anywhere else in the world.

"Thank you."

Rory blinked in surprise. "For what?"

"For Hannah. I haven't seen her this happy in—I'm not sure I remember when."

She shook her head. "It's not me. It's Hillcrest. This place is magical that way."

When Jamison offered a disbelieving snort in response, she held up a silencing hand. "Hear me out." And when that hand came down and she entwined her fingers with his, he couldn't have said a word anyway.

Holding hands hadn't made it into his fantasy, but it might have if he'd known how something so simple would make his pulse skyrocket, his heart race, his stomach muscles tighten in response. The softness of her skin seemed to telegraph through his entire body until he swore he could feel her caress…everywhere.

He wasn't sure how he got his feet to move as she led him over toward a white wrought iron bench. Tucked off to the side of the garden, the shaded spot offered a perfect view of Hannah playing a few yards away.

"Rory—" His voice was a strangled croak, and even when she let go, the feel of her hand gliding away branded him. It was all he could do not to scrub his palm against his pressed khakis.

She patted the spot beside her. "Have a seat. Please," she added when he stood ramrod straight at her side.

Somehow, he made his muscles move and forced himself to sit on a bench too small for the arm's-length distance he needed between them. So small the cool breeze carried the sunshine-and-wildflower scent of her skin closer and a strand of her hair danced over his biceps like a caress.

It took everything in his power to focus on the words she was saying rather than following the tantalizing movement of her lips, but the seriousness in her blue eyes soon caught his complete attention. "I have an older brother, Chance, who I adore. He's four years older than I am, and growing up he was always my hero. The big brother who looked out for me. When I was a few years older than Hannah, he was in an accident."

Even though years had passed, Rory sucked in a deep breath before telling the next part. "He was showing off for his friends, fell off his skateboard doing some crazy jump and hit his head. He ended up in a coma. The doctors did everything they could, but for a long time, they didn't know if he would wake up or what kind of shape he would be in if he did."

"I can imagine how hard that must have been on you and your parents." Hannah's injuries hadn't been that severe, but it was the months leading up to the accident when he hadn't known if he would ever see his daughter again and the agonizing hours after that final fight with Monica when he hadn't even known if Hannah was still *alive* that gave him an idea of what the McClarens had gone through.

"It was. Our family had always been so together, so strong, but Chance's accident proved how everything could change. Like that," she said with a snap of her fingers. "As the weeks went by, and his condition didn't change, eventually my dad went back to work. Not because his job was more important than Chance, but because—I just don't think he could sit there, feeling so hopeless, anymore.

"My mom refused to leave my brother's side—eating, sleeping, living at the hospital. She never came out and said so, at least not when I was around, but I think she resented my dad for not doing the same."

"And what did you do," Jamison asked, "during all that time?"

Rory met his gaze before ducking her head, looking almost embarrassed that he'd asked about her. He could imagine she must have felt like the forgotten child, the healthy, happy one no one had the time or energy to pay much attention to.

"I split my days between school and the hospital. I mostly tried to be quiet and stay out of the way, but as the weeks went on… I don't know, maybe I got to be more like my dad, where I couldn't sit there and watch anymore. And then one day, after my mom had run down to the cafeteria for coffee, she came back and I was kneeling on the bed, shaking Chance and shouting at him to stop messing around and to wake up."

"Rory."

Shaking off his sympathy, she talked faster, as if eager to get through the worst of it. "After that…incident, my aunt and uncle, Evie's parents, brought the two of us here for an extended vacation. We ran and laughed and played and explored every inch of this place.

"Not that I forgot about Chance. Every game of pretend Evie and I played over the summer had something to do with breaking a curse or casting a spell or rescuing him from a dragon. I knew if I believed strongly enough, one day Chance would open his eyes and wake up… And one day, he did."

"I'm glad your brother got better, and I can see why, as a little girl, this place would seem so magical, but Rory—" Jamison stopped short and heaved out a heavy sigh. "Hannah's mother isn't going to open her eyes and wake up. Not for all the faith or magic or fairy tales in the world."

"No, she isn't. And Hannah's been through a horrible tragedy, but she's still a little girl who wants to run and laugh and play again, and she needs to know it's okay for her to do those things."

"Of course it's okay."

"And she knows this…how? By watching you? When was the last time you ran or laughed or just enjoyed life a little?"

"Give me a break, Rory. I'm a grown man, not a kid."

"Right. But you're a grown man *with* a kid. A child who's lost her mother. She's looking to you to see how she's supposed to react to a loss she isn't old enough to understand."

Jamison jerked away from Rory's imploring gaze to focus on Hannah. She was no longer dropping petals but was instead gathering them up, one by one. Picking up the pieces…

He didn't want to admit Rory was right, but the truth

was he'd spent his entire life burying his feelings. Was it any wonder he'd done the same when Monica died?

But he hadn't thought about how his emotions—or his lack of emotion—were affecting Hannah. He'd seen how she had retreated into herself after the accident, so different from the smiling, laughing girl he remembered.

How had he not seen his own reflection staring back at him when he looked at his daughter?

"Even before...Monica," he confessed, "I wasn't the running and laughing kind of guy."

A small smile played around Rory's lips, telling him she wasn't shocked by his confession. "And that's why I wanted you to come along today. So you could see that here, at Hillcrest House, you can be."

"Wait a minute." Jamison reared back against the wrought iron bench and waved a hand in the direction of the path they'd taken. "You're telling me this whole tour was for my sake and not for Hannah's?" It was by far the most ridiculous—and quite possibly the sweetest—thing anyone had ever done for him.

"Hillcrest House is special that way," she told him. "Its magic seems to touch whoever needs it the most."

Somehow his scoffing laugh stuck in his throat. There was no magic, and hadn't he already decided there couldn't be any touching? He wasn't the kind of romantic fool who would buy into such whimsical nonsense.

But in the peaceful setting with the dappled sunlight streaming through the trees and the gentle understanding reflected in Rory's midnight blue eyes, Jamison almost wished that he was.

Chapter Five

Jamison Porter had to think she was the world's biggest fool. Had she really spent the past five minutes trying to convince a corporate lawyer, a man who lived his life based on rules and regulations, to believe in magic?

No wonder he was staring at her. The poor man was probably trying to figure out a way to grab his child and run before the crazy lady totally fell off her rocker. She would have been more embarrassed—probably *should* have been more embarrassed—except she believed every word she said. Hillcrest *was* magical, the kind of place to bring people together, and if he gave it half a chance, Jamison might feel that, too.

A tug on her skirt broke the moment, freeing her from that intense silver stare, as she turned to Hannah.

"Miss Rory?" The little girl ducked her head shyly as she pointed to a glimpse of white showing between the trees in the distance. "What's that?"

"That, Miss Hannah, is my favorite spot in the world."

"Your favorite spot in the whole, whole world?"

After pressing her knuckles to her chin and pretending to think for a moment, Rory nodded. "The whole, whole world."

Hannah offered a lightning-quick smile, one Rory couldn't help returning. Playing to the child's curiosity, she stood and held out her hand. "Do you want to go see?"

After hesitating for a moment, Hannah asked, "Can Daddy come, too?"

Without looking his way, she offered, "I bet your daddy would love to come with us."

Jamison made a sound Rory decided to take as an agreement as she led the way down the flagstone path. "What about you, Hannah?" she asked the little girl. "Do you have a favorite place?"

The little girl gave a soft giggle. "The hidey-hole in Daddy's office."

Rory laughed. "A hidey-hole, Jamison? I mean, I've been known to duck behind an ice sculpture to avoid a bridezilla or two, but I've never had to install a hidey-hole."

"It's not a hole, it's—" He shook his head. "Your favorite spot, Hannah? Really?" he asked, surprise softening his expression.

His daughter nodded as she swung the two adults' arms back and forth in time with her steps. "Yep. It's just my size an' when I'm real quiet, nobody knows I'm there. Like the time I hid from Nana."

"Yes, well, your grandmother isn't as good at hide-and-seek as you are," Jamison said, his wry tone telling Rory the older woman hadn't been as amused with her granddaughter's game as Hannah was, either. With a glance at Rory, he said, "And it's not a hole. The furniture set in my home office came with a liquor cabinet. I'm more a beer-on-the-weekend than a three-martini-lunch kind of guy, so I never bothered to stock the cabinet. Probably a good thing, since someone—" he gently shook Hannah's arm "—thinks it's a fun place to hide."

Jamison thought he was struggling as a father, but he must be doing something right. Didn't he realize Hannah's favorite place was one she associated with him?

As they rounded a bend along the flagstone pathway, Rory announced, "And here it is. My favorite place in the whole, whole world."

Rory was accustomed to breathless reactions at this point, and Hannah did not disappoint. "Daddy, look! It's a playhouse."

"I see it, Hannah," Jamison answered, and Rory couldn't help wondering *what* he saw.

With its crisscross latticework, carved pillars and wide steps leading toward the circular platform, the gazebo was breathtaking. The gleaming white woodwork could be transformed by wrapping the columns with gorgeous flowered garlands, adding colorful organza swags to the decorative eaves or bunting to the airy facade.

It was one of the most romantic spots Rory could imagine, and she'd shown it to dozens of couples in her short time as Hillcrest's wedding coordinator. But showing it to Jamison felt…different.

She felt oddly vulnerable, as if she were revealing a part of herself to the enigmatic, troubling man at her side.

Needing to create some distance, she let go of Hannah's hand and tried to pretend this was no different from any other tour. "It does look like a playhouse, but it's a gazebo, and this is where Lindsay is getting married." Pointing to the wide steps, she added, "Ryder and your daddy will be standing right up there, waiting. Because you're the flower girl, you'll go first—"

"An' get to throw my flowers."

"You'll throw your flowers and Robbie will carry the rings. Lindsay's bridesmaids will walk down the aisle and finally Lindsay."

"'Cause she's the bride and gets to eat cake for breakfast," the little girl piped with a definitive nod.

"That's right, and she'll walk right up here and—" Rory had barely set foot on the first step when she heard a creak and a crack. Neither sound registered until the board splintered beneath her sandal and pain shot up her leg. Her abbreviated cry got stuck in her throat as she lost her balance and fell—

Not to the solid ground but against Jamison's solid chest as he caught her in his arms. For a stunned moment, neither of them moved.

"You okay?" His low murmur stirred the hair at her temples and the vibration set off tiny shock waves in her belly.

Staring breathlessly up into his silver eyes, Rory could do little more than nod. Her heart pounded, and she wished she could blame the reaction on her near fall. Instead, she was pretty sure it had everything to do with the man who'd caught her. She braced a hand against his chest, knowing she should move, but her body refused to listen to her brain. The soft cotton was warmed by the morning sun and held the scent of soap combined with 100 percent pure male.

His face was inches from hers, so close she could feel the kiss of his breath against her lips, a prelude to the touch of his mouth against her own…

"Miss Rory!" Hannah's startled cry broke the moment so quickly Rory wasn't sure she hadn't imagined it.

"Stay back, Hannah. It's not safe," Jamison instructed. Bending down, he carefully maneuvered Rory's foot from between the jagged, cracked boards. She winced at the raw scrape on the outside of her ankle.

"She's all bleedy."

The wobble of tears shook Hannah's voice, and Rory focused on the little girl instead of the throbbing pain. "Hey, Hannah, do you—do you know what would make me feel better? If you'd sing a song. Can you do that for me?"

Nodding her head with a big sniff, she started singing a song Rory had heard her humming under her breath on their walk. She wasn't sure which was the bigger distraction—Hannah's sweet voice or the feel of Jamison's hands against her bare skin. She swallowed hard at the sight of the gorgeous man kneeling at her feet and swayed slightly.

Jamison caught her around the waist and lowered her to the first step. "Here, have a seat while I take a look at your ankle."

"Thank you. I—I don't know what happened."

"I can tell you that. The wood's nearly rotted through."

She shook her head. "No, that can't be. Earl, our handyman, just finished remodeling the gazebo last week." She had noticed some wear and tear and had put the gazebo on the handyman's to-do list.

"I'd say all your handyman did was slap on a coat of white paint. Judging by the way that step cracked beneath your feet, that new layer of latex is about all that's holding this thing together."

Dismayed, Rory struggled to push to her feet, but Jamison held her in place. "But this is where Ryder and Lindsay are getting married. It's where I—"

Where *Rory* wanted to get married. Okay, she wasn't even dating anyone and her last relationship had ended in disaster, but none of that meant she'd given up hope of finding true love. She wanted love, marriage, a family… and it all started here. She'd imagined dozens of scenarios for her perfect dream wedding, and while the dress, the flowers, even the guy had changed numerous times, the one constant had been speaking her vows beneath the lacy, romantic gazebo.

"Hey, it's going to be okay." Jamison's voice cut into her thoughts, and only as she met his silver gaze did Rory realize how close he was sitting.

He'd taken the step below her and slipped the sandal from her foot. He cradled her instep in one large hand while he brushed sharp slivers of wood from her abraded skin. The warmth of his body seeped into hers, radiating out from his palm, and Rory shivered in response. She caught the scent of his aftershave again, mixing with the pine-scented breeze surrounding them.

She drew a quick breath in through her mouth, trying to somehow stop inhaling the heady combination, but that only made matters worse as Jamison focused on her parted lips. Her pulse pounded and it was all Rory could do not to lean closer, to close the narrow gap between them, to press her mouth against the temptation of his.

The wind shifted again, rustling through the trees and carrying the sound of Hannah's sweet voice as she started singing a new song…

Jamison reared back, a look akin to horror flashing across his features so quickly, Rory wasn't sure what she had seen. But just like that, it was as though the tender moment never happened.

"You're lucky it wasn't a guest nearly breaking an ankle on that step," he was saying. "This whole thing is a lawsuit waiting to happen. You need signs and a barricade cordoning off the area until someone can tear—"

"Tear it down?" She stared at him as she jerked her foot away. Instantly, the warmth of his touch disappeared, and the throbbing in her ankle multiplied. Was this the same man who'd come to her rescue, catching her when she would have fallen? The same man who'd cradled her foot in those big, warm hands? The same man she'd thought was going to kiss her?

With his arms crossed over his broad chest, *he* might as well have had signs and barricades warning her off.

"I am not letting anyone tear down the gazebo!" She'd as soon rip her own heart out and douse all her dreams of finding true love. Without the gazebo—

He reached out and gave the wobbly railing a good shake. "You won't have to let anyone tear it down. A stiff breeze, and the whole thing will fall over."

Still feeling foolish over the almost kiss she was starting to think had only happened in her own head, she glared at him. "You'd like that, wouldn't you? After all, you've made it clear how you feel about this *whole wedding thing*. You'd probably just as soon tear it down yourself."

"You're being ridiculous," Jamison muttered, but the baleful look he cast at the gazebo told Rory he was considering doing some damage to the structure—with his bare hands.

Pain shot up her leg the instant she pushed to her feet, and Jamison shot her a frustrated look. "Would you sit back down? You're lucky you didn't break your neck, thanks to your beloved gazebo, and you should go to the hospital—"

"No, Daddy!"

Jamison started at his daughter's shout. "Hannah, what?"

The little girl rushed over, but instead of latching onto her father, she threw her arms around Rory's legs, almost knocking her off balance.

Jamison frowned as Rory flinched. "Hannah."

"Don't make Rory go to the hospital! Don't make her go! Mommy went to the hospital and she never, never came back!"

* * *

Jamison froze at his daughter's cry, the sound piercing straight through his heart. In those first dark days after the accident, he'd tried to be there for Hannah, to be the one to care for her, to hold her when she cried. But her tears had been for her mother, and Jamison's fumbling, painful attempts to explain that Monica was now in heaven didn't seem to penetrate Hannah's sorrow.

"No! I want Mommy!" Accusation had filled her dark eyes, as if Jamison was the one keeping Monica away, the one responsible…and in so many ways, he was.

He'd seen the sympathy of the doctors and nurses at the hospital. *Give her time*, they'd advised. *She'll come around.* Before long, he'd learned to step back, to let someone better prepared handle Hannah when she was upset. One step, and then another and another, and before long, he'd stood on the fringes of his daughter's life. Present but accounting for nothing.

"Hannah." He could barely get the word out, barely make himself move to brush a hand against her curls. Half afraid to touch her and 100 percent certain she'd pull away.

Rory had no such fear. "Oh, Hannah, sweetie." Despite her injured ankle, she dropped down to his daughter's level to give her a hug. "I'm fine! All I need is a Band-Aid or two."

She brushed away Hannah's tears, reassuring the little girl who managed a watery smile in response, her ease with his daughter making Jamison feel like even more of a failure as a father.

"See, Daddy? Miss Rory doesn't need to go to the hospital." Hannah stared up at him, her chin set at a stubborn angle.

Jamison fought back a sigh. How did he end up the bad guy in all of this when he was only trying to help? "Hannah…"

"Your daddy was worried about me. And even if I did have to go to the hospital, I promise you I would come back."

He caught sight of the wince she tried to hide as she pushed to her feet and warned, "You need to get some ice on that ankle to keep the swelling down."

"I'll be fine," she repeated with a big smile, and Jamison couldn't figure out if it was for his benefit, his daughter's or her own.

At her first awkward step, he sighed again, wrapped an arm around her waist and under her knees and lifted her against her chest. Her startled gasp brought them face-to-face. Close enough for him to count the freckles dusting her cheeks. Close enough to feel her breath against his skin. And Jamison wondered how long he could have resisted before pulling Rory into his arms—banged-up ankle or no banged-up ankle.

"I'm not letting you hobble all the way back to the hotel."

"Well, you can't carry me back!"

He gave her a light toss, fighting a grin at the way her arms tightened around his neck. "I'm pretty sure I can."

"Not into the hotel. I can't—please, Jamison."

His smile faded. Rory was more than simply flustered by the idea. Pained embarrassment etched her pretty features. He didn't know the reason for the lack of confidence he'd sensed earlier, but he could understand why she wouldn't want her coworkers to see a guest carrying her through the hotel—regardless of the situation. Still, he couldn't let her limp back on her own. "Rory…"

"You, um… My place isn't far from here."

"Your place? You don't have a room at the hotel?"

She shook her head. "Evie does. She's staying in my aunt's room while she's…away. But I wanted a place of my own. I thought it would be easier."

"Easier?" he asked.

He did his damnedest to ignore the dizzying thought of taking Rory back to her place, but that was as impossible as ignoring the feel of her in his arms as she gave him directions to something called the caretaker's cottage.

She's injured, you idiot, he warned himself. *And your daughter is right beside you.*

Hannah skipped along the path, carrying the shoe he'd slipped from Rory's foot and still humming the song she'd switched to earlier. A song Monica used to sing to her.

It might not have been his dead wife's voice calling out from the grave, but it had still chilled him to the bone.

"I thought it would be easier keeping my professional and personal lives separate," Rory was saying, "if I wasn't staying at the hotel." She didn't meet his gaze, but judging by the color in her cheeks, she was well aware whatever was happening between them was a serious mixing of the two.

She wasn't simply the wedding coordinator any more than he was just the best man.

The best man… He wasn't anywhere near the best man for a woman like Rory. He needed to keep his distance, so how the hell had he ended up with her in his arms, about to carry her into her home?

"Yeah, how's that working out for you?"

She lifted her chin, but the stubborn angle only emphasized the pulse pounding at the base of her neck. "Just fine," she insisted, but as he rounded a curve on the path and the small cottage came into view, he thought he heard her whisper under her breath. "Until now."

Rory had always loved the caretaker's cottage, as the place was still known even though many years had passed since Hillcrest had live-in staff. From what her aunt had told her, the tiny wood-and-stone structure had nearly fallen into disrepair, but decades ago, Evelyn had saved it from the brink of destruction and had kept it up over the years.

Still, it had needed some sprucing up and some serious elbow grease to turn it into a place Rory called home, but now it was her sanctuary. A place she could retreat to where she didn't have to deal with demanding brides, cold-footed grooms or the mess she'd left behind in LA.

As Jamison set her down on the tiny porch, she insisted, "I'll be fine from here."

He'd said little on the walk from the gazebo, but Rory had felt the rock-hard tension gripping his muscles—a tightness she doubted had anything to do with carrying her weight.

She'd practically thrown herself at him thanks to the broken step, and he probably had whiplash from pulling away from her so fast.

"There are still splinters stuck in your ankle. If you won't let me take you—you know where—you're going to need some help."

She felt the weight of his frown as she hop-stepped over to the door and slipped the key out from beneath a brightly colored mosaic pot of pansies. She held her palm out in the universal stop sign as he moved closer. "I'm good. I've got it."

The very, very last thing she needed was Jamison Porter carrying her over the threshold!

"I like your house, Miss Rory," Hannah announced before bending down to take an exaggerated sniff of the pansies.

"Thank you, Miss Hannah."

"She probably thinks seven dwarves live here," Jamison muttered under his breath as Rory pushed the door open.

She shot him a look over her shoulder, though she had

to admit the tiny cottage in the woods did have a fairy-tale feel. The front door opened into the living room, a comfortable space Rory had filled with secondhand finds from the Hope Chest, an eclectic consignment store in town. Two floral-print sofas faced a steamer-trunk coffee table, all in pastel shades with white accents. Hannah was drawn to the patchwork bear sitting in a miniature white wicker rocking chair in the corner, both mementos from Rory's childhood.

"I have a first-aid kit in the bathroom." Rory waved a hand toward the partially open door down the narrow hallway.

"I'll get it. You sit."

Rory flopped onto the sofa with a huff. Sit? What was she, a dog? But as she reached down to massage the bruise already forming on her ankle, she had to admit it felt good to take her weight off. A clatter sounded in the bathroom—something falling into the porcelain sink—followed by Jamison's curse.

"Everything okay in there?"

"Fine. I dropped the—never mind."

Groaning, Rory dropped her head back on the back of the couch as she tried to remember what else she kept in the medicine cabinet along with the Band-Aids and iodine. Just what she wanted—a superhot guy getting a peek at her anti-aging wrinkle cream, Midol and other assorted feminine products.

He returned a moment later, first-aid kit in hand, and while Rory couldn't be sure, she thought his face was a shade or two more red than when he'd entered.

Great.

"Find everything?"

"Uh, yeah. I think so."

And then Rory wasn't so worried about Jamison's embarrassment or even her own as he knelt down in front of her and placed her foot on his khaki-covered thigh. She could feel the muscles and heat beneath her foot and it was all she could do not to flex her toes like some kind of attention-seeking kitten. And while Jamison might have made reference to Snow White, Rory couldn't help feeling a little like Cinderella as he cradled her foot in his large hands.

"How's that?" he asked.

A perfect fit…

Rory snapped herself back to reality as she realized he'd already removed the last of the splinters with a pair of tweezers, dabbed some antibiotic ointment on the scrape and was getting ready to smooth a Band-Aid over the area.

"Good. Fine. Thank you."

His nod sent a lock of hair falling over his forehead, and she gripped the cushions at her side to keep from reaching out. Jamison glanced up and their gazes locked, and Rory knew.

"I'm not imagining things."

His forehead wrinkled in a frown. "I wouldn't think so. I've never heard of a twisted ankle causing hallucinations."

"You were thinking of kissing me earlier."

This time it was Jamison's turn to look like he'd taken a blow to the head. He sucked in a breath that fanned the flames burning in his quicksilver eyes. "Rory. That's not—" His gaze shot to Hannah, who was sitting in the rocking chair, her attention still captured by her newfound stuffed friend. "We can't."

Maybe Rory should have been more disappointed as he turned his attention to cleaning up the cotton balls and wrapping from the first aid, but instead a tiny kernel of hope bloomed in her chest.

Because *can't* was a different story than *didn't want to.*

Chapter Six

"What do you mean, you fired Earl?" Her head pounding almost as loudly as her ankle, Rory stared in disbelief across the wide expanse of her cousin's cherrywood desk. She'd spent a painful half an hour searching for the handyman before stopping by her cousin's office, where Evie had stunned her with the news that she'd let the man go.

"Is that—" Evie frowned as Rory hobbled over to a chair and reached down to rub her ankle. "Why on earth is there toilet paper wrapped around your foot? And why are you limping?"

Rory straightened, heat rising to her cheeks. "Never mind."

Before Jamison and Hannah left the cottage, the little girl had ducked into the bathroom and returned with a long length of the paper trailing behind her. Her blond brows had pulled together in concentration as she'd tried to wrap the "bandage" around Rory's ankle before her father stepped in.

The last thing she'd expected was for Jamison to indulge his daughter's attempts to play doctor, but he'd showed the same seriousness using the toilet paper as when he'd applied the antibacterial ointment and Band-Aids.

Yes, she should have ripped the silly "bandage" off already, but she'd been touched by Hannah's sweetness. Not to mention Jamison's…

"How could you fire Earl without telling me?"

"We agreed when we both started working here that staffing decisions fall under my purview." Evie gazed back at her, slender hands folded in front of her. Sometimes her cousin's crystal-cool demeanor was enough to make Rory want to scream. It made her want *Evie* to scream, to show some emotion, to go back to being the warm, funny girl Rory remembered instead of the calculating woman she'd become.

"Earl wasn't a handyman you can replace with a snap of your fingers." The potbellied, fiftysomething man had worked for the hotel almost as long as Rory could remember. "He was—"

"He was stealing from the hotel," her cousin cut in.

Rory's jaw dropped. "Stealing?" she choked, the word lodging against the lump in her throat.

Pamela Worthington's voice whipped through her mind so clearly, she half expected her former employer to be looming behind her, anger and disappointment written across her aristocratic features. *I trusted you, Aurora. I gave you a chance despite your limited experience, and this is how you repay me? By stealing from our clients?*

"Are you—" Rory cleared her throat before her words could break into ragged shards. "Are you sure? Maybe there was some kind of mistake—"

But Evie was already shaking her head. "He turned in an invoice from Hendrix Hardware a few weeks ago." She tucked a strand of perfectly straight dark hair behind her ear. "Not long after that, I ran into Howard Hendrix, who told me he was sorry the parts Earl special ordered for the new irrigation system didn't work out and if we needed him to order more, to let him know."

"Maybe the parts didn't work. Maybe he bought them somewhere else."

"Where? And why wouldn't Earl have a copy of that receipt? You know Hendrix gives us a better deal than the big-box store over in Redfield. No, Earl returned those parts and pocketed the money."

"But I saw him working on the irrigation."

"And for all we know, he patched everything together with duct tape and used chewing gum. I already have a call in to a landscaping company. Which means spending even more money."

Focusing on the money side of her job was not Rory's strong suit, but Evie had been clear on how tightly the two were tied together.

I know you like picturing yourself as some kind of fairy godmother, but you can't solve things with a wave of a wand. Aunt Evelyn wants to expand the wedding destination aspect of the hotel, but doing so only make sense if it makes money.

Her cousin had also told her about an offer on the hotel. Their aunt Evelyn had fielded offers from large hotel chains before, but with her recent health issues, Rory feared she might be considering it. Selling Hillcrest…

Rory couldn't even imagine not having the hotel in her family.

"I spoke with Susannah Erickson this morning. She's almost committed to having the ceremony here," Rory told her cousin. "I'll give her a call this afternoon. If I can get them to sign off on the paperwork, I can request a deposit—"

"Rory," Evie said slowly.

Just the sound of her cousin's voice had her stomach sinking. "What is it? What's wrong?"

"As Earl was leaving, he said something under his breath."

Rory frown in confusion. "You just fired him, Evie." She held up a hand as her cousin opened her mouth to protest. "Rightfully so, but I'm sure he had a whole bunch of things to say."

"It wasn't about his being fired, at least not exactly."

"What did he say?"

Evie dropped her gaze to her hands, her inability to make eye contact making that sick feeling in the pit of Rory's stomach even worse. "He said that if his last name was McClaren, he wouldn't be getting fired. He'd be getting promoted to wedding coordinator."

Rory sucked in a quick breath that fanned the flames of humiliation rising in her cheeks. "How—how could he know? How could anyone here know?"

Silence had been a stipulation in keeping the Worthingtons from going to the police. The last thing they wanted was for their clients to know one of their employees had stolen from the multimillion-dollar homes they were hired to stage.

Somehow, though, word had gotten out. And the Worthingtons quickly pointed the finger at Rory—the designer they had fired after finding pictures of the stolen items posted to online auctions from her computer.

She'd not only lost her job, but her career, her friends, her boyfriend, as Peter had taken his mother's side. Only later, once the hurt and humiliation started to wane, had Rory realized why he'd turned on her so easily…

"I don't know, Rory," Evie said, pulling her from the dark memories and how badly things had ended in LA. "I certainly haven't said anything."

A touch of self-righteousness underlined her cousin's words. Of course, Evie wouldn't say anything. Evie would never do anything wrong. Evie would never cross a line and date someone she worked with. Evie would never find herself framed for a crime she didn't commit.

Rory blinked back the tears burning her eyes. She'd thought she'd left it all behind her—the accusations, the whispers, the "thanks but no, thanks" responses to every job she applied for.

But it was her family's reaction that hurt the worst. Not that they didn't believe she was innocent. But she couldn't shake the feeling they thought she'd somehow brought this on herself. By being too naive, too trusting, too *something*.

"Regardless of what Earl does or doesn't know… I think it would be best if I'm the one who deals with collecting the deposits from now on."

"Evie…" Rory gaped at her cousin, as stunned now as she'd been when Pamela Worthington had confronted her with the "proof" that Rory had been behind the rash of thefts.

"It's not that I don't trust you. You know that."

"Do I?" She couldn't help asking.

Evie lifted her gaze and straightened her shoulders. "You should. But these couples are spending a great deal of money, and it's their trust we can't afford to lose. Besides, collecting deposits falls more into my job description."

That's not the point! The words were on the tip of her tongue, but Evie had already turned back to her computer screen. *I didn't do anything wrong. I didn't deserve to be fired, to be blacklisted from every design firm in Southern California!*

But deserved or not, those things had still happened. Yes, she'd been glad to come to Clearville to help her aunt Evelyn, but the truth was, she'd slunk out of LA with her tail between her legs. And now the fallout had followed her, and Rory felt she had no choice but to duck and run once more.

She was halfway to the door when Evie asked, "Why were you looking for Earl, anyway?"

"I'd asked him to fix up the gazebo last week."

"The gazebo?"

For a split second, Evie's gaze lost focus, a sadness shadowing her expression, and Rory couldn't help wondering if her cousin was thinking about her own plans for her wedding and the ceremony that was to have taken place there years ago. And how, back then, it had been her relationship—and not the gazebo—that had ended up in shambles.

"It was looking a little worn around the edges, and with Ryder and Lindsay's wedding coming up..." She shook her head. "Anyway, it turns out it's in worse shape than I first thought."

Rory didn't know if Evie picked up on the sympathy in her voice, but if she did, her cousin knew all too well how to make people stop feeling sorry for her. "If the gazebo is in bad shape, that makes it a liability. A—"

"A lawsuit waiting to happen," Rory filled in, recalling Jamison's words earlier.

Her throbbing ankle echoed its agreement. Not only did they have to protect their guests, they also had to protect themselves. If Aunt Evelyn were still in charge, she would feel the same way Evie did. The two strong businesswomen didn't have any trouble following their heads. And maybe they had it right. After all, where had following her heart gotten Rory except into a boatload of trouble?

"Lindsay and Ryder's wedding can still take place as planned," Evie said pragmatically. "They can always use the rose garden."

The garden was lovely. A place where numerous weddings had taken place. But it wasn't the gazebo. It wasn't where Lindsay and Ryder wanted to say their vows. It wasn't where Rory dreamed of having her own ceremony.

Rory wasn't giving up. Not on her dreams of the future and not on the wedding Lindsay and Ryder wanted. "There's still time."

Evie raised a disbelieving eyebrow. "Less than two weeks."

"Like I said," Rory responded with a confidence she didn't entirely feel, "plenty of time."

Her cousin shook her head. "I know you want to believe everything ends in happily-ever-after, but you need to be practical about this. Talk to Ryder and Lindsay about moving the ceremony now. Don't put it off with the hope that a bunch of talking rodents are magically going to fix the place."

Rory offered a quick curtsy. "As you command, my evil queen."

Her cousin rolled her eyes and turned her attention back to her spreadsheet. Evie might not believe in fairy tales, but Rory still did. She wasn't about to lose faith in giving Ryder and Lindsay the wedding of their dreams.

"Ready, Robbie?" Ryder Kincaid called out to his son. "Okay, go long!"

Cocking back the golden arm that had carried him all the way from small-town Clearville to a college football scholarship, Ryder threw a perfect spiral to his son. The ball arced through the late-afternoon summer sky, hitting the boy right in the hands…and then bounding off to land in the sand a few feet away.

Smiling sheepishly behind too-long bangs and pair of wire-rimmed glasses, Robbie scrambled after the pigskin. "Almost had it!"

"So close, bud!" Ryder called back, his smile as wide as if his son had caught the winning touchdown in the Super Bowl. "Kid's smart as a whip. Can't catch to save his life."

Jamison couldn't help thinking the boy's skills would have benefited from playing catch with his dad from the time that he was Hannah's age, instead of just over the past few months. "Maybe if he—"

"Maybe what?" Ryder asked as Robbie chucked the ball back in an end-over-end toss.

"Maybe Robbie takes after Lindsay."

"You got that right." Ryder's grin was just as big as he thought of his fiancée, and Jamison knew he'd made the right decision in not speaking his mind.

Ryder was crazy about Lindsay. That much Jamison could see, but he couldn't understand it.

In the months after he and Monica separated, she'd done everything she could to keep Jamison from seeing Hannah. Canceling visits, conveniently forgetting when he was scheduled to come by the house, insisting Hannah was sick, asleep or any other excuse she could come up with to keep him from seeing his daughter.

He hadn't wanted to fight with Monica. After his parents' endless battles, he'd learned to bury all emotion, knowing even as a kid that anything he said or did would only throw fuel on an already out-of-control fire. He'd retreated into himself, playing the childish game of closing his eyes in the hope no one could see him.

He'd never intended to fall back into that same pattern

with Monica. He'd done his best to ignore her constant complaining, her out-of-control shopping sprees, the way she'd started spending more time out with friends than at home with Hannah. He'd buried himself in his work, not wanting to admit his own marriage was headed down the same rocky path as his parents'. By the time he'd finally opened his eyes, his daughter had grown from a toddler to a little girl he hardly recognized.

He glanced over to where Hannah was playing off away from Robbie and his cousins, building a Leaning Tower of Pisa sandcastle on her own. Was that missing time the reason why he struggled so much to connect with her now? Or was it something more, something lacking in him, that all his relationships seemed destined to fail?

All Jamison knew for sure was that he'd never forgive Monica for keeping Hannah from him for all those months. And if he'd been Ryder, and Lindsay had kept Robbie away from him for years… There was no way.

"I'm sorry we haven't had more time to hang out since you've been here," Ryder said as his older nephew took over and the three boys started a game that looked far more like dodgeball than football. "But we'll have time with Cowboy Days coming up."

Jamison had seen the signs advertising the event during his trips into town. Normally attending a benefit rodeo—any kind of rodeo—would be last on his to-do list. Here in Clearville, it was evidently a can't-miss event, but his response was noncommittal. "We'll see," he told Ryder. "Hannah isn't comfortable in big crowds. And I know you're trying to get as much as you can done before the wedding and honeymoon."

"Yeah, I can't believe the wedding's coming up so soon. But when Rory told us about a cancellation, we couldn't pass up the chance to have the wedding at Hillcrest House even if it did mean putting a rush on things."

"It did happen fast, didn't it?" Jamison couldn't help murmuring. And why was he somehow not surprised Rory had a hand in the abbreviated engagement?

"Depends on how you count. As far as Lindsay, Robbie and I are concerned, we've already waited almost ten years to be a family."

Jamison's gaze cut to Ryder as his friend spoke those words, but no buried anger, no lasting bitterness over the past lingered in his expression. Nothing but excitement and anticipation for the future.

"We're lucky Rory was willing to work with us, and she's done an amazing job with the wedding preparations."

"What's her story, anyway?"

Ryder's eyebrows shot upward. "Seriously? You're interested in Rory McClaren?"

"I didn't say I was interested. I'm…curious. Hannah thinks she's some kind of fairy-tale princess and fairy godmother all rolled into one, and I want to know more about her."

"Well, from what Lindsay says, the woman can perform miracles when it comes to weddings." Ryder shot him a sidelong glance. "It's a pretty sure bet Rory's got plans for her own dream wedding someday."

Jamison felt his face heat. He needed to put on some more damn sunscreen. "Not interested," he repeated, "just curious."

And maybe if he kept telling himself that, he'd start to believe it.

You were thinking of kissing me.

Thinking about it? Jamison still didn't know how he'd escaped her house without pulling her into his arms and tasting those lips that had tempted him from the start.

"Right… About Rory. Her family's owned Hillcrest for years. Her aunt's been running it the past three decades or so, but she recently brought Rory and her cousin Evie in to help out with the wedding destination packages they're promoting. From what I've heard, Rory had been living in LA. She worked for some hotshot interior design firm—the kind that decorates houses for Hollywood stars and stages million-dollar mansions for putting them up to sell."

Jamison could picture Rory in the role—dream weddings, dream houses, all part of her belief in happily-ever-after. "Sounds like a job she'd be good at."

"Yeah, well…"

"What?" Jamison asked when his friend's voice trailed off.

Ryder shook his head. "Small-town gossip about the reason why Rory was let go from the job. Like you said, not a whole lot else to do around here."

"Hey, Uncle Ryder, catch!" One of the boys tossed the ball back, an end-over-end lame duck Ryder still managed to deflect up into the air at the last minute and catch one-handed—much to his nephew's delight.

Ryder grinned as he spun the ball between his hands, cocked back his arm and returned the ball in a perfect spiral.

"Show-off," Jamison muttered under his breath, more annoyed by his burning curiosity about the gossip about Rory than he was by his friend reliving his golden years.

It was hard to imagine any scandal connected to Rory McClaren. She had such a sweetness, such an air of innocence surrounding her. But he'd seen a hint of the shadows hiding behind her wide blue eyes.

If his marriage to Monica had taught him anything, it was that everyone had secrets. Had he paid more attention in the final months of his marriage, maybe he would have seen what was coming. Maybe he could have stopped her, and if he had—

Jamison looked over at his daughter, carefully crafting her sandcastle, the expression on her sweet face so serious, even as the boys yelled and laughed and raced around her.

Maybe if he had, Hannah's mother would still be alive.

"What can I say?" Ryder raised a shoulder in a negligent shrug. "Some of us have still got it. Hey, man, you okay?"

Jamison pulled in a deep breath. He couldn't close his eyes and pretend everything was going to be okay. If Rory was going to be in his—in *Hannah's* life—even for a short time, then he needed to learn everything he could about her. For his daughter's sake.

"You were telling me about Rory and her life in LA."

"Oh, yeah. Look, I'm sure it was nothing, but the story goes that she got involved with the boss's son and it didn't end well." Ryder shook his head. "As someone who once worked for his in-laws, I can sympathize. I guess things got pretty ugly at the end, with lots of accusations being thrown around about Rory stealing some stuff...not that I believe it for a second."

The whole thing sounded rather petty and ridiculous. What had Rory done—refused to return the gifts her ex had given her? Kept some of the things he'd left at her place? Ryder was right. The rumors were likely nothing more than a bad breakup blown out of proportion thanks to the Clearville grapevine.

"Has Rory talked to you about the gazebo?"

"She said it's in bad shape and even asked if she could hire me to do the work, but with trying to get our scheduled jobs finished—" Ryder shook his head "—I don't see how I can squeeze another project in. Lindsay's disappointed, but she understands. Plus, Rory's done such a fabulous job on short notice that she doesn't want to make her feel bad."

The image of blue eyes flashing wide with hurt and disappointment jabbed at Jamison's conscience. *He* had made Rory feel bad, snapping at her the way he had when she'd been nothing short of amazing with Hannah.

And before Jamison realized what he was saying, he told his friend, "I could do it."

"Do what?"

"Fix up the gazebo."

"Seriously? You haven't done any remodeling work in years. I bet a judge's gavel is the closest thing to a hammer you've been around since we were in college."

Although it was quite possibly the worst idea he'd ever had, Jamison insisted. "It'll all come back to me the minute I put on a tool belt."

The two of them had met while working construction part-time. Despite the differences in their backgrounds and the fact that Jamison was a few years older than Ryder, they had struck up an instant friendship.

And it was that friendship that had him saying, "Consider the gazebo your wedding present."

That was the reason he'd made the offer. It had to be. No way should he be doing this as a way for Rory to see him as some kind of hero when nothing could be further from the truth. He was simply helping out a friend.

Nothing more.

Right. Helping out Ryder by fixing up Rory's favorite place in the whole, whole world.

A wide grin split his friend's face. "Hot da—dog!" he exclaimed with a glance at the kids. "You have made my day. No, my wedding! Lindsay is going to be thrilled, and this is much better than some high-tech coffee maker ordered off the bridal registry!"

His face heated at how closely his friend had him pegged. A perfectly wrapped present had been delivered to the hotel the other day, compliments of his assistant's efficiency. He had no idea what the box contained or even what the card said. "I would never buy something so lame."

"Are you sure about this, though? Isn't the point of this vacation for you to spend time with Hannah?"

Jamison rubbed at the back of his neck. "I'm going a little stir-crazy here, Ry. I'm used to nonstop meetings and calls and conferences. This is all getting to me."

Restlessness and frustration stacked one on top of the other inside him, like the brightly colored blocks Hannah used to play with. Higher and higher until a crash was inevitable. He had too much time on his hands. Too much time to worry about Hannah. Too much time to—

You were thinking of kissing me.

"Right..." his friend drawled. "I can see how tough this is, you know, when life is literally a walk on the beach. Tell the truth—you've been dying to check your phone the whole time we've been out here."

"There's no reception," Jamison grumbled as Ryder laughed. "Doesn't it drive you crazy? This small-town living?"

"This small-town living has given me the chance to know my son."

"You could have done that in San Francisco," he argued even as Ryder pinned him with another knowing look.

"I'm not that far removed from the corporate world, Jamie," he said, breaking out the childhood nickname only Jamison's father still used and only to remind him of who he used to be. "You can't tell me you'd be doing this in San Francisco." His friend tipped his head toward the kids running along the windblown beach.

"I have a job," Jamison argued. "A career—"

A child. One he'd already let down so many times in her short life.

With his gaze locked on Hannah and her precarious sandcastle, Jamison admitted, "I don't know if I can do this, Ry."

His friend was silent for a moment before he advised, "Do your best, Jamison. That's all any of us can do as parents."

Jamison nodded as his friend clapped him on the shoulder before jogging over to join the boys in their game. *Do your best...* Good advice, but other than in his professional life, doing his best had never been enough. Not for his mother, who tried to fill the emptiness in their lives with one failed marriage after another. Not for Monica, who'd taken to wild spending sprees and late-night partying with friends during the final months of *their* failed marriage. And not for Hannah, who would grow up without a mother thanks to the choices he had made.

You're her father. Rory's gentle yet insistent voice seemed to echo in the ocean breeze at his back, a warm, buffeting push in his daughter's direction. *She's still a little girl who wants to run and laugh and play again...*

"Hey, Hannah Banana," he said as she upended another bucket of wet dark sand to start another tower of her leaning castle. "Can I give you a hand?"

She squinted up at him in the sunshine, her sweet face adorably wrinkled, and Jamison stepped to the side so his shadow blocked the glare. "I dunno. Do you know how to play?"

His own father had taught him how to fix, repair, build any number of projects. How to start with the best materials and use the right tool to guarantee what he crafted was solid, sturdy, dependable. Built to last...

But when it came to forming lasting relationships—with his father, his mother, Monica...Hannah—Jamison felt as though every foundation rested on shifting, unstable sand, always ready to give way at any moment.

I have faith in you.

Rory's words rang in his ears. He didn't have that kind of faith in himself. But maybe he didn't need to. Maybe for now, for as long as he was in Clearville, Rory's faith in him would be enough…

Sinking down onto his knees in the cold, damp sand by his daughter's side, he brushed some dried grains from her pink cheek. "I was thinking maybe you could teach me."

Chapter Seven

"As you can see, the rose garden is a beautiful spot for a wedding. In fact, we have a ceremony scheduled here in a few days." Rory forced a smile as she turned her gaze to the young couple who'd come to tour Hillcrest.

The rose garden was beautiful, and if they had to move Lindsay and Ryder's wedding to this location, the ceremony would still be as touching and emotional as it would be taking place in the gazebo. But it wouldn't be the wedding Lindsay and Ryder had imagined, and that was the problem. Rory wanted to give every couple the wedding of their dreams, not some kind of runner-up.

The couple exchanged a glance. "On the website, we saw pictures of a gazebo. It looked like the perfect backdrop. We'd love to see it in person."

Her heart sinking, Rory admitted, "I'm sorry. The gazebo isn't available at the moment. We have some renovations in the works. I'm sure it won't be long before the work is completed, and there's still plenty of time before the two of you plan to get married. For now, why don't we take a look inside at the ballroom?"

Twenty minutes later, the young couple left…without signing a contract. It was a big decision, and Hillcrest House wasn't the only option for couples looking to get married, but Rory couldn't help feeling like she'd failed. Again.

She'd hated having to call Ryder to tell him about the sorry shape the gazebo was in, but in the back of her mind, she'd hoped he might have a crew she could hire. Evie would blow a gasket if she learned Rory had tried to solicit a Hillcrest groom to do manual labor at the hotel, but construction work *was* Ryder's job. But he was also in high demand, booked solid and rushing to get several jobs completed before he left on his honeymoon.

He had told her he would see what he could do, but Rory hadn't heard back, and her other efforts to find someone on such short notice had turned up empty. She didn't want to admit defeat, but maybe Evie was right. Maybe she needed to be practical—and not just about the gazebo.

She hadn't seen Jamison and Hannah in the past two days, and she hated how much she missed them. More than once, she'd done a double take when she spotted a dark-haired man out of the corner of her eye or stopped midsentence at the sound of a child's voice only to be disappointed that it wasn't the man or the child she was instinctively looking for.

She was getting too close, too fast. She'd made the same mistake with Peter, certain she could overcome the obstacles between them and trying to make molehills out of mountains. She'd fallen hard—and landed even harder. If she wasn't careful, when Jamison and Hannah returned home after the wedding, she'd be left behind nursing something far more painful than a bruised ankle.

If only Evie's "be practical" advice didn't feel so much like quitting without trying her best. How could she give up on having the gazebo ready for Ryder and Lindsay's wedding before she'd exhausted every possibility of getting it fixed?

And how was saving herself from heartache later more practical if it meant being miserable now?

Rory was still waging that internal battle as she headed for Evie's office, tucked back behind the registration desk. A group of hotel employees had gathered over to the side near an empty luggage rack, and Rory recognized the tall redhead in the middle.

Trisha Katzman had worked at the hotel for years. The thirtysomething woman had made it clear she, and not Rory, should have been the one to take on the expanded wedding coordinator role. Rory had done her best to smooth things over, to reassure Trisha she wasn't taking over her job and the increase in weddings would create more than enough work—and reward for a job well done—for everyone.

Her efforts had met with little success. The redhead was coldly polite face-to-face, but Rory could feel the daggers the other woman shot her way the second her back was turned.

And something had changed lately. The subtle disgruntled looks were no longer so subtle, and Trisha's smug expression reminded Rory of her last miserable months in LA.

The other women in Trisha's clique returned Rory's greeting before picking up their conversation. "I still can't believe that store's computer got hacked and some loser stole my credit card number," one of them was complaining as she walked by.

The other two made sympathetic sounds, but Trisha pointedly looked over her shoulder, tracking Rory's movements as she said, "Hard to know who to trust these days, isn't it?"

Rory froze.

She knew.

The patterned carpet shifted beneath her feet as her stomach listed and sank. Rory didn't know how the other woman had found out about what happened in LA, but she had no doubt Trisha was responsible for the rumors swirling around the hotel.

Once Rory would have walked over and confronted the group. She'd learned back in junior high that showing fear in front of a group of mean girls was the worst thing she could do. But after everything that happened in LA, when nothing she said made any difference and keeping silent had ended up her only defense, the words stuck in her throat.

Ducking her head, Rory headed away from the group and down the narrow hallway to Evie's office. Her cousin glanced up at her quick knock. "Oh, good. I was about to come looking for you—what's wrong?"

"It's—nothing." Rory didn't need to see the "I told you so" look in her cousin's eyes. She'd been fooling herself thinking she could have a fresh start in a place she'd always loved.

Evie's gaze narrowed, but she didn't press. "Good, because right now we have enough trouble. Mrs. Broderick called. She swears she and her daughter requested veal *piccata* and not chicken as part of the reception menu."

"They went back and forth before deciding on chicken." Rory specifically remembered. The conversation had gone on so long, by the time the two women made up their minds, she thought she might scream if she heard the words *veal*, *chicken* or *piccata* ever again.

Evie lifted an eyebrow. “That's not what she says.”

“I'll talk to the chef. Hopefully it won't be too late to cancel the order.”

“And if it is? They signed the contract, which states chicken,” her cousin pointed out. “If you talk to them…”

“What difference would that make?” If Mrs. Broderick didn't believe what was in front of her in black and white, what was the likelihood the woman would believe anything Rory had to say?

“Then I'll talk to them,” Evie decided.

“No, Evie, this is my job. I'll handle it.”

Rory held her breath, waiting for her cousin to take yet another responsibility away from her because she couldn't be trusted—

Finally, her cousin gave a short nod. “All right.”

Half an hour later, after dealing with their disgruntled chef and butcher, Rory stepped outside. She inhaled a deep breath, taking in the scents of forest pine and salty ocean and hoping the combination would clear her head.

She had a dozen phone calls and emails to return on everything from placing orders with the florist to confirming the chairs and bunting with the rental company to sending a new song list to the band for a wedding. But nothing needed to be done right that second. And with Trisha and her clique still inside the lobby, Rory wanted a few minutes to herself.

But as she followed the meandering walkways leading from the hotel, she didn't take the curve that would lead toward her cottage. Instead, she found herself walking down the tree-lined path toward the gazebo.

Her steps slowed on the flagstone steps, not wanting to

see the caution tape she'd asked one of the groundskeepers to put up, cordoning off the damaged and dangerous steps.

It was a simple wooden structure. Her hopes and dreams for a future and a family with a man she loved were not tied into its decorative pillars or carved eaves. Even if it might feel that way…

"Miss Rory!"

Her mood lifted, concerns about Trisha and the gazebo melting away when she saw Hannah tugging on Jamison's hand as the father-daughter duo headed her way. Maybe she should have been worried how happy the simple sight of them made her, but Rory had never been one to question a good thing. She'd always been more inclined to embrace it—easy enough to do when Hannah broke free the last few steps and threw her arms around her legs.

Bending down to return her hug, Rory breathed in the scent of little girl, baby shampoo and sunshine. Words spilled out of Hannah as she filled Rory in on the past two days—time spent going into town, including an all-important trip to the café for a cookie, and a day at the beach.

"Me and Daddy builded a sandcastle this big!" Hannah threw her arms out wide, and Rory met Jamison's gaze for the first time.

"You did?"

"We *built* a sandcastle," he automatically corrected.

"Daddy," Hannah sighed, "I just tol' her that. And it was this big!"

"Well, I am very proud of you," Rory said, her words not for Hannah alone, something Jamison picked up on based by the eye roll he gave her.

She had a hard time imagining Jamison on the beach, let alone playing with his daughter in the sand. And yet she could see a hint of sun in his cheeks and on the forearms left bare by the shirtsleeves he'd pushed up to his elbows. She wouldn't go so far as to say he looked relaxed—his silver eyes were too intense, too watchful to fit that description—but he did seem more at ease than when he'd arrived at the hotel.

He was even dressed more casually in a faded gray Henley and jeans. The comfortable clothes molded to his broad shoulders and muscular legs and had Rory wishing he would sweep her up into his arms again…and not because she'd injured her ankle.

As if reading her mind, he asked, "How's the ankle?"

Rory lifted her leg. "Almost as good as new. The scratches are healing and the bruises are already starting to fade…" It hadn't been her intention to draw Jamison's gaze to her legs or the strappy white sandals she was wearing despite the still-tender ankle, but she couldn't argue the results or the masculine appreciation in his expression.

"Toilet paper must have done the trick."

The wry humor in his voice did as much to set the butterflies in her stomach fluttering as the heat in his gaze. "I couldn't agree more."

"I'm glad you're all better, Miss Rory, 'cause me and Daddy have a surprise!"

"Hannah, you're not supposed to tell her. That's what makes it a surprise."

Her big brown eyes wide with innocence, Hannah protested, "But I didn't tell her, Daddy! I didn't tell her about fixing—oops!" The little girl clapped her dimpled hands over her mouth to keep the words from spilling out.

Rory laughed. "Okay, well, someone needs to tell me! What are the two of you up to?"

With a nod at his daughter, Jamison said, "Go ahead."

Throwing her hands out wide, she exclaimed, "Daddy's gonna fix the playhouse!"

Rory looked from the exuberance written across Hannah's face to her father's much harder to read expression. "Fix… You mean the gazebo?" she asked, her voice filled with disbelief. And then even more disbelief as she asked, "You?"

But if she'd offended Jamison, he didn't let it show as he stepped closer and bent his head toward hers. "What's the matter? You don't think I'm up for the job?"

A day or two ago, she might have said no, but in the T-shirt and jeans, he looked the part of a calendar-worthy handyman. This ruggedly physical side of him was something Rory would never have imagined. So different from the cool, composed lawyer. Add a tool belt and a hammer swung over one broad shoulder and—

She had to stop herself right there. No need for a hammer when her heart was doing all the pounding.

"I'm sure you're—" Rory snapped her mouth shut, his turn of phrase getting stuck in her throat. Feeling a rush of heat rise in her cheeks, she finished, "Perfectly capable."

Desperate to ignore the glint in his eyes that said he knew what she was thinking even if it wasn't what she was saying, she said, "But I don't understand—"

"I was talking with Ryder, and I offered to fix the gazebo. You know, for their wedding."

"Oh, Jamison…"

As if hearing the wobble of tears in her voice, he quickly went on. "Ryder's going to provide any of the materials or tools I need so long as I swear not to cut my fool hand, foot or head off."

Rory laughed in return even if she was still blinking back tears. "You're not, um, likely to actually do any of those things, are you?"

"It hasn't been that long since I had my hands on a power tool."

There was nothing overtly sexual about that statement,

but Rory had to pull her gaze away from the muscular arms and chest his T-shirt put on display. Definitely some powerful tools there, but it was his offer—his thoughtfulness—that had her throwing her arms around his neck.

"I can't believe you'd do this. It is so sweet of you."

He started, caught off guard by her impetuous hug before wrapping his arms around her waist. "It's hard, sweaty, manly work. Nothing sweet about it."

"You're helping give your friends the wedding of their dreams."

"Don't you dare call me Ryder's fairy godfather. I'd never live it down." His wry smile faded as he pulled back far enough to meet her gaze. "Besides, I'm not just doing this for him."

"No?"

Rory counted out the time it took for him to respond by the rapid beating of her heart. "No." He frowned as if annoyed by his own admission. "I'm doing this for you."

She sucked in a quick breath. "For me?"

"You know," he clarified, "for all the help you've given me with Hannah."

"Oh. You don't owe me for that, Jamison." She took a step back, brushing at the material of her full skirt where it clung to his denim-covered thigh. She could have used the reminder that he was a guest—a member of the wedding party—before she'd thrown herself into his arms.

She turned her focus to Hannah, who'd wandered a few feet down the path toward the rose garden. "I've enjoyed spending time with her, and since she's one of my flower girls, it's part of the job."

"Is it?" he challenged. "Because if that's the truth, then maybe I'm the one imagining things."

"Imagining things…"

His hand closed around her wrist, trapping her palm

against the muscular strength of his thigh. "Yeah, like that you're thinking of kissing me right now."

Her breath caught in her throat, and her fingers instinctively flexed, her nails digging into warm denim. Jamison's eyes darkened from silver to steel and suddenly she was imagining so much more than kissing—

"But we still can't," she echoed his words from the other day.

Can't, not *didn't want to*, because, oh, how she wanted to.

Without taking his eye off her, Jamison called out to his daughter. "Hey, Hannah, how'd you like to play a game of hide-and-seek? Close your eyes and count to one hundred."

"One hundred?" she asked as Hannah's singsong voice filled the air.

"She only knows up to twenty."

Turning her wrist until her hand clasped his, Rory tugged Jamison toward the closest tree. "Then we better make this fast."

She was already breathless with anticipation by the time they circled around the large pine, and he hadn't even touched her. By the time he pulled her into his arms, Rory thought her heart might explode. Yet despite her instructions to hurry, Jamison didn't kiss like a man in a rush.

He kissed like a man who'd traveled far and had finally, at long last, come home. Like a man who'd thought of nothing else, who had dreamed only of this moment. He caught her bottom lip, tugging in a gentle tease, before delving farther. His tongue swept inside, and her senses reeled, spinning off into a world she'd never known existed.

A world of pleasure. A world of sensation. So bright and startling all else seemed dull and gray.

And Rory had to have more.

Digging her hands into his dark hair, she pulled him closer. Arousal poured through her veins, centering low in her belly and striking sparks wherever their bodies touched. But the contact, her mouth eagerly seeking his, her breasts straining against his chest, wasn't enough. She had to have more and almost cried out in protest when Jamison broke the kiss.

"Rory," he ground out, words barely registering beyond the pulse pounding in her ears, "we better stop..."

Though the haze of desire, Rory heard Hannah's voice. On a breathless whisper, she said, "We still have ten seconds left."

"Nine," Jamison corrected, his breath warm against her skin as he trailed kisses down the length of her throat.

Her head fell back in pure pleasure. She thought she just might melt into the rough bark of the tree at her back, but Jamison pulled her tight and she melted into him instead. "Nine?" she asked weakly.

"Hannah always skips fifteen."

Sure enough, the little girl missed the number, and Rory started her own countdown. "Four, three..."

Recognizing the challenge, Jamison covered her mouth with his in the hottest, fastest kiss of Rory's life. One that left her gasping for air even as Hannah yelled out, "Twenty!" and started to search for them.

Ready or not.

Rory stepped back and sucked in a single lungful of air that wasn't superheated by the attraction burning between them before Hannah rushed around the tree and stopped short at the sight of them.

"Daddy, you're s'posed to hide." Shaking her head in disappointment, she said, "You and Miss Rory aren't very good at this game."

Jamison met Rory's gaze, and beneath the shared amusement was enough heat to set another round of fireworks shooting off in her stomach. Rory didn't want to argue with a four-year-old, but this game was one Jamison was very good at.

As it turned out, Jamison was quite as bad at hide-and-seek as his daughter feared. That wasn't as much of a surprise as the enjoyment he found in the game. Of course, part of that was the grown-up version he and Rory were playing—stealing kisses while Hannah's eyes were closed, finding a hiding spot of their own before tracking the little girl down in the rose garden.

But they'd both been careful to keep those stolen moments lighter, more playful. Not that the spark had dimmed. If anything, it built with every touch, every glance.

A controlled burn instead of an out-and-out wildfire like their first kiss.

"You know, I was so excited earlier—" Catching sight of his raised eyebrows, Rory rolled her eyes, but not before her cheeks turned a flattering shade of pink. "About the *gazebo*," she stressed, "that I didn't ask what you plan to do about Hannah while you're working."

Hannah had skipped ahead on the flagstone path only to get distracted by a colorful butterfly flitting by. The joy and awe on her sweet face brought a lump of emotion to the back of his throat. He'd seen his daughter break free and spread her wings over the past few days, and he was terrified of doing anything that would send her back into the cocoon of sadness and loss.

"I talked to Ryder about hiring a teenage girl they've used before."

Seeming to remember how reluctant his daughter sometimes was to leave his side, Rory asked, "Do you think Hannah will be okay with someone new watching her?"

"I hope so. If not—" Then he might soon have bigger problems than finding time to fix the gazebo.

"Does she have a babysitter back home she's comfortable with?"

"I haven't used any sitters back home…not since before the accident. Hannah's been staying with her grandparents. With everything that was going on, it seemed better that way."

"She's here with you now. That's what matters."

"Yeah." He sighed. "She's with me for now."

"For now," Rory echoed, "but not for long? Is that what you're saying? What happens when you go back to San Francisco, Jamison?"

Even though she'd asked the question, the disappointment in her expression said she knew the answer as well as he did. "Monica's parents want Hannah to live with them."

And they didn't even know about the promotion, one that would mean long days and even longer nights. Times when he would be leaving for work while Hannah was still asleep in the morning and wouldn't be home until after she was in bed in the evening.

"Hannah's grandmother is a retired nurse. She can be with her all day, every day. And Hannah loves her grandparents. After Monica and I separated, Hannah spent as much time with them as she did with Monica. And far more time than she spent with me."

Something Louisa was quick to point out. He carried around plenty of guilt on his own and didn't need his in-laws piling on, but Louisa knew what button to push—reminding him what a detached and absent father he'd been even before he and Monica separated. And now that Hannah needed him to be both mother and father…

"I'm sure they do love her, but Jamison, you're her father and your daughter needs you. I'm not trying to compare what I went through to Hannah losing her mother, but after Chance's accident, I needed my parents, too. As an adult, I get it. They could only handle so much, and almost all of their time and energy was focused on Chance getting better. But for me, as a kid, I felt like they were as lost to me as Chance was in that coma."

Even after so many years, Jamison picked up on the tremor in Rory's voice, the whisper of a little girl who'd gone unnoticed, unheard. He hated thinking of her feeling that way. Hated thinking of *Hannah* feeling that way.

"Rory—" He swallowed against a lump in his throat. "I—I just want what's best for her."

"I know. I see that, Jamison. I do." The certainty in her gaze turned sorrowful as she added, "What I don't understand is why you don't think that would be you."

Rory knew she shouldn't have been surprised when Jamison didn't answer her question. Just because he'd kissed her senseless didn't mean he was going to spill his guts. And just because she'd poured out the old ache in her heart when she spoke of the horrible days following Chance's accident didn't mean Jamison would pour out his.

Instead, his expression closed off, reminding her of the man she'd first met and not of the man she'd just kissed. Avoiding the emotional discussion, he'd gotten down to the business of inspecting the gazebo. Or at least trying to with Hannah hanging by his side, wanting to "help."

"Got it, Hannah?" he asked, as he ran a measuring tape along the length of the gazebo railing. "Are you holding on tight?"

"Got it, Daddy!" Stretched up on her tippy toes, Hannah held on to one end of the tape.

Jamison jotted down some figures in the small notebook he'd pulled from his pocket. "Okay, kiddo. You can let it go."

Hannah released the small tab and the yellow metal tape zipped back into the casing, bringing a giggle from the little girl and drawing a smile from Jamison, but the shadows lingering in his expression made Rory's heart hurt.

Did he think Hannah would break if he were to unbend enough to hug her—or was he afraid that he would? His love for the little girl was obvious, but so was the fear.

He needed more time. Time with Hannah, not time spent fixing the gazebo. As touched as she was by his offer to help his friend, to help *her*, his daughter needed him far more than Ryder and Lindsay needed the perfect setting for their wedding.

Swallowing against the lump of disappointment in her throat, she opened her mouth, but Hannah beat her to the punch.

"Did ya see, Miss Rory?" The little girl bounced on her toes. "I'm being a big helper!"

Rory met Hannah's wide smile with one of her own as the perfect solution bloomed. "I did see, Hannah. You are such a good helper, and I just had the best idea ever!"

Chapter Eight

Maybe it was something in the water.

Something that made him say yes to harebrained schemes and even come up with a few of his own. Bad enough he'd offered to fix up the gazebo, but what the hell was he thinking yesterday when he agreed to let Rory and Hannah help?

I just had the best idea ever!

Rory's eyes had glimmered with such hope that Jamison had found himself holding his breath in a combination of dread and anticipation. Even before she started talking, he'd had a feeling that whatever the crazy idea swirling in her pretty little head was, he was going to hate it. And an even worse feeling that whatever it was, he was going to be fool enough to agree to it. Just to keep that light in her eyes and the smile on her face...

Jamison fought back a groan as he and Hannah made their way down the flagstone path. He adjusted the tool belt at his waist even as he gave serious thought to smacking himself upside the head with a hammer. How was he supposed to work and keep an eye on his daughter…when he couldn't keep his eyes off Rory?

He'd reached for his phone a dozen times already, prepared to call Rory and then Ryder and tell them both the whole thing was off. He could tell his friend the work was too much and the ceremony could take place in the rose garden with Lindsay and the guests none the wiser.

There was only one problem.

"I'm going to be a big help, right, Daddy?"

Even if Ryder was smart enough to keep his mouth shut with the woman in his life, Jamison had already blown it by telling the pint-size girl in his.

Excitement radiated from her tiny body as she bounced by his side, jumping from one flagstone to the next, one hand holding the oversize yellow hard hat on her head.

"I get to help Miss Rory fix the playhouse."

"It's a gazebo," he corrected. "And I'll be the one fixing it," he added before realizing he sounded like a total jerk.

In the months since Monica's death, Jamison couldn't think of a single suggestion he'd come up with that Hannah hadn't met with *I don't want to.* Even her favorite activities back home—going to the park or the zoo—had all been shot down.

But not this chance to work on the gazebo.

Did it matter that Rory was the bigger draw when it came to Hannah wanting to lend a hand? Wasn't his daughter's happiness, no matter the reason, most important?

And what happens when you go back home? When there is no Rory around to add a hint of sweetness to everything she touches and to make more than smiley-face oatmeal happy?

Construction wasn't easy work, and Jamison had had

his share of injuries—the worst of them a pair of broken ribs and a punctured lung thanks to a fall through some rotten floorboards. But the sharp pain and struggle to breathe were nothing compared to what he felt when he thought of trying to care for Hannah on his own.

"But we get to help, right, Daddy?"

"Sure thing, Hannah Banana. I need all the help I can get," he sighed, wishing the words weren't so blatantly true.

And that was why he found himself trailing after his daughter as she raced ahead toward the gazebo.

"Hi, Miss Rory!" Hannah cried out as she rounded the curve in the path.

Jamison should have been prepared, thanks to his daughter's early-warning signal, yet somehow he was still caught off guard. Because standing in front of the gazebo, gazing up at the aging structure as if the rotting wood and cracked paint had already been stripped away and restored to its once-gleaming glory, Rory turned to greet them with a brilliant smile.

"Look, Miss Rory! We both have hard hats!" Hannah clamped both hands on top of hers as if expecting her sheer excitement to blow the thing right off her head at any second.

And Jamison couldn't help feeling like he should hold on to his own, considering how the sight of Rory in a pair of faded skintight jeans and a pink—hot-pink—hard hat was threatening to blow his mind.

"I see!" And then meeting his gaze over his daughter's hard hat, Rory shot him a wink. "Safety first, right, Jamison? After all, it has been a while..."

She had no idea. If she had, she would have brought a fire extinguisher instead. Something in the intensity of his gaze must have given him away because her smile faded.

His heartbeat quickened as the awareness between them grew. Try as he might, he couldn't keep his eyes from drifting down her body.

He'd never seen her dressed so casually—couldn't have imagined her wearing denim, a fitted white T-shirt, that outlined her breasts far too clearly for his comfort, and honest-to-God work boots. And yet there she was, like some kind of construction worker Barbie.

"This is never going to work," he mumbled under his breath.

Despite the rush of color blooming in her cheeks, Rory pretended she hadn't heard him. She waved a hand at a shaded area several yards away from the gazebo where a picnic basket and blanket waited. "Are you ready to get started, Miss Hannah?" At his daughter's nod, she said, "We have a big bucket of screws and nails we need to separate so all the same sizes are in their own little cups. And then we'll use scissors to cut sandpaper to the right size to fit your daddy's super noisy sander.

"When we're done with that, we have paper and pencils and paint so we can draw pictures of the gazebo and practice on them until your daddy is ready for us to help him paint the real thing. And then we can make sandwiches with the stuff I brought in that basket over there, because all that hard, hard work is going to make us all hungry. What do you think?"

Jamison shook his head. He thought she was amazing. All those little projects would keep Hannah engaged and entertained. And he never would have thought of any of them. Somehow, though, instead of his inadequacies as a father casting a dark pall over his mood, gratitude rushed through him.

He caught Rory's hand as she walked by and gazed down at her in that ridiculous hat. Her blue eyes sparkled and her pale pink lips curved in a smile that had him thinking about their kiss…

She might not have been dressed like one, but he couldn't help asking, "Are you sure you aren't some kind of magical fairy-tale princess?"

"Why, Jamison, I didn't think you believed in fairy tales."

"I don't," he insisted. "But I believe in you. You have this way of making things—even the most everyday, average things—special."

And if that wasn't magic, then he didn't know what was.

Despite Jamison's initial concerns over the shape of the gazebo, a more thorough inspection revealed the overall structure—the support beams, most of the main floor and the roof—was sound. The steps, the lattice facade and the railing needed the most work, but he'd assured her the repairs were all doable and could be fixed before the wedding.

With Hannah occupied on the blanket with some of the little games she'd come up with, Rory had worked at Jamison's side, hoping effort made up for what she lacked in experience.

"Admit it…you're impressed." Rory pointed a plastic water bottle Jamison's way as they took a short break.

He gave his typical snort of disbelief as he raised his own bottle. But before he took a long swallow, he murmured, "Only every time we're together."

She took a quick sip of the cool liquid, thinking it might do her more good to dump the whole thing over her head. Her heated thoughts at watching Jamison do something as simple as drink from a bottle didn't bode well for completing the gazebo without her jumping his bones.

I believe in you.

How long had it been since someone had that kind of faith in her? Months? Years?

Evie had always been the practical one, Chance the adventurous one and Rory the dreamer. The girl with her head in the clouds, whose ideas were always too impractical, too over-the-top, too silly to be taken seriously.

But Jamison believed in her.

With Hannah close by, they had no chance to repeat the kiss from the day before. But the little girl's presence wasn't enough to keep Rory's thoughts from straying in that direction or to keep her from imagining Jamison felt the same way.

More than once, their gazes had locked over some small task—their fingers brushing as he handed her the hammer, his chest pressing against her shoulder as he reached around her to help with a particular stubborn nail, his breath against her neck raising gooseflesh on her skin as he offered some words of instruction.

"You told me you're a jill-of-all-trades, but this seems a bit much for a wedding coordinator."

"Well, I wasn't always a wedding coordinator," she told him, only to instantly regret it. She didn't want to talk about LA. Didn't want to think about Pamela or Peter or the thefts she'd been accused of.

"So what did you do before this?" Jamison asked.

"I worked for an interior design firm." She forced a smile. "Way too girlie for you to find interesting."

"Still not sure how carpentry falls under interior designer… And for the record, I happen to find girlie very interesting."

His appreciative glance coaxed a genuine smile out of her, and she sighed. "I started at the bottom with big dreams of working my way up. As low designer on the totem pole, I was stuck with all the jobs no one wanted—

including getting my hands dirty to get a remodel done on time. If that meant ripping out carpet because the subcontractor no-showed or repainting an entire kitchen because the client changed her mind at the last minute and the painter had already walked off the job, then I was their girl."

"So what happened?"

Rory started. "What makes you think something happened?"

Jamison shrugged casually. "You're here, aren't you? Something must have happened."

"I had the chance to work at Hillcrest with my family. This place means so much to me, I wouldn't have missed that for the world." Even if she hadn't been without a job and weeks from running out of rent money for the ridiculously expensive studio she'd called home.

"So…no heartbroken guy left behind?"

"Heartbroken? Definitely not."

"But there *was* a guy."

Rory squeezed the water bottle, the thin plastic crackling in her hands. "His name was Peter, and he's the boss's son. I should have known better than to get involved with someone at work." But some lessons were hard to learn. By no means could she classify her relationship with Jamison as strictly professional.

"Pamela, his mother, had far greater aspirations for him than dating a lowly assistant in her company. I tried not to let it bother me, and Peter assured me his mother would come around. All I had to do was to give her some time."

"But that didn't work?"

"The longer we dated, the more uncomfortable things became at work. I don't think it was coincidence that I was always assigned to the most difficult clients. My friends all thought I should quit, but—I don't know. I guess I was too stubborn and the job wasn't the problem. Quitting wouldn't make my relationship with Pamela any easier. If anything, it would have proved to her that I could be run off."

"And you weren't willing to give up on Peter."

"I thought he was the one. So I put up with so much crap from his mother. She'd turned a job I loved into one I hated. I dreaded waking up in the morning, knowing I'd have to do battle with that dragon, but I did it. I did it for months, because I told myself it was worth it. I was willing to fight for our relationship, but Peter..."

The worst of her ex's betrayal caught in her throat, as did the humiliating circumstances that had led to her leaving LA. She should tell Jamison the entire story, she knew she should, but—

I believe in you.

She didn't want to lose the faith he had in her, not when it meant so much, not when there was a chance he *wouldn't* believe in her once she told him the whole truth.

"Looks like someone's ready for a nap."

Lying back on the picnic blanket, his eyes closed to the bright, cloudless sky overhead, Jamison said, "You have no idea."

Muscles he hadn't used in years groaned in protest at the slightest movement, thanks to the hard work he'd put in over the past three days, but Jamison was determined to have the gazebo ready by Ryder's wedding. If he had to throw in the towel, his friend would never let him hear the end of it.

Rory's low chuckle brushed over his skin on the warm summer breeze. "Like father, like daughter."

He cracked an eye open to see Hannah slumped to one side, half-eaten peanut butter and jelly sandwich in hand.

She looked angelic, peaceful. Pushing up onto his elbows, he said, "It's hard work being a number one helper."

The title was one his daughter wore with pride, overcoming her shyness with strangers to tell anyone who would listen—the big, burly guy at the lumberyard, the skinny teen in the paint department, the gum-popping cashier at the hardware store—that she was the best helper ever.

He'd had his doubts about taking Hannah along on those trips, certain he could get in and out much faster and more efficiently on his own, but Rory had insisted. And since he seemed incapable of saying no to either of them, the two ladies had accompanied him. And yeah, maybe it had taken more time, but it was time spent with Hannah…and with Rory. She'd pushed Hannah around in a basket, managing to turn even the countless trips up and down the aisles in the huge home improvement store while he looked for the right L-bracket into some kind of adventure.

"When will we be ready for the big reveal?"

"I'm sure we'll be done at least an hour before the rehearsal dinner next Friday."

Rory tossed a crumpled napkin at him. "Very funny."

He grinned as the wadded-up ball sailed past without hitting its mark. Despite having to work around Hannah's nap time and Rory's scheduled fittings, tasting and meetings with clients and potential clients, they'd made real progress.

They'd torn out the splintering lattice fasciae and trim, and pried up the rotted steps and any warped boards on the circular platform. He'd cut the replacement boards and had spent the morning sanding them smooth, filling the air with the slight scent of burning wood. A fine layer of sawdust covered just about everything. Including Rory's toned arms, left bare by the pink-and-white-striped tank top she wore.

Suddenly not feeling so tired, he could think of better things to do while Hannah slept than to take a nap of his own…

"So tell me the story," Rory said, catching Jamison off guard.

Talking wasn't where his mind had gone.

"You sound like Hannah," he said with a laugh, "but if she were awake, she'd tell you I suck when it comes to fairy tales. I can't tell her a bedtime story without the CliffsNotes in front of me."

Rory laughed. "Don't worry. You already know this one. It's the origin story of a successful lawyer with a hidden background as a blue-collar construction worker."

"Not hidden," Jamison argued, feeling his face heat at the lie.

"So this is something you do a lot?" she pressed. "Help friends with projects or volunteer with Habitat for Humanity?"

The simplest thing would have been to agree and hope Rory would leave it at that. But from the moment they met, she'd challenged him not to take the easy way out. Not when it came to Hannah and not when it came to telling the truth about himself. "I haven't picked up a hammer in almost a decade," he confessed.

"But once upon a time…"

A gruff laugh escaped him at the teasing look in her eyes. "Once upon a time," he began, "I worked construction while I was in college. That's how Ryder and I met."

"So you weren't—" Rory cut herself off, but Jamison had a feeling where her thoughts had gone.

"Born with a silver spoon in my mouth?" He shook his head, hardly offended by the assumption when he spent most of his life trying to give that very impression. "Not even close. My parents had me when they were barely out of their teens. Neither one of them took more than a few college courses. My mom worked as a receptionist off and on, and my dad was a handyman, taking on whatever jobs he could find."

"And he's the one who taught you how to do this," Rory said, waving a hand at the gazebo with an expression of pride that sent guilt stabbing through Jamison's heart.

"Yeah, my dad taught me a lot of things." And Jamison had repaid him by being ashamed and spending most of the past fifteen years pretending the man didn't exist.

"But the things my dad could do… It was never enough for my mother. They fought all the time. Over everything, it seemed, but mostly over money. My mom was the one who always encouraged me to do more, to be better, to—"

Do whatever you have to do so you don't end up spending your life cleaning toilets like your father.

Jamison shook his head, trying to dislodge his mother's bitter words from his memory. "Anyway, when I was ten or so, she got it in her head that public school wasn't good enough and that I needed to go to prep school."

"Prep school? As in matching uniforms with jackets and ties and argyle socks?"

He gave a mock shudder. "It was that bad and worse."

"Hard to imagine worse."

"Worse was knowing I didn't belong in that uniform. That I was the charity case—the kid who could only afford to go to Winston Prep because my dad took a job there as a janitor and my tuition was waived.

"My mother was the one who was so determined I go to that school, and my dad made it happen the only way he could. But that wasn't good enough for her, either. She hated that he worked there, was always putting him down, and after a while, I started to feel the same way. I didn't want the other kids knowing he was my dad."

"It's hard to think of anyone other than yourself when you're a kid."

"When they divorced my freshman year, I thought the constant fighting would be over. But in some ways it got worse. Like they no longer had to even pretend that they cared about each other. I got caught in the middle and felt like I had to make a choice, and I chose to stay with my mom.

"After so many years of hearing how we deserved better and how I had it in me to 'be something' so long as I didn't let my dad bring me down… I don't know. I guess I started to buy into it. I wanted the expensive shoes and the latest electronics and the fancy cars like everyone else at Winston had, and when my mom remarried that first time, to a rich guy she met thanks to her making friends with the parents of kids who went to Winston, I got all that stuff."

"The first time your mother remarried?"

"First, but not last. She's on her fourth marriage. Fifth, I guess, if you count that she married number three twice."

"Ouch."

"It's made Father's Day interesting."

"I'm sorry, Jamison."

"Don't be. I made my choice. I could have gone to live with my dad, but I liked have all those shoes and toys and cars." Jamison shook his head. "You know, even after my mom remarried, and my stepdad was footing all the bills and could afford to pay my tuition a thousand times over, my dad kept working at that school. A thankless, low-paying job he must have hated…just so he could still see me."

"I'm guessing that made it all worth it for him."

"I wish I'd appreciated all he was willing to do for me and that I hadn't cut him out of my life the way I did."

"But that was then. What about now?"

"It's been better…especially over the past few years.

Mostly thanks to Hannah." A smile touched his face as he said his daughter's name. "I reached out to him after she was born, and he's made a real effort to get to know her, to be there for birthdays and holidays. He enjoys being a grandfather."

"I'm glad…for Hannah, but also for you and your father."

"Yeah, me, too," Jamison agreed, but he couldn't help thinking of the years he'd lost—both with his father and with Hannah.

Two of the most important people in his life, and he'd failed them both. First as a son and then as a father.

As much as he'd enjoyed the past few days and as familiar as a hammer felt in his hand, Jamison couldn't see giving up everything he'd worked for—the struggle to put himself through college, the countless hours of studying to get through law school, the prestige of working at Spears, Moreland and Howe, and the promise of the partnership—even if it would be best for Hannah.

His dad had made that kind of sacrifice, but Jamison couldn't help feeling he was very much his mother's son. He loved his daughter, he did, but Jamison couldn't help feeling something lacking inside him kept him from loving her *enough*.

Chapter Nine

The first annual Clearville Cowboy Days was in full swing by the time the sun started sinking behind the horizon, painting the sky with a pinkish-orange hue. Warm summer air carried the sound of laughter and, as long as the wind wasn't coming from the arena, the mouthwatering scent of smoky barbecue. Along with the draw of the rodeo, walkways led toward a fenced-off petting zoo and a carnival-style midway lined with cheesy stuffed-animal prizes. Bells and whistles rang out mixed with groans and cheers from the spectators gathered around the games.

"I still can't believe this turnout."

"Yeah, it's impressive," Jamison responded, trying to match his friend's enthusiasm as he, Ryder and Lindsay dodged the boisterous crowds checking out the Rockin' R benefit rodeo.

"The chamber of commerce has worked with Jarrett Deeks and his wife, Theresa, on the event," Lindsay chimed in. "The hope is to raise money and awareness for their horse rescue, but it's also a chance for Clearville to shine."

"A chance for you to shine," Ryder told his fiancée with a proud smile that had Lindsay shaking her head.

"Theresa and Jarrett already had much of this in place before I moved back and came on board. They're the ones who deserve credit."

"Says the woman who's been working tirelessly on promotion and sponsorship and vendors—"

"All right, all right! I'll take some credit if it'll make you hush up!"

"I bet you can think of better ways to shut me up," Ryder challenged with a suggestive lift to his eyebrows.

"You do realize other people can hear you, right?" Jamison's pointed comment had his friend grinning even more unrepentantly while Lindsay gave his shoulder a quick shove.

"You're crazy, you know that?"

"Only about you."

At that, Lindsay showed she did indeed know how to shut Ryder up as she rose onto her tiptoes to keep his mouth occupied with a kiss.

Jamison jerked his gaze away to focus on a trio of dusty cowboys, complete with hats, chaps and bandannas, laughing with a group of wide-eyed, flirty girls, none of whom looked old enough for all the makeup they were wearing, let alone the beers they were drinking.

All in all, Jamison felt as out of place as…well, a corporate lawyer at a rodeo.

But it wasn't the retro Wild West setting that had him feeling so uncomfortable. It was playing third wheel to Ryder and Lindsay, an unnecessary cog to the obvious affection and attraction between them.

"Are you sure the kids are okay going off by themselves?"

"They're fine, Dad," Ryder teased.

Lindsay's response was more sympathetic. "I know Robbie, Tyler and Brayden are still young," she said, referring to her son and his two cousins, "but they're good boys. They'll keep an eye on Hannah, and the carnival games are all being run by locals who'll watch out for them, too."

"Yeah, I'm sure you're right."

He'd worried about Hannah's reaction to the loud noises, huge animals and large crowd, but his concerns had been misplaced. After little more than a brief hesitation, Hannah had taken off with the boys, leaving Jamison feeling… bereft. Suddenly, he was the one feeling out of place and overwhelmed.

They'd spent so much time together the past few days, he missed having his daughter at his side…as much as he found himself missing Rory.

He still didn't know why he'd agreed to go to the rodeo—other than the thought that Rory might be there. And if that wasn't the stupidest move ever, he didn't know what was. Going to the rodeo on the off chance of catching a glimpse of the beautiful brunette when he could have gone *with* her.

She'd issued the invitation as she'd packed up their picnic lunch the day before. "From what Lindsay says, they'll have all kinds of music, food and even games planned for the kids. Anyway, I was wondering if you and Hannah would like to go. You know—" she rolled her eyes, a hint of color brightening her cheeks "—with me?"

Jamison had swallowed the instant agreement that came to mind. "Rory… I'm leaving in just over a week."

"I know," she'd shot back quickly, her eyes and smile still bright. "But fortunately for us, the rodeo is tomorrow. You're still here tomorrow."

He should have expected she wouldn't give up easily,

not a woman who'd been willing to fight for a man she thought was *the one*. But like the ex who had let her down, Jamison knew he'd done the same.

The disappointment in her gaze should have been enough to make him keep his distance. Rory wasn't the type of woman to have a summer fling, and he couldn't offer her anything more. He'd be going back to a life that already felt overbooked with the pressure of the upcoming promotion and the responsibility of raising Hannah on his own.

"Lookie, Daddy, Tyler won me a fuzzy unicorn!" Hannah's voice broke into his thoughts as she raced toward him, and Jamison wondered what it said about him that he was as eager to see his daughter as she was to see him.

"He did, huh?" Jamison bent down to examine the purple-and-white stuffed animal she proudly held out.

"Uh-huh! For me!" His daughter nodded, her ponytail bobbing exuberantly. She didn't seem to care that the poor thing was slightly cross-eyed, its golden horn already bent, as she gazed at the older boy with a look of pure hero worship.

The brown-haired boy trailing behind her with his younger brother and Robbie scuffed his oversize tennis shoe against the loose gravel. "No big deal. It was one of those dart games where you have to pop the balloons. The prizes were all lame—uh, kinda girlie."

Ryder smiled at his nephew's deflection of Hannah's praise. "Way to go making a little girl's night, dude."

Tyler ducked his head, but he still held up his hand for his uncle's high five.

"I think someone might have a little crush," Lindsay teased, and Jamison didn't know which of them was more horrified—ten-year-old Tyler or his thirty-one-year-old self.

Just the thought of makeup, short skirts and puberty

had panic racing through him, and he longed to hold on to the unicorn and hope for a miracle that would keep his daughter a little girl forever.

"Hey, Dad, can we have some money to go get something to eat?"

As Ryder handed the boys some cash, Lindsay warned, "Not too much junk food."

"Yeah, right," Ryder snorted as the boys took off, jostling each other as they went. "I'm sure they're heading straight for the booth selling the organic quinoa."

A few yards away, Robbie turned back. "Hannah, you wanna come?"

"Can I, Daddy?" She looked up at him, her eyes filled with happiness and hope, and something caught inside his chest.

"Yeah," he said, his voice husky. "Go have fun."

She turned to race after the boys before circling back. "Here." She thrust the unicorn into his arms. "You can hold Uni. He'll keep you comp'ny."

Bending down to her level, he tapped the mythical creature's bent horn against her forehead. "Thanks, Hannah Banana."

She giggled at the nickname and threw her arms around him in a quick hug that had Jamison swallowing against the sudden lump in his throat.

Rory might not have been by his side, but she was there. He could feel her presence in Hannah's smile. She'd given his little girl back her laughter, her sense of adventure, her willingness to try…and he wondered at what might be possible if only he was half as brave as his daughter.

"Come on!"

Rory stumbled, trying to keep up with Debbie Pirelli as her friend dragged her through the Clearville fairgrounds toward the sound of country-western music. Boots might have been the right fashion choice, but they weren't the most comfortable. She slipped more than once on the fair-ground's loose gravel before they reached the stage. A local band had taken their place in the spotlight, and a dozen or so wannabe cowboys were boot scooting their ladies across a makeshift dance floor.

"I'm not sure this is a good idea," Rory protested.

"Trust me! This will be fun!"

Following at a slower pace a yard or so behind, Drew Pirelli laughed. "I can't tell you how many things she's talked me into with those same words!"

The vivacious blonde sent her husband a grin over her shoulder. "Like you're complaining!"

"Um, he might not be," Rory said after Drew offered to stand in line for drinks at the nearby booth, "but did I mention I'm not a fan of country music?"

Her friend laughed again. "You do know this is a rodeo, right? I don't think they'll be playing too much classical music around here tonight!"

Debbie was Hillcrest's exclusive wedding cake designer, and Rory had gotten to know the talented baker and café owner over the past few months. She'd been surprised and pleased when Debbie had called to see if she wanted to go to the rodeo. The last thing she wanted was for her new friend to think she wasn't enjoying her company. "Thanks again for inviting me. I'd been looking forward to this night, but I wouldn't have come by myself."

"Ah, now I get it," Debbie said as she bounced on her toes in time with the music.

"Get what?"

"You wanted to come with someone else."

"No, I—not really," she mumbled. She'd hoped to go with Jamison and Hannah. Rory loved seeing the little girl come out of her shell, how her first few steps in trying something new were always a little hesitant, but once she found her footing, she was ready to hit the ground running.

And Jamison…he was running, too. Only he was running away.

"I can't figure him out," she muttered, not realizing she'd spoken the words out loud until Debbie jumped on them.

"Who?"

"What?"

"Who is this mystery man we're talking about? The one you can't figure out but would like to be two-stepping across the dance floor with right now."

That was enough to startle a snort right out her. "Two-stepping is the last thing I can picture Jamison…"

Rory swallowed a curse as Debbie crowed with laughter. "I knew it! I knew there was some guy you'd rather be with right now." Her eyes widened further. "Wait… Jamison. Isn't that the single dad who's been bringing his adorable daughter into the café for cookies this week? No wonder you're not into cowboys if a guy like that is your type."

"That's part of the problem. Jamison is the exact opposite of my type."

Debbie raised a knowing eyebrow. "Funny. That's what I said about Drew. Once upon a time."

Ignoring her friend's words, Rory said, "He can be so serious, so logical, so lawyery…" And he probably would have been the first to call her on making up words, had he been there.

"Not to mention seriously sexy, practically gorgeous—"

"Okay, stop. I don't need to hear all of that. Especially not after making a fool out of myself over him yesterday."

"Ooh, that sounds promising." Debbie's blue eyes lit up with curiosity. "Give me the gory details."

Rory might have made it seem like Debbie was pulling the information out of her, but deep down, she needed someone to talk to. No way could she go to Evie when her cousin's line between business and pleasure was more like the Great Wall. And Rory didn't feel comfortable talking to Lindsay about her fiancé's best friend.

She was careful, though, not to reveal too much of Jamison's past. He'd opened up to her in a way she doubted he did with too many people, and she would hold fast to what he'd told her in confidence.

"I know this attraction between us isn't meant to last, that he'll be going back to San Francisco after the wedding." And if she wasn't careful, she'd be heartbroken when he left her behind. "Maybe he's right. Why bother to start something that's destined to come to an end?"

Debbie glanced past Rory and her grin widened even further. "We need to find you a dance partner."

Thrown by the abrupt change in topic, Rory said, "I'm not sure how that's going to help."

"Oh, believe me, it will. Jamison thinks he's being all noble by keeping his distance, but that's sure to fade fast when he sees you in the arms of another guy."

"Sees me?" Rory's heart skipped a beat even before she glanced over her shoulder to what had captured Debbie's attention a few seconds earlier. Or more specifically who…

Jamison stood outside the crowd gathered near the beer garden. His chestnut hair gleamed even in the artificial light. He wore a black T-shirt and jeans, perhaps in an effort to fit in, but for Rory, he still stood out. He was more masculine, more striking than the men around him, and that was even with the stuffed unicorn he held in one long-fingered hand.

She jerked her attention back up to find her gaze snagged on his lips and the memory of his kiss. Thirty feet and two dozen or so people separated them, but the distance, the crowd, the music, all of it faded away until only the two of them existed. Right up until the moment he turned away…

"Dance," Debbie commanded and just like that, the rest of the world rushed back in. Only it was too close, too crowded, too noisy.

"I don't feel like dancing," she protested weakly as she lost sight of Jamison in the line of people milling around the drink booths.

Debbie shook her head. "This isn't about how you feel. This is about making Jamison face how *he* feels."

"I don't even see him anymore. He's probably not even paying attention."

"Oh, trust me, he's still watching." Her friend grinned "And it's up to you to make sure there's something to see."

He couldn't stop watching. Try as he might to pull his gaze from the crowded dance floor, to stop staring at Rory like some kind of stalker, his attention returned to her time and again. In the brief seconds when he would lose sight of her during the turns and twists of complicated line dances he couldn't begin to follow, his heart would stop…only to start racing double time when he once again caught a flash of her ruffled denim skirt or the red bandanna material of her sleeveless top.

She was far from the best dancer on the floor. She'd stumbled once or twice, turned the wrong way and even bumped into a dancer next to her. But through it all, she kept smiling, laughing despite her embarrassment, her blue eyes sparkling and her dark ponytail swaying in time with the music.

"Here you go," Ryder said as he handed Jamison the chilled bottle of beer that had brought them over to the area by the dance floor in the first place. "Sorry it took so long. Man, those lines are crazy."

The brew was cold and crisp but did little to douse the fire in his gut as the music changed, switching from a boot-scooting beat to the slow, mellow strains of a waltz. Like some kind of switch had been flipped, the crowd of people who'd been standing side by side started pairing off, leaving Rory alone. But only for a moment…

A split second in time when her gaze met his, the pull strong enough he caught his body swaying in her direction.

I'm leaving soon.

His reasoning for keeping his distance hadn't changed, but neither did Rory's response. He didn't need to hear the words to read what was written in her expression.

You're here now.

A blond cowboy stepped between them, blocking Rory from his sight. The other guy was tall and wide enough that Jamison couldn't see Rory's answer to the question the cowboy asked, but a second later, her slender hand curved over the guy's broad shoulder as he took her into his arms.

Dragging his gaze away with a curse, Jamison sucked in a lungful of air, suddenly realizing he'd forgotten how to breathe in the last few moments. He needed to get out of there before he made the best worst mistake of his life. "I need to check on Hannah," he said, but Ryder was shaking his head.

"Lindsay's already talked to Robbie. They're having a great time. They've left the food court and are heading over to the kiddie rides."

"Maybe I should go—"

"She's fine, man. She doesn't need you to hold her hand…but maybe you need her to hold yours?"

"What the hell is that supposed to mean?"

"Just that strangling that unicorn isn't helping your mood any. Maybe you think having Hannah around will keep your mind off a certain wedding coordinator strutting her stuff out on the dance floor."

"I'm not—she's—" Cutting himself off, Jamison set the stuffed animal he'd forgotten he was still holding on a nearby table and took another long pull of the beer he no longer wanted. "Rory's free to dance with whomever she wants."

"Yeah, right," Ryder gave a doubting scoff, and Jamison couldn't blame his friend. Even the cross-eyed unicorn seemed to be gazing at him disbelief, but it was the truth…

"Go ask her. Unless you're afraid she'll say no."

He was afraid she'd say yes. Rory might have been in the arms of another man, but it didn't matter whom she danced with or how many times.

That could have been me.

It *should* have been him.

"Hannah! Oh, sweetie, what happened?"

Lindsay's cry jerked his attention from the dance floor in time to see three guilty-looking boys leading a sniffling Hannah their way. Tyler and Robbie exchanged a quick glance before Tyler said, "She, um, kinda got sick after we went on the merry-go-round."

"Yeah," the youngest boy chimed in, "it was super gross and—"

"Brayden, dude."

"Oh, right." The boy ducked his head at his uncle's reproach and mumbled, "We're real sorry she got sick."

"Daddy, I don't feel so good." A flood of tears balanced on Hannah's lower lids, and Jamison froze.

The sight of his daughter's tears instantly sent him back to those first horrible days after the accident when all

Hannah could do was cry for her mother and there'd been nothing—*nothing*—Jamison could do to soothe her fears.

Lindsay reached out to smooth Hannah's hair back from her sweaty forehead in the way all mothers seemed to know how to do. "Poor thing. They have a first-aid station set up near the front entrance—"

Alarmed, Jamison broke out of his paralysis. "You think she's that sick?" Knowing Hannah's fear of hospitals—the place where her mother had died—he didn't want traumatize her further unless a trip to the doctor was absolutely necessary.

"No, not at all. I think she had too much junk food combined with too much excitement, but they can help clean her up and maybe give her something to settle her stomach."

Bending down, he tried to keep his own stomach from roiling as he took in the bluish-purple mess staining the front of his daughter's T-shirt. What on earth had she eaten that would be that color coming back up? "What do you think, Hannah? Do you want to go get cleaned up and see what we can do to make you feel better?"

But Hannah shook her head, her lower lip protruding in a trembling pout. "No." She wobbled. "I want—I want m—"

Jamison braced himself only to be blown away by a request he never saw coming. "I want Miss Rory."

Chapter Ten

Her heart still in her throat, Rory ducked into the first-aid tent. She barely took in the small space with its two empty cots and a rolling cart stacked with bandages, gauze and bottles of peroxide and iodine before her gaze locked on the third occupied bed.

"Miss Rory..." Hannah's brown eyes filled and her lower lip trembled as she spotted her. "I got sick."

"I know, sweetie. I heard, and I'm so sorry you don't feel good." Hazarding a glance at Jamison, standing like a sentinel near the foot of his daughter's bed, Rory added, "Your daddy called me and said you wanted me to come see you."

She'd heard the reluctance in his voice as he explained how the little girl had gotten sick and that he'd taken her to the first-aid area. How he hadn't wanted to bother her...

But Rory had the feeling Jamison was the one who was bothered—by Hannah needing her. And maybe, just maybe, by how he needed her, too...

The little girl nodded, giving a watery sniff and wiping at a tear with the back of her hand. She was wearing one of the Rockin' R souvenir T-shirts. The oversize sleeves hung down to her elbows, making her look even smaller and more vulnerable.

As soon as Rory sat down on the cot, Hannah climbed onto her lap…and right into her heart. Closing her eyes against the undeniable realization, she breathed in the sweet scent of baby shampoo combined with mint toothpaste. Little more than a week, and Rory had fallen hard, and she didn't dare think about her feelings for the sad-eyed girl's father…

"I'm feeling better now," she mumbled into Rory's shoulder.

"Don't count on it."

At Jamison's dry comment, Rory couldn't help but glance up at him. He too looked a little pale and green around the gills, and she finally noticed Hannah wasn't the only one wearing a brand-new souvenir T-shirt.

She pressed her lips together to keep from laughing, but judging by the way he shook his head, she didn't succeed in hiding her amusement. "So glad you—and everyone—find this so funny."

"I don't think it's funny, Daddy." Hannah wrinkled her nose in an exaggerated expression of disgust. "I think it was yucky."

"And that," a female voice chimed in, "is what we in the nursing field would call a spot-on diagnosis."

Rory looked up as Theresa Deeks handed Jamison a plastic bag containing Hannah and Jamison's damp shirt. She hadn't realized the pretty nurse would be overseeing the first-aid station, though Theresa was certain to be on hand after all the work she and her husband, Jarrett, had put into making the rodeo such a success.

"I rinsed them out, but they'll still need a good washing."

"That wasn't necessary."

The dark-haired woman laughed. "It was if either of you hoped to wear them again."

"That's my favorite shirt," Hannah chimed in, her voice forlorn.

Jamison looked slightly exasperated by his daughter's "woe is me" sigh but merely said, "Then I thank you for saving my daughter's favorite shirt."

"You're welcome, and as long as Hannah is feeling up to it, you can take her home."

"Come on, kiddo." Jamison reached out, but the little girl burrowed deeper into Rory's arms.

"I want Miss Rory."

"Hannah—"

"It's okay, Jamison. I'll ride back to the hotel with the two of you."

"Are you sure?"

At her nod, he leaned down to reach for Hannah. The move brought Rory and Jamison face-to-face, and even with his daughter between them, her breath caught at his nearness. Nerves danced in her stomach as if she'd been the one to have way too much junk food.

Jamison stood, lifting his daughter from her lap, and Rory was surprised at how empty her arms felt. Picking up the unicorn that had been tucked against Hannah's side, she was glad to have something to hold on to. Something to occupy her hands and to stop her from reaching out to smooth the oversize shirt over Hannah's back…or to try to ease the frown from Jamison's forehead.

"This is my fault. I should have been paying closer attention to Hannah and not—"

Watching you.

He didn't say the words, but Rory still heard them, and

even though he was blaming himself, she couldn't help feeling like he felt she, too, was somehow at fault. She'd taken more than her fair share of blame when she'd done nothing wrong, and this was one time where she wasn't going to keep quiet.

"Mrs. Deeks..."

"You can call me Theresa," the dark-haired woman offered over her shoulder as she wheeled the cart out of the way.

"Theresa, is Hannah the only child to come in with a bellyache tonight?"

"Are you kidding? We've had half a dozen or so little kids come through already. And don't even get me started on the big kids," she added as she crossed her arms over her chest. Offering a sympathetic smile, she told Jamison, "Your daughter's going to be fine. In a little while, you can try to get her to drink some flat soda to keep hydrated and crackers or dry toast if she's hungry. By morning, I'm betting she'll be back to her old self."

Jamison didn't say much once they left the first-aid tent and headed for his SUV. He strapped Hannah into her car seat, tucking her stuffed unicorn in next to her, and had pulled out of the parking lot before he glanced Rory's way.

The fairgrounds were located outside town, connected by a two-lane highway lined with towering pines but not the typical streetlights. Without the passing glow, the interior of the car was too dark for Rory to read his expression.

Hannah drifted off to sleep, and Rory might have found the soft sound of her breathing soothing if not for the tension she sensed coming off Jamison in waves.

Was he still blaming himself for Hannah getting sick? For not paying more attention to how much junk food one little girl could eat in a very short time span? They were almost back at the hotel when he spoke.

"I'm sorry. I'm sure this isn't what you had in mind for how tonight would end."

"And what do you think I had in mind?"

"I saw you earlier. Dancing. Having fun."

She must have been a better actress than she gave herself credit for if Jamison had thought she was enjoying herself. She'd tried. She had, appreciating the effort Drew and Debbie had put into including her.

But that hadn't stopped her from wishing Jamison had been on the dance floor beside her, that he had been the man to pull her into his arms and hold her body close as they swayed in time with the music.

And when her phone rang and his name lit up the screen—

"Actually, this is exactly how I hoped tonight would end."

She didn't need passing streetlights to recognize the incredulous look he shot her. "Leaving early with a sick kid?"

"With the three of us spending time together."

"Rory." Jamison made a sound that was half laugh, half groan. "I'm trying to do the right thing here."

"And if we disagree on what the right thing is? Then what?"

"We're leaving in just over a week. If we start something—if we—then what?"

She knew the answer as well as he did and couldn't deny the ache in her heart at the thought of saying goodbye. But worrying about the future wouldn't stop it from coming. All they could do was make the most of the time they did have. As far as she was concerned, that was the only right thing to do.

"If you left tomorrow, I wouldn't miss you any less."

Rory heard his quick intake of breath, but he didn't reply as he pulled into the Hillcrest House parking lot and cut the engine. The golden glow from the safety lights bathed the SUV's interior, and she could see what she'd missed before. The muscle working in his jaw, the tendons standing out in stark relief along his forearms, his hands tight on the steering wheel as if they were flying down the freeway. Holding himself back when every fiber in her being ached for him to hold her…

Deciding to put her cards on the table, Rory shifted on the passenger seat to face him. "I adore your little girl, Jamison, and I—I like you."

His hands clenched around the wheel tight enough that the leather squeaked beneath his grip.

"I know that makes me sound like a twelve-year-old with a foolish crush—"

Now he responded, quickly cutting off her words. "I think you're smart and brave and amazing. Which is why I can't do this."

"Do what?"

"Pretend to be the kind of man you deserve. A good father…a good husband…a good son… Name any kind of relationship, and it's one I've already failed. I don't know what this is between us, but I don't want it to be—I don't want *you* to be one more person I fail."

Debbie was right, Rory realized. He really did think he was being noble by keeping his distance. She might have admired his effort if she wasn't so tempted to smack him upside the head.

"You only fail when you stop trying. You haven't stopped trying with your father and you won't stop trying with Hannah. Not because that's the kind of man I deserve, but because that's the kind of man you are. And as for the two of us…" She sucked in a deep breath of her own. "I know how this ends, Jamison. With you and Hannah saying goodbye. Whether we spend those days together or not, that doesn't change. Whether you kiss me right now or not, that doesn't change. So the only question is…why not kiss me?"

Why not kiss me?

The words, the temptation, pounded through Jamison's veins in time with the blood beating from his heart. At the moment, he wasn't sure which was more vital. His heart had maintained the steady rhythm for the past thirty-one years, but he'd never felt this…aware. This alive.

Fortunately—or unfortunately, damned if he knew which—he hadn't had a chance to answer Rory's question. With the motion of the vehicle no longer lulling her into sleep, Hannah woke up and he'd lifted his sleepy, grumpy daughter against his chest. She held on tight to her new toy and the stuffed unicorn rode along his shoulder as she wrapped her arms around his neck.

The warm weight of her in his arms, combined with the trust and faith she placed in him, brought an ache to his throat. He pressed a kiss to her tangled curls as he breathed in her baby shampoo scent. Rory was right. He wasn't quitting on his little girl. He didn't know how he'd manage being a full-time single dad and a full-time lawyer, but he'd find a way.

Even though it wasn't very late, the hotel lobby was quiet—most of the guests were either at the rodeo or out enjoying dinner. Even so, Jamison was conspicuously aware of Rory walking by his side toward the Bluebell suite.

They needed to talk, to finish the conversation they'd started in the car but—

Why not kiss me?

Jamison sucked in a breath as they turned down the narrow hallway. He was going to have one hell of a time focusing on talking when he had Rory alone in a hotel room.

He carried Hannah straight into the suite's connecting bathroom and, within minutes, had her surrounded by a tub full of bubbles. Rory joined them a few seconds later, making the small space positively claustrophobic as she placed a hand on his shoulder and set a pair of pajamas on the toilet seat.

"Can you, um, hand me that washcloth?" The folded cloth at the edge of the tub wasn't so far that he couldn't have reached it, but Jamison found himself wanting Rory to stay. As she knelt by his side, helping Hannah hold the washcloth against her face as he rinsed the warm, sudsy water from her hair, it hit him this was the first time he'd ever shared Hannah's bath-time duties.

Before their separation, Monica—or, he later suspected, the nanny the Stiltons hired to "help out" their daughter—had been responsible. Now the nighttime duty was his alone.

I won't miss you any less if you left tomorrow.

God, wasn't that the truth, he thought as Rory wrapped his daughter in an oversize towel, drawing out a sleepy smile. Within minutes, she had Hannah dressed and still giggling from her first attempt to put the little girl's pajama top on inside out and backward.

But once Jamison tucked his daughter into bed and Rory kissed her good-night, Hannah hugged her unicorn to her chest, huge tears filling her brown eyes.

"Oh, Hannah, do you still feel yucky?"

Nodding her head vehemently, Hannah gave a watery sniff. Then, with a single blink, the dam burst. Silent tears coursed down her chubby cheeks.

"Sweetie..."

As Rory sank down on the bed beside her, the little girl threw her arms around her neck. "Can you sleep in my bed tonight?"

"Hannah," Jamison started but he could already see

Rory melting like Hannah's cotton candy at the first splash of water. He didn't doubt his daughter wasn't feeling well. He had a souvenir T-shirt and a possible lifelong aversion to brightly colored spun sugar to prove it.

But that didn't mean Hannah wasn't playing on the grown-ups' sympathy and using tears to get her way. After all his years with Monica, he'd built up a slight tolerance. Rory had no such immunity.

"Of course, Hannah." Curling up on her side next to the little girl, she promised, "I'll stay right here until you fall asleep."

Having done their trick, Hannah's tears performed a magical disappearing act as she snuggled beneath the covers.

"Daddy, too."

Hannah patted the empty spot on the other side of the bed, and Rory's eyes flew wide. The startled look and instant color heating her cheeks were reminders that she wasn't as bold as her words.

He knew he should play this smart and keep his distance. Starting something determined to end in such a short time made no sense in his logical, well-ordered world. But then again, he'd never met anyone like Rory McClaren in his logical, well-ordered world.

A little over a week ago, he wouldn't have believed such a charming, magical woman existed. And the chance to spend eight days—hell, even another eight minutes—with her would make spending the rest of his life missing her a price he was willing to pay.

The last thing Rory expected when she closed her eyes and pretended to sleep was to drift off. But as she lay on the bed with Hannah curled up against her side, keeping her breathing slow and steady—thinking that might encourage her rapidly beating heart to do the same—trying to lull the little girl into a peaceful slumber, she somehow followed right along.

She woke slowly, taking in the unfamiliar warmth pressed against her side and something soft and furry brushing her face. She blinked as she waited for her eyes to adjust to the dim light shining in from the doorway. Brushing the unicorn's fluffy tail aside, Rory smiled at the sight of Hannah's angelic features, sweet and soft in sleep. She looked over the little girl's blond head to Jamison's handsome face. Not sweet, not soft.

Not asleep.

Her mouth went dry as she met his glittering gaze. "Um, what time is it?" The question wasn't the one she wanted to give voice to, but she couldn't quite bring herself to ask how long he'd been watching her sleep.

She was tempted to pull the blanket over her head as the humiliation of another question she shouldn't have asked throbbed in the stillness of the night. She might as well have begged him to kiss her, and that was after he'd already turned her down once!

"Late…or early, depending on how you look at it."

"I should go." Sliding out of the bed, she placed the stuffed animal under Hannah's arm and smoothed out the blankets, wishing she could smooth her rattled nerves as easily.

Focused on getting Hannah ready for bed, Rory had pushed the final minutes of their conversation out of her mind. But now the words pinballed through her skull, pained embarrassment flashing all around. She'd thought the way Jamison had kissed her, the way they'd opened up to each other, sharing hurts and fears from their pasts, had meant something.

But she'd been wrong before.

Ducking out of the bedroom, Rory hurried down the

shadowed hallway as fast as her boots could carry her. She'd keep her attention where it should have been all along, on Ryder and Lindsay's wedding, on getting through the next week, and then she could forget all about Jamison, all about Hannah, all about how her heart was breaking inside her chest…

She'd barely made it to the living room when Jamison caught her by the shoulders, stopping her short and drawing her back against him. His warm breath stirred her hair and sent shivers running down her spine as he murmured in her ear. "If you leave now, I won't miss you any less."

For a split second, she allowed herself lean into the warmth and strength of his body before growing a backbone and pulling away. He let her go, and Rory spun to face him, ready to remind him he didn't want this, didn't want *her*, but the sheer longing in his expression sucked the words right from her chest.

"Jamison—" The whispered sound of his name hovered in the charged air between them. A connection drawing them closer as he reached up to cup her face in his hands.

His thumbs caressed her cheeks, her lips, charting a sensual path that held her captivated. Her heart pounded, running a hundred beats a minute, but she couldn't even move. "Jamison—"

Light as a feather, his lips moved against hers as he spoke. Her stunned senses barely recognized the words. "So why not kiss me?"

Rory didn't know what it was about this man that was magic, but one kiss and she'd swear she could fly. She fisted her hands in the crisp cotton of the Rockin' R T-shirt as if he might somehow keep her grounded, but how could he when it was his touch, his kiss that had her body, her heart, her soul soaring? And then her feet really did leave the earth as she sank onto the couch cushions, Jamison following her down, his body strong, warm, *perfect* above hers.

He deepened the kiss as her mouth opened to his—touching, tasting, teasing. His hand found the narrow gap between the bandanna-print shirt tied at her waist and the top of her skirt. Her skin sizzled at the contact, and it was all she could do not to arch her body into his, wanting, demanding, needing more—

But she could feel him holding back. Like a kite with a string still tethered to the ground, Rory could feel the tug of resistance, the slow, unrelenting pull reeling them back to earth as he broke the kiss.

This time she didn't let old insecurities get in the way, didn't doubt his desire for her. "Jamison," she whispered softly once she'd found the breath and ability to speak.

He dropped his forehead against her shoulder, his body rock hard as he fought for control. "We can't," he started as he lifted his head.

"I know," she smiled, his willingness to put his daughter first one of the reasons why she loved hm.

Loved him?

No! She couldn't—she didn't—she—

Loved him.

Rory slammed her eyes shut, too afraid of the emotions Jamison might see. "I should go."

The cushions shifted beneath her as he pushed into a sitting position and lifted her up beside him. She felt as well as heard the words he spoke against her ear. "Rory… I wish—I want—"

"I know." Her heart was suddenly filled with wishes and wants, but closing her eyes wasn't going to be enough to make them come true. Lifting her lashes, she repeated, "I should go."

"As long as you know how much I want you to stay.

You were right before. I want us to spend the time we have left together."

Rory didn't know if she wanted to laugh or cry. She'd convinced Jamison—straitlaced, logical Jamison—to take a leap, and now she was the one who wanted to play things safe. To protect her heart, to take a step back from the edge rather than risk a nasty fall.

"Tell me you still want that, too, Rory," he urged, his hands bracketing her shoulders. "I'm here now, and I don't want to start missing you until I have to."

If you leave tomorrow...this won't hurt any less.

"I want that, too," she promised.

"Good." Pulling her back into his arms, he pressed a kiss to her temple. "Good."

Rory wasn't sure how long she stayed in his arms, her head resting on his chest as she counted out the beats of his heart. If only it didn't seem like the steady rhythm was going backward, counting down the time they had left…

It was still dark and Jamison was still sleeping when Rory eased out of his embrace and slipped out the door. The old-fashioned hallway sconces had been dimmed for the night, casting a soft golden glow on the familiar dark walnut wainscot and richly patterned carpet.

So overwhelmed by the emotions still careening through her, Rory barely noticed the two women she passed in the hallway until their sharp laughter stabbed her in the back.

"Guess those stories Trisha heard were right. She really can't keep her hands off the merchandise."

Chapter Eleven

Jamison jerked awake, startled by the unfamiliar ring of a telephone. Pain shot down his spine as he lifted his head, blinked a few times and realized he'd fallen asleep on the couch.

Rubbing the kink at the back of his neck, he pushed into a sitting position on the too-soft blue floral cushions. He hadn't planned to spend the night on the couch, but then again, much of what happened last night had been completely unexpected…

He took a quick look around to confirm what he already knew. Rory was gone. He didn't blame her for leaving. The last thing she would want was for someone to see her slipping out of a guest's room in the middle of the night.

That didn't mean he didn't wish she'd stayed. Call him selfish, but he'd had the pleasure of falling asleep with her in his arms. He wanted to know what it was like to wake up the same way.

Still, maybe she was calling to check on Hannah and see if she felt up to another batch of smiley-face oatmeal. Anticipation wiped away the last traces of sleep as grabbed the hotel phone off the end table.

"Jamison, my boy! How are you doing up there in Smallville?"

He cringed at the sound of his former father-in-law's voice. Gregory Stilton was as big and imposing in person as his booming voice was over the phone. When Jamison first met Monica's father, he couldn't help being impressed by the businessman's wealth, status and importance. At the time, those things had still mattered to Jamison. Having just passed the bar and eager to make his mark, Jamison had seen Gregory Stilton as having it all.

"It's Clearville, Greg," he told the older man, "and everything's fine."

"Good, good. Glad to hear it. And how's our granddaughter?"

His hand tightened around the phone. "She's doing fine."

His gaze locked on a piece of paper on the coffee table, a project Hannah had worked on the day before. It took some imagination, but even he recognized the lime-green grass, turquoise sky and silver gazebo. Three stick figures held hands in front of the structure. He might have wondered at his daughter's Picasso-like image of him if not for the big red smile filling up half his face.

"Better than fine," he added, hearing the pride in his voice. "She's doing great. She's looking forward to her role as a flower girl in Ryder's wedding."

"Well, that's great."

Over the years, Jamison had learned to distrust Greg's over-the-top friendliness. More often than not, he was hiding his own agenda behind his smile. He'd come to appreciate Louisa's open disdain. At least with his mother-in-law, he never had to guess where things stood.

Proving his suspicions correct, Greg casually commented, "Of course, this vacation of yours couldn't come at a worse time—what with the junior partnership up for grabs."

"How do you know about the partnership?"

Gregory's laughter ratcheted up Jamison's suspicion even more. "You're nearing the big time now, Jamison. The law firm of Spears, Moreland and Howe taking on a new partner is news. People have been taking about it at the club."

The firm's partners ran in a tight-knit circle of powerful men and women in San Francisco. It was possible Greg had heard the rumors. But it was also possible that, as a powerful man himself, Gregory Stilton would use his considerable influence to weigh in on which direction he wanted the firm to go.

"Greg..."

If the older man heard the warning in Jamison's tone, he ignored it. "You know if you get the promotion, you'll be spending even more time at the office—long hours, weekends. Have you thought about what you'll do with Hannah?"

"We've talked about this. She'll be starting preschool once I get back."

"Half days in the mornings," Greg pointed out dismissively. "And that's if you can get her to stay. You know how leery she is around strangers."

"Hannah's getting better about that."

Silence filled the other end of the line, and Jamison realized what he should have known all along when his mother-in-law's voice came across the speaker. "Getting better? What strangers have you been leaving her with up there?"

"Not strangers. What I meant is she's getting better about meeting new people." Knowing his in-laws would dig the information out of Hannah given the chance, he added, "Rory McClaren is the hotel's wedding coordinator, and Hannah's taken a shine to her. She's made the whole idea of being a flower girl fun for Hannah. That's a good thing, Louisa."

"Is it? I thought this trip was about you spending time with your daughter, not about finding someone else to watch her while you go off and—do whatever."

"I'm the best man. The only *whatever* I've been doing is lending a hand with the wedding, and I wasn't always able to do that without someone to help with Hannah."

Jamison heard Louisa mutter the words *party planner* and *responsible sitter* under her breath before Greg came back on the line. "We're glad our little girl's looking forward to the wedding. How about you put her on so we can both say hello?"

A loud yawn sounded from the bedroom doorway as Hannah shuffled out, rubbing one eye before she pushed some serious bed-head curls out of her face. "She's right here, but don't expect too much. She just woke up and might be a little cranky."

He held the phone away from his ear rather than listening to what Louisa thought of him letting his daughter sleep in late and past her scheduled breakfast time. "Hey, Hannah Banana, want to talk to Nana and Papa?"

Giving a sleepy nod, Hannah took the phone and scrambled onto the couch next to him. Some of the tension caused by speaking with his in-laws faded as she snuggled by his side. "Hi, Nana. Hi, Papa."

Jamison might have questioned if he'd done the right thing in bringing Rory up in a conversation with his in-laws, but his daughter proved he'd little choice as she launched into a recitation of everything she'd done over the past few days—with almost every sentence filled with "Rory this" or "Rory that."

And after his daughter capped off her story with a detailed account of throwing up the brightly colored cotton candy, Jamison figured Louisa was about ready to faint.

"I didn't feel good, so I wanted Miss Rory to spend the night. Daddy, where is Miss Rory?" Hannah frowned before thrusting the phone back at him. "Nana wants to talk to you."

I bet she does, Jamison thought grimly.

"What kind of example are you setting, having some strange woman spend the night—"

"She didn't spend the night, Louisa. She stayed until Hannah fell asleep."

No need for the woman to know what happened after Hannah fell asleep. Covering the mouthpiece, he told Hannah, "Rory had to go back to her house, but we'll see her in a little bit if you're feeling okay."

"I feel good, Daddy. But I don't think I should have cotton candy for breakfast."

"Wise decision, kiddo."

He'd barely paid attention to the final minutes of Louisa's tirade. He was sure he'd heard the lecture about strict schedules and maintaining routines a dozen times before. "It was one night of too much sugar and too much excitement," he finally interrupted. "She's fine now, Louisa. In fact, I'd say Hannah's happier than she's been in a long time."

I'm happier. And he refused to feel guilty about that even as a cold silence filled the other end of the line.

"And I suppose you think this Rory person has something to do with that."

"It's not about what *I* think, and if you were listening to anything your granddaughter had to say, you'd know that."

"My granddaughter is four, a child who can be easily manipulated and fooled. As her father, it's up to you to know better."

Jamison rolled his eyes. "No one's manipulating or fooling anyone."

"I guess we'll see about that."

"What does that mean?"

"It means I hope you know what you're doing," she told him before ending the call, the warning in her voice making it clear she didn't think he had a clue.

Jamison hopped down from the stepladder after putting the final touches of paint on the trim along the gazebo's roof and tossed the paintbrush into an empty bucket. "What do you think?"

"It's be-yoo-tiful, Daddy!"

Rory couldn't agree more. The gazebo gleamed against the bright blue midday sky as it never had before, shining like new and yet still maintaining all the old-world charm and romance that made it a perfect part of Hillcrest. She loved the elegant scrollwork along the eaves, a more delicate pattern than what had been there before. Jamison had found matching spindles to replace the loose railing, making the stairs as good as new.

But it was the special touch he'd added, one no one else could see, that meant the most. Beneath the top step, on the underside of the tread, Jamison had carved all their initials.

He hadn't inscribed them within a heart, but he didn't need to. He and Hannah had already etched a permanent spot within her own.

He smiled when he got a good look at his daughter's

face. "Hannah Banana, I think you have more paint on you than on the gazebo."

Their roles as helpers had involved touch-up work, painting over screw and nail heads with Hannah doing her best and Rory following behind to fix any missed areas and clean up any drips.

"Uh-uh!" the little girl argued before wrinkling her paint-splattered nose and turning to Rory. "Do I, Miss Rory?"

"Well, maybe not that much." Dipping the tip of her finger in an open paint can, Rory said, "But you do have some here…and here…and here."

Hannah giggled as Rory tapped her nose, cheeks and chin. "Now look, Daddy!"

Shaking his head with the slightest bit of exasperation, Jamison said, "Nice polka dots, kiddo."

"I like poky dots."

"Well, you can't have poky dots if we're going to go into town for something to eat, so we better get cleaned up."

"Yeah, pizza!"

"With lots of anchovies, right?" Rory teased as she grabbed a semiclean cloth and a bottle of water off the top of a cooler.

The little girl made a face. "Anchovies, yuck!"

"Hannah, you don't even know what anchovies are," Jamison pointed out.

"Are they good?" his daughter demanded, her doubt obvious.

"Well, no," he admitted, clearly failing to prove his point.

Hannah turned back to Rory in triumph. "No anchovies!"

"All right. How about—" Rory paused for a moment to think "—pepperoni?"

"Okay!" With the promise of pizza in the air, Hannah

bounced on her toes, making Rory's efforts to clean off her face like a new version of pin the tail on the donkey. "No anchovies, just pepperoni."

Once Rory had Hannah's face as clean as she could get it without a tub full of bubbles, she cupped her cute cheeks in her hands. "There you go. All clean."

Hannah responded with a definitive nod. "Daddy's turn."

Jamison had dropped down to sit on one of the stepladder's lower rungs, and when he brushed a hand across his damp forehead, he left behind a streak of white.

"Hannah is right." Lips quirked in a smile, she told him, "You're wearing almost as much paint as she was."

He took in his white-flecked shirt with a careless shrug as he cracked open the water bottle she handed him. "What can I say? Construction work is an ugly process."

Ugly was not the word that came to Rory's mind as she grabbed the damp towel and walked to his side. "Come here."

He leaned forward, and she lifted a hand to brush his dark hair back from his forehead. His gaze caught hers, and she paused, almost forgetting why she'd embarked on this task.

She dabbed at the paint just as she had with Hannah. The actions might have been the same, but Rory's response was completely different. Her hand trembled as she traced a path across Jamison's forehead, his temple and along one cheekbone. She lowered the towel but didn't back away, staying whisper close, as his gaze searched hers.

"Better?" he murmured.

"Not quite so ugly anymore." She'd meant the words as a tease, but the huskiness in her voice gave her away.

Hannah had grabbed the empty water bottle, seeming to enjoy making the thin plastic crackle and pop in her small hands. Crouched along the edge of the pathway, her interest soon turned to scooping loose dirt into the narrow container.

Rory had learned the little girl's attention didn't stay captured for long, but for now…

She brushed her lips against Jamison's, their equal height giving the illusion of equal footing until Jamison caught her face in his hands, took control and shattered any pretense of staying grounded.

It was a quick kiss. A prelude for what was to come. A promise of more…but enough to send her head spinning into the clouds, leaving her breathless and dizzy with desire. She didn't know if her feet would have actually left the earth, but Jamison held her fast. He caught her hips and pulled her into the cradle of his thighs.

The gazebo had always been her favorite place, and that was before. Now every time she closed her eyes, Rory would see Jamison leaning against the carved post, paint streaked across his forehead and a gleam in his eyes. His low voice would echo through the whisper of wind in the trees and Hannah's lilting laughter would ring out with the trilling call of the birds. Pizza would never taste the same again, and paint fumes would always bring her back to this moment and this man.

Her favorite place and her favorite people in the whole, whole world…

"Ryder's bachelor party is tomorrow night."

"I know, so is Lindsay's bachelorette party."

"Do I even want to know what goes on at a bachelorette party?"

"Probably not." Rory was touched Lindsay had invited her and had been looking forward to hanging out with a group of women who weren't pointing and whispering behind her back.

Ever since the night of the rodeo, she'd lost count of the conversations that had stopped the moment she stepped into a room or neared a group of Hillcrest employees. As usual Trisha Katzman was right in the middle, surrounded by her flock. Whenever the redhead spoke, the other women leaned in like hungry birds, eyes wide and mouths open, pecking over a tasty morsel of gossip as they whispered back and forth.

Thrusting the thought aside, she asked, "What do you have planned for Ryder's last night as a free man?"

"You know me, something wild and crazy."

Rory couldn't help but laugh at his deadpan delivery. "It's always the quiet ones you have to watch out for."

Jamison smirked a little. "Per the groom's specific instructions, we're having a guys' night out at the Clearville Bar and Grille for a debauched evening of pool, darts and beer."

"Hmm, if not for the beer, you could invite Ryder's son and a few of his school friends along."

"Oh, you are funny."

She was glad he thought so. The bachelor and bachelorette parties were among the last events leading up to the wedding. The rehearsal dinner was scheduled at Hillcrest House the evening before the wedding, and after that—After that, it would all be over.

Lindsay and Ryder's life as a married couple would just be starting, but her relationship with Jamison would come to an end.

A smarter woman might have tried to keep her distance, to guard her heart, but Rory didn't have that kind of strength. She did know she was right about one thing, though. Ending their relationship now wouldn't make her miss him any less, so she was determined to enjoy what time they had together now.

She was afraid she'd have plenty of time to be miserable later.

Jamison cleared his throat and glanced over to where Hannah was now sprinkling the collected dirt along the walkway. "I, um, talked to Ryder. His parents are watching Robbie and his cousins tomorrow night. He said they'd be happy to add a girl to the mix."

"Do you think Hannah will be okay staying with them?"

Jamison huffed out a sigh. "Ever since the night of the unicorn, Hannah's been asking when she can play with Robbie and his cousins again."

Rory laughed. "But that's a good thing, isn't it?"

"A good thing for Hannah…and I'm hoping a very good thing for us."

Their time alone since the night of the rodeo had been limited to stolen kisses when Hannah was preoccupied with some game of make-believe or in the evening after the little girl had gone to bed. But Jamison was careful not to go too far, pushing them both to the brink before pulling back from the edge.

If Rory didn't know better, she might have thought he was trying to drive her out of her mind.

But if Hannah was happy staying with a sitter for a night…

"Don't tell me," Rory said, keeping a light note in her voice despite the bass drum beating inside her chest, "you have something wild and crazy planned?"

"Oh, sweetheart, you have no idea."

Chapter Twelve

"Am I the only one who thinks this is a bad idea?" Rory's words fell on deaf ears as she and the rest of Lindsay's bridal party scrambled out of the SUV amid constant chattering and bursts of laughter.

"I'm afraid so," Sophia Pirelli Cameron said. The petite brunette met Rory's exasperated glance with a sympathetic look. "You've been out-Pirellied."

"I had no idea that was even a thing."

Sophia laughed. "When you have as much family in town as I do, you learn to go with the flow."

At the moment, the five women, including Sophia's sister-in-law, Debbie, were flowing toward the Clearville Bar and Grille, a local watering hole offering beer, chips, an assortment of burgers and every sport imaginable on large-screen TVs. The place was popular with locals and tourists alike, and for tonight, it was the hot spot for bachelor parties. As in Ryder's bachelor party.

The girls were supposed to be out for their own night on the town, but halfway to Redfield, Debbie had had the great idea of crashing the guys' night out. The exuberant blonde's enthusiasm was contagious, and it hadn't taken much convincing for Lindsay's future sister-in-law, Nina, to turn the car around and head back to Clearville, where all of their guys waited.

Well, not her guy.

Jamison would be there, of course, but the other women were all married or about to be married to the men inside. While she and Jamison…

"That's a pretty heavy sigh for a Saturday night," Sophia commented as the two of them fell into step a few paces behind Lindsay, Debbie and Nina, who were already racing toward the bar. "I don't suppose it has anything to do with a certain best man, does it?"

"Jamison is part of the wedding party and a guest at our hotel—"

"Not to mention single…and hot…at least according to Debbie and my cousin Theresa."

Rory groaned. "You're right. Your family really has taken over the town, haven't they?"

"Pretty much," Sophia said. "But what can I say? Clearville's home, and I'm glad to be back. I'm only sorry I stayed away so long."

Music and light spilled out from the open double doors leading into the bar. Their steps slowed as they neared the entrance. "Considering how much family you have here, why did you stay away?"

The brunette lifted a shoulder in an easy shrug. "Small towns have long memories. When I was in high school, I screwed up. I trusted the wrong person and did something I shouldn't, and when we got caught, I took the blame. I'm not proud of what happened, but the thing I regret the most is the guilt that drove a wedge between me and my family. I never should have let that happen, especially not when they forgave me long before I got around to forgiving myself."

I trusted the wrong person.

Boy, did Rory know how that felt! And maybe she had carried her guilt around for too long—when that was the only thing she'd done wrong.

"Thank you, Sophia."

The brunette shot her a curious glance. "For what?"

"For helping put the past into perspective."

"You're welcome, and while I'm doling out pearls of wisdom, let me tell you that trips to the past are best served with fruity cocktails."

Rory's laughter faded away as they stepped inside the bar and she spotted the combined bachelor and bachelorette parties gathered near the pool tables. Music blared from the jukebox in the corner, making it impossible to hear what they were saying. But even in the dim lighting and neon glow cast from the beer signs hanging on the walls, what she saw made her heart sink.

Ryder was furious. Lindsay stood in front of her fiancé, her pretty face distraught, as the rest of the bridal party milled awkwardly around the couple.

He couldn't be so upset because Lindsay had crashed his stag party! In all the time Rory had worked with the groom-to-be, he'd been nothing but laid-back and relaxed, happy with whatever made Lindsay happy. Watching them together, Rory had thought they were the perfect couple…

In an instant, she switched from member of the bachelorette party to wedding coordinator. There had to be something she could do to fix this!

Cutting through the crowd gathered in front of the bar, Rory reached Bryce Kincaid's side. "Bryce, what is going on?"

"One minute everything was fine, and then in the next—" Ryder's brother shook his head. "All I know is that I heard Ryder tell Jamison he's not sure if he even wants Jamison to be at the wedding, forget having him *in* the wedding."

Jamison? This was about *Jamison*?

A tearful Lindsay caught sight of Rory and hurried to her side. "This is awful! Jamison is the best man. Ryder's best friend! I know how much he wants Jamison standing beside him." She brushed the backs of her fingers beneath her eyes. "I'm not going to be so dramatic as to say Jamison's absence will ruin the wedding, but I know how much it will hurt Ryder if he's not there. Something like this could ruin their friendship."

"Do you know what the fight was about?"

"Other than me?" Lindsay asked with a sad little laugh. "No clue."

"Okay. You keep working on Ryder and see if he'll open up. I'll find Jamison. Between the two of us, they don't stand a chance."

"Thank you, Rory."

"Wedding coordinator to the rescue," she promised, glad to hear a genuine laugh from her friend as she gave her a quick hug.

Oh, Jamison, what did you do?

Turning to Bryce, she asked, "Do you know where Jamison is now?"

"He drove separately from the rest of us in case he had to leave early to pick up Hannah." At her questioning glance, he added, "I've already called my folks. They haven't heard from him, and Hannah's asleep on the couch after somehow talking my boys into watching a princess movie with her."

"I rode over with the rest of the bachelorette party—"

"I can give you a ride if you know where he might have gone."

"Let's start at the hotel."

Once Rory spotted Jamison's SUV in the parking lot, she convinced Bryce she could handle things from there. Faint moonlight lit the way to the lobby, but a gut feeling had her veering away from the elegant building and following a familiar path instead.

She ducked under the yellow caution tape barring the way to the gazebo. The elegant structure was draped in shadows, still and silent, and a dark figure sat hunched on the top step. Her heart ached at the loneliness, the isolation he seemed to have wrapped around him like a moth-eaten-yet-familiar blanket.

Oh, Jamison, she thought again. *What did you do?*

She set foot on the first step, noticing the six-pack of beer, and sank down beside him. Smoothing her skirt over her knees, she kept her gaze focused straight ahead as she asked, "Come here often?"

Jamison tipped his head back to take a swallow from the beer in his hand before stating, "I'm not even going to ask how you found me here."

"I think the better question would be *why* are you here?"

"I'm getting drunk," he said, the clarity of his words and the barely touched bottle belying his words. "Isn't that what tonight is all about?"

"Actually, tonight is about spending time with your best friend and celebrating his upcoming marriage."

"I don't think Ryder would call me his best friend anymore. Even though all I was trying to do was to look out for him."

A bad feeling sinking into the pit of her stomach, Rory asked, "Look out for him how?"

"I told him it wasn't too late—"

"To call off the wedding?" She reared back in shock and might have tumbled from the step if he hadn't steadied her with his free hand.

"No, no, not to call it off. Just to have one of the lawyers at the firm draft a prenup."

"Oh, Jamison."

"I didn't think he'd—I'm trying to protect him, you know? Isn't that what a best man—a best *friend*—does?"

"I think a best man should be happy his friend has found the love of his life."

Wincing, he ran a hand through his hair. "I tried to have a good time. I did, but all I could think about was that I'd been there, done that, and look how it ended."

"Been there?"

"I was best man at Ryder's last wedding, too."

"Oh."

"Yeah. And that time, I did keep my mouth shut, even though I sensed Ryder was feeling pressured into the marriage. I told myself it was cold feet and everything would work out."

"And everything did work out."

He shot her an incredulous look. "They were miserable together. They ended up getting divorced."

"Yes, so Ryder and Lindsay can get married now."

"You are incredible."

"Thank you."

"Not a compliment. You can't be that naive."

Rory sucked in a lungful of cool night air and tried not to let that arrow strike her heart. He thought she was naive for believing Ryder and Lindsay's love was meant to last. How foolish would he think she was for falling for him when she'd known all along their relationship was destined to end?

Keeping her voice steady despite the trembling inside, she said, "Believing in love isn't being naive any more than being cynical makes you smart. All it does is blind you to the good things in life. I don't know anything about Ryder's first marriage, but I do know he's crazy about Lindsay."

"Lindsay kept his son from him for nine *years*! Ryder didn't even know Robbie existed. At least Monica only—" Cutting himself off, Jamison shook his head and took another drink.

"What did Monica do?" Rory asked, her words blending in with the rustle of wind through the trees, the distant rush of waves against the shore.

For a long moment, she didn't think he would answer, that he would keep his words—like his heart—locked up in the past. But finally, he started to speak. "We'd been fighting a lot, so much that I was afraid it would start to affect Hannah."

"And you didn't want that…not after the way you'd grown up."

"It's the last thing I wanted for Hannah. I did my best to ignore the worst of Monica's habits—the extreme shopping, the time she'd spend out with friends instead of at home with Hannah, her complaints that I was the one who spent too much time at work to be a good husband and father. Although she was right about that…"

Jamison still didn't know if his marriage had failed because of all the time he put in at work or if he put in all that time at work because his marriage was failing. But he did know Hannah had paid the price.

"Jamison—"

Ignoring her softly voiced protest, he continued, "Before long, Monica and I couldn't seem to be in the same room together without arguing, and I felt like I had no choice. I moved out. We called it a separation, but I think we both knew we wouldn't be getting back together. I don't know why I didn't ask for a divorce right then."

"Maybe because you still were holding out hope you would work things out."

Jamison gave a rough laugh, his hand tightening on the beer bottle. "Well, if that is the reason, it was a foolish hope. We might not have fought as often, but when we did, it was as bad, if not worse. That's when she started keeping me from seeing Hannah. It was small things at first. Dropping her off a few minutes late, picking her up early. But before long, she was canceling visits altogether. Hannah was sleeping or not feeling well or had a playdate with friends. One excuse after another until I was lucky to see Hannah once a month instead of every weekend."

It was his father who had warned him not to make the same mistakes he had. "I let your mother convince me you were better off without me," he'd told Jamison. "I was never going to be rich or successful. I was never going to be the kind of man she would be proud of. But the one regret I have is that I didn't fight as hard as I could for you, Jamie. You are rich and successful, but I can promise you, none of that will mean a thing if you don't have that little girl in your life."

Rory shifted closer to him, slipping the cold, hard bottle from his hand and replacing it with the warm, soft reassurance of her own. "And that was wrong of Monica, but—"

"That's not all she did, Rory." Jamison had to take a deep breath to get out the words, buried deep in his memory where he tried his damnedest not to think about them. "I couldn't let things continue the way they were going. So I told Monica I was filing for divorce. I was prepared for her to go ballistic, but she barely reacted. I left that day feeling this huge sense of relief and went on an out-of-town business trip, thinking everything would work out. I should have known better."

The wind picked up, drawing a curtain of clouds over the full moon. Dark memories crouched in the shadows, trying to drag him back into the past, but Jamison held on tight to Rory's hand, her touch, her presence keeping him present.

He thought of the first time he saw her, how her smile, her beauty had warmed him like a summer day… She was his sunshine, his ray of light.

"I tried calling while I was gone, and when she didn't call me back, I started to get this bad feeling. She'd been so calm when I left, acting so out of character… I tried her parents to see if they could get ahold of her, but they couldn't reach her, either. Finally, I left in the middle of a meeting and took the first flight I could get home. I didn't know what I would find."

"Oh, Jamison."

Even though he had moved out, he'd convinced Monica to allow him to keep a key in case of emergencies. "When I got there, everything was the same as when I left, and I felt foolish for overreacting. It's not like it was the first time Monica had avoided my calls. But then I found her phone on the counter. She never went anywhere without that phone."

He'd torn through the house after that, the missing items as telling as the phone she'd left behind. Suitcases, clothes, Hannah's favorite toys… "Monica was gone, and she'd taken Hannah with her."

"Jamison… I am so sorry. How awful for you to have to go through that!"

There was more. There was what happened the day of the accident, but Jamison couldn't bring himself to tell Rory about that. Couldn't watch the sympathy and understanding in her beautiful face fade into the condemnation he saw whenever he looked in the mirror.

"How long were they gone?"

"Almost four months. One hundred and seventeen days."

Gazing at his granite profile, Rory could still see the toll that time had taken on Jamison written in his tense jaw, the brackets around his mouth and the hand fisted at his side. Her heart ached for all he—and Hannah—had been through, emotion building inside her as she wished for something to say to wipe those bad memories away. Instead, she scooted closer to him on the step and rested her head on his shoulder.

"I know it doesn't sound like a long time—" he started.

"It sounds like an eternity," she protested and felt a small sense of victory when Jamison sighed and some of that tension eased out of him. And when he leaned his head against hers, Rory wished this was a moment she could make last.

"Between the separation and the time she was gone, I only saw Hannah a handful of times in almost eight months. She'd grown so much, when I first saw her in—when I first saw her again, I hardly recognized her."

"But all of that happened to you and Monica. It didn't happen to—"

Us.

Monica had let him down, betraying him in the worst way possible, but Rory wanted him to know he could count on her. That he could trust her with his heart, and even more important, he could trust her with his daughter. She would never let either of them down.

"To Lindsay and Ryder."

"I don't know how he can forgive her."

But it wasn't Lindsay Jamison needed to forgive. He needed to find a way to forgive himself.

"It's not your fault."

But instead of soothing his pain, her words caused Jamison to jerk away. He vaulted off the steps only to turn back and point an accusing finger at her—as if condemning her for trusting him, for loving him. "You don't know, Rory—"

"I know you." She stood slowly before she deliberately made her way down the steps. "I might not know the man you were, but I know the man you are. A good father, a good friend, a man who—"

"A man who killed his wife!"

"What?" Rory stumbled on the final step, but this time Jamison wasn't there to catch her. She regained her balance at the last second, her legs, her entire body trembling at the force of his words. Words that couldn't be true. "I don't understand. Monica died in a car accident. Were you—were you the one driving?"

His arm fell to his side, and his chin dropped to his chest. "I was a thousand miles away."

"Then how—"

"Monica called me. When she figured out I had a detective looking for her, she called me. We were yelling at each other, ugly, hateful things—and then I heard her scream."

"Oh, my God. You heard the accident?"

"Heard it? I *caused* it."

"Oh, Jamison, you can't believe that! You know it isn't true. Monica called *you*. You didn't know she was behind the wheel."

"I should have. I should have realized she'd take Hannah and run again—"

"Maybe, maybe you could have guessed she'd do that. But you couldn't know that she would crash."

He closed his eyes as if that could block a truth guilt wouldn't allow him to believe. He might not listen and he didn't want to see, but Rory could still make him *feel*. She lifted her hands to his face, and the scrape of his late-night stubble sent chills up her arms. The sensation was as powerful as if he'd run his jaw over her sensitive skin from her wrist all the way to her shoulder.

And she knew in the split second before she raised her mouth to his, that this kiss wouldn't be the caring, consoling kiss she intended. But then their lips met, and she stopped worrying about what the kiss was supposed to be and focused on what it *was*.

Raw. Intense. So close to perfection, she could have been dreaming. But the tension in Jamison's body, the lingering anguish, was all too real. The need to take that pain away had Rory parting her lips beneath his, as if she could somehow draw out the darkness trapped inside him.

Touching and tasting, the kiss grew more and more heated, and the air seemed to sizzle around them. It burned in her lungs until she had to break the kiss and gasp for breath.

"Rory." He groaned her name in what might have been a protest, but the plea in his rough voice and a tiny thread of hope let her know how much he wanted to believe.

"There are a million things you could have done differently then, but there's not a single one you can do now to change what happened."

"So I'm just supposed to forget?"

"No, you're supposed to remember. To remember how lucky you are that Hannah survived and that she's okay."

"I am. You have no idea how damn grateful I am that she wasn't badly hurt."

"I know. I know." Rory swallowed hard, knowing the words she needed to speak and knowing how hard they would be for Jamison to hear. "And you have Monica to thank…because no matter how angry she was, how determined to run, she still took the time to buckle Hannah into her car seat. To make sure your daughter was as safe as possible in case of an accident no one could see coming."

His fingers flexed at her hips, and Rory tensed, waiting for him to push her away. To reject her and the forgiveness she wanted for him. Instead, he pulled her body to his. Close, then closer until she could hear his ragged breathing and feel his heart thundering. Until she resented every article of clothing, every millimeter of distance separating them.

"I can't. I know you want me to forgive Monica, but I can't."

"It isn't about what I want, Jamison. It's about what you need."

"I need you, Rory. All I need is you."

He swept her up in his arms, but instead of carrying her away from the gazebo, he climbed the stairs to the shadowed platform. It was dark, and the secluded gazebo seemed a million miles away from the hotel and its slumbering guests. As he sank down onto the top step—the one with their hidden initials carved in the wood—and drew her into his lap, no one else existed outside the world they created for each other.

He murmured her name against her mouth, her cheek, her throat. Each husky whisper sent shivers running up and down her spine. The seductive, potent promises set off tiny explosions along her nerve endings—fizzy and sparkling and all building to a grand finale. She tugged his shirt from his jeans and shoved her hands beneath the soft material. The tight muscles and smooth skin of his back made her greedy for more.

His eyes blazed at the proof of her impatience, and he

reached behind his back with one hand to pull the shirt over his head. She smothered her startled laughter at the unexpected move against his neck, breathing in the scent of his skin and the anticipation of what was to come.

With his shirt gone, she had the freedom to explore his broad shoulders, muscled chest and stomach, first with her eyes and then with her hands. His hair-roughened skin tickled her palms, but it was Jamison who flinched as she worked the button on his jeans.

"Rory." He caught her hand, his grip a little rough as he held her fingers against his rock-hard abdomen. He didn't ask the question, but the words were written in his glittering gaze.

I'm leaving...

Leaning forward, she gave her answer as her lips found his. *You're still here...*

Their affair might not last, but Jamison seemed determined to make it one she would never forget as his hands slid beneath her skirt and he set out to brand every inch of her body. He stripped away her panties and found her wet and waiting for him. Heat flooded her bloodstream, a tidal wave of desire that washed away the worries of what tomorrow might bring and left her bathed in his kiss, his touch…

Until the tide turned, and Rory was the one painting kisses over his chest, shoulders and stomach. She'd studied dozens of swatches over the years—paints, fabrics, ribbons—but she'd never before realized that kisses came in colors. The innocence of pink, the glorious revelry of gold, the rich decadence of red…

She'd nearly completed a rainbow when Jamison stopped her. She muttered a protest that was silenced when he reached for protection and then lifted her above him. Her body sank onto his, and Rory welcomed him just as she'd welcomed his kiss, his touch, his heartache. Her arms and legs wrapped tight, never wanting to let him go...

With his hands at her hips, he slowly began to move, increasing a pace destined to drive her wild. Her body rose and fell with every thrust, and a kaleidoscope of colors burst behind her eyelids as the pleasure broke, showering down over them in a burst of fireworks.

His breathing was still rough in her ear, his heart pounding against hers, when Rory pressed her lips to his shoulder, fighting a smile he evidently felt against his skin. "What's so funny?"

"I was thinking we should do something to celebrate the gazebo's reopening, but this is so much better than anything I had in mind!"

Chapter Thirteen

Jamison woke slowly, blinking against the early-morning light. The sun streamed through the curtains, and he suffered a moment's disorientation. He never slept this late. Hannah never let him sleep this late. At the thought of his daughter, his eyes flew open and took in the unfamiliar, feminine surroundings. Lace curtains. White wicker furniture. Pale pink walls and sheets embellished with tiny pink roses. At the sound of a soft sigh, the memories from the night before came rushing back.

Rory. In his arms at the gazebo last night. Rory. In bed with him this morning.

Wide-awake now, he rolled his head on the pillow. They'd made their way back to her cottage after leaving the gazebo, stumbling through the darkened rooms before falling into her bed and making love a second time. She slept on her side facing him, one hand cradled against her cheek. Her dark hair spilled in disarray across the pillowcase, her eyelashes forming soft shadows against her cheeks. Sheer amazement filled him. He'd never seen a lovelier or more amazing sight.

He felt the ridiculous urge to wake her, as if that might somehow prove last night hadn't been a dream.

As if she could read his thoughts, her eyelids fluttered, then drifted open. Unlike his momentary confusion, her eyes were clear. "Morning," she whispered.

"Hi," he murmured, almost afraid to break the silence.

"What time is it?"

"Early," he insisted, ignoring his previous admission.

She smiled at his white lie. "Not that early. When are you supposed to pick up Hannah?"

"We didn't have a set time, since no one knew how late we'd stay out."

Reaching out, she cupped his face in her hand. "You know you have to make things right with Ryder."

Jamison didn't want to lose his oldest and best friend, but Ryder wasn't first on his mind as he pressed a kiss into Rory's palm. "I didn't plan for this, you know."

"Uh-oh." Her smile trembled a little as she tucked the sheet beneath her arms. "Do I hear another 'do the right thing' speech coming?"

"Too late for that," he sighed.

"But not too late for this." Leaning forward, her dark hair framing her face, she brushed her lips against his. The gentle, giving kiss still had the power to kick his pulse into overdrive and send desire crashing through his veins.

"Rory…"

"I know you're leaving, Jamison." Was it his imagination or was the shine in her blue eyes the glitter of tears? Before he could know for sure, she ducked her head again, punctuating her words with kisses on his face, his throat, his chest. "But not today…and not tomorrow…"

And before long, leaving Clearville—leaving Rory—was the last thing on his mind.

An hour later, Jamison pulled up in front of the Kincaid residence. Ryder's parents lived outside town in a ranch-style house with a wraparound porch and lush green front yard. The sounds of laughter and a dog barking filled the air as he headed for the front door.

"Kids are all out back." Ryder stepped through a side gate, coffee mug in hand, and let the door slam shut behind him. "Hannah has the boys playing some kind of game where she's a princess and they're trying to rescue her from a dragon. Who in this case is my brother's Border collie."

"Sounds like they're being pretty good sports about the whole thing."

Ryder shrugged as he climbed the steps to the porch. "Robbie's been begging for a dog, so any game that includes Cowboy is one he's up for."

Jamison opened his mouth, the apology stalling in his throat. "Seems like you survived last night."

"Yeah, it was a real blast." Ryder's poker face folded slightly as a wry smile kicked up one corner of his mouth. "Especially once the bridal party showed up."

"So that's what happened." He'd been too caught up in the moment last night to wonder how Rory had found out about the argument at the bachelor party.

"Huh?"

"It's—nothing. I was an ass last night."

Ryder took his time, lifting the mug, blowing on the steaming dark roast, taking a swallow before saying, "Got that right."

Jamison sighed. He was going to make him say the words. "I'm sorry. I know you love Lindsay and she loves you, and I…hope everything works out."

His friend tipped his mug in Jamison's direction. "But you don't think it will."

"Dammit, Ryder, I'm trying really hard not to get into another fight with you."

"Good thing, since I'd kick your ass."

"And I'd sue yours until you didn't have a penny to your name."

Ryder smirked, and Jamison figured they could call their insult battle a draw. His friend lifted the mug for another drink, and Jamison noticed the gold trophy and the words *World's Greatest Father* on the side.

"You want to know how I can forgive Lindsay? The truth is, that's the only way I could expect her to forgive me. The only way I could forgive myself."

It's not your fault. Rory's words whispered through his mind. *And you have Monica to thank...*

He couldn't. Maybe if he had Rory's capacity for love, for hope, for forgiveness, he could forgive Monica. But he was a man who lived the law—right and wrong, black or white.

Jamison shook his head. "You didn't do anything wrong! You didn't know Lindsay was pregnant."

"I didn't want to know," Ryder stressed. "I slept with her. I knew the baby could be mine—forget what the Clearville grapevine had to say. But I had plans, big plans, and you better believe being a teenage dad wasn't part of them." He rubbed his thumb over the trophy emblem on the mug. "That's not an easy thing to admit, even now, but it was something I had to face when Lindsay told me about Robbie. Something we both had to get over in order to move on."

And he was moving on. To a life with the woman he loved with a confidence and faith Jamison...envied. "I really was trying to look out for you."

"I get it. I do. Your head was in the right place."

"Isn't the expression your *heart* was in the right place?"

"Oh, hell, no. Your heart's all messed up, dude."

"What is that supposed to mean?"

"Just that half the stuff you were saying was way more about what's going on with you than anything to do with me."

Bits and pieces of his argument echoed across the lush green lawn.

You have to protect yourself.

You made a mistake before.

Don't leave yourself open to getting hurt again.

Jamison swore under his breath. "When did you end up being the smart one in this friendship?"

"I was always the smart one. Playing the dumb jock was how I got all the girls."

"You are so full of it."

Jogging down the porch steps, Ryder spoke over his shoulder. "Yep. But I'm right."

He'd always had a bit of showman in him back in his college football days, and Jamison couldn't help thinking his friend hadn't lost his touch as he followed him around to the side of the house. Ryder pushed the gate open wide, and Jamison saw what was behind door number one.

In the middle of a green tree-lined lawn, Hannah held a beat-up red Frisbee over her head, running and laughing as the black-and-white dog and three boys chased after her.

Her pure joy grabbed hold of Jamison, and he didn't want to let go. Didn't want to step back from the emotion pouring through him. He wanted to embrace it for all it was worth, and he only wished he had Rory at his side to share in this miracle.

Hillcrest's magic touches whoever needs it most.

She was magic. She was his princess and fairy godmother

rolled into one, and Jamison didn't know what he would do without her in his life.

As if reading his thoughts, Ryder said, "You have a good thing going with Rory, Jamison." At Jamison's questioning glance, his friend added, "Your daughter isn't exactly a vault when it comes to Miss Rory and how much time you are all spending together."

"Rory's…amazing. She's been so good for Hannah."

"She's been good for *you*. That's what's made the biggest change with Hannah. Kids are smarter than most adults give them credit for. She's taking her cues from you. If you're happy…"

"She's happy," Jamison finished, but he still wasn't sure he believed it. Or maybe he was too afraid to believe it. Too afraid he couldn't be this happy in San Francisco. That he wouldn't be this happy anywhere that Rory wasn't. "When we get back home…"

"What happens when you get back?"

"I don't know." Hannah had come so far, and maybe Ryder was right. Maybe he too had taken some serious strides when it came to being the kind of dad Hannah deserved, but without Rory…he didn't know if he could keep going in the right direction.

And yet… "Rory and I both agreed. After the wedding, we go our separate ways. No hard feelings." And no broken hearts.

It didn't take a genius to figure out a woman like Rory wanted more than a short-term fling. The woman lived and breathed weddings and had made her belief in romance and a love of a lifetime clear.

All of which asked the question of what the hell she was doing with him.

He was jaded, cynical, so wary of love he'd almost blown a longtime friendship because he wasn't ready to believe Ryder had found a love that would last beyond the honeymoon stage.

"So that's it?" Ryder twirled the now-empty mug around by the handle, and Jamison had the feeling his friend was thinking of chucking it at his head. "You meet this amazing woman and you're going to kiss her goodbye?"

Thoughts of kisses and goodbyes took him right back to Rory's bed that morning. Their relationship was temporary. It had to be. They'd agreed. And nothing this good could last.

He might not know much about fairy tales, but he knew what happened when the clock struck midnight. Their magical night would be over.

"What else am I supposed to do, Ryder? My life is back in San Francisco."

"Your *job* is back in San Francisco. Don't fool yourself by calling that a life. And if you're going to walk away from the best thing that ever happened to you, at least be honest about the reasons why."

"I wanna see Miss Rory!"

Jamison sucked in a breath, struggling for patience—with his daughter and with himself. *He* wanted to see Rory. He wanted to talk to her about his conversation with Ryder, to let her know he was back on track as Ryder's best man and as his best friend. He wanted to thank her for that… and for a whole lot more.

A handful of hours had passed since he'd left her bed that morning, and his eagerness to see her again surprised him. Worried him.

I won't miss you any less if you leave tomorrow.

He wasn't leaving tomorrow. The wedding was Saturday and his reservation lasted through the weekend, but he couldn't deny their time together was coming to an end.

He wasn't worried so much about missing Rory as he was about finding the strength to leave.

"Daddy!"

"Hannah—" Catching himself before he could snap at his daughter, he reminded her, "We can't see Rory right now. She's working."

She'd told him about the small afternoon wedding taking place in the rose garden. She'd spent most of the day yesterday preparing for the event in the hours leading up to the bachelorette party.

"But I wanna tell her about the sleepover! We played games and watched princess movies and Mrs. Kincaid doesn't know how to make smiley-face oatmeal, but she made smiley-face pancakes instead!"

Pancakes... Jamison closed his eyes with a sigh. That explained the sugar rush that had the little girl bouncing around their suite like the Energizer Bunny. "Why don't we go outside for a walk?"

"To the gazebo?" Hannah asked, her brown eyes wide.

What kind of father was he that he wanted to keep the memory of his night with Rory and the gazebo to himself? That he wasn't ready to see the magical spot in the full light of day?

"How about down to the beach instead?"

"Can we hop like bunnies?"

"If we do will it make you super sleepy so you take a big nap this afternoon?"

Hannah wrinkled her forehead. "I don't think bunnies take naps, Daddy."

"Of course they don't," he muttered as they headed out of the suite and into the hallway. All the time wondering at the odds of convincing his hopping daughter to be a giant sloth instead.

With Hannah tugging at his hand, Jamison stepped out of the lobby and into the sunny, cloudless day. A slight breeze blew off the ocean, cooling the sun's rays and adding a hint of sea salt to the air. He couldn't help giving a slight chuckle at the first thought that came to mind.

It really was the perfect day for a wedding.

As they headed down the path leading to the rocky shoreline, a familiar sound rang out in an unfamiliar setting. Reaching into his pocket, he pulled out his cell phone. He still kept the thing charged, carried it with him everywhere, even though away from the hotel, he rarely had reception.

In San Francisco he could count on one hand the number of times he didn't respond to a call within half an hour. Here, he'd gotten used to missed calls, lengthy messages and unreturned emails. Most of the time, he waited until the evening when Hannah was asleep to respond.

But not last night.

Last night, San Francisco and the law firm had been the last things on his mind.

But when he saw the name on the screen, he swiped his thumb to answer the call.

"Jeez, Porter, where the hell are you, the dark side of the moon?" his friend and fellow lawyer Donnie Lipinski demanded. "I've been trying to get ahold of you for days!"

"Sorry, cell coverage is pretty spotty around here."

His friend swore so loudly Jamison automatically looked to Hannah who was tugging on his arm. "Give me a second, will you, Hannah Banana?"

"I wanna see Rory!"

"In a minute."

Hannah dropped to her butt in a pout, arms crossed

over her chest and bottom lip stuck out as far as it would go. "Count to one hundred and I'll be ready to go," he promised.

Lifting the phone back to his ear, Jamison caught Donnie midstream. "…middle-of-nowhere vacation?"

"One! Two! Three!"

Hannah's counting reached an almost-obnoxious volume, and Jamison covered his ear with his free hand. "I'm here for a friend's wedding," he reminded Donnie.

"A wedding lasts what, a day? Maybe two if you get suckered into going to the rehearsal dinner. You've been there almost two weeks." Lowering his voice, he added, "Do you know how many clients Martinez and Harris have met with in two weeks? And word has it Martinez grabbed the Langstone account."

Jamison took his turn swearing, though he was careful to do it under his breath. The firm encouraged competition between its employees, with a "may the best man win" mentality. Langstone Communications was a coveted account, one he'd thought he had a good shot of landing… two weeks ago.

"They're pushing hard toward the finish line, and you're still stuck in the blocks, man."

Hannah finally reached twenty, and Jamison dropped his free hand. "I needed to come here, Don. It was important."

"More important than your career?" Incredulity filled his friend's voice, as if he couldn't image what could top that. The thrill of the chase, the euphoria of landing the biggest, brightest account had been a rush beyond anything Jamison could imagine.

But he never could have imagined a woman like Rory. Making love to her, kissing her, hell, even making her smile made him happier than any client, any account ever had.

But he'd been a lawyer for years, and everything he felt for Rory was so new, so fragile. And hadn't the personal relationships in his life taught him that nothing lasted? His feelings for Rory would fade, and he would need the comfort, the security of his career to fall back on. "I'll be back on Monday," he told Donnie.

His friend snorted. "Who knows how many accounts your competition will have brought in by then? Forget the promotion—you'll be lucky to still have a job."

Jamison opened his mouth to retort, but Donnie had hung up. As much as he loved modern technology, what he wouldn't give for an old-fashioned phone he could slam back into its cradle right now. Instead, he dropped the cell into his pocket.

He wasn't in danger of losing his job. Donnie was busting his balls with that comment. But the promotion… Yeah, he had a feeling he could kiss that goodbye.

You're destined for bigger things, Jamison. Never forget that. Never settle for less when you can take more.

His mother's words echoed through his thoughts as he ran a hand through his hair. He didn't want to end up like her—grasping and grappling to hold on to something fleeting that had already passed him by. He'd worked hard for that partnership, dammit! He'd put in the long hours, the nights, the weekends. He'd given his all! He'd sacrificed—

He'd sacrificed his marriage just to be considered.

What would he be expected to sacrifice to win it all?

Reaching into his pocket, he powered down his phone.

"Hey, Hannah—" His shoes crunched on the loose gravel as he turned. "Are you ready—"

His words—his heart—stopped at the sight of the empty path behind him.

Chapter Fourteen

"Hannah!" He called her name, but this was no game of hide-and-seek with his daughter giggling, hardly out of sight, a few feet away. She was gone. "Hannah!"

He froze, unsure where to go, what to do…but then he knew.

Hannah had gone to find Rory.

He had to believe that, just like he had to believe he'd find the two of them together. He couldn't bear to think anything else. The rose garden wasn't far from the front entrance of the hotel, and he ran the distance in record time. His heart pounded in his ears so loudly he could barely hear the strains of a harp floating on the air. But that sound and the activity around the wedding had to have drawn Hannah to the one spot where Rory was sure to be.

She *had* to be there.

He stopped short as he rounded a curve, his shoes skidding beneath him. Two dozen people filled the white chairs lining the lawn, all focused on the couple standing beneath the delicate arched trellis. He scanned the crowd but didn't see Rory. Didn't see Hannah.

The bride's tremulous voice barely carried to the back row. It was all Jamison could do to not hold his peace and to start calling out for his daughter…

"Psst, Daddy."

At first, he thought he'd imaged the faint whisper blending in with the breeze rustling through the trees. That the sound had come from one of the guests, murmuring under their breath about the bride or her dress or the ceremony. But then he heard it again.

"*Psst*, Daddy! Over here!"

The call was louder this time, enough for a few heads in the back row to turn his way. Jamison paid them no attention as he scanned the garden off to his right, where he finally spotted golden curls amid the verdant green bushes and red roses.

"Hannah."

Too relieved to have found her, Jamison didn't care about making a scene as he wound his way through the fragrant bushes until he could crouch down at his daughter's side and yank her into his arms. "Hannah, what are you doing? You know better than to go off without me!"

Her lower lip sticking out in a pout, she said, "I wanted to see Miss Rory's wedding."

"Hannah, this isn't Rory's wedding."

"Uh-huh," his daughter insisted. "See? She's right over there."

Jamison followed his daughter's outstretched hand and spotted Rory standing off to the side. His breath caught at the sight of her—her hands clasped in front of her chest and a beaming smile on her face. No one was supposed to be more beautiful than a bride on her wedding day, but as far as Jamison was concerned, no woman was more beautiful than Rory—ever.

Her outfit—a pale yellow sweater and narrow cream-colored skirt—was a little more sedate and businesslike than the flowery dresses she usually wore, and her hair was caught back in a professional-looking bun. But nothing she wore could ever downplay how stunning she was, and that was only on the outside.

Her inner beauty—her kindness, her compassion, her caring—that would shine through even in the darkest moments. Wasn't that why his first instinct when Hannah was missing was to run to Rory? Yes, he'd figured that Hannah had gone to find her, but even more than that, *he* had wanted to find Rory. To have her tell him that everything would be all right. To make it all better, the way she'd made everything in his life better.

And he couldn't help wondering if he was only fooling himself. If his feelings for Rory were destined to fade, then why did they grow stronger every time they were together?

"You know, we've never had a Hillcrest House wedding crashed before." Up until a minute ago, Rory wasn't sure how she'd feel the next time she saw Jamison. She hadn't imagined she'd be fighting laughter, but she found herself doing just that as she confronted the guilty-looking duo crouched at the back of the rose garden.

"Look, Daddy! It's Miss Rory!"

"So I see." His silver gaze swept over Rory with an intimacy and something…*more* that left her trembling in her sensible shoes. The wedding guests were focused on the bride and groom, but it still wouldn't do for her to launch herself into Jamison's arms in the middle of the ceremony. Even if she wanted to…

The soloist had started singing about the power of love,

providing enough ambient noise for Rory to feel comfortable murmuring, "You're not planning to rush the aisle when the pastor asks if anyone objects to this wedding, are you?"

"I wouldn't be anywhere near this ceremony if a certain someone—" he landed a pointed gaze on his oblivious daughter "—hadn't decided she wanted to come to your wedding."

"*My* wedding?"

"That's what she said."

"So this is my fault?"

"Clearly. My daughter is obsessed."

"With weddings?"

"I wish it were that simple."

As much as Rory wanted to deny she was a complication in Jamison's life, it was hard to do when his daughter scrambled over to take her hand. "Did you see the flower girl, Miss Rory?" Hannah asked. "She had a blue basket for her flowers and ribbons in her hair and she went like this!" Throwing out an arm, she exuberantly mimicked the other girl's flower-tossing technique.

Raising an eyebrow, Jamison murmured, "Was she throwing rose petals or a ninety-five-mile-an-hour fastball?"

"You hush," Rory scolded under her breath but with a smile. "I did see her, Hannah. But you don't have to lurk in the bushes."

"Are you sure?" Jamison asked. "As you pointed out, we aren't guests."

"You're my guests. Wedding coordinator's prerogative. Besides, it's not like the bride and groom will notice."

The young couple only had eyes for each other, and Rory led Jamison and Hannah closer in time for her favorite part.

"As long as we both shall live."

The tall, thin pastor beamed as he announced, "I now pronounce you husband and wife. You may kiss your bride."

The guests burst into applause as the groom cupped his bride's face and pressed his lips to hers in a kiss that was as much of a vow as the words he'd spoken.

It was a moment that would never get old, no matter how many weddings she witnessed, and one that never failed to bring tears to her eyes. The love, the hope, the promise of a future where two lives joined together as one… Her heart was filled with so much emotion, she couldn't stop some of it from overflowing.

She was struggling somewhat blindly with the clasp on the tiny clutch hanging from her wrist when Jamison's hand flashed in front of her face. Rory blinked, dislodging a tear or two, when she saw what he was holding out to her.

Snatching the tissue, she touched it to the corners of her eyes, trying not to do too much damage to her makeup. "Don't make fun. I always cry at weddings."

"Tears of joy that all the hard work is over?"

"No!" Her protest faded into laughter as she admitted, "Well, maybe. A little."

"I've also started carrying wet wipes if you really feel the need to break down."

"Hmm, those would have come in handy at the rodeo. Goes to show you're learning."

A muscle twitched in his jaw as he glanced down at his daughter. "She got away from me, Rory. I was on the phone. I swear I only turned away for a second, and when I looked back…"

She could only imagine the panic that must have raced like wildfire through Jamison's veins. Hannah's disappearance, even for a few minutes, must have taken him back to those long, agonizing months when his daughter had been gone and he'd had no idea when or if he'd see her again.

"Look at her now, Jamison." The little girl was focused on the ceremony taking place, throwing her arm out and tossing imaginary flower petals. "She's fine."

"No thanks to me."

"Jamison..."

"I don't know if I can do this, Rory. To be the kind of father Hannah deserves. I've already made so many mistakes. I wasn't there when she needed me most—"

"You're here now."

"But when I get back home..."

Jamison raked a hand through his hair. How was he supposed to juggle being a full-time father and full-time lawyer when he couldn't keep an eye on his daughter during a five-minute phone call?

"You can do this." Rory caught his hand in hers, her blue eyes shining with the faith that had been there from the start. A faith that made him believe he could do anything...as long as she was by his side.

"I can't—I can't do this without you. I don't want to do this without you," he blurted out. "I don't want to say goodbye."

"What?"

Pulling Rory into his arms, he pressed his forehead against hers. "After Ryder and Lindsay's wedding, I don't want that to be the end."

"Jamison, what—what are you saying?"

"Rory, I—we can make this work, right? Somehow?" He heard the desperation in his own voice but couldn't make the words stop spilling over one another. "We can call and text and maybe I can make it up here for Labor Day weekend..."

"Labor Day," she echoed weakly.

"We're good together, Rory. I want to give our relationship a chance."

Reaching up, she traced her fingers along his jaw, her touch tender, but her smile as sad as he'd ever seen. "Labor Day is a holiday, Jamison. Not a relationship."

"Rory—"

"We agreed, remember? When this is over, we say goodbye."

He stepped back, his hands dropping to his sides. She was turning him down? Sticking to the rules as if this was some kind of game they were playing?

"You can't mean that."

"I know you're scared, Jamison."

"Scared?"

"Of taking care of Hannah on your own."

Scared? Hell, he was terrified! But that wasn't why he wanted Rory in his life…was it? Okay, maybe his words had come across like a knee-jerk reaction to the panic rushing through him, but he'd still meant them.

"Miss Rory," Hannah piped in, breaking the moment. "Are you crying?"

Lifting her chin and turning her face away from him, she murmured, "Just a little." More now than when the couple had spoken their vows a few minutes earlier.

Vows joining two lives as one, to have and to hold, from this day forward… Vows of forever.

Not for a weekend. Not for a holiday.

Was he really surprised Rory had turned him down when he'd offered so much less than she deserved?

Gazing up at the two adults, the little girl said, "You hafta kiss her, Daddy. Like when my tummy didn't feel good. You kissed me and the next day—" Hannah threw her arms out wide "—I was all better."

"Listen to your daughter, Jamison." Rory offered him

another sad yet tender smile. "You can do this. You already know how to make it all better."

If this was better, Jamison thought as he followed his daughter's instructions and gave Rory a heartbreaking kiss that already felt too much like goodbye, he'd sure as hell hate to see what he could do to make things worse.

Hannah twirled back and forth in the middle of the bridal shop, the full skirt swishing around her knees. The cream-colored taffeta with its burgundy velvet sash and hint of matching lace at the hem fit perfectly. "Do I look like a real princess?"

"The prettiest princess ever." Rory and Hannah had met up with Lindsay at the shop to double-check the alterations and pick up the dress. The little girl beamed back, and her joy was enough to bring the sting of tears to Rory's eyes.

The days leading up to Ryder and Lindsay's wedding were the best and worst of Rory's life. She lived each day they were together—whether it was window-shopping in town, having a picnic at the gazebo, buying clothes for Hannah. But a part of her mourned the moment she closed her eyes, knowing each morning meant one day closer to Jamison and Hannah leaving.

But, oh, those nights…when Jamison pulled her into his arms, determined to remind her just how *good* they were together…

Making love with him was so magical, so amazing, Rory almost gave in. Almost agreed to what he offered. To late-night phone calls, video chats between meetings, the occasional stolen weekend. And she would have—if he'd told her he loved her.

"I think I'm the one who's supposed to tear up at this part," Lindsay said gently as she handed Rory a tissue once Hannah went to change back into her regular clothes.

"Although I can't blame you. If I didn't know better, I wouldn't even think that was the same girl from just a few weeks ago."

Rory dabbed at her eyes. "Time here in Clearville has done wonders for her."

"*You* have done wonders for her. For her and for Jamison."

She crumpled the tissue in her hand. Oh, how she wanted to believe Jamison had changed but, forcing a laugh, she said, "The same Jamison who wanted Ryder to get a prenup?"

Lindsay gave her a chiding look along with another tissue. "The same Jamison who apologized to Ryder and to me. He was looking out for Ryder—I can't really blame him for that."

He was a good friend, a good father, a good man… Was it any wonder she'd fallen so in love with him?

"We agreed. When our time together is over, we say goodbye."

"Well, it's not like it was written in stone. You can change your mind. Something tells me you *have* changed your mind."

"It doesn't matter if I've changed my mind. Not if Jamison hasn't changed his."

"And you're so sure he hasn't?"

I can't do this without you.

She'd heard it before from grateful brides and grooms. How Rory was the glue bringing together all the thousands of tiny details that made up a wedding. How they never could have managed it all on their own. But then the big day was over, and the newly married couples went on with their lives.

It would be the same for Jamison and Hannah. They would go back to San Francisco, back to their lives.

Without her.

"You're sure he hasn't changed his mind?" Lindsay pressed.

"He—he said he doesn't want our relationship to end after the wedding."

Lindsay's brows shot to her hairline. "But that's huge!"

"It's not—he said we're good together..." Aware of Hannah on the other side of the curtain, she mouthed, "As in—in bed."

An impish smile played around her friend's lips. "And are you?"

"Not helping!"

"Look, Rory." Turning serious, Lindsay said, "I can only imagine how Jamison had to bury all his feelings, all his emotions simply to get through a single day when Hannah was missing. And considering how long she was gone, that's digging pretty deep."

Rory's heart hurt for all he had gone through. "I know."

"So how close do you think you have to get for a man whose feelings are buried that far down to admit he needs you—even a little?"

Chapter Fifteen

"Last chance, man," Ryder warned. "Speak now or forever hold your peace."

The groomsmen had gathered in a small room at the back of the hotel to get ready for the ceremony. Standing in front of the full-length mirror, Ryder was straightening his bow tie for the tenth time. Jamison might have thought his friend was nervous if not for the huge grin on the other man's face. "Still don't know why we couldn't have gone with clip-ons."

"Leave the stupid thing alone, will you? It's fine. And the only speaking I'll be doing is when I give the best man's toast."

"I'm not talking about that. I'm talking about…her." Ryder tipped his head to the right, and Jamison felt his heart jump to his throat, pressing against his own too-tight tie.

Rory had slipped in the back. Like at the previous wedding, her dress was simple, understated, a sleeveless beige-colored sheath she probably thought would help her fade into the background. As if that could ever be possible.

She smiled at Robbie, giving the boy a high five when he showed her the rings carefully tied to the pillow he would carry. She adjusted Drew's bow tie, helped Bryce with a cuff link and made Lindsay's and Ryder's fathers laugh at something she said.

It was ridiculous to feel jealous, but he was. Of all of them. Of the ease and laughter they were sharing with Rory. An ease that had gone out of their relationship as the tension of a ticking clock marked each moment they were together.

"No hard feelings, right?" Ryder mocked after taking one look at whatever was written on his face.

"I told her I'd changed my mind." But he knew now what he'd only started to figure out then. It wasn't his mind Rory needed him to change.

Seeming to come to the same conclusion, Ryder reached over and gave the back of his head a light tap. "Did you tell her you love her?"

From the very beginning, from the first moment they met, Rory had told him she was a woman who lived and breathed love, romance and happily-ever-after. Little wonder she'd turned his half-baked, half-assed offer down.

Never settle for less.

Maybe his mother had had one thing right after all. And maybe it wasn't too late to grab hold of more.

"One final touch!" Rory announced as she faced the groomsmen. They all looked so handsome, from Robbie to his grandfathers, but Jamison… She didn't know if her heart could take seeing him so suave, so stunning, so *San Francisco.*

If Hannah had changed into a girl Rory hardly recognized, well this—this was a man she didn't know. The other groomsmen looked somewhat uncomfortable in the formal wear, clothes that didn't quite fit despite quality tailoring. But Jamison… The tuxedo suited him, and why not? This was who he was. Jamison Porter, hotshot corporate lawyer.

Her hands trembled as she reached for the white florist's box. The pair who had brought the flowers were putting the final touches on the centerpieces in the ballroom and had asked if she might deliver the boutonnieres. She handed out a single burgundy rosebud to each of them, leaving Jamison for last.

He caught her wrist as she reached out to hand him the flower. "I think I could use some help."

Ryder muttered, "You got that right," as the groom turned toward the mirror, but the words hardly registered. Her pulse pounded in her ears as Jamison's fingers stroked the underside of her arm.

You can do this, Rory. It's part of the job.

The pep talk didn't steady her nerves, but it was enough to jolt her into action. She slid her fingers beneath the lapel, doing her best to ignore the strength of his chest against her knuckles, the body heat transferred to the smooth fabric.

"We need to talk."

She shook her head. "Not a good idea when I'm pointing a sharp instrument at your heart."

His chuckle vibrated against her fingers as she finally, finally slid the pearl-tipped pin into place. "After," he qualified. "Tonight."

It would have to be tonight. Because there wouldn't be any *after* tomorrow.

Rory didn't know how she made it through the wedding. Hannah was the perfect little flower girl, practically skipping down the lace runner toward the gazebo, tossing the petals up in the air and then giggling as they rained down over her. The guests laughed along with her only to fall reverently silent as Lindsay stepped into view.

She was a beautiful bride, but it was the love shining on her face that was truly breathtaking. And Ryder—the groom had laughed and joked his way through the rehearsal dinner the night before, but this time he was the one Jamison had to hand a handkerchief to as Lindsay walked down the aisle.

Rory couldn't meet Jamison's gaze, not if she had any hope of smiling her way through the ceremony. She'd told the truth when she said she always cried at weddings, and if the tears streaming down her face when the couple spoke the words *to have and to hold from this day forward* weren't tears of joy, well, no one else had to know.

"Did you see me, Miss Rory? Did you see me throw the flowers?"

Rory managed a genuine smile as Hannah raced into the ballroom, darting between the white-covered tables and fancifully dressed wedding guests. She'd been double-checking with the band, the servers and the bartender while the bridal party finished with the pictures. Everything was running smoothly, something Rory normally appreciated, but tonight, she could have used a minor emergency. Something to get her mind off the best man.

She wanted to believe Lindsay could be right, that Jamison cared for her more than he was able to admit. But she was afraid of fooling herself again, of building another relationship on a lie—this time one of her own making.

Bending down, she scooped Hannah into a hug and spun her around. "You were the best flower girl ever! I am so proud of you."

As Rory set her back on the ground, the little girl

reached up to touch the crown of flowers circling her blond curls. Her eyes were wide as she said, "There were *lots* of people!"

They'd talked about that at the rehearsal dinner. How the empty chairs would be filled with wedding guests watching her walk down the aisle. "Was that scary?"

"Kinda scary. But then I saw my daddy waiting for me, and I wasn't scareded anymore."

Rory wasn't sure what made her turn at that moment, but as she did, Jamison walked through the ballroom's carved double doors. His chestnut hair gleamed in the wall sconces' warm lighting, and she knew the instant he spotted them. The joy, the anticipation…

How many times had she seen it before—on the face of a groom waiting for his bride? Nerves trembled in her stomach, and Rory wrapped her arms around her waist. Not trying to still the overwhelming, frightening emotions swelling up inside her, but embracing them instead.

Jamison was waiting for her…and maybe she didn't have to be afraid anymore.

Hillcrest House's dark-paneled ballroom was decked out in all its finery for the reception. White tablecloths covered a dozen or so round tables. Each chair had a large bow tied at the back. Burgundy and cream roses sparkled in cut-glass vases beneath the crystal chandelier, and a matching garland draped the front of the band's raised platform stage, the cash bar and the tables offering a mix of appetizers and crudités.

But for all the romantic touches and tasteful decorations, he could see only Rory. She might as well have been the only woman in the room. The only woman in the world. The only woman for him…

Their gazes locked, and even from across the room he

could see a slight shudder shook her slender body at the powerful impact.

That's it. You can do it. One foot in front of the other.

But this time it wasn't Hannah who needed the silent encouragement. He wove his way through the round tables and milled with wedding guests, his heart thundering in his chest. Past a growing collection of brightly wrapped wedding gifts, past the towering three-tiered wedding cake, past the photographer setting up to capture the moment when Lindsay and Ryder walked into the room as husband and wife…

So focused on the beautiful wedding coordinator, he barely heard his name over the romantic ballad being played by the band.

"Jamison!"

But when a hand clamped down on his shoulder, he turned and did a quick double take, hardly believing what he was seeing. "Louisa? Greg?" He stared at his in-laws. "What the—what are you doing here?"

His beefy, sterling-haired father-in-law blustered about missing Hannah and wanting to see their little flower girl. Jamison raised a brow at his mother-in-law, wanting to know the real story.

Blonde and trim with classic features she had passed down to her daughter and granddaughter, Louisa lifted her chin. "We want to make sure Hannah is being properly cared for while she's here."

"Properly—is this because she got sick at the rodeo? Good Lord, Louisa! Hannah is fine! See for yourself."

Waving a hand toward his daughter, he expected Louisa's rigid stance to loosen once she spotted her granddaughter. Instead, the woman froze, her expression icing over until Jamison half expected her to shatter. He followed her chilly gaze, his own reaction completely different as he saw Hannah and Rory together.

Standing on the edge of the parquet dance floor, Rory held Hannah's hand overhead as the little girl spun around, making her full skirts flare out from her skinny legs. Their combined laughter rippled through the elegant ballroom, washing over him like a warm wave.

"I take it that's your wedding coordinator."

"That's Rory McClaren, yes." Jamison sighed, trying to hold on to his patience.

She's lost her daughter. It can't be easy for her to see Hannah so happy with a woman who isn't her mother, who isn't Monica.

Rubbing his forehead, he said, "I still can't believe you came all this way when we'll be home on Monday."

"That isn't what Hannah said."

"What?"

"She said you didn't want to say goodbye."

Jamison swallowed a curse. Clearly he needed to pay more attention to the conversations his daughter was having with her grandparents. Maybe he shouldn't have been surprised by his mother-in-law's overreaction, but he wouldn't have expected Greg to go along with it. "And you came all this way because of that?"

"So are you saying it's not true? That you're not planning to come back?"

"My plans are none of your business."

"You're a fool, Jamison Porter."

"Excuse me?"

"You've been here just over two weeks, and you've already let that woman get her hooks into you. Worse, you let her get to you through your daughter."

"Now, Louisa—"

"Don't!" She raised a silencing hand, and her husband

took a step back as if to avoid the blow. "This has to be said."

"No, it doesn't." Steel undercut Jamison's words as he stepped closer and lowered his voice. "If you're here for Hannah, that's fine. But my relationship with Rory is my business. You don't know her—"

"Oh, and you do? Did you know the hotel is losing money and that one of those massive hotel chains has made an offer to buy it?"

Jamison glanced at his father-in-law, who merely shrugged. "Word gets around."

"Right. Probably something you heard at the club," he added sarcastically. "Even if that is true, it doesn't have anything to do with me and Rory."

"Oh, really. So you don't think she'd be interested in a wealthy lawyer who could save her family business?"

"She isn't like that."

"This isn't even the first time she's latched onto a rich man. Did you know that? She went after her boss's son at her last job."

Jamison swore under his breath. "Yes, she told me, Louisa, but who the hell told you? You have no right—"

"I have every right where my granddaughter is concerned!"

"Nana! Papa!" Hannah's happy voice bubbled over the harsh whispers, and Jamison forced himself to take a deep breath and a step back as she rushed over. "Look, Miss Rory, it's my nana and papa!"

Rory laughed as Hannah tugged her over toward the older couple. She looked so happy, so beautiful. He wished for a way to warn her Louisa was on the warpath.

Louisa was wrong about Rory. He was sure of it. He trusted Rory. He trusted her with his daughter. He trusted her with his heart. He couldn't be so wrong about her… couldn't be so wrong a second time.

"Welcome to Hillcrest House," Rory said as Greg lifted his granddaughter for a kiss. "Hannah has told me a lot about you."

Louisa's greeting was less exuberant, patting Hannah on the back as the little girl leaned over for a hug. "Yes, well, our granddaughter has had quite a bit to say about you, too."

Picking up on the tension, Rory crossed an arm over her chest as she fingered the pendant she was wearing. "All good, I hope," she said with a tentative smile.

"Hannah, my girl, why don't we go take a look at that big ol' wedding cake?" Greg suggested, leaving a heavy silence behind as he and Hannah walked away.

"It's funny how small the world can be sometimes," Louisa stated, but Jamison knew he wouldn't find anything amusing in what she had to say. "I used to live in LA, and it turns out we have a mutual acquaintance—the Van Meters. You know them, don't you, Ms. McClaren?"

Rory went pale, the color leaching from her face, as she took a stumbling step backward.

"In fact," Louisa continued, "the Van Meters hired the company you used to work for to stage their house. Johanna Van Meter has wonderful taste. She was devastated to realize some of her priceless antiques had been stolen."

Ignoring the uneasy feeling worming its way through his stomach, Jamison demanded, "Louisa, what are you talking about?"

"Ms. McClaren knows. Would you like to tell him… or should I?"

This was a nightmare. It had to be. Standing in front of Jamison as his mother-in-law blamed her for stealing from the Van Meters.

This couldn't be happening and yet—

Rory had to swallow a burst of hysterical laughter. God, Louisa Stilton even bore a slight resemblance to Pamela Worthington. And the look of disdain—well, that was identical.

"Rory." Jamison grabbed her arm, shaking her from the dreamlike paralysis that, no matter how far or how fast she ran, she could never escape. "Tell me this isn't true."

He loomed over her, a commanding presence in the dark tuxedo he wore so well, and she was struck again that this was the real Jamison Porter. Not the hard-body handyman with paint splattered on his jeans and T-shirt. Not the tortured soul who'd made love to her by the gazebo. Not the laughing father who'd played hide-and-seek with his daughter. This was Jamison Porter, Esquire—a man of wealth and power and status.

One who suddenly reminded Rory how it felt to be powerless.

"Tell me!"

Shock had wiped all reaction from his expression as Louisa spit out her accusations, but now Rory could see the emotion creeping back in. She could see the questions; she could see the doubt.

Trust me, she silently pleaded. *Believe me... Love me.*

But he'd never said the words. She wanted forever, and he wanted a weekend. A holiday. A fairy tale…

But this was one without a happy ending. "What do you want me to say, Jamison? That it's all true? That thousands of dollars' worth of belongings disappeared from a house I staged? That I was fired when pictures, receipts, transactions from online auctions were found on my computer at work?"

Tears clogged her throat and burned her eyes. "Fine, I'll tell you. It's true. It's all true."

* * *

"Go ahead and say it," Rory told her cousin the next morning as she sank into one of the chairs in her office. "I know you want to, and I deserve it."

Evie had pulled Rory out of the lobby on the verge of a breakdown. She'd overheard one of the porters speaking with a new hotel guest as he wheeled a loaded luggage cart past her. "You're lucky we had a family check out early. The Bluebell suite is one of our best..."

The Bluebell...

Gone. Jamison was gone. He'd already left. Without giving her a chance to explain. Without giving her a chance to say she loved him before saying goodbye...

Maybe it wouldn't have mattered. Maybe their relationship was destined to end from the start.

Evie handed her a box of tissues before circling behind the refuge of her desk. "You're right. You deserve to hear this...so here goes." She took a deep breath. "I'm proud of you."

"Yeah, right." Rory pulled out one tissue and then another. "Real proud."

How many times had Evie warned her not to mix business and pleasure? She still hadn't learned the lesson and totally deserved an *I told you so* from her know-better cousin.

"I am. It wasn't that long ago that you and Peter broke up."

"And here I am—" she waved a tissue in surrender "—four months later, stupidly falling in love again."

"Bravely falling in love again." Evie glanced away, swallowed hard and glanced back again. Her professional demeanor dropped away, leaving her looking vulnerable, raw, real... "It's been two years since my engagement, and I haven't had the courage to let a man close since."

"I didn't think you wanted a relationship," Rory

murmured, embarrassed she'd been so caught up in her own troubles that she hadn't seen the loneliness her cousin tried so hard to hide.

Evie gave a short laugh. "It's a lot easier to tell yourself you don't want what you can't have."

"But you could… You're smart, beautiful, sophisticated. Any man would be lucky to have you in his life."

But Evie was already shaking her head. "It doesn't matter whether some guy would or wouldn't get lucky with me. I can't bring myself to put any kind of faith into a relationship, and what guy is going to put up with a woman who doesn't trust him?"

"Maybe one who understands what you've gone through? One who's willing to earn your trust?"

"No one wants to work that hard."

"Someone will. The one man who's worth it will."

Evie shook her head again. "Never mind all that. This isn't about me, anyway. It's about you and the way you never let life get you down. That even after everything that's happened, you still believe in love and romance and happily-ever-after."

This time, it was Rory who shook her head as she wiped the tears from her eyes. "I don't know about that…"

"I do. I know you, and I know you won't let some corporate lawyer jerk change who you are."

"He's not a jerk," Rory murmured. He was the man she loved. The handyman, the lover, the father, even the lawyer—all were different sides of the man she'd fallen in love with.

And maybe Lindsay had been right. Maybe Rory had touched something inside Jamison, but she hadn't reached deep enough. She hadn't been able to grab hold of the trust he'd buried so deeply, and without that…

"See?" Evie announced triumphantly. "You still have

faith in people. That's what makes you so good at your job. I know we don't always see eye to eye, and that sometimes it seems like we're too different to agree on much of anything. But the truth is, your strengths are my weaknesses, and vice versa. And that means if we work together, we're pretty damn unstoppable."

"I had no idea you felt so strongly about the hotel after… everything."

"The truth is, I haven't let myself feel much of anything in a long, long time. But this is where I belong. Where we belong."

Where we belong... "Now if we could get Chance to come back."

"That would be the icing on the wedding cake. But for now, it's just the two of us, and heaven help any guy who gets in our way."

Chapter Sixteen

"Hannah, you need to sit still." Jamison struggled to cling to his patience as he tried to figure out how to keep hold of the brush with one hand, the neon-green rubber band with the other and his squirming daughter with his third, nonexistent hand.

"That's too hard!" The little girl cringed away from the soft-bristled brush as though he held a branding iron to her head. "It hurts!"

"I'm trying not to pull your hair, but you have all these tangles." How was it that every strand of his daughter's blond hair seemed to be tied in knots? How was it that his whole freaking life seemed to be tied into one giant knot since he'd left Clearville?

As if reading his thoughts, Hannah argued, "Rory did it better."

Jamison wished he could convince himself his daughter was simply talking about the uneven, frizzy ponytail springing from the top of her head, but he couldn't. Rory had made everything better.

"We've talked about this, Hannah." And they had. Incessantly in the week since they'd been home.

Hannah's frown and saucer-size pout told him what she thought about that, but like it or not, Jamison gave a final tug to tighten the haphazard ponytail before grabbing his briefcase and Hannah's backpack and ushering her out the door.

"I don't wanna go to school."

"You like school," he reminded her—or maybe he was trying to convince himself—as he belted his daughter into the booster seat in the back of his SUV. "And after school, your grandmother is going to take you for a girls' day out."

Jamison didn't know what that entailed and didn't want to know. He was grateful to his in-laws, he really was. But by giving in and having them watch Hannah in the afternoons, he was playing into Louisa's hands. He might have viewed it as a short-term solution, but he didn't fool himself that she had given up on her long-term plan.

She needs you to fight for *her.*

Rory's voice rang in his memory along with the stricken look on her face at the wedding. She had needed him to fight for her…and he'd failed miserably. She hadn't stolen those items, no matter what the evidence might have said.

And if she'd told him what had happened, if she'd trusted him with what had happened, he would have been prepared for his in-laws' accusations. Instead he'd been blindsided by the secret Rory had kept. And for a moment, when faced with the realization that maybe he didn't know her as well as he thought, that maybe—like with Monica—he didn't know what she was capable of, he'd shut down.

He'd retreated back into the shell that had surrounded him in the final months of his marriage and during the desperate, agonizing weeks when Monica and Hannah were missing.

Somehow, he'd found his way back home, where the familiarity of work waited. Where Hannah had started preschool and where, for a while, Jamison had thought he was going to have to enroll himself after spending the first few sessions seated in a humiliatingly tiny chair beside his daughter, who refused to let him leave.

He'd interviewed almost a dozen nannies, but none of them had been right. None of them had been… Rory. He couldn't see any of them knowing how to turn a boring breakfast into smiley-face oatmeal. He couldn't imagine any of them showing the patience Rory had when Hannah asked her to watch her practice walking down the aisle for the twentieth time. He couldn't picture any of them healing old hurts, breaking through a protective shell, making him feel again…

And that was the real problem. Not that those women couldn't be the nanny Hannah needed, but because they couldn't be the woman *Jamison* needed. The woman he loved.

"I don't want a girls' day with Nana! I want Rory!" Hannah's petulant demand so closely echoed the one in his heart that it was all Jamison could do not to snap at his daughter.

Instead, he finished buckling her in and climbed into the driver's seat. "We can't always have what we want," he muttered under his breath as he jammed the key into the ignition.

Traffic into the city was a tangled mess, with cars locked bumper to bumper on the freeway. Not that that stopped other vehicles from trying to weave through the lanes, cutting off drivers and jamming on their brakes. When a red sports car nearly took off his front bumper while slicing toward one of the exits, Jamison swore and slammed on the horn.

Hannah's scream nearly sent his heart through his throat. "Hannah, what—"

"Don't go, Daddy! Don't go!"

Glancing into the rearview mirror, he saw the tears streaming down Hannah's chubby cheeks. The hysteria in her voice told Jamison this was more than worry about him dropping her off at school.

Taking the same exit as the sports car, he pulled off into the first parking lot he came to. Hannah was still crying when he climbed into the back. Strapped in her booster seat, she reached out, clinging to him as tightly as she could.

"Hannah, honey…" Jamison undid the buckles at her chest and pulled her into his lap. "I'm right here, and I'm not going anywhere."

Another horn blasted from the nearby freeway, and Hannah cringed again. Swearing under his breath, Jamison asked, "Did I scare you when I honked the horn? I'm so sorry, sweetheart."

Her chin tucked against her chest, Jamison could barely make out the words his daughter was saying. "What did you say, Hannah? What was that about Mommy?"

"Mommy was mad on the phone. She said we weren't coming home. Never, ever, ever again."

His fight with Monica… The accident… Jamison had heard the whole thing. How stupid of him not to realize that, sitting in the back seat, *Hannah* had also heard her parents' final, fateful fight. "Oh, Hannah…"

"I tol' her I wanted to go home. I wanted to see you and Nana and Papa. Mommy said I had to stay with her." Tears streamed down her face. "But I told her I didn't want to, so she went to heaven without me."

"Hannah, sweetie. Mommy—Mommy didn't want to leave you." His heart broke at the thought of his little girl thinking her mother had left because of something she'd said, something she'd done. "It was an accident."

The words lifted a weight from his chest, and he sucked in a deep breath. The first he'd taken without the crushing guilt pressing on him since the day he walked into an empty house and realized Hannah and Monica were gone. They'd both made mistakes, but he was lucky. He had the chance to make up for them, while Monica—

"She loved you." The words Rory had spoken that night in the gazebo, words he hadn't been willing to embrace, came back to him. "She loved you so much, and she wanted you to be safe so that you could come back to me and Nana and Papa. Because we missed you."

"Like I miss Mommy?"

"Yeah, like that."

"I don't want you to miss me anymore."

"Neither do I, Hannah."

Not when he'd already missed so much. "What do you say we play hooky today?"

"I don't know that game."

Jamison laughed. "It's a fun game. One where you skip school and I skip work and we have a daddy-daughter day."

"Really? Then what do we do?" Hannah's eyes lit up with hope, and for a moment, Jamison panicked. He didn't know any more about a father-daughter day than he did about a girls' day out.

All you have to do is be there for her.

"We can go to the park and have a picnic. We can color in your coloring books and then watch one of your videos."

"An' have ice cream and popcorn?"

"Maybe ice cream *or* popcorn," he offered, not wanting a repeat of the night at the rodeo. "Does that sound like fun?"

"That sounds like the best! I love you, Daddy."

Breathing the words against his daughter's blond curls, he murmured, "I love you, too, Hannah Banana."

It wouldn't always be so simple. But maybe it wasn't always as hard as he made it out to be. Maybe he did have a chance of making things right…and not just with Hannah.

He'd finished belting Hannah into the booster seat when the sound of his phone ringing jarred him from his hopeful thoughts. His boss's name flashed across the screen, but Jamison didn't immediately reach into the front seat for the device.

"Are you okay now, Hannah?"

His daughter nodded, but even he could see she wasn't as excited as she'd been seconds before. "I bet Miss Rory would like to go on our picnic."

"I bet she would, too."

Slipping back into the driver's seat, Jamison reached for his phone. "Mr. Spears."

"Jamison, good of you to pick up."

He heard the dry reproach in his boss's voice but refused to make excuses. "I'm glad you called. I was about to phone in to let you know I won't be coming in today."

"Jamison—"

"I'm spending the day with my daughter." Catching Hannah's gaze in the rearview mirror, he shot her a wink.

"We're gonna watch a princess movie!" she shouted, and he grinned, not knowing—or caring—if his boss could hear her.

Silence filled the line before the older man commented, "You do realize the partners are going to make a decision about the promotion soon."

"I do."

"You've worked hard for this, Jamison. I'd hate for you

to lose out now when you're so close. I probably shouldn't be telling you this, but you're first in the running."

"Why?"

"Well, we want to let all the candidates know at the same time—"

"No, I mean why am I first? Harris has seniority, and Martinez landed the Langstone account. So why me, Charles?"

"I don't understand what you're asking," Spears said stiffly, but Jamison had a good idea the other man knew exactly why he was asking, just like Jamison knew exactly why the older man wasn't answering.

"You can tell my father-in-law I said thanks but no, thanks."

Jamison didn't wait for his boss's response before ending the call. He didn't know for sure that his father-in-law had influenced his boss's decision and would probably never know, but if he took the promotion, he would always wonder. But it was more than stubborn pride keeping him from accepting, more than a need to know that he'd earned the partnership on his own merit.

Taking the job would be taking a step backward—back to the man he'd been before he and Monica separated, back to the man he'd been before the accident, back to the man he'd been before Rory.

He didn't want to go back. He wanted to go forward, to step toward a future that a few weeks ago, he wouldn't have dreamed was possible.

Jamison paced his office impatiently, his hand tightly gripping the phone as he counted out the rings. "Come on, pick up."

The masculine space with its solid furniture and shelves

lined with law books used to be his sanctuary. But now he saw it for what it was. *His* hidey-hole.

He'd had to wait until Hannah went down for a nap after their impromptu daddy-daughter day to make this call, and he didn't want to wait anymore. Just like he didn't want to hide from his emotions anymore.

"Hi! Hello," he almost shouted out a greeting when he heard the voice on the other end of the line. "It's Jamison Porter, and I need your help."

Silence answered his desperate plea before Evie McClaren asked, "Why exactly would I want to help you, Mr. Porter? You broke my cousin's heart."

His own heart gave a painful jerk at the thought of hurting Rory. "I know. I made a mistake. When my mother-in-law told me what happened—"

"You thought Rory was guilty."

"No! Not really. Not once I had a chance to think about it. But Louisa sprang the information on me, and I was—I was blindsided by it."

The same way he'd been blindsided by Monica. By coming home to find the house empty. To find Monica had left without a word and taken Hannah with her.

"It totally caught me off guard, Evie, and I didn't handle it well. I know I was no better than her ass of an ex, who didn't stand by her—"

"Stand by?" Sharp laughter pierced Jamison's eardrum. "Is that what you think happened? You think Peter didn't come to Rory's defense when she needed him?"

Jamison swallowed, suddenly fearing whatever happened might have been so much worse. "Isn't it?"

"Peter didn't let Rory down. He set her up."

"You mean he—you mean the boss's *son* is the one who stole from their clients? And he framed Rory for it?"

"I don't know if he was framing her or simply covering

his tracks. But all of the proof—the online auctions, the storage shed, the emails—all of it traced back to Rory's computer."

Jamison swore under his breath. "How could he do that to her? When she trusted him—"

Like she trusted you? Like she counted on you to be there for her, to believe in her the way she believed in you from the very beginning?

Sick to his stomach, Jamison sank back into his chair.

"Guys are jerks," Evie said succinctly. "Unfortunately, Rory was so shocked by the accusations, by the evidence planted against her, she didn't realize until later Peter was the only one with that kind of access. And by then, it was too late. Anything she said would have seemed like she was simply trying to throw blame on someone else.

"Rory came here for a fresh start. Instead the stupid rumors followed her, and if that wasn't bad enough, your mother-in-law had to show up—"

Jamison closed his eyes. "I have even more to make up for. So I'll ask again, Evie. Will you help me?"

"What do you need me to do?" she asked, suspicion still underlining her words.

Even so, he felt the first kernel of hope start to sprout. "I'm looking for my very own fairy godmother."

Evie let out a short scoff. "And you called me? Mr. Porter, you must be even more desperate than I thought."

"You have no idea."

"Oh, there you are, Rory." Evie breathed out as she reached Rory's side in the middle of the lobby. "I've been looking everywhere for you."

"Why? What's going on?" Rory had tried to take her cousin's words to heart, to believe her unshakable faith in people and her belief in happily-ever-after were her greatest strengths. But some days she felt like the only news was bad news.

It wasn't easy dealing with so-in-love couples, with helping them make their wedding dreams come true, when her own heart was broken. She knew it wasn't their fault. That they hadn't somehow stolen her happiness and taken it for themselves. But she couldn't help wondering how their relationships seemed to be smooth sailing when falling in love had left her beaten and broken, stranded on the ragged shoals.

Evie rolled her eyes but wouldn't meet her gaze, her attention focused across the lobby. "Oh, you know. The usual. We've got some crazy-in-love guy who wants to plan an over-the-top, surprise proposal for his girlfriend. He's waiting to meet with you at the gazebo to go over all the details."

"A surprise engagement. Well, that could end badly…"

That statement caught Evie's attention, and her cousin turned to meet her gaze. "Stop being so cynical. That's my job. And something tells me this guy has nothing to worry about. So go!"

Great. Just what she didn't want to deal with. A crazy-in-love fiancé-to-be gushing over the woman he loved.

Don't make comparisons, she sternly warned herself. *What you and Jamison had wasn't love. Not really. Not on his part. Which is why you're going to get over him... someday.*

Catching sight of Trisha and her friends huddled near the concierge desk, Rory straightened her shoulders. First things first.

Surprise lit the other woman's eyes when Rory walked toward the clique instead of hurrying by with her head ducked down as if she were invisible. No, worse…as if she were guilty.

Tell me it isn't true, Rory. Tell me!

She'd been so sure he wouldn't believe her. So afraid Jamison saw what they had as some kind of escape from the real world. That his feelings for her weren't strong enough to survive the challenges of everyday life. But the truth was, it wasn't Jamison she hadn't trusted.

"Trisha, I'd like a word with you."

The redhead raised her sculpted eyebrows before glancing at her friends with a smug smile. "I'm kind of on break here."

Rory met their laughter with a smile of her own. "Break's over."

The three other women exchanged startled glances before murmuring their goodbyes and heading off in opposite directions—hopefully to get back to doing their jobs.

Trisha huffed out a breath before demanding, "So what do you want?"

"There have been some rumors going around, rumors that might have been intended to hurt me, but that could end up hurting Hillcrest."

Trisha blanched slightly, as if she hadn't considered the more far-reaching consequences.

"This hotel has been in my family for decades, and I'm not going to let anyone damage its reputation. So if you—" The threat stalled in Rory's throat as Evie's words played through her memory. Her cousin was right. She did still have faith in people. "If you hear anyone spreading those rumors, I'm counting on you to help put a stop to them. You've worked here for years, and the staff looks up to you. I'm sure we won't have any of these problems going forward, will we?"

Trisha blinked. "I, uh—no, no trouble," she agreed, clearly startled by the turn of the conversation. "I'll make sure none of those rumors get spread around."

"Good." Rory sighed with relief. "I'm glad to hear that."

As Trisha hurried away, Rory straightened her shoulders and turned toward the lobby doors. One confrontation over, one more to go.

She'd avoided the gazebo in the week since Jamison left, but she couldn't stay away any longer. Lindsay and Ryder's wedding had brought even more attention to Hillcrest House, and Rory was fielding call after call from couples looking to plan their ceremonies there. More brides would say their vows framed by the elegantly scrolled woodwork.

But not Rory. Not when she couldn't look at the graceful structure without thinking of Jamison… Picturing his sexy smile as he teased her about his abilities. Remembering the thoughtful way he'd included Hannah in the work… Torturing herself with the memory of making love in the moonlight…

Evie was right. Rory wasn't going to give up. She still had faith that she would fall in love again, have a family of her own. But while her cousin admired her ability to get over Peter as quickly as she had, Rory didn't think getting over Jamison would be nearly as easy.

The sun was sinking behind the horizon, painting the sky with a gorgeous pink-and-purple haze and casting a golden glow over the gazebo. The groom-to-be stood with his back to her, one foot on the first step and a hand braced on the railing. His tailored dark suit was a stark, masculine contrast to the delicately carved white spindles.

Rory's heart seized at the sight. How long would it be before she stopped imagining Jamison in every tall, broad-shouldered man she saw?

"Good evening, I'm—" The introduction stuck in her throat as the man turned and the faint rays highlighted his face. "Not imagining things…"

"Hello, Rory."

"What—what are you doing here?" she asked, still unable to believe he was real.

"Didn't Evie tell you?" he asked.

"Yes! I'm meeting a man who's planning to propose to his girlfriend at the gazebo. Which is why I can't do this with you right now. He'll probably be here any minute and—"

A small smile played around Jamison's lips. "What?" Rory demanded.

"He's here."

Throwing her arms up in the air in frustration, she demanded, "Who's here?"

"I'm here, Rory," he told her.

"You—you're—"

"I'm the guy who was an idiot not to trust you, not to fight for you. I'm the guy who couldn't let go of the darkness of the past long enough to see the bright future right in front of him. I'm the guy who never should have left and the guy who will do anything it takes to convince you to forgive him."

Tears flooded her eyes, but Rory quickly brushed them aside. After seven days, she was too starved for the sight of him to let anything get in the way. "Oh," she said softly. "That guy."

"That guy," Jamison agreed. "The one who loves you. I love you, Rory. I love your openness, your faith in people, your willingness to see the best in them. In me, even when I probably didn't deserve it."

Rory blinked again, but nothing could keep the tears from spilling down her cheeks.

"I said it all wrong before, and you were right to turn me down. I don't want a holiday or a weekend. I don't want to reach for a phone when I want to talk to you at night. I want to reach for *you*.

"Evie told me what happened at your last job, but I didn't need her to tell me the whole story. I know you wouldn't have stolen from a client. I know *you*." He shook his head. "I've been miserable since I left, Rory. Even after the partners at the firm offered me the promotion, I wasn't happy."

"You turned the partnership down?"

"Turned the partnership down and turned my resignation in."

Rory's jaw dropped in shock. "You…resigned?"

"The job wasn't right for me, not anymore, and it was never what was best for Hannah."

If Rory had ever had any doubt Jamison deserved all the faith and belief she'd had in him, his words brushed them away as easily—as tenderly—as he brushed away her tears.

"I can't believe you quit."

"Well, fortunately I won't be unemployed for long. Turns out a lawyer over in Redfield is getting ready to retire and is looking to take on a partner."

Rory wasn't sure how much more her heart could take. "You mean you'd move here? To Clearville?"

Jamison shrugged a shoulder as if giving up his life in San Francisco to live in the small town was no big deal. "I'd move wherever you are. I missed you, Rory. Hannah missed you, too." He smiled, but a hint of vulnerability reflected in his sterling gaze. "I realize I've sprung all this on you suddenly, but I'm hoping at least some of it has come as a good surprise."

Realizing she'd been too shocked to do much more than echo what he'd told her, Rory reached up to cup his face in her hands. "Well, there is one problem."

"Yeah, what's that?"

"I came out here because Evie told me a man was looking to propose to the woman he loves…"

Turning his head, Jamison pressed a kiss to her palm before lowering to one knee. Despite what her cousin had told her, Rory still gasped when he pulled a small blue box from his suit pocket. "Rory McClaren, you might not be a princess, and I know you're not a fairy godmother, but Hannah and I think you would make a wonderful stepmother.

"I love you, Rory. In such a short time, you've brought light and laughter back to both of our lives, and if I can spend the rest of my life making you as happy as you've made me over the past few weeks, I'll be the luckiest man alive."

Her heart ready to burst from her chest, Rory sank down in front of him and threw her arms around his neck. "I love you, Jamison Porter, and I can't think of anything that would make me happier than to be your wife and Hannah's stepmother. I've spent my whole life imagining the perfect wedding, but you're the one who's made my dreams come true. You're the best man, the *only* man, for me."

Epilogue

One year later

"That's the fifth time you've looked at your watch in the last ten minutes," Ryder murmured as he adjusted the cuff link on his tuxedo. "Is this my turn to remind you that it's not too late?"

Jamison met his friend's cocky grin with a wry look. "Very funny." And no less than he deserved now that their roles had been reversed. Now that Ryder was the best man and Jamison—

He sucked in a deep breath and ran a finger beneath the starched collar and bow tie. He was the groom.

"So no cold feet?"

No cold anything.

The summer day was perfect for a wedding. The sun shone down on the gleaming white gazebo with only a hint of clouds above, and the scent of roses carried from the garden on the warm breeze. Dozens of chairs lined either side of a lace runner as their friends and family had gathered to celebrate his marriage to Hillcrest House's very own wedding coordinator.

Rory's parents sat in the front row. So, too, somewhat surprisingly, did his parents. And Monica's.

A lot could change in a year.

"I'm not nervous," he insisted. Despite the way the second hand on his watch seemed to move in slow motion and the bow tie threatened to cut off all the air to his lungs, the words were true.

He'd been waiting for this moment—for this woman, for Rory—his entire life. He didn't want to wait anymore.

His heart jumped in his chest as the familiar music began to play, and his wait was over. Oohs and aahs rose from their guests as they caught sight of Hannah, looking like an angel in her lacy white dress, and a huge grin split Jamison's face at the overwhelming rush of emotion he felt for his daughter.

She met his grin with a dimpled smile of her own. A flowered crown perched on her riot of curls was already slightly askew, and a white wicker basket swung from side to side as she skipped down the aisle, remembering to drop a rose petal or two on the way.

The music swelled, and Jamison's breath caught as the guests all rose to their feet. But then at his very first glimpse of Rory in wedding white, the rest of the world fell away.

He'd told her once that he didn't believe in fairy tales, and in a way, that was still true. Because this was no fantasy, no game of pretend, no story that would come to an end on the final page. The emotions pouring through him as Rory climbed the gazebo steps and placed her hand in his were as solid and as real and as lasting as anything he could ever hope to build.

Even if she did *look* like a fairy-tale princess…

Sunlight glittered on the lace and beads, the shimmering white satin hugging her curves. Her skin was as luminous as the pearls around her slender neck, and her dark hair was held back from her beautiful face by a rose-adorned headband.

"Did you see Hannah?" she whispered, her sapphire eyes sparkling, as the minister began his greeting. "She was perfect."

"I knew she would be."

Hannah had been as eager—almost as eager—for this day to arrive as Jamison.

"You did?"

He nodded. "I had faith."

Those were the same words Rory had spoken a year ago, but so much had changed since then. For him and for Hannah. Gone was the shy, fearful girl he'd first brought to Clearville. She'd blossomed beneath Rory's care, growing happy and confident, blooming into, well, the perfect flower girl.

And why not? He and Rory weren't the only couple to be touched by Hillcrest's magic. His daughter had had plenty of practice in the past few months.

So, yes, Jamison had faith. He had hope…

And when he vowed to take this woman to be his bride, when he sealed that promise with a kiss, and when Hannah turned back to the happy crowd, tossed the rest of her bright red rose petals straight up into the air and shouted, "Now we get cake!" Jamison couldn't help but throw his head back and laugh.

He had love.

* * * * *

MILLS & BOON

Coming next month

CAPTIVATED BY THE BROODING BILLIONAIRE

Rebecca Winters

Unable to sit there any longer, she stood up. "Thank you for dinner and the opportunity to see the Salon de Dionysus. I feel very privileged that you would allow me a glimpse inside your *saint des saints.*" She'd tried to pronounce it correctly. "But it's getting late and I'm positive you're tired after our long drive today. I'd better go back to my room."

Lines darkened his striking features. "Now that I've been honest with you, why do I get the feeling you're running away from me already?"

He could see through her with those piercing black eyes. She started to tremble. "Because I'm questioning my own judgment. Since we arrived at the estate, nothing feels right."

"That's because what we felt for each other when we first met was like a clap of thunder out of a blue sky. I was reminded of a line in *The Young Fools*, by Verlaine."

"What line was that?" She'd enjoyed much of the French poet's translated work.

"Suddenly a white nape flashed beneath the branches, and this sight was a delicate feast for a young fool's heart."

"Raoul—" Where had he pulled that from? He never ceased to amaze her.

"The reverberations have been growing stronger with every passing minute, so don't deny it." He got up from the couch and reached for her with his strong hands. Their mouths were only centimeters apart.

"I don't deny it, but I'm not looking for any kind of complication. I never want to go through the pain of betrayal again."

She heard his sharp intake of breath. "I'm positive my father lied to me to get his own way. You think I don't understand betrayal?"

Abby shook her head, not immune to the tortured tone in his voice. "I don't know what to think," she cried.

"Then don't," he said before covering her mouth with a kiss so hungry and full of desire, she moaned. Finding herself immersed in sensations her body had never known before, she slid her hands up the silk covering his chest and wrapped her arms around his neck.